Alice

Alice

NANCY ROSS

POOLBEG

Published 2006
by Poolbeg Press Ltd
123 Grange Hill, Baldoyle
Dublin 13, Ireland
E-mail: poolbeg@poolbeg.com

© Nancy Ross 2006

The moral right of the author has been asserted.

Typesetting, layout, design © Poolbeg Press Ltd.

1 3 5 7 9 10 8 6 4 2

A catalogue record for this book is available from the British Library.

ISBN 1-84223-224-X
ISBN(from January 2007) 1-84223-224-8

Typeset by Patricia Hope in Bembo
Printed by Litografia Rosés SA, Spain

www.poolbeg.com

About the Author

Nancy Ross is the only child of the well-known musician and songwriter, BC Hilliam. After a career in the WRNS, followed by several high-powered secretarial jobs, two marriages and three children, she started out on yet another career – writing.

Her previous novels, *Still Waters Run Deep*, *The Enchanted Island* and *Love and Friendship* are also published by Poolbeg.

Also by Nancy Ross

Still Waters Run Deep

The Enchanted Island

Love and Friendship

To my daughter,
Imogen Mary Lompad

Part One

Chapter 1

In later years when Olivia looked back to a day in the late fifties when she met Alice she thought her life altered its course from that particular moment. From then on it took on a momentum of its own, and the events that followed were out of her control and she had no power to stop them.

Up until then nothing much had happened to her, a happy but uneventful childhood and the transition from child to young woman passing without clashing of cymbals or claps of thunder. She gave no anxiety to her parents. She was not interesting-looking or beautiful, but she was not plain either and her rather vapid good looks and sweetness meant that she had admirers. Like her contemporaries, her knowledge of sex was sketchy, and she was content to leave that puzzling complication on the back burner, thinking that it must be an agreeable activity to look forward to in the future.

She was shy, so she felt lost and alone on the third day of the secretarial course she was taking in London. A country girl, she was not used to living in the city, and leaning new skills was daunting. All around her were groups of girls chattering like a flock of starlings, in that high-pitched drawl peculiar to middle-class young women of the time, for this establishment in Exhibition Road provided a grounding in shorthand and typing that was not cheap, and inaccessible to most girls who aspired to be secretaries. It was the last costly step taken by parents who did not know what to do next with their daughters.

Suddenly Olivia became aware that a girl had disengaged herself from the crowd, and she was surprised when she came and stood by her side.

"I'm Alice Mountjoy," said the girl, "and I know your name – Olivia Anderson. I looked it up on the register."

That was flattering, especially as Olivia, alone and more able to observe, had noticed how popular this particular girl was with the other students. From the first day she had been the centre of a group. She made remarks in class that made people laugh, a relief when the work was so tedious. She made no effort to fathom the intricacies of shorthand, and her typing was terrible. She did not appear to take the course seriously, and this was borne out by her next statement.

"Isn't this the most boring place imaginable? Don't you absolutely hate it?"

"I don't know," replied Olivia truthfully, pushing a strand of fair hair from her forehead, a gesture she often made when unsure of herself, or when someone unfamiliar to her was addressing her. She felt something more was expected of her, so she said rather tamely, "I suppose it's a means to an end."

"I'll tell you what the end will be," said Alice emphatically, "a boss chasing you around the desk – that is what this course will lead to. Secretaries are fair game for that sort of thing."

Olivia had never thought of this aspect, and she was sure it had not occurred to her mother who had instigated the idea of her taking the course. "Why are you doing it if you don't like it?" she asked curiously.

"Blackmail," the girl answered cheerfully. "My stepfather is paying for me to come here. He wanted me out of the house before I spilt the beans to my mother. Dirty brute!" She laughed, her open friendly face lighting up with amusement at the words she had just spoken. A loud bell sounded, indicating the end of a fifteen-minute break.

"Oh dear . . ." began Olivia.

"I'm off," cried Alice. "Be seeing you!"

Olivia watched the mane of bright hair mingle with the other heads making their way to the classroom. She regretted the end of a conversation that had just begun to be interesting. A stepfather who abused her? Surely that was what she had implied? Olivia longed to know more about this fascinating girl. She wondered, what sort of family background did she have? It intrigued her because it sounded so different from her own.

Olivia's father, Kenneth Anderson, was a doctor with a country practice in the New Forest. He was thirty-six years old when he met his wife, Joan, and, at that time, was a resident physician at a London teaching hospital. Joan, a nurse, was a lively girl in her late twenties. She was just beginning to think it was time she got married. In the years just before the war women had acquired a certain amount of independence, but spinsterhood was still regarded as an indication of failure. Joan had no desire to be an old maid, and she took one look at the lanky rather shy Kenneth and knew exactly what she wanted. He took a little longer to fall in love, but when he did it was with a depth of emotion that surprised them both. They married before the longing became too much to bear, as couples like Kenneth and Joan did not sleep together before marriage.

Four years later Kenneth was offered a partnership in a practice in Hampshire. He seized the opportunity with excited joy. It was what they both wanted, to escape from London. The dark clouds of war on the horizon made the move even more desirable. They had no children and, except for the endless enquiries from both sets of parents, this did not concern them greatly. They decided philosophically that perhaps it was not meant to be, and stoutly maintained that it was their lack of offspring that bound them so closely together. It never occurred to Kenneth, a doctor, or Joan, a nurse, to question their childlessness. Fertility was still a matter of chance.

As soon as Kenneth took over his new job, they

started looking for somewhere to live. They found a house on the edge of the New Forest in a village called Annesley. It was a muddle of a house: six bedrooms, many adjoining each other, one small bathroom and no central heating. In winter the only warm room was the kitchen. There was a small strip of garden at the back dominated by a snowy cherry tree, but who needed a garden with the New Forest on the doorstep? Their windows looked out on to a garden of ancient trees and sunlit glades stretching for miles and miles. No stately home in the land boasted more than this.

Kenneth paid the princely sum of fifteen hundred pounds for his house, and the initial payment on the mortgage was hard to find. They had hardly any furniture but the vendor sold them large pieces to fill the empty spaces. He was generous, and Kenneth said it was because he fancied Joan. They acquired a Welsh dresser for eight guineas, a corner cupboard for five pounds and a big mahogany dining table with six Victorian chairs for ten guineas.

The time of their move to the new house coincided with the Munich agreement and Mr Chamberlain's promise of 'peace in our time'. Kenneth listened to the news on the wireless with feelings of apprehension, but Joan was too happy to worry about what the politicians were up to; she had her lovely home and, to her mind, the perfect husband – and although they were not at all well off they were able to afford a live-in maid.

Only sceptics like Kenneth thought the war had not

been successfully averted. When it came it changed everything. Kenneth became a Surgeon-Lieutenant in the Royal Navy Reserve, and while he was on a mine-sweeper in the North Sea, the most demoralising and dangerous job imaginable, he thought constantly of his wife battling with the problems of evacuees in their large cold house. And now, miraculously, bearing his child.

Olivia was three months old when her father saw her for the first time, and it was a moment he would remember and cherish all his life. "Kenneth dotes on her," Joan confided to a friend many years later when they were trying to think of a suitable career for Olivia. "If he had his way she would stay at home and do nothing."

It was true, and perhaps he loved her more because the war had prevented him from seeing her for so much of the first precious years of her childhood. On one leave she was a baby, sitting in a high chair, on the next she was a happy child, running rather than walking, and laughing a lot. Like most of the English babies in wartime she was the picture of health, with clear skin and corn-coloured hair. When the evacuees left (their misguided parents believing an unlikely bomb attack was preferable to being stuck in the country) Olivia became a solitary little girl. She began to talk to imaginary friends and fairies. When her father came home they walked in the forest together and looked for fairies in the boles of trees. On his next leave Kenneth found the fairies had disappeared from her life, and she became scornful when he mentioned them. Their demise could be attributed to her new-found friendship with Adam Bowlby, the vicar's unruly son who had no truck with fairies.

During the war years Joan never ceased thinking of Kenneth. She convinced herself that if she forgot him for one second of the day something would happen to him. She went to sleep at night with him on her mind, and when she awoke in the morning her first thought was to wonder what he was doing at that moment. When he came back for good she honestly believed that she had kept him alive with her thoughts and prayers.

Kenneth returned thankfully to the job he had barely begun before the war, and the elderly General Practitioner who had been doing everyone's work at the surgery was able to retire at last. Life was filled with wonder and hope, as before, but now had another dimension, gratitude. Kenneth left all religious matters to Joan; he had an ambivalent attitude to God and had not sought help from that direction even in the worst hours, but after all he had witnessed he would never cease to be grateful.

Olivia spent the last two years of her education at a boarding school. Kenneth had been reluctant, but Joan had insisted. The walks he took with his daughter were for a time limited to school holidays; then when the final exams were taken (with only fair results) she came home and the walks were resumed on a more permanent basis. Kenneth was delighted, but Joan pointed out that a girl couldn't spend the rest of her life going for walks, bicycling to tennis parties and attending local dances with Adam Bowlby. "Olivia must do something," was her constant cry.

From Olivia's bedroom she looked on to a greensward, about the size of a village cricket pitch (the real cricket pitch was on the other side of Annesley) and beyond was a little lane, winding between the giant oaks and beech trees. In the winter the lane became a quagmire, and was named, appropriately, the Muddy Lane by the villagers. This was the start of the walk Kenneth and Olivia took over the years, always accompanied by two dogs. The dogs changed, and they changed as well. Kenneth became a little grizzled and even leaner, and Olivia lost the sunlit beauty of her childhood but retained the sweet disposition and shy charm.

"Come, Rufus! Come, Rusty!" No need for dog leads as there was no traffic anywhere near. Along the Muddy Lane and then straight into the forest. It was quiet but, when you listened carefully, full of small sounds, like the leaves in the trees above rustling and sighing and the scrunching underfoot of little sticks. And the dogs, golden retrievers, snuffling and snorting in the tall bracken on either side of the wide grassy path, returning at intervals to make sure the walkers were still there.

Of course, on this particular day, they had to disturb the perfection by talking about Olivia's future. It was a subject much discussed by her parents, by her mother especially, and she wished they would leave it alone.

"I can't imagine anyone will give me a job," she said, exasperated. "I'm so ordinary and stupid." Of course she did not believe this to be true; she was too aware of the love and respect her parents and friends had for her to undervalue herself in this way, but the words were uttered in defiance of the pressure that was being brought to bear on her.

Her father found her words disconcerting, and he hastened to say, "You are not ordinary and you are not stupid," and then went on to quote some book or other, as he was apt to do. Olivia did not recognise the quotation, as she did not read books, a fact Kenneth found hard to understand. In his busy life he had always found time to read. He suspected that even as a child Olivia had not been interested in books. In her girlish bedroom there was a shelf containing childhood classics such as *Black Beauty* and *What Katy Did*. Her mother had placed them there, and Kenneth believed they had never been touched.

"Maybe if you read more," he said gently, switching at fronds of bracken with his stick, "you would learn about life and people, and not feel so ordinary."

Olivia was silent. She did not feel reprimanded, as she was too secure in her father's affection to believe he was seriously finding fault.

"It's just that I hate the idea of leaving all this . . . again," she said sadly, remembering the strange pain in her chest she had experienced when she went away to school, a sort of nagging ache which did not go away until she was back home.

She had told no one of this phenomenon but if she

had mentioned it to Kenneth he would have diagnosed the problem at once, for it was akin to his own. Sometimes when Olivia was away he had peeped into her bedroom, and the forlorn tidiness of it smote his heart. No clothes lying across the chair and on the bed, no shoes and tennis racquets cluttering the floor. If he had had his way she would never have gone away to school, but Joan had decreed otherwise and Joan was always right. He appreciated the dangers of being overprotective of an only child.

"We will always be around, you know," he said, "and you want a career, don't you? To be your own person and not dependent on others?" He felt he must instil some ambition into his girl.

"I suppose so."

"I know I'm right," he said firmly, "and one day you will see it for yourself. It is important that you do something." He was aware that he was echoing his wife's words, and suddenly he found himself thinking of an old aunt, his mother's sister, long since dead, who had never wanted to leave home. She had stayed, eventually living alone, apparently contented. Could it be that Olivia took after her? But, in a modern age this course was no longer open to young women, and could not be considered.

They arrived at a river called the Highland Water. The name was a mystery for they were in Hampshire, not in Scotland. A narrow wooden bridge with a new handrail, which had recently replaced the old one when it became unsafe, spanned the river. Even so, care had to be taken when crossing the bridge. Kenneth, in his endless endeavours to educate Olivia (and also to give himself pleasure) had told her several times that the Highland Water was mentioned in a play called *Journey's End*. Two army officers in the First World War, waiting to go over the top, in order to distract their minds from what is going to happen to them, talk about the places they know and love the best. One of them describes the Highland Water. Olivia loved this story; she could relate to the way the soldier felt about the place and how his mind would turn to it at such a tragic moment. She did not mind how many times her father described to her the last heart-rending scene of the play, for although she did not read books she was a wonderful listener. Years later, when she was catching up on all the reading she had lost, she remembered Kenneth talking about *Journey's End* and she made a point of looking for it among his books.

The brackish water beneath the bridge chattered over brown shiny stones, and into it dashed the dogs, spraying globules of water in all directions, then jumping on to the bank and shaking themselves vigorously. After a heavy rainfall the river became a noisy monster, torrents of water swirling and rising every day until it almost reached the level of the bridge. The child Olivia had longed for it to get there, but it never did.

The problem was what was this 'something' that Olivia should do? Although quietly happy she was aware of a slight feeling of restlessness, an unspoken fear that time was slipping by, that something was expected of her but she did not know what it was.

"What do you think I should do?" she asked her father.

He did not know the answer. She was not a girl with a fixed ambition, certainly not clever enough to go to university. For instance, there was no chance of her becoming a doctor or lawyer. Kenneth had never faced this dilemma; he had known from the age of twelve that he wanted to be a doctor. How proud he would have been if his daughter had chosen the medical profession! Sometimes he thought, rather guiltily, if only they had a son! But, for some reason, hard to understand, they had not been able to repeat the miracle of birth.

He said, "Mummy has suggested a secretarial course in London. It lasts a year. In fact she has made enquiries, and you could start in a few weeks. Does that appeal to you?"

He held his breath.

"What do you think?" She was cursed with indecisiveness and uncertainty, and of course it was her mother, not hampered by such characteristics, who had decided what she should do.

"I think it is a good idea," he said. They walked without speaking. He was wondering if it was the right decision and she was feeling relieved that a decision had been made.

"If the course is in London," said Olivia at last, "where shall I live?"

"Mummy suggested that we might ask Aunt Patience if you could stay with her."

He and Joan had discussed it the previous night – in the place where they had all their discussions, the bedroom.

Patience was Joan's sister and Olivia's godmother. Kenneth had reservations about her being asked to act as guardian and landlady. He had an abiding memory of her at Olivia's christening in the village church. She had brought a whiff of sophistication to the quiet little ceremony, appearing in a long fur coat and high-heeled shoes, making everyone else look threadbare and war weary. He had made some comment about her, and Joan had been quick to point out that Patience was living in London at the time, barricaded in her house in Queen's Gate with only her maid, Hilda, for company. The two women lived in freezing conditions on the lower floor with sandbags outside the front door, one room having been turned into an ARP meeting place. Patience went to the Ministry of Defence every day where she was doing some secret war work.

Joan was right, of course, but there were things about Patience's life that made Kenneth uneasy. Most of all, the fact that she had been married to Sir Cosmo Lucas, a much respected Member of Parliament, and when the marriage failed Sir Cosmo manfully took the blame for its inadequacies and a divorce was granted. He provided evidence of adultery by spending a short time with a young woman in a hotel bedroom in Brighton. This was the behaviour of a gentleman, but Kenneth thought the whole thing incredibly tawdry, and it irritated him that his sister-in-law had profited by the sordid business, getting a generous allowance and the gift of a substantial property in Queen's Gate.

The allowance would cease on her remarriage, and wisely Patience did not embark on matrimony again. In the early years she visited Joan and her husband from time to time, but she was the first to admit she was not a country person. After the war, when English houses began to warm up slightly, she found the house in Annesley cold and uncomfortable. Perhaps she sensed Kenneth's feelings about her, for gradually she grew apart from them. The two sisters occasionally communicated by telephone and scrawled messages on Christmas cards. The cards sent by Patience were designed by her, and loyally preserved each year by Joan, for that is what she did after the war – painted pictures for calendars and cards.

"I'm not sure she is the right person to ask," Kenneth had said to Joan.

"Of course she is. She is my sister and I have complete trust in her."

"We've heard stories, love affairs, that sort of thing."

"If there is any truth in those stories Patience will be discreet, you may be sure of that."

"I hope you're right."

When he told Olivia about the proposal that she should live with her aunt, she turned a radiant face towards him. "Oh, that would be wonderful!"

"But you have not seen her for so long. I'm surprised that you remember her."

"I remember her very well, Daddy. Surely you haven't

forgotten her coming down here with the man who owned the red sports car, and how they took me for a drive in it?"

"That was years ago. You were only a child."

"I liked her very much," said Olivia.

"Well, don't get your hopes too high," said Kenneth dryly. "She may say no."

Patience was approached, and, rather surprisingly, consented to having her niece to stay with her during the term time, and the sum of four pounds a week was agreed upon for her keep.

Once everything was arranged Joan and Olivia were soon busy choosing clothes suitable for London. It was like going back to school again, thought Olivia, the same indigestion and uncomfortable feeling that she did not want to go through with it.

Her parents came to see her off at Southampton station. She felt she wanted to register their dear faces on her mind forever, and it seemed to her she was leaving them for good instead of only thirteen weeks. Sensing how she was feeling, her father pointed out that she could visit them at weekends whenever she wished. Olivia looked at her mother's serene face, the dark hair cut very short, and her father, shaggy grey hair in need of a cut, a well-worn suit hanging on his lean body, his hand so cool and comforting, loving her with every squeeze of the fingers. Then her lips on her mother's soft cheek and her father's rough one.

"Give Patience our love."

"Ring us."

They had already given her money, much more than she needed, and her two suitcases were crammed with new clothes. In a way it was a relief when the train pulled out of the station, and she could settle into the corner seat of the carriage and glance at the magazines her mother had insisted on buying for her at the last moment.

How silly I am, she thought, of course everything will be perfect. She acknowledged to herself that she felt a nervousness out of proportion to the very small adventure ahead of her. Since leaving school, she told herself, she had been at home too long and that made it difficult to make a fresh start. She wanted to see new places and meet other people, but at the moment home seemed very attractive, a place where she was assured of love and did not have to prove anything.

After a while she started gazing out of the grimy window, seeing her rather wan reflection in the glass, and, behind it, passing rapidly, fields and little houses with gardens and sheds sloping down to the railway line. Soon smoky tenements replaced these, and brick walls with messages chalked on them, telling her that she had left the peace of the countryside and had entered a world containing angry and defiant people.

At Waterloo she was lucky enough to catch the eye of a young man in the taxi queue. Obligingly he helped her with her heavy suitcases, and insisted on waiting with her until a cab arrived to take her to her aunt's house. She gave him a sideways glance, quickly so that he would not notice, and she decided he was rather good looking. She waved to him through the window as the taxi moved away, and he stood, rather forlornly, on the pavement, wondering why he had not found out more about her. He had thought it too forward to ask for her name and address. Life is full of such lost moments, and if he had been more enterprising everything might have been different. It was a chance encounter that came to nothing, but it gave Olivia a frisson of excitement and she began to think living in London might not be so bad after all.

Chapter 2

Olivia pressed the front door bell of the house in Queen's Gate. It was a house with an imposing façade in a terrace of similar houses, all alike in their elegant simplicity. Her two large suitcases were at her feet. Darkness was beginning to fall, and the long beams of the streetlights were slanting across the pavements. There was a night chill in the air.

Someone familiar to Olivia opened the door. Although she had never met her, she had heard her mother mention her many times. Her name was Hilda and she was a kind fat lady who was her aunt's maid. Except when she ventured out to the shops or to the pictures she always wore a multicoloured flowered overall, tied tightly under her large bosom. To Hilda everyone was 'dear'.

"Come in, dear. Let me help you with those cases."

"Please don't worry. I can manage."

But Hilda insisted, and together they dragged the suitcases into the narrow hall and then up one flight of stairs.

Hilda opened a door, and said, "This is your room, dear, and the bathroom is opposite."

"Thank you."

"Take your time, dear, and come down when you are ready."

"Thank you," Olivia said again.

The bedroom was sparsely furnished and cold, but as most English bedrooms were cold in the fifties Olivia did not notice the temperature. She unpacked her dresses, skirts and blouses and hung them in a white-painted wardrobe. She put other items – underclothing, stockings and a bulky packet of sanitary towels – into the drawers of a small painted chest of drawers. There was a dressing table in the room on top of which stood a three-sided mirror, nothing else. She soon filled the empty space with her jars and bottles, hairbrush and comb and a photograph of her parents in a leather frame. The single bed was covered in a pretty patchwork quilt, and beside the bed was a little table, on it a lamp with a pink shade. She put her travelling clock, a present from her father, on to the table. The walls of the room were painted white, and there was only one picture, a Monet print of the *Thames below Westminster*. A hanging bookcase was filled with rather dog-eared books. She read two of the titles, *Chrome Yellow* by Aldous Huxley and *Strong Poison* by Dorothy L. Sayers.

She peered at her reflection in the mirror from all angles, and dabbed powder on her nose and applied lipstick to her lips. Then she stood in the centre of the room, thinking she ought to venture downstairs. She felt her confidence diminish slightly, but the feeling was instantly dispelled by a loud rap on the door and the entrance of her aunt who enveloped her in a warm embrace. Olivia found herself pressed against a soft plump body, and she took a deep breath of musky scent.

Patience Lucas was dressed in a way that was well ahead of her time. The word "hippy" was unknown then. She wore a loose-fitting garment, heavily embroidered in bright colours. Around her neck and in her ears were heavy pieces of jewellery. Her thick mane of curly hair was bunched at the back and held by a silver clasp.

"How lovely to see you!" she said, stepping back and looking at Olivia. "And what fun it will be having you to live with us." She sounded as if she meant it.

The girl replied politely, "I've been looking forward to coming, Aunt Patience."

A slight frown appeared on the other's face. "Darling, I must ask you not to call me 'aunt'. It sounds so stuffy. And I do not like the name Patience. When you have known me longer you will realise the name does not suit me at all. I have no patience."

Olivia was surprised to hear this, and wondered why her mother had never mentioned it. At home she had always been Patience. Perhaps it was a whim her aunt had acquired lately, together with the strange attire. Olivia had been quite young when she had seen her last and she remembered the clothes she wore then, and the shoes, and she remembered 'thin' as well – did her mother know about the increase in weight? She could not help glancing down to see what was worn on the feet now, and she spied flat thonged sandals.

However, she was a guest and anxious to please, so she said, "What would you like me to call you?"

"Pat. Everyone calls me Pat."

Olivia was disappointed. The name Pat evoked a drunken Irishman whereas Patience was romantic. But it was settled, and Pat it was from that moment, and very soon she could not imagine calling her by any other name.

"Now we'll have supper," said Pat, "and I'll show you around the rest of the house tomorrow."

All meals were eaten in the kitchen which was spacious, with room for an old-fashioned dresser, and even a desk, strewn with papers, in one corner. The three women, Pat, Hilda and Olivia sat at a plain wooden table, enjoying the warmth of a nearby Raeburn stove. It was unusual, the lady of the house eating with the servant, and the thought passed through Olivia's head that Pat must be a Socialist.

Hilda did not remove her apron, and before sitting down with them stood by the stove spooning a delicious concoction of meat and gravy straight from the pot on to warm plates. With it they had chunks of brown bread and a bowl of salad.

"This is so good," murmured Olivia. "We never have food like this at home."

"Hilda is a marvellous cook," said Pat. "I am so lucky. She has a marvellous touch with herbs and spices. Even during the war we ate well, didn't we, darling?"

"That we did, dear."

Olivia was impressed that her aunt had a maid. Her mother had told her that in the late thirties they had been able to afford a live-in servant, but she had gone into munitions during the war and they had not had one since.

While Hilda was carrying the plates into the little scullery adjoining the kitchen she asked Pat, "How long has Hilda been with you?"

"Oh, years," replied Pat carelessly. "I can't remember how many years we have looked after each other."

They were so sweet together, but Olivia noticed that Hilda did not join in the conversation. She remained silent while Pat rattled on about Joan and their childhood together, asking Olivia a lot of questions about their life in Annesley. "I'm a Londoner," she said, "through and through. I've got everything I want here."

It was true. Pat was a happy woman, content with her life, her work and her many friends. She treasured her independence, being inclined to forget Sir Cosmo's contribution towards it. Her unfortunate marriage had been a blessing in that it provided her with the means to do what she wanted.

At first, when approached by Joan about having Olivia

to stay, she had been dubious. It would interrupt the routine that was important to her and, supposing the arrangement proved intolerable, it would be hard to withdraw without embarrassment. However, she felt slightly guilty that she had neglected her only relatives over the years, not because she did not love them but because they lived a different life from hers and she had not bothered to bridge the gap. Perhaps she had been given this opportunity to remedy the situation before it was too late.

She studied Olivia, sitting quietly at the table, and she reflected that an enchanting child had grown into a pleasing if not out of the ordinary young woman. No backbone though, she thought, and wondered how her determined sister had managed to produce a shrinking violet. Kenneth, of course, was charming, but a mild-mannered man and no doubt his daughter took after him.

Olivia, in her turn, was thinking that Pat was a very attractive woman, and it was hard to know why she came to this conclusion. She knew that Pat was five years younger than her mother, and she could see the likeness between the sisters. That was surprising too, and she could not put a finger on where it lay. In most respects they were completely different, so maybe it was the turn of the head or the voice. Pat was not as good-looking as Joan. In fact she was quite ugly with a face wrong in every feature. Her eyes were too small, her mouth too wide and her nose was lumpy and bumpy. Her skin was sallow and, as to her figure, she had shapely breasts but her movements were ungainly and she had chunky legs. It was astonishing that so many people of both sexes considered her almost beautiful. It may have been her hair that gave them this impression. A wonderful mass of intractable curls, she knew it was her greatest, her only, asset and she refused to have it cut, wearing it in an untidy bun when she got too old to have it hanging down her back. No, it was her warm voluptuousness that was so alluring, and a man only had to look at her to know that richness lay in that soft compliant body. She had women friends as well, and they loved her because she was a good listener and there was no problem she could not relate to, understand and advise upon. She did not care for women as much as men, and sometimes they irritated her and she was quick to criticise. But, even so, they sensed she was without malice, and she prided herself that she did not get involved with husbands.

The next morning, as promised, Pat showed Olivia the rest of the house. First of all, they went into the room that was meant to be a drawing room but had become a studio. It was a large light room of graceful proportions, an empty marble fireplace at one end and beautiful plaster mouldings on the ceiling. A Valor oil stove heated it during the winter months. It was empty of furniture except for an easel, a chair and a big table covered with pots and tubes of paint, brushes stuck in a chipped white jug, pencils, chalks, rags and other paraphernalia.

"This is what I'm working on at present," explained

Pat. It was a screen and on it was a half finished picture of a woman kneeling in a garden. It was done with broad-brush strokes and was a medley of blues and greens in the sky and the foliage, and pinks and yellows in the flowers in the border the woman was weeding.

"The painting is lovely," said Olivia.

"Oh, it's not mine, I'm afraid. I copied it from a painting by Alfred Sisley. It's for an order from Harrods, and the colours complement the room where the screen will stand. I do a lot of orders, mostly screens, like this one, or panels. They are made for me by a little man in Camden, then I decorate them and sell them for a big profit." There was no doubt she was talented, and if she had been obliged to live on her earnings, without Sir Cosmo's allowance, she would have been able to manage, but not in a house in Queen's Gate.

"And the cards and calendars?" Olivia asked.

"They are not important. I do them to keep the pot boiling."

Next to the studio was a smaller room, which must have once been the dining room. Now it was used for sitting in after supper and it contained two shabby armchairs and a sofa. Big cushions were scattered around on the floor for people to sit on. Olivia noticed there were no photographs anywhere, and the room was strangely empty. On one wall hung a single large painting. She did not know the name of the artist, and therefore had no idea of its value. She was attracted to it in a strange way, but she thought it very peculiar, and decided her father would not like it at all. Later, much later her aunt told her how much it was worth, and Olivia wondered why she did not sell it. She could not know that a time would come when the painting would belong to her, and she would not dream of selling it. Characteristically, Pat had decided it needed no rivals and it occupied most of the space of one wall, and there were no other paintings in the room. The opposite wall had a gas fire fitted to it, with white gas mantles, which had to be changed from time to time when they became discoloured. The fire made a hissing sound when it was lit, but the chatter in the room was usually so loud that no one noticed it.

On that first day in London Olivia was left to her own devices. Having shown her over the house Pat retired to her studio, shutting the door behind her. Olivia decided to venture outside, and she walked along Cromwell Road and spent an hour wandering around the Victoria and Albert museum. Then she jumped on to a 74 bus, a bus that was to become very familiar to her, and she went to Harrods. It was so fascinating for a girl like Olivia, the exotic clothes, expensive handbags and shoes and the heady scent of the make-up department. By the time she started the return journey to Queen's Gate the shops were closing and lights were being turned on all over the city. The streets were jammed with brightly lit buses and taxis, and the crowds jostled each other on the pavements. She wondered if Pat would be worried about her, if she had stayed out too long. She was accustomed to her parent's concern if she was away from home for more than a few hours and they did not know where she was.

She let herself in with the key Hilda had given to her. She hoped she had not caused them anxiety on her first day. She put her head round the door of the kitchen, and Hilda looked up from rolling out pastry on the table, and said, "Had a nice day, dear?" When Pat appeared she asked the same question, and it was apparent she had not been in the least troubled by Olivia's long absence.

The following day was the first day of the course. Pat usually stayed in bed until about eleven o'clock, but on this day she made the effort to come downstairs at half past eight. In her dressing-gown she gave Olivia a hug, and wished her luck. After that, every day started the same way. Hilda insisted on cooking her breakfast and when Olivia protested she said, "Begin the day with a full stomach, dear. That's my motto." After she had eaten and thanked Hilda, Olivia let herself out of the front door, quietly so as not to disturb Pat, and walked along the street, and across another street to the secretarial college.

There were two classes, the typing class and the shorthand class. The girls were taught to type rhythmically, and each one sat bolt upright in front of a weighty manual typewriter bearing the name in gold lettering: *Imperial*. Popular tunes were played over and over again on a record player. The favourite was "Put Another

Nickel In" as it had a suitable jerky tune. No looking at keys was allowed. The girl sitting next to Olivia seemed to have the ideal temperament for touch-typing and rapidly tapped from one exercise to the next, whereas Olivia, towards the end of a passage, began to think too much, faltered, hit the wrong key and had to start again. She had been the same playing tennis, starting to lose when with a little more confidence she could have gone on to win.

She was more proficient with the shorthand, and sitting on top of a bus she found herself mentally transcribing the advertisements on the hoardings. Shorthand, like riding a bicycle, is never forgotten, and long after those pencil markings became obsolete she would use them for lists and messages.

Life at Queen's Gate was interesting. There was a dinner party almost every night, and even though the food was served in the kitchen the women wore evening dresses and the men dinner jackets. Hilda ate with them but, as always, hardly uttered a word. She served the delicious food she had cooked from a row of pots on the top of the stove. When the diners retired to the poky sitting room, with a polite 'Thank you, Hilda, that was lovely', she set to work clearing the plates and silver from the table, and then putting them all in a sink fully of hot soapy water. Washing up for so many people was a daunting task for an elderly lady, especially as the guests did not rise from the table until late at night.

When she could escape from the others, Olivia

would help with the drying, Hilda protesting all the time, saying, "It's not right for you to do this, dear." Then the usually taciturn Hilda would become talkative, and tell Olivia about her childhood in Somerset, and how when she was fifteen she went into service for Lady Lucas, Sir Cosmo's mother. "She was a real Tartar, dear." When Lady Lucas died Hilda started working for Pat, and when the marriage broke up she asked if she could stay with her. "I've never regretted it, dear, not for a moment."

Olivia heard how Pat and Hilda stayed in London during the war, and how they dug themselves into this house in Queen's Gate with sandbags around the front door and all the big windows equipped with blackout frames which had to be fixed every evening before it got dark. How the big room, now Pat's studio, was the headquarters for the local ARP, and how Pat did hush-hush war work.

"We were here all during the Blitz," Hilda told her, "and every night we wondered if our end would come. A big bomb dropped on the corner of our street, where it meets Cromwell Road. It was like a gaping tooth that corner, until they built Baden-Powell House."

Olivia loved hearing all these stories.

All sorts of people came to the dinner parties. Like Hilda, Olivia did not say much but she listened. For instance, she noticed that although Pat was always standing up for the rights of women, that they should have equal pay and the same opportunities as men, and more support in the home (like many childless women, she considered looking after children a mindless occupation), she did not welcome opposition to her views, especially from her own sex. Olivia thought it strange that the men almost with one voice agreed with everything she said. If there was dissent, it always came from a woman in the party, and Pat was quick to quash it.

One evening she was elaborating on one of her favourite themes, that a girl should live with a man before marrying him. She would have been gratified to know that in a short time it would become the norm. To Olivia's dismay she had no compunction in telling how she and her sister, under misguided parental influence, had both been virgins when they married. Everything had worked out well for Joan, but for Pat it had been disastrous, a marriage never consummated. Olivia hardly knew what this meant, but she could guess, and she felt herself blushing.

A woman opposite her said to Pat, "I would not like you to influence a daughter of mine with your views."

Pat gave her a withering look, turned to her niece and said, "You don't think I'm a bad influence, do you, darling?"

"Of course not."

The men laughed and Olivia concentrated very hard on hiding her embarrassment. It would not do to appear discomforted

On another evening a black man joined their table, his face shining like ebony in the candlelight. Pat always had candles on the kitchen table. Olivia's neighbour, whose name was Bob, informed her in a quiet voice, "He is a famous cricketer. He is not allowed to stay at any of the good hotels in London even though he has come over here to play at Lords. It is a disgrace."

Olivia thought so too. "How awful!"

"That is why he is staying here with Pat. She has the right idea about such things."

"One day," said Bob, sipping his wine, and then holding his glass near a candle so that the red liquid was reflected in the glow, "one day there will be no racism in this country, and blacks will mingle with whites. The streets of London will be teeming with people of all colours. It will be a cosmopolitan city."

Olivia found this hard to believe, as she seldom saw a foreign face in London. The day before had been an exception when a black man had got on the bus in which she was travelling. There had been a little flutter of interest among the other passengers, and Olivia noticed a child nudging his mother as he stared at the stranger. Surely that reaction would never change? But now she looked at the black man with new interest and thought she would like to know him better. It was her shyness, not the colour of his skin that stopped her from speaking to him.

In the middle of that night she saw Bob again. Lying in her narrow bed she was awoken suddenly by a floorboard creaking in the passage outside her bedroom door. She got out of bed, and quietly opened the door.

She saw the rear view of Bob tiptoeing along the corridor, and he had nothing on! How she knew it was Bob she did not know, but she recognised him instantly. Olivia had never seen a naked man before, and she was struck by the absurdity of his retreating bottom and spindly legs. When she climbed back into bed she lay in the dark laughing silently to herself. Mother would have a fit, she thought, and of course she would never tell her.

Olivia felt none of the pangs of homesickness she had experienced at school. Her life was so full she did not have time to appreciate the extent of her happiness. The truth was she hardly ever thought of her parents, the dogs and the forest. Pat had to remind her to telephone her mother and father once a week as they had agreed. She became completely engrossed in all that went on in the house in Queen's Gate, and in her work at the college. Learning to type and to write shorthand was not too taxing, and she had made friends at last. When she arrived at the college each morning she was greeted by friendly faces.

And then, of course, there was Alice.

Chapter 3

Olivia sometimes had a small suspicion that Alice's friendship with her was largely due to her intense curiosity about the occupants of the house in Queen's Gate. Olivia, flattered to be singled out from so many as a companion to such a popular girl, was happy to fuel the interest. Alice never tired of hearing about Pat and Hilda, and, most of all, the people who came to dine every night in the kitchen. It was as if she was starved of stimulating company, and she was always complaining about the girl she shared a flat with in Cromwell Road. "She's so boring," she said. 'Boring' was a favourite word of hers.

She wanted to know the smallest detail. "What is Pat's bedroom like?"

"Lovely. The furniture is painted a sort of deep turquoise with lots of gold leaf and carving. She has an enormous bed. No blankets, just a puffed-up eiderdown affair, very soft and downy."

A group of girls met in a coffee bar during the lunch break for a hot drink and a cream pastry. Olivia and Alice usually managed to get a small table on their own because Alice, who was older than most of the students by a few years, thought them woefully immature and, for this reason, not worthy of her companionship. It was true that many of them were like overgrown schoolgirls, but Alice did not count Olivia among them, although she was the same age, and maintained she was more adult. They had two free hours to fill (including the walk back and forth to college) so they made their cups of coffee and pastries last, finishing up with cigarettes. Olivia had never smoked until now, as her father considered it a health hazard, despite the general belief that it did not harm, and, according to one famous advertisement was beneficial to the throat. Alice smoked, so Olivia did too, rather self-consciously and with a faint feeling of guilt.

Although Alice liked to think of herself as grown-up, it was the raw youthfulness of her that was so devastating. There was a healthy warmth about her that was very seductive – glowing skin, shining hair, breathing life and sunshine. She had round blue eyes, which she opened very wide to good effect, and a rather sharp pointed nose. Her hair was naturally fair, long and very straight. She brushed it to one side so that a heavy hank fell over her shoulder and on to one breast. She had a habit of shifting the mane from one shoulder to the other with a deft movement of hand and head. When she smiled, and she smiled often, it was an endearingly wide smile revealing rather large even white teeth.

She liked to shock, and because of her youth there seemed no harm in it, it was just silliness. Olivia did not entirely believe her when she recounted stories about the men she had known, but she enjoyed listening. She had doubts about Alice's 'bad reputation' and she suspected that Alice herself had promulgated the rumours that circulated about her. As there were no men in the college it was hard to know how Alice behaved in male company. Occasionally she bestowed her gleaming smile on a chap at the next table in the coffee bar, but it went no further than that.

"You have such a lovely voice," she said to Olivia. "I hate my voice."

She had a sweet light voice and a boisterous laugh. She was continually denigrating herself in this way, and Olivia found it hard to understand. It seemed so out of character, as if she was trying to convince people that she thought little of herself despite the blatant self-confidence.

Olivia had little self-confidence, and she felt she could learn from Alice. Like most of the girls of her generation, she had become adept at warding off hands struggling with bra-straps and suspenders, usually in the back seats of cars. Adam Bowlby was beginning to be a problem in this way, and it was a relief to be in London away from him, although he was threatening to come and see her. She did not know how to put him off. He was a childhood friend and she did not want to hurt him. Alice would have known how to deal with the situation. There was very little honesty in the fifties – that came later in the enlightened sixties. The love game was a mixture of pleasure, ignorance and desire. The girls divined they had powers to entice and reject, and they used these powers mercilessly and with no understanding. Alice may have gone further but it was doubtful. The fear of pregnancy was very real.

When news of Queen's Gate had dried up the girls turned to another topic, the teacher who taught them typing. She was called Miss Drake, and they discovered her first name was Marcia, and for some inexplicable reason this name caused amusement. She was a youngish plain woman with a suspicion of a moustache on the upper lip. There was no doubt that she admired Alice greatly, and it was assumed she had a 'thing' about her. She was always praising Alice when she did not deserve it, and she looked at her with a peculiar expression, a sort of dog-like devotion.

Of course Olivia had come across Marcia's type at school. Some of the mistresses were inclined to be that way about their pet pupils, but she had never been one of the favourites. Alice, by her own account, was a magnet. "Frightful lesbians," she said scornfully, "they always fall for me."

One morning Alice appeared with her hair up – it was a fashion much followed at that time – but her hair was too long, too straight and kept slipping out of the pins. Marcia was quite upset. "Your lovely hair . . ."

"Bloody cheek," said Alice to Olivia later, having freed

her hair with one flamboyant shake of the head. "What has it got to do with her, how I do my hair?"

"She was right though, it looked awful."

"She is supposed to teach us typing, not make comments about our appearance."

Olivia had to admit her friend went too far at times, and her outrageous behaviour was an embarrassment. For instance, the day after the hair incident she said to Marcia, "Miss Drake, do you mind my asking what colour knickers you are wearing today?"

It was so absurd and childish and a ripple of amusement went around the class. Surely she would not reply?

Marcia however remained cool. "No, of course I don't mind, Miss Mountjoy," she parried. "Why should I? The answer is beige."

The revelation (beige!) was almost unbearable, and some of the sillier girls held handkerchiefs to their mouths to stifle giggles. It was soon after this that Marcia failed to appear. They were told she was ill, but the rumour circulated that she had been dismissed.

"If she has lost her job," said Alice, now on Marcia's side, "it is very unfair. She can't help having unnatural tendencies and should not be made to suffer for them. I think we should all sign a petition saying we want her back." They all thought it a good idea, but in the manner of the young did nothing about it.

Then Olivia ran into Marcia sitting at a table on her own in Lyons Corner House. In front of her were a pot of tea and a wedge of iced walnut cake.

"Hello, Miss Drake."

Marcia gave her a watery smile of recognition, and Olivia sat down opposite her.

"Are you better?" she asked in the sort of voice her mother might have used.

"Oh, I wasn't ill," replied Marcia. "That was an excuse. In fact, I was asked to leave. Someone complained about me. Rather unpleasant really."

"I'm sorry."

"So am I. It was the perfect job for me, not far from Gloucester Road where I live with my mother. Now I have to look for another post."

Olivia hoped that she would not start weeping, but Marcia managed to control her tears and went on bitterly, "They will have no difficulty in finding a replacement. Supervising typing classes and putting on records requires no skill."

"Who could have complained?" Olivia wondered.

"I shall never know who it was." She paused. "How is Al – Miss Mountjoy?" The teachers were not supposed to be on familiar terms with the students.

"She is very well," Olivia told her. "As a matter of fact she was thinking of getting up a petition to have you reinstated."

An unbecoming flush travelled up Marcia's neck to her face. "How sweet of her, but it would do no good. Thank her for me, will you? And give her my love."

When Alice heard this she said, "There is simply no way to help that pathetic creature."

And that was the end of Marcia Drake as far as the girls were concerned. She was soon forgotten, and Olivia did not think of her again until her name came to mind, years later.

Something far more interesting had happened at Queen's Gate. One evening Olivia returned from college to find that someone called Captain Nigel occupied a place at the kitchen table – at least that was Pat's name for him.

Nigel Benton was a Captain in the Territorial Army, one of his many interests, and originally Pat had named him Captain Nigel so as not to confuse him with another Nigel of her acquaintance. Not that there could be any confusion, and Olivia soon realised how special he was to Pat. Also, Olivia could not help noticing that after Captain Nigel's arrival Bob disappeared from the scene.

Pat radiated happiness in the presence of Nigel, and it became evident that he was not just another visitor but a resident. He had his own room, and a cupboard full of Saville Row suits, and Hilda took pride in washing and ironing his handmade shirts.

Olivia liked him at once. He was immensely tall, about six feet five inches, and had a baldish head and pale blue eyes. On the first day she met him, he said to her in that clipped Army voice that was to become so familiar to her, "Tell me about the college you go to every day. Do you like it?" He was the first person in that house to take an interest in her day-to-day activity. Pat could not bring herself to be enthusiastic about shorthand and typing.

He was indulged in every way. He was particular, so rooms were tidied and cushions plumped for his benefit. Hilda worshipped him, and he teased her, slapping her bottom and undoing the strings of her overall. Her stout body shook with laughter at his antics. He called her 'the boss' and 'What's the boss cooked for me today?' was the sort of question she loved to hear.

Olivia learned that he had been away from Queen's Gate for three months on an archaeological dig in Greece. During his absence Olivia had come to stay, unaware of his existence, but she now realised his importance in the house and that his return was the reason for much rejoicing.

Alice was agog. "Does he sleep with her?" she wanted to know.

Olivia admitted that she had discovered that he slept with Pat.

"Do you mean he sleeps in her room every night?"

"Not every night, but quite often. When I am in my room I can hear him walking along the passage to Pat's room. He makes no secret of it. In fact he is rather noisy, heavy on his feet. It is usually about one o'clock when he goes to her room, and he returns just before I get up."

"Why don't they share a room and be done with it?" declared Alice. "I suppose she is worried about her reputation."

"Oh, no," cried Olivia jumping to her aunt's defence. "She would never worry about that. She believes, you see, that sharing a room destroys the romance." It was an opinion expressed by Pat at one of the dinner parties, before Nigel appeared on the scene. Olivia had thought about it carefully, and decided she might be right. Surely, however much you loved someone it must be nice to be alone in your bed sometimes? Not always having to listen to a man's breathing, or, God forbid, perhaps his snoring.

"How utterly stupid!" was Alice's view.

Olivia had an uneasy feeling that she was being disloyal to Pat, but Alice's avid interest was gratifying and hard to withstand. However, she was glad that she had never told her about Bob. The idea of her aunt having one lover was acceptable, but Bob was another matter. She knew Alice would revel in a description of Bob's naked form padding down the passage, but she kept that incident to herself.

"Has she had other men?" asked Alice, as if reading her thoughts, something she was very good at doing.

"Oh, no. I don't think so," Olivia replied, and received a sideways glance, which seemed to say: I know you are lying.

"What would you do if Nigel came to your room one night?"

It was a mischievous question, and Olivia thought it very funny. No, she did not know what she would do. "It's an education living in that house," she said.

"Why don't you ask me to dinner so that I can meet these people?" It was an oft-repeated plea. For weeks now Alice had been angling for an invitation to Queen's Gate. "They entertain their friends, why aren't you allowed to entertain yours?"

"It's not a question of being allowed," said Olivia. She was not sure. She wanted to ask her, but she could not help feeling nervous about introducing Alice to Pat and Nigel. Alice was unpredictable, they would be surprised by her, Olivia was sure of that. Not the sort of friend they would expect her to have. She wondered – what would they make of her? Nigel was very straightforward and Army-like and Pat had enough of her sister Joan in her make-up to detest vulgarity. She was unconventional, but she never indulged in smutty humour.

Olivia approached Hilda first. "Do you think I could invite a friend to supper one evening?"

"Of course, dear. Talk to Pat about it. I'm sure she'll say yes."

Pat's reaction was to blame herself for not thinking of it before. "Please ask anyone you like, darling. How selfish I have been not to think of it. This is your home while you are in London."

So Alice was invited to dine in the kitchen at Queen's Gate.

Chapter 4

Olivia was amazed to see how much Captain Nigel took over the running of the house, and even more amazed that Pat allowed him to do it. She seemed content to let him organise everything, and that is what he appeared to enjoy best: organisation. He and Hilda went into a huddle every morning to decide on the meals and the food to order, and he even sorted out the bills that had accumulated on Pat's desk during his absence, and she signed the cheques as he handed them to her.

He wanted to convert one of the bedrooms to a second bathroom, and Pat indulged him in this scheme as well. One of his most endearing qualities was his enthusiasm, and he spent hours chatting to builders and poring over plans. Olivia wondered who was going to meet the costs of the alterations, but this factor did not seem to worry either of them. They were completely happy and at ease with each other. Olivia was sure her parents had no knowledge of the relationship, and she felt if they had known they would have approved.

"It's a joy to see them together," Hilda said.

Both of them were anxious to make Alice welcome. Pat reiterated that she felt guilty because she had not told Olivia she could have friends to the house whenever she wanted. "I thought you would take it for granted, darling. It was wrong of me."

Before Alice's arrival Captain Nigel scuttled around the kitchen table, laying out silver and damask napkins and replacing the candles. He loved doing these tasks, which had once been Hilda's responsibility.

It was obvious that Alice was anxious to make a good impression. She was dressed in a pristine white shirt, open at the neck, and a floral skirt, her tiny waist clinched by a wide belt. With her clear skin and squeaky-clean hair there was one word to describe her: wholesome. Pat sat in her usual seat at the end of the table. She was wearing an orange kimono and a necklace of brown beads around her neck.

Kindly, to put the girl at ease, Pat asked Alice about her family. To Olivia's relief, Alice did not elaborate about her stepfather's shortcomings, as she was apt to do to anyone who would listen, but instead described the house where they lived in Cornwall and made it sound picturesque and rather grand.

"I hope Livvy will come and stay there," she said.

"You call her Livvy?" said Pat. "I like that."

Captain Nigel was writing a book about his experiences in Greece, and he talked amusingly about his secretary. "She is unbelievably bad. She spells Delphi with an 'f'. Hurry up and finish your course, girls – then I can employ one of you instead."

"Not me," said Alice. "I'm hopeless. Livvy is very good." She went on to describe the girls in the typing class, tapping away to tunes on the record player. "Touch-typing is a mindless occupation," she told them. "Only people who have the ability to empty their heads of thought are any good at it."

She has just said *I'm* good at it, thought Olivia.

"How interesting," said Pat. "Like people who never dream – I always think they must be unimaginative."

Alice enthused about the food. "It is so delicious," she said. She turned to Hilda, "You *are* clever." Hilda beamed.

Well, she has got what she wanted, thought Olivia. She is here with the people she so longed to meet, here at this table with the candlelight casting shadows on the ceiling. The conversation flowed easily, and Olivia did not know at what stage in the evening everything changed.

Alice was on her mettle, and she talked. How she talked! In the short pauses when she was airing her views, something Olivia had never had the nerve to do, she listened. Eyes widening with fascinated curiosity, on the alert to break in, like a bird waiting for a moment to swoop.

Captain Nigel admitted to an interest in fossils. He

enjoyed chipping away at bits of rock with a little hammer. He had a collection of ammonites, a fact that Olivia had never managed to discover in all their conversations. In no time at all he was telling Alice about his hobby, directing his words at her, moving his chair slightly sideways so that he faced her when he was speaking.

Alice talked so much and with such animation, and she encouraged Nigel to talk as well, so that, for once, even Pat had little to offer. She sat, stony-faced, fiddling with the brown beads. For the first time, Olivia realised that her own reserved manner was an asset in Pat's house. She willed Alice to shut up, but Alice went on and on, face aglow, voice slightly affected.

They moved to the sitting room, but before they sat down Alice requested to see Pat's studio. Olivia wished she had warned her not to do this, as Pat was sensitive about showing people her sanctum; she liked to issue the invitation herself.

However, she nodded in agreement, and they followed her to the next room. As they tripped behind her, Olivia could not help noticing Pat's ungainly stride and the faint absurdity of the orange kimono flapping around her ankles.

Olivia knew that Pat was finishing a commission for a calendar. The painting of three kittens sitting on a blue velvet cushion was on the easel.

Alice was enchanted. "Oh, how some cat lover will like this!" she cried.

"It is a successor to this one," explained Pat, and she produced another canvas depicting the same kittens playing with a ball of wool.

"I've seen this before," exclaimed Alice, excited. "My mother was given this calendar last Christmas."

"That's nice to hear," said Pat dryly. "It all adds up."

"These things are not representative of your work, darling," interrupted Captain Nigel. "Why don't you show Alice one of your panels?"

"Yes," said Olivia desperately. "Show her that one." There was an example of Pat's work, loosely wrapped in paper, leaning against the wall.

"No," said Pat stubbornly. "It is ready for despatch, and I don't want it unwrapped. Leave it, please."

Captain Nigel insisted on escorting Alice to her flat in Cromwell Road. Pat expected this of him; he was a gentleman and, although it was not far, it was not pleasant for a young girl to walk alone in London after dark. They set off together at about half past eleven.

Olivia helped Hilda with the washing up, and when they had finished she went into the hall and found Pat halfway up the stairs, on the way to bed. She stopped and turned when she saw her niece, and Olivia forced herself to say, "Thank you for having Alice this evening. I hoped you liked her?"

Hearing the anxiety in the girl's voice Pat said kindly, "I thought her a very pretty girl, and clever." There was a little pause while Pat hovered on the stairs, hand resting on the banister. She seemed suddenly weary and dispirited. Then she said thoughtfully, before going upstairs, "She has wonderful teeth."

The next day the girls treated themselves to doughnuts with their coffee. Neither of them had any misgivings about eating fattening food; they were happy in the knowledge that they could eat what they liked and not put on an ounce of weight. "The evening was not a success," said Alice decidedly. "I could tell that from the beginning Pat did not like me."

"That is so untrue," answered Olivia. "Why are you always putting yourself down?" She went on to tell her how Pat had pronounced her 'pretty' and 'clever'. "And she said you have the most wonderful teeth!"

"She hasn't got very good teeth herself," Alice observed.

There was a short pause while they concentrated on the doughnuts.

Alice spoke next in a slightly reproving voice. "You know, you should not dismiss her work as rubbish. It is very difficult to paint that sort of thing."

Olivia had never dismissed her aunt's work as rubbish, and she said so. "She paints such a lot, and you only saw a few . . ."

"And it is so profitable," Alice continued, ignoring the protest. "People lap it up. That's appropriate when you think of those kittens." She laughed.

Olivia was beginning to feel nettled. "Pat does some fascinating work," she said on the defensive, "and she gets orders from Harrods and Liberty's, as well as private buyers."

"Oh, I can believe that." Alice's strong white teeth (her best feature) sank in to the last bit of doughnut, and little bits of white sugar settled delectably on her top lip. She chewed for a moment, looking straight ahead. When she could speak, she said, "Nigel, what does he do? For a living I mean, apart from digging, playing soldiers and collecting fossils?"

"I don't know. Maybe he doesn't have a proper job. I have a feeling he is rich and does not need to work." Olivia leaned over the table and lowered her voice. "I often wonder when he started living with Pat. He must be years younger than she is."

"Twelve years younger," replied Alice triumphantly. "Twelve years! They met six years ago, and they have been together ever since, except for the time he has been abroad. He asked her to marry him, but she didn't want to lose her allowance from her ex-husband."

Olivia was astounded to hear this. She marvelled that Alice had managed to glean so much information during the short walk between Queen's Gate and Cromwell Road. She could not help wondering why Captain Nigel had imparted so many personal details to someone he had just met.

Alice looked sharply at her, and Olivia had the uncanny feeling that she knew exactly what she was thinking. "People talk to me," she said. "I don't know why."

She stood up and brushed crumbs off her short skirt. As well as having marvellous teeth, she had marvellous legs and she liked to show them off. For the first time, Olivia was aware of her sexuality, the skirt taut across the flat belly, the jacket fitted tightly to round breasts.

"I want to stop at the bookshop on the way back," Alice told her. "I won't be a minute."

Olivia waited for her outside the shop, and when her friend finally emerged she was carrying a flimsy paper bag containing a book. Through the thin paper Olivia was able to decipher the word 'Fossils'.

A few days later Alice invited Olivia to say a long weekend with her family in Cornwall. It was half term, and although Olivia had been to see her parents on two weekends since being in London, this was special because it started on Friday morning and ended on Monday evening. She did not want them to be disappointed.

"I don't think they will feel like that," said Pat when the plan was mentioned to her. "Cornwall is beautiful, and you have never been there. I think you should go."

"Yes, you go," said Captain Nigel, "then you can tell us all about it when you get back."

So Olivia telephoned Kenneth and Joan and told them about the invitation, and, as Pat had predicted, they were delighted for her. If they felt disappointment they were careful not to show it. Her kind father sent her the money for the train fare.

During the long journey from Paddington to Penzance, Alice talked about her family. "My father was unique. As well as being good-looking he was kind and generous, and had a fantastic sense of humour. I have the most perfect memories of my early childhood. We lived in a big house with our own park and woodland. Daddy and I used to go for walks in the woods." Olivia could relate to that.

"My father and mother were so happy together," Alice continued. "You know how rare it is for two people to really love each other? They were completely devoted, always. When Daddy died my mother was devastated."

"How old were you when that happened?"

"I was seven years old, and I remember it clearly. I can hardly bear to talk about it. To make matters worse, he had a partner in his business who turned out to be an embezzler. Daddy trusted him and he was let down. My mother and I were left with hardly any money. We had to sell everything and after that life was a hard struggle. That is why she married George, my stepfather. She thought it would solve our problems, but it just increased them. As I have told you, he made my life a misery, and my mother is an unhappy woman. She made a terrible mistake because no one could take the place of my wonderful father, least of all George."

"What a sad story," said Olivia.

"Well, she must make the best of a bad choice." Alice stared fixedly at the passing landscape on the other side of her carriage window. "This is such a boring journey," she said impatiently.

"When did your mother marry . . . George?" Olivia

felt she wanted to know as much as possible about the people she was to visit.

"Ten years ago. He was a widower, and he has a son who is my stepbrother. Bill Randall. He is staying with them now, so you will meet him this weekend."

Chapter 5

The two girls arrived at Penzance Station after a long tedious journey. The train was unheated and there was no buffet car. Even Alice's conversation had dried up after the first two hours. When, at last, they stepped on to a rather bleak platform they were buffeted by a strong cold wind gusting in from the sea. They were thankful to see Alice's very presentable stepbrother there to meet them.

Bill Randall was handsome in a conventional English way – that is, he did not look like a film star but more like the hero of a boys' adventure story. He was fairly tall and had dark brown eyes, the sort of eyes where the pupils are hardly discernible. His hair was luxuriant, straight and blondish with a tendency to fall over his forehead.

He grabbed their suitcases, one in each hand, and

they followed his striding figure to the car park. The wind tore at their clothes and blew their hair into their eyes. They held down their billowing skirts with their hands, before thankfully settling into his battered Morris Minor, Alice in the front seat and Olivia squeezed into the back with the luggage. As he slammed the door, Bill turned and bestowed on her a brilliant smile. It occurred to him that his duty visit to his father and irritating stepmother had suddenly taken a turn for the better.

Bill was an erratic driver, travelling too fast along the front, a long straight road with the cold grey sea merging with the cold grey sky on one side, and a row of desolate white seaside hotels on the other. They turned into narrow lanes with steep inclines and dips, and he was forced to slow down. When he met a car coming towards him he had to back into a space by the side of the road, which he did with much reluctance and swearing. They came to a village near Newlyn, and Bill turned into an open gate. Ahead of them was a square Georgian house, very plain and perfect. He stopped the car opposite a heavy front door, and the three of them clambered out. They went into what seemed like the main room — a stone floor, scattered rugs and a smouldering fire in a vast open fireplace. The walls were covered with paintings, and Alice pointed to one and whispered to Olivia, "Stanhope Forbes!" Olivia tried to appear impressed by this information, which meant nothing to her.

George Randall greeted them cordially, and Olivia could not help remembering that Alice had called him a 'dirty brute'. He looked harmless, a big tweedy man (Olivia noted the same dark brown eyes of the son), pipe in hand, standing squarely, legs apart, with his back to the fire. There was a big black Labrador at his feet, and Olivia at once fell to her knees beside it. When she was with dogs she was instantly at ease, and she stroked its soft head and muzzle.

"The dog's name is Rastus," said Bill's father, thereby placing him in an era before the giving of such a name would be unthinkable. "And mine is George, and this is my wife Maureen, Alice's mamma."

A figure emerged from the shadows and held out a limp hand. Olivia took it, and for a moment it lay in her own, like a small damp fish. The first thing she noticed about Maureen was that she was incredibly thin. She wore a shapeless cardigan, which she hugged to her body as if she could not get warm. Her nose, which Alice had inherited, was faintly pink at the sharp tip, and she wore spectacles. Olivia could not have been more astonished. Except for a chilling resemblance, it was hard to believe that this sad-looking creature was the mother of the vibrant Alice.

The girls shared a bedroom, and after they had unpacked and changed they went downstairs. George Randall was poking ineffectually at the ashes in the fire, and Olivia, shivering, thought, why doesn't he get more wood?

"It's freezing," said Alice. "Can't something be done about that wretched fire?"

"Bill! We need more logs!" shouted George.

Bill appeared at once, and, before picking up the empty basket, rewarded Olivia with one of his all-enveloping smiles. She smiled back.

Dinner that evening was served in an icy dining room. George doled out the food from an enormous old-fashioned sideboard, and he took so long about it that by the time it reached the table it was almost cold. Olivia despaired at having to eat slivers of fatty beef swimming in greasy gravy, surrounded by blobs of watery potato. Runner beans when they arrived were etiolated and stringy. Suddenly she felt unhappy – absurdly unhappy. She felt as if tears might come to her eyes, and in another second she would have to blink them away. She hoped that she was not going to make a fool of herself, and let Alice down. She could not understand why she felt so abjectly miserable for no good reason, and she could only think it was because she had the beginnings of a sore throat.

The conversation did not rattle along in the easy way it did at Queen's Gate. George made a few attempts to talk to Olivia, and asked her about the college. "I expect you will make a fortune when you are a secretary," he said.

"I don't think so."

Bill Randall contributed very little to the general conversation, which limped along at a desperately slow pace. Olivia wondered if he was sulking about something, and she noticed how his mouth turned down at the corners. It was a look he had when displeased, and later she was to know it very well. It completely altered his handsome face. Even Alice was not her usual ebullient self, and, as for her mother, she sat in disgruntled silence, prodding at her food and putting little piles of gristle and fat on the side of her plate. It was disgusting, and Olivia felt she disliked them all. All except Alice of course – she could never bring herself to dislike Alice.

The situation did not improve after dinner when a very long game of Monopoly was played. Olivia, coping with the complexities of hotels, houses and railway stations, now found she was battling with a headache as well as a stinging sensation when she swallowed. She thought the evening would never end, and it was a relief to say a polite goodnight and go upstairs to bed. She wondered how she was going to manage to get through the rest of the weekend.

"I'm so sorry," said Alice when they were alone. She plumped herself down on one of the single beds. "I should never have asked you here to meet my ghastly family. How could I have been so silly? I can see you hate them."

Olivia wanted to reassure her, but found it difficult because of feeling so rotten. She said, "Please don't say that. If I appeared subdued it's because I think I am getting a cold."

Alice ignored this. Apart from a few childish ailments she had never been ill in her life, and, like most healthy people, she shied away from ill health.

"My mother is so dreary," she went on. "I know it is hard to believe but she used to be a live wire. Marriage to George changed all that. He is the most selfish man I know, and so mean."

"Is he?" Olivia got into the other bed and laid her aching head on the pillow. "His son seems quite nice."

"He is even worse than his father. I hate him."

"I suppose it is hard, the stepbrother-stepsister relationship."

"Any sort of relationship would be hard with him." Alice got into her bed, and started thumping her pillow. "Even the pillows are hard in this house."

"Do you mind if I go to sleep?" asked Olivia wearily. "Right away, I mean, without any talking. I don't feel so good."

In the morning she felt less good. Her head was hot, her body cold and she could hardly speak. "I don't think I can come down to breakfast," she croaked, feeling she was in the middle of a nightmare.

Alice flounced out of the room; creating the impression that Olivia was purposefully leaving her to the mercy of the family.

Much later that morning Maureen appeared, waking Olivia from a muddled sleep. Maureen stood at the end of the bed. "Do you want me to send for the doctor?" she asked.

"No, no, of course not. Thank you. I'm so sorry."

"I'll bring you something to eat."

"Please don't bother."

"Soup," said Maureen decidedly, "soup would be best." She shuffled out of the room, and Olivia huddled further down into the bedclothes.

Alice appeared some time later, carrying a tray, on it a lonely bowl of soup with a spoon beside it. Chicken noodle, thought Olivia, eying the green specks floating in the yellow liquid, but she was hungry and finished it. It was salty and made her long for water. The empty bowl with its vestige of golden scum remained on the bedside table, and Olivia, finding it distasteful, wished someone would come and take it away. At last Alice appeared with a mug of tea.

"You are like Jane Bennett in *Pride and Prejudice*," she said.

"I don't know her," whispered Olivia, "because I have never read the book." She thought of her father urging her to read the book. If only he could be with her now!

"You have never read *Pride and Prejudice*? How amazing!" Alice left the room, and Olivia was sure she was hurrying down to impart this extraordinary piece of information to her family.

Olivia's next visitor was George. By now the room was getting dark, and he had come to ask if she needed supper. "It makes it easier for Maureen if she knows."

Olivia thanked him and said she did not think she could eat any supper. She pressed her cheek against the pillow, even making this small decision and trying to be polite was a heavy burden.

"It's bad luck," he said. He sounded genuinely

sympathetic, and if Olivia had not been told differently, she would have judged him a kind man. The knowledge that a human being could be so deceptive deepened her depression.

She pretended she was asleep when Alice came to bed. The next day there was no improvement. She experimented with her voice, and found it almost non-existent and there were frightening noises in her head, like the clattering of distant tin trays, and she recognised these as symptoms of a high fever. No one had suggested taking her temperature, and in a house like this there was probably no thermometer. She thought of her kind mother, a nurse, who would deal with the situation in a sensible way. Even Pat would do something to help her, and Hilda would bustle around being comforting. Olivia felt full of self-pity, and scared. Her chest hurt and she wondered if she was getting pneumonia – if that happened they would have to do something.

At noon on Saturday (or was it Sunday – she had lost count of the days) another bowl of chicken noodle soup appeared, the other half of the packet. Olivia finished every drop of the oily liquid, and put the bowl with the other one left from the day before. Then she pressed her face into the pillow to try and block out the strange noises and dancing lights, and she slept.

That evening she felt better. When Alice put her head around the door she said, "I think I'll live."

"Oh, darling, I'm so glad," replied Alice, and was gone.

Olivia struggled out of bed and looked in the mirror

on the dressing table. A sad pale girl gazed back at her. She combed her matted hair, put on her dressing gown and tiptoed down the passage to the bathroom. After washing her face and cleaning her teeth she felt revived. When she got back to the bedroom she summoned up enough energy to straighten the sheets. There was a loud rap on the door, and she hurriedly got back into bed, calling out "Come in!"

It was Bill. He was carrying a tray on which reposed a platter of bread and cheese, two glasses, a bottle of whisky and a jug of water.

"My cure for the 'flu," he said, sitting on the edge of her bed, the tray between them. The food was a welcome sight for Olivia. "I'm famished," she told him.

"No wonder in this house," Bill said. "They must have learnt their housekeeping in Belsen. My stepmother is a canny shopper, no extravagances there. By staying in this bed you have missed no gastronomic delights, I can assure you. Let me see, for lunch today we had a slice each of very unpleasant pink ham which had been heated under the grill, and on top of it a round of pineapple – cold pineapple, mark you, straight from the tin."

"Oh dear," said Olivia laughing, "and what did you have yesterday?"

"Um, what did we have yesterday? Ah, I know, curry. Now, I absolutely adore curry, but this was a sloppy beef stew with a dash of curry powder thrown in and a handful of sultanas. I think I disliked that meal more than the ham. Sacrilege to give it the name of curry."

"What about your father? Does he approve?"

"I think his stomach started to shrink after he married Maureen. Now he no longer notices the economies, he just falls in with everything she does. God knows why he married the wretched woman. What could he have seen in her?"

The meal was very satisfying and the whisky lifted Olivia's spirits. She said, "I like Alice very much."

"Well, I do not," he said emphatically. "I think my dear stepsister is the person I like least in the world. Her mother is an angel of goodness compared with her daughter —she's a snake, she's a spider. She would betray her best friend to get her own way."

Olivia was startled by the vehemence with which he expressed his opinion, and she was worried that he did not lower his voice. It would be heartbreaking if Alice should overhear him uttering those words about her. He must have sensed her anxiety because he said, "For heaven's sake forget her, will you? I'd rather talk about you. I'm surprised you look so good. Downstairs they were all telling me you were at death's door."

"I thought I was, but I'm better now. I'm so grateful to you for bringing this food and drink. I was beginning to feel very low."

"I can imagine. This is a family you do not want to be with when you are not feeling on top of the world, but you seem almost recovered, sitting up in bed and looking quite dishy."

"Like Jane Bennett?"

He hooted with laughter. "Oh, yes, we heard about Jane Bennett. Who the hell is she, anyway?"

Olivia thought him a delightful creature. During the short pause that ensued she resorted to the familiar dance floor question, "Do you come here often?" and then qualified it by saying, "To stay, I mean?"

"Seldom. I like to keep in touch with my father – that is the only reason I come. Well, it's a sort of duty, and I'm fond of him as well. He is such a good-natured old boy; I can't turn against him because he has made a rotten marriage. As you have probably gathered by now, I don't like coming here very much. This visit looked more promising, but then you had to go and get 'flu." He smiled at her his sweet boyish smile.

"What do you do?" she wanted to know.

"I'm a solicitor with a firm called Abbott and Cunliffe in Arundel Street, just off the Strand. It's a well-known old-fashioned firm – you may have heard of them." She had not. "Very prestigious," he said, "lots of important clients. I don't want to stay there for ever, but it's good experience."

"Where do you want to go, when you leave?"

"I think to the country eventually. I don't like London, too much traffic, too many people, too expensive, all the usual reasons. I'd rather settle for a nice country house and a wife and children." Again he smiled at her, conscious that he had spoken quite openly and was looking for a reaction. Although he was sincere in expressing his hopes for the future, it was a device he often used with girls with marked success.

Olivia was no exception. She coloured slightly and murmured, "Oh, the country . . ." She suddenly had a picture in her mind of her father taking his walking stick from the stand in the hall, calling the dogs, and setting off for a walk without her. "I love the country," she told Bill. "My parents live in Hampshire, and our house looks straight on to the New Forest. It is so beautiful. But what about round here? It is beautiful too. Perhaps you would like to live in Cornwall?"

"I wouldn't mind it at all," he replied. "There are some lovely parts of Cornwall. It's a pity you have come all this way and haven't had the chance to see any of them. Do you think you could recover sufficiently so that we could do a bit of sightseeing tomorrow, before you go back?"

Olivia felt she could manage that, but, for the present, was having difficulty in keeping her eyes open. "I'm sorry, I feel so tired," she said. "I expect it's the whisky."

"If you're going to make a comeback tomorrow," said Bill gently, "I think it's important you have a good night's rest tonight."

He leaned forward and kissed her lightly on the forehead. Whether from the effect of the alcohol or because she still had a slight temperature, Olivia felt very hot. She hoped her skin did not feel damp under his cool dry lips.

After he had gone, she noticed he had left the tray covered with the remains of the bread and cheese, the two glasses and the jug. He had taken the whisky bottle with him. Never mind, she thought, forgiving him and adding the dirty soup plates to the pile – perhaps Alice will take them all away when she comes.

She tried to keep awake so that she could talk to Alice. It occurred to her that because of her indisposition she had been neglectful of her, and she thought she might remedy the situation with a little late night gossip, now that she felt up to it again.

But sleep overtook her, and she did not hear Alice come in, undress and get into the bed beside hers.

Chapter 6

The following day the world seemed a brighter place.
For one thing, the leaden sky Olivia had managed to
glimpse through the window when she was lying in bed
had been replaced by a blue one, with a few cheerful
little clouds scudding across it. For another, she felt so
much better in health and spirits, and with a light heart
she stepped out of bed and put on her dressing gown.

She closed the bedroom door quietly so as not to
wake the sleeping Alice. She was pleasantly surprised that
there was hot water for her bath. In all other respects the
bathroom was very uninviting, cold black and white tiles
everywhere and no lock on the door. The idea that
George Randall might invade her privacy suddenly
worried her at first, but there was a chair in the room
and she propped it against the door. She ran the water
into the bath, which was vast and had green stains below

the taps, and slipped in. Afterwards she rinsed her hair in the basin and by that time the water had become cold which was rather unpleasant. She dried her hair as best she could with her towel. All this activity made her feel slightly debilitated, and she decided this would be remedied by a cup of tea and toast and marmalade. When she returned to the bedroom she found that Alice was still asleep. She dressed very quietly so as not to disturb her.

Olivia picked up the tray of leftover food and dirty dishes, and went downstairs. A door was open and she saw it was the kitchen. It was empty. She would have done the washing-up but was discouraged by a sink full of pots and pans soaking in oily water. She moved things on the wooden draining board so that there was room for the tray.

She found George and his son sitting by one glowing log of wood. They sat very close to it, newspapers in hands. The dog, Rastus, had his nose almost buried in the surrounding ash, his long body stretched on the hearth in search of warmth.

Both men rose to their feet when Olivia entered, and so did the dog, putting a cold nose against her leg. She bent down and patted him. She decided breakfast must be over as it was not mentioned, and neither (she could not help noticing) was the state of her health mentioned.

She thought she knew Bill well enough to say, "Any chance of a cup of tea?" He went for it at once, and she sat in a chair by the fizzing damp log, and tried not to shiver. She had hoped there would be a roaring fire so that she could dry her damp hair. Her host returned to his seat, but he put his newspaper to one side.

Bill returned with a mug of tea. "I'm going to show Olivia a bit of Cornwall," he announced to his father.

"Good idea. Where are you taking her?"

"I thought Marazion and St Michael's Mount. It's an obvious choice, but if you have never seen it . . ."

"Marvellous place. I haven't been there for years. I've a good mind to come with you."

"Why not?" asked Bill doubtfully.

"No, no. Too much to do."

What did he do, Olivia wondered, but she was relieved he was not coming with them.

"I expect Maureen would like to go though," suggested George brightly. "It would do her good to get out for a change."

He heaved himself to his feet, and started shouting her name. She appeared through the front door, bringing a blast of cold air with her. She was wearing gumboots and a very old grubby raincoat. In her hand was a blackened pot that presumably contained kitchen scraps. For chickens, ducks? Olivia did not have the energy to enquire.

"How about going for a drive to Marazion with Bill and Alice's friend, dear?"

"I'm too busy," she replied shortly.

Olivia roused herself. "Please may I help? We don't have to go just yet."

70

George answered for his wife. "She wouldn't let you," he said.

"That's settled then," said Bill briskly. "I don't suppose Alice will be interested, having been there so many times."

His father gave him a quick glance. "I think she will want to be with her friend. At any rate, I suggest we give her a chance to make up her own mind."

"She may be still asleep," volunteered Alice.

But when she went upstairs to see, Alice was no longer asleep, and, within a short time, she came skipping down the bare oak stairs in front of Olivia, looking very fetching in a tight fitting pink jersey and black slacks. Perhaps because she was not feeling robust herself, it seemed to Olivia that Alice exuded rude health and abounding energy. Yes, of course she would love to go with them.

They wrapped themselves in coats and, before they set off, Alice explained that she always felt sick in the rear seat of a car and would Olivia mind very much if she sat in the front with Bill? Of course Olivia was happy to scramble into the back, and she was gratified to see Bill's scowl.

He parked the car in the little village of Marazion, and the three of them hired a small boat to take them over the narrow strip of water to the castle on St Michael's Mount. The boats were like taxis ferrying people over before the tide changed.

They climbed a very steep rocky path to the castle,

and Bill took Olivia's hand. It was a small gesture but it made her feel secure and happy. Alice strode on ahead, anxious to get on and already showing signs of boredom. However, Bill was determined that Olivia should see everything, and he kept referring to a tattered old guidebook he had brought from home. He steered her through the Blue Drawing Room of the castle, elegantly furnished and with many family portraits on the walls and into the Chevy Chase Room where the monks took their meals, a more sombre room and curiously airless. Olivia wondered if the monks had felt claustrophobic in such surroundings.

How wonderful to live in a place like this, thought Olivia, a fortress with views of the sea from all sides, and the waves lashing against the stone walls. The place breathed high romance. She enthused about it when they were having coffee and cake in the tourist café.

"It is rather special," admitted Alice. "I wonder if the owners have a son?"

"Are you thinking you would like to live there?" asked Bill. There was more amusement than sarcasm in his voice, which made Olivia think that he and Alice understood each other quite well, and that their mutual dislike was not so deep-rooted after all.

"No," said Alice, "I would not like to be stuck on this rocky island, so maddening to be cut off just when one didn't want to be, but I would not mind being in another stately home in a more accessible place. However, I think a millionaire would suit me better than a lord – he would probably have a big house in London which I would like very much."

"You would only like it if you loved him," Olivia pointed out.

"Oh, I don't care about love," replied Alice airily. "I want to *be* somebody. Let's face it; I'm not likely to do anything unusual so I shall have to succeed through marriage. It is the only route for me. I know I am going to have a long life and I must make the most of it. It is so easy to let the years slip by without doing anything, and I do not intend to fall into that trap. My ambition is to have a rich husband, a beautiful home and lots of children."

Fortunately for Bill, who was becoming increasingly irritated by this talk, the tide had turned and people were beginning to stroll back to the shore along the causeway. They joined the crowd and walked back to the car.

Bill seemed touchingly pleased that Olivia had enjoyed the morning. When he managed to get a moment alone with her, he clasped her hands and promised to telephone her during the week. There was no doubt about the admiration in his eyes, and it excited her. He was leaving for London on the following day, and he was tempted to alter his plans so that he could travel with the girls. He knew his father would be disappointed, so he said nothing. Instinctively, Olivia knew what he was thinking, and liked him for his decision.

After lunch at the house (limp lettuce, canned salmon and salad cream from a bottle), Bill drove them to the station. Olivia sat behind him, looking at the nape of his neck where the hair grew in an endearing little point.

Olivia and Alice spoke little during the long train journey. Olivia was content to quietly consider the past few days and the impact they had made on her. Even Alice seemed absorbed in private thoughts. Eventually, both girls managed to get snatches of uncomfortable sleep, and it was late when, thankfully, they stepped out into the glare of Paddington Station. The underground was eerie, almost deserted, their footsteps echoing along the passages. At last the escalator and into the cold night air of South Kensington.

"Do you want to come in?" suggested Olivia doubtfully. "I expect Pat is waiting up for me, and I know she would be pleased to see you."

"No," said Alice decidedly, "although it is very nice of you to ask me, but I have other plans."

Olivia could not imagine what plans she could have at that time of night, but she was too weary to care. It was probably Alice just being mysterious. They parted in the Cromwell Road at the turning into Queen's Gate, Olivia saying truthfully that she had enjoyed the end part of the visit and Olivia apologising once again for the shortcomings of her relations.

Walking slowly back to Pat's house carrying her suitcase, Olivia thought, it's true, they are an odd family. She compared George and Maureen with her own father and mother, so welcome to everyone, so considerate of other people's feelings. How lucky she was to have such parents!

"You do look pale, dear," said Hilda as soon as she saw her. She, as well as Pat, had waited up for her. Olivia's explanation produced consternation from both women, and she was ordered to bed at once. It was bliss to slip between clean white sheets, to be propped up by soft pillows and to have kind-hearted Hilda appear with a tray of delicious food – scrambled eggs and triangles of toast.

Then Pat came in and sat on the end of the bed and Olivia told her about George and Maureen, the strangeness of them, and of her own despair because of feeling so ill in that cold inhospitable house. She mentioned Bill Randall from time to time, and Pat was suitably interested. Olivia felt free to talk about him, so certain was she that he would telephone her as soon as he returned to London.

"Where's Captain Nigel?" she asked.

"He's gone to see a friend who may be going on an expedition with him in the spring. I doubt if he will get back early enough for you to see him before you go to sleep. Of course he will want to hear all your news but, darling, I don't think you should trouble yourself about him tonight. Just settle down and get some rest." Pat got up, and, leaning over the bed, pressed her lips to Olivia's forehead. Then, taking the tray, she left the room, turning off the light and quietly closing the door.

Olivia was asleep almost immediately, her thoughts tumbling over each other and merging into dreams. The shorthand test she would have to take the following day, the waves lashing against the castle on St Michael's

Mount, and the young man with brown eyes who would telephone and say, "Olivia?" Whether her imagination would have supplied the rest of the conversation she was not to discover, for she was in a deep sleep before either of them could say another word.

Chapter 7

Two weeks passed and Bill had not telephoned. A sort of melancholy settled on the household, and everybody was more subdued than usual, Hilda because she was, by disposition and situation, a quiet body, and Pat and Olivia because they harboured private thoughts which were interrupted from time to time by the telephone ringing. Pat would look at Olivia, and she would go to answer it, careful not to hurry her steps and trying to still the beating of her heart. Most times the call was for Pat, a talkative friend or a customer.

Life went on, of course. The days spent at college and the evenings with Pat and Hilda. Captain Nigel was often absent as he was doing a project which took him almost every day to the British Museum. Olivia discovered he had small bachelor flat in Pimlico, which he seldom used as he preferred to be at Queen's Gate, but which he now occupied most nights, saying he wanted to do his work without distraction. Pat insisted she was happy about this arrangement which he told her was only temporary, and she was used to him being away for long periods.

"We respect each other's freedom," she told Olivia, "after six years we know each other too well to have doubts or fears." But, somehow, this separation was different, and Olivia noticed that Pat did not entertain her friends any more.

Then the uneasy stillness was broken by the arrival of the workmen who had come to install the new bathroom. It was unfortunate that Captain Nigel who had devised the plan was not around to see its fruition.

For the first time Pat displayed signs of exasperation. "He should be here while all this is going on," she said, trying not to mind the sound of heavy boots on the stairs and the constant noise of hammering and sawing. Hilda was kept busy supplying cups of tea, at the same time issuing warnings about the disposal of cigarette butts.

In the midst of the chaos Pat found time to be concerned about the soulful expression on the face of her niece. She knew only too well the cause of it. "Why don't you telephone him?" she suggested.

It was a fairly outrageous suggestion. These were times when it was not considered permissible for a young woman to telephone a man; the first move must come from him. The theory, promulgated by mothers, was that nothing could be gained by the girl taking the initiative.

If the man wished to get in touch with her he would do so. That premise still holds good today, but there are some notable exceptions and girls tend to grasp them in desperation: the man may be painfully shy, he may have lost her telephone number (unlikely) or he may feel unworthy of her (most unlikely). Olivia did not even consider telephoning Bill, but she wished, how she wished, that there was some way of making him remember her existence.

Her only link was Alice, and on the day after their return from Cornwall Alice did not turn up at college, and she had not been there since. Olivia telephoned the flat and the reply was always the same: "She is not here, and I don't know where she is."

After several attempts and many messages left with the flatmate, the call was returned.

"Are you ill?" Olivia asked anxiously.

"No, of course not."

"Why haven't you been to college? I worried about you."

"I have given up the course. It was so boring; I couldn't stand another moment of it. Who wants to be a secretary anyway?"

"What will your stepfather think? You told me he is paying for it. Surely he will not be pleased if you fall out during the first term?"

"He doesn't mind because he knows I am doing something worthwhile instead."

"And what is that?"

"Research. I've got a job doing research."

It sounded impressive, and Olivia was impressed. What sort of research she wanted to know, but Alice was evasive and quickly changed the subject. "Have you seen Bill?" she asked.

"No."

"I wonder why? He seemed so keen. Shall I ring him and ask him what he's doing?"

"Please don't do that," Olivia pleaded, clutching at the last remnants of her pride. "There is no reason for him to telephone, no reason at all."

"Oh, very well."

"I telephoned you," explained Olivia, "because I had not heard from you for so long, and I was beginning to wonder if we are still friends."

"Livvy!" Alice's voice, rising with emotion, conveyed her genuine distress. "How can you say such a thing? You know we shall always be friends, always and always."

It was such a relief to hear her say that, and made the other disappointment seem less important. They ended the conversation with assurances of eternal friendship and promises to meet in the near future.

Olivia came to a philosophical conclusion that there was nothing she could do about Bill. There was no clear way open to her except to anguish and dream and finally give up hope. It was when she had reached the last part that he surprised her by telephoning.

"Hello," she said, her voice cracking.

"I've not rung you before because I have been so busy."

A flimsy excuse but she accepted it gratefully.

He asked her to have dinner with him. "That would be lovely," she said, hoping she did not sound breathless or too eager.

For Olivia the magic started early in the day of her first date with Bill. It was a day full of expectation and self-indulgence. Such days in a lifetime are rare and sometimes passed unnoticed, but Olivia savoured every moment of that precious time. It started with a lie, a day off college because of a dentist's appointment in Southampton, a lie shared by Pat and approved by her. Pat knew all about special moments, and that they must not be allowed to escape because of a silly formality.

Olivia set off for the shops feeling she travelled on wings. In a remarkably short time she had purchased a black dress and a pair of strappy shoes. Then she went to a hairdresser's recommended by Pat where she had a shampoo and set before returning home to prepare herself, in a leisurely fashion, for the evening ahead.

"You look beautiful," said Pat truthfully when she saw the result of the day's activity. Hilda was called in to look and admire.

Pat could not analyse her feelings towards this young girl. Childless, she had never regretted her state, and had always thought children must get in the way of so much pleasure. Now she was experiencing an emotion almost like that of a mother for a daughter.

"Do you suppose," she said wryly to Hilda, "that I shall lie awake tonight, listening for her return?"

There had been hasty introductions when Bill arrived. Pat liked him instantly. She recognised the type at once – personable, intelligent and full of self-confidence. He had been to a minor public school and knew how to behave, and he had obtained a degree by dint of hard work rather than intellect – now he was on the brink of a lucrative career. He had a boyish enthusiasm, which was very appealing, and Pat was sure her sister Joan would approve.

Olivia and Bill had a delightful evening. He talked of his work, recounting in detail stories of legal cases in which he had been involved. She was happy to listen to him. Like her, he hardly ever read a book, seldom went to the theatre, did not appreciate the opera and thought the ballet was 'for queers'. Every weekend in the summer he played cricket, and she was not expected to be knowledgeable about that.

After dinner, they sat over minuscule cups of coffee and looked into each other's eyes. Then they went on to a nightclub and danced, very close, to the music of Edmundo Ros. Olivia felt, for the first time, the desire and longing to be with a man. The hardness of him pressed against her produced sensations which were new and exciting. Her legs felt leaden and it was an effort to move them around the dance floor.

Her hands clasped the back of his neck and his hand was low on her back. In the semi-darkness they were oblivious to the other couples shuffling past them. They were alone, moving very slowly to the music. It was an almost unbearable ecstasy only broken by having to return, rather dazedly, to their table.

When Bill took her to the front door of Pat's house, having paid the cabby, he drew her behind one of the pillars that flanked the steps and kissed her. He was not a man of the world in any sense but he was experienced enough to know how to kiss, and he did not kiss like Adam Bowlby or any of the other boys Olivia had known. He felt her respond, and inwardly cursed the nosey old aunt and the caring parents he had not yet met and all the other niceties which prevented him from taking her straight to bed. It was the early hours of the morning so she did not ask him in, but, before she shut the door, she looked at him half-imploringly, and he suggested they meet on the following evening.

After that they saw a great deal of each other. They did not go to a nightclub again as Bill could not afford such luxuries, except on special occasions or when he wanted to impress. They met each Saturday or Sunday and visited the zoo in Regent's Park, went to the cinema or for a row on the Serpentine. In the evenings they ate at a little bistro in Clareville Street. Olivia found it difficult to concentrate on shorthand and typing; her thoughts were so full of him. Sometimes when she came out of college she found him outside, waiting for her. She would take his arm, so proud of him, aware of the glances of the other girls, who thought he was 'very handsome' and 'had a lovely smile'.

One evening he came to supper at Queen's Gate, and

Pat was able to confirm her first favourable impression. As for Hilda, she regarded Bill fondly from the beginning. Captain Nigel was not around to indulge and spoil, and she missed him.

Pat missed him too. She knew he made every effort to 'escape' as he called it, and when he did appear there was much joy in the household. Now, she wished he could have been present to meet Olivia's young man. Watching the two young faces she felt a pang of regret; growing old was hard for her, a warm passionate woman. She looked down at her hands which betrayed the telltale marks of age, and then she glanced at dear faithful Hilda, and Hilda smiled lovingly back at her as if she understood.

After the meal, Pat remained tactfully in the kitchen, saying she had work to do at her desk, and Olivia and Bill went into the sitting room. They sat close together on the sofa, Bill with his arm around her shoulders.

"You finish term the weekend after next," he said. "That's right, isn't it?"

"Yes."

"What are your plans?"

"To go home, I suppose." A little hope entered her mind that perhaps he might come with her, to meet her family.

Evidently this was not part of his plan, for he said, "I think you should go home the following week, on Tuesday, say, then we could go away together for the weekend."

"Goodness!" was all she could find to say.

"Well?"

"They would not understand. How could I tell them I was not coming home at the end of term?"

"It's only two days, for God's sake, and you will be with them for the rest of the holidays."

"I'd like to think about it," she said.

"Do you want to go to the country or the sea?" he asked, completely ignoring her last remark.

"The seaside."

"That's settled then. I wish I could take you abroad, but I can't afford it. It will have to be an hotel in England."

"Not Brighton," she said. Brighton had sinister connotations for her.

He laughed. "All right, not Brighton. What about Worthing? Very respectable."

"You must let me think about it," she parried.

He kissed her on the back of the neck. "Don't think too much. Just do it. You want to be with me, don't you?"

Of course she did, and, after he had gone, she decided to talk to Pat about it. "Do you think I should go?" she asked.

Pat had not anticipated being faced with such a question. In her view, the arrangement with her sister to look after Olivia did not include having to make a decision of this sort.

"Why don't you ask your mother?" she said rather sharply.

"I couldn't do that," Olivia said, shocked.

Pat was not the sort of woman to shirk a challenge and, after a few moments' thought, she said seriously, "It seems like a serious relationship, and if you feel the same way about each other, and perhaps marriage is in the offing, you should find out whether you are suited." She felt quite pleased with herself, having tempered her advice with a reference to marriage, knowing that this was an important factor in Joan's ambitions for her child.

Olivia knew in her heart that her mother would not share Pat's view. "It's so difficult," she said.

Pat, who had never had any problems fulfilling her desires, decided that someone had to take the lead, so she said decidedly, "I think you should go." That being settled she turned to a more practical matter. "Have you a Dutch Cap?"

No, of course Olivia had never possessed or felt the need of such a thing. Pat took her to see a woman doctor, someone she had known for years. She muttered in the ear of her old friend before Olivia was ushered into the surgery. There she was fitted with a diaphragm and given a tube of ointment. It was not pleasant squatting on the floor, having to insert an uncomfortable object into her poor defenceless body, which had never known abuse before. Olivia wondered if she wanted to go ahead with the plan, all this discomfort for the sake of love. And she reminded herself that Bill had not said he loved her. That was something she could not bring herself to tell Pat, and she wondered if it would have made any difference if she had mentioned it.

That evening her misgivings were slightly mollified by his kisses and caresses and evident delight that she had decided to go. She made an excuse to leave him early and return to Pat's house to experiment with her new acquisition in the privacy of the bathroom.

"Do you think we should go as Mr and Mrs Smith?" Olivia asked Pat half-flippantly, half-seriously. By now, she was leaving all decisions to Pat.

To her surprise, Pat seemed dismayed. Like many broad-minded people she could be unexpectedly conventional about some things. "Of course not! You must have separate rooms. Anything else would be tawdry."

Secretly, Olivia was beginning to think the whole venture was getting out of hand. She had envisaged a double room with a bathroom, but she supposed Pat knew best.

"One thing, darling," she said to Bill, rather shyly. She was proud that he was her darling, although she had never heard him use that term of endearment himself. "I would like a room to myself in the hotel, a single room. Pat thinks that is how it should be."

A look passed over his face, a mixture of incom-prehension and exasperation. If he had not been in love, he would have spoken his mind against Pat and her ridiculous advice and against Olivia for being squeamish.

"I've already changed one booking," he said. "Now I'll have to start again." He went on to explain that he could not afford two single rooms, a fact which Olivia relayed to Pat.

"I'll treat you," was Pat's solution. "No, don't argue, it is something your mother would want me to do, I'm sure." Olivia found this hard to believe, but when she told Bill he beamed with pleasure.

"In that case," he said, "I'll book a double room for you and a single for me." Much heartened, he went off to telephone the hotel and managed to get the two rooms on the same floor, and, after some negotiating, next to each other. Without Olivia's knowledge he arranged also for meals and drinks to be included in her bill.

Olivia telephoned her mother and explained she would not be coming home on Thursday as they had arranged.

"I thought you were breaking up on that day?" said Joan.

"Well, yes, I am, but I'm staying with someone over the weekend." So far the truth.

"Oh, I see."

"Well, Alice, as a matter of fact."

"Are you going to Cornwall again?"

"No, she is having a party, here in London." Like all lies, this one grew heavier every moment, and the weight was increased by the fact that she had not seen Alice for weeks. She wanted to see her very much, and had telephoned her flat so many times the flatmate had started to get annoyed. "How often do I have to tell you? I don't know where she is."

Olivia yearned to talk to Alice, someone of he own age who would understand better than Pat how she was feeling. Life had become complicated for Olivia. She suspected she had lost a friend, someone she really loved, and it was a hard loss to bear. At the same time, she realised her relationship with Bill had reached a point where it had to progress or come to an end. She supposed, rather sadly, that going away with him was progress. Of one thing she was certain: she did not want to lose him.

Chapter 8

They booked into the Bedlington Hotel, Worthing, as Mr William Randall and Miss Olivia Anderson. Olivia had a large stark room with a double bed and an adjoining bathroom, which Bill, in a single room next door, would have to share unless he chose to use the bathroom at the far end of the corridor. After they arrived he went to his little room and she stayed in hers, unpacking her case and then lying flat on the top of the brown counterpane until she heard his knock on the door. They had arranged earlier to go for a walk along the seafront before dinner.

The sea was bitterly cold and unfriendly, and the sky like a sheet of metal. The pavement was wet and slippery because it had been raining recently, and they descended some steps until they were on a lower level and sheltered from the biting wind. It was high tide and the waves beat on the sea wall, occasionally cascading and spreading in front of them like a fan, stinging their faces with spray. They held hands. Very soon it became so cold they decided to return to the warmth of the hotel, and silently they went to their respective rooms to change for dinner. Olivia had a bath, and locked the door before removing the Dutch Cap from its round tin box. She thought, better to attend to the wretched thing now rather than later.

There was a constraint between them during dinner, although they both did their best to be natural. It was hard to be animated as the other guests were so quiet, all speaking in low voices. The waiters made a welcome noise clattering the dishes and passing between the tables, and they could hear the tapping of knives and forks on the plates. It had been better in the dark cosy atmosphere of the bistro in London when there had been nothing at stake. Now they both felt their spirits drop to zero.

"I'm afraid the food is not very inspiring," he said.

"It's fine. I'm not very hungry, that's all."

The thought crossed Bill's mind that, as Pat was paying for most of the weekend, he could have booked into a better hotel. Too late to think of that, though, and because of his stupidity he had to endure Windsor soup, overdone roast beef with cardboard Yorkshire pudding followed by a pathetic Peach Melba. Coffee was served in the lounge, which had a patterned red carpet, and chairs covered in a shiny pink material grouped around small round tables. Again, the atmosphere in the lounge was quiet, terribly quiet. The other guests were mostly families, tiptoeing about, hushing their children who were out of sorts after a disappointing day at the seaside.

Going up in the lift Olivia became convinced that the whole thing was going to be a horrible anti-climax. Of course she loved Bill, but that just made the certainty that she was going to disappoint him even harder to bear.

She put on the sheer nightdress she had purchased the day before, and the first thing he did was to remove it and throw it on the floor. Until she saw Bob padding along the passage at Queen's Gate in the buff she thought all men wore pyjamas in bed, as her father did. Now she was to learn that Bill did not possess a pair.

Lying in bed, their bodies together, the old feelings returned. In truth, Bill had only slept with two women and both of them had been married. He found Olivia's virginity unnerving, and was not sure if he knew how to cope with the situation. His insensitive approach left her bewildered and unhappy, and afterwards she lay in the darkness, eyes wide open, with Bill's sleeping form beside her.

Her body felt sore and surrounded by dampness. Her arm was trapped beneath Bill, and she feared she could not extricate it without waking him. She knew that sleep was impossible, and she thought longingly of the single bed in the next room, clean white and inviting. If she had been able to move she would have gone to it.

She thought of her mother and father, how happy they were. They must have done this many times, and enjoyed it. She had a vague childhood recollection of the war when her mother had scooped her up and taken her into her own bed, saying that she could not bear to be alone, and now, years later, her daughter longed to be alone. Olivia's eyes filled with tears at the thought of her own inadequacy. She imagined she would lie awake all night, listening to the wind outside the window and to Bill uttering scraps of conversation in his sleep. Eventually, he turned over and her numbed arm was released. Then she must have slept because morning came quite quickly, and she watched the light edging the curtains with a sense of relief that the night was over. Bill gave a little snort as he awoke, and immediately turned to her.

"Don't worry," he whispered , his mouth against her ear, "it will get better." She was grateful.

Breakfast in the dining room consisted of a perfectly formed fried egg, a sculptured piece of bacon and a sausage. The hot coffee revived her a little. She wondered if Bill noticed her pallor and black-rimmed eyes (when she knew him better she would realise he did not notice such things) but, glancing at her quickly over his newspaper, he may have thought she looked less pretty than usual.

After breakfast they went to their respective rooms to collect coats and scarves. Olivia felt embarrassed because a chambermaid had removed the soiled sheets and was in the process of making up the bed with crisp clean linen. She did not look up when the girl entered, but hurriedly finished making the bed, bundled the dirty sheets under her arm and left the room. Illogically, Olivia felt the whole world, and the Bedlington Hotel in particular, was hostile towards her.

They went for another walk along the seafront. The weather had improved a little, and they stood and watched children, wearing woolly cardigans over swimsuits, playing with tin buckets and wooden spades on the beach. Most of the grown-ups were huddled in deckchairs, their coats wrapped around their knees, hats covering their ears. There were no bathers venturing into an icy sea.

Arm in arm, Olivia and Bill walked into the town, like a married couple keeping their troubled thoughts to themselves. They gazed idly into shop windows displaying garish seaside paraphernalia, and studied the postcards on the revolving stands. Olivia wondered if she would send one to Pat, but dismissed the idea at once as utterly ridiculous. What would she say? 'Having a lovely time. Wish you were here'?

It was Saturday, and a new batch of tourists was starting their holidays; the main street was jammed with cars stuffed with luggage and children. Drivers, watching the lights change from red to green and then to red again, without making any progress, optimistically hoped the weather would change and be kind to them.

"Let's get out of here," said Bill suddenly. His hand tightened on Olivia's arm, and he steered her through the crowds at a brisk pace until they reached his car in the hotel car park.

It was a relief to sit in the car and be driven out of

the noisy town into the peace of the countryside. Olivia felt herself beginning to relax. Bill drove a long way, through sprawling villages and along winding lanes. Neither of them spoke very much except to comment on a picturesque cottage or a spectacular view, but their silences were less strained, almost companionable, as if they had both resigned themselves to the inevitable and were determined to make the best of it.

Bill turned the car into a car park of a public house bearing the cheerful sign 'The Jolly Farmer'. "Can't be bad," he commented

There was a fire blazing in the hearth, a real fire where the big logs crackled and shifted over a pile of ash under the grate. They chose a table near it, and both ordered the same things from the blackboard – steak and kidney puddings. They came in individual earthenware dishes with a good helping of chips and a side salad. They shared a bottle of red wine, and gradually their bodies became infused with warmth and love. Olivia could not believe what was happening to her. Their eyes met, their hands met and their knees touched under the table. While they were drinking their coffee they both agreed they could think of only one thing: the big white bed at the Bedlington Hotel.

Olivia put her hand on his knee during the journey back. She thought how nearly they had lost each other, how easy it was get to a point of no return in a relationship, and, thankfully, she knew that this one could be saved.

They almost ran into the hotel, and in the lift they

kissed as if they had never kissed before, his back pressed into the corner, she leaning against him. "Let's make love, here, in the lift," she said laughing. When they arrived at their floor they drew apart. An old lady was waiting for the lift and they smiled at her, and she smiled back.

With arms around each other they walked to their room, Olivia's room, number eighty-seven. She would remember that magical number forever. The longing for her body to be joined with his body, and the relief when it did, brought joy beyond all expectations.

The following day was Sunday and a day of rest for most of the staff in the hotel, and no maid appeared to do the room. Olivia and Bill had a bath together and then went back to bed. In the evening they were late for dinner and reproachful looks were levelled at them. As they were both ravenous, they devoured prawn cocktail, roast pork and strawberry gateau but they decided to miss the coffee in the lounge. Their haven was room eighty-seven.

The tragedy was that Monday was their last day. They did not go down for breakfast but ordered tea and toast in their room. When the waiter arrived they had completely forgotten about Mr Randall and Miss Anderson and the empty single bed in the next room, and Bill confidently instructed the man to leave the tray on the bedside table.

After breakfast they locked the door in case the maid came to clean the room. She did come, rapping loudly on the door, and they lay, moist bodies clasped together and hearts hammering, until they heard her go away.

Then came a telephone call from Reception telling them they must vacate their rooms, pointing out that they should have left by noon and it was now half past twelve. Suitcases were packed in great haste, and, when they got downstairs, Bill settled his own account and Olivia paid hers with the money Pat had given her.

"Where's my jacket?" Bill said, looking around wildly.

"Don't worry, sir. The boy will fetch it."

But Bill was worried. It was the sort of thing that instantly put him out of temper.

"It can't be lost," Olivia reassured him, in her new role of comforter and supporter.

Sure enough, the boy returned with the jacket over his arm. "On your bed, sir," he said cheerfully.

Bill looked at Olivia. "I thought you looked all around the room . . ."

"Your bed, sir," repeated the boy, grinning.

By the time they got back to London they were engaged. It was a natural sequence of events, and Bill realised it was the only way open to him if he was to keep Olivia by his side, and by now he desired that very much. Living together was out of the question, and he sensed the parents, whom he had not yet met, would be unhappy if they knew he had spent a weekend with their daughter. He did not want them to be critical of him. He felt himself fortunate that Pat was so broad-minded, but he had no desire to push his luck with her either.

He made a joke about not being able to kneel while driving, but he promised to make a proper proposal later.

Olivia's acceptance did not affect his driving skill, so certain was he of her answer. She sat quietly at his side, savouring the moment, which she felt was the happiest in her life. She clasped her hands very tightly on her lap, as if trying to convince herself that it was real, it was happening to her.

Pat took one look at her niece and knew that all had gone well. It was a relief to her as she had suffered misgivings all during the long weekend Olivia had been away. The dark circles under Olivia's eyes did not diminish the radiance, but even Pat did not expect to hear of an engagement.

"My God!" she cried as she kissed Bill and hugged Olivia. "This is so exciting. Whatever will Joan say, I wonder?"

She called for Hilda.

"Hilda, they are going to be married and we must open a bottle of champagne."

But Olivia did not want champagne. At that moment her only desire was to fall into her narrow little bed, and sleep. She had never been so tired in her life.

Chapter 9

The next day, rested and happy, Olivia telephoned her parents to let them know she was going to be married. Kenneth answered the telephone and was so taken aback by the news that he could not speak, but just laid the receiver on the table and went to fetch Joan. Joan was incredulous and asked to speak to Patience, and Pat came on the line to tell her sister about the suitability of the match. Then Joan wanted to speak to her daughter again, and eventually the call was ended by Olivia telling her mother that she was not returning home just yet, as she and Bill were going to choose the ring that afternoon.

An understanding senior partner at Abbot and Cunliffe gave Bill the time off, and they searched the jewellery shops in Hatton Gardens until they found the ring they liked best. Three small diamonds perched on a gold hoop was within Bill's price range. Olivia was so proud of it, and could not resist extending her fingers, from time to time, so that the diamonds caught the sunlight.

It was getting late when they returned to Pat's house. Olivia put her key in the lock, and as soon as they stepped into the narrow hall she sensed something was wrong. The workmen had departed at the end of the day, and she and Bill had to pick their way through piles of tiles, ladders and tools, which had been left in an untidy muddle on the ground floor. A hush had fallen over the house. Olivia peeped into Pat's studio but she was not there.

They found a disconsolate Hilda sitting at the kitchen table, one hand clutching her apron as if for strength, the other cupping her chin as if she had an aching tooth.

"What is the matter, Hilda?"

"Olivia, dear, I think something bad has happened. Pat is in her room, and won't come out. She has been there for hours, and it is so unlike her. I have pleaded with her, but she won't move. Am I glad to see you, dear! I have been so worried." She favoured them both with a sad little smile.

"Have you any idea what the problem could be?" asked Bill.

"I think it is something to do with the Captain. I can't make it out. Pat is really upset."

"You go and see her," Bill urged Olivia.

She went upstairs to Pat's bedroom, knocked on the door and called out, "It's Olivia. Please may I come in?"

"Yes," came the reply. Pat was in bed, her eyes swollen with crying, the tears wet on her cheeks, glistening in little furrows Olivia had never noticed before. She looked a mess and quite old, and, in the midst of her own happiness, Olivia was deeply disturbed by the sight.

"Don't worry," said Pat, seeing her distress. "I'll be all right." She heaved herself into a sitting position, putting a pillow at her back. Olivia noticed she was in her nightdress, although it was hours before she would normally go to bed.

"Tell Hilda not to fuss," went on Pat, and then she asked, "Is Bill with you?"

"He's downstairs."

"Ask him to bring me a large whisky, please, with very little water. No, on second thoughts, ask him to bring me the bottle, a glass and a jug of water."

As Olivia was leaving Pat caught hold of her hand, and examined the ring.

"It's beautiful, darling," she said, her voice suddenly choked with sobs. "*Hail, wedded love. . .*" and then, "I need that drink."

Bill took the tray up to her, and when he came downstairs again he said, "I don't know what has happened, but whatever it is she doesn't want to talk about it at the moment."

Olivia said to Hilda, "She says you are not to worry."

"She must have something to eat," replied Hilda unhappily.

"No," Bill told her firmly. "She doesn't want food."

Hilda insisted on make omelettes for the three of them, and after a rather subdued meal Bill said he would return to his flat. Olivia made him accompany her upstairs again, and together they looked in Pat's room. She was sleeping. "No wonder," said Bill eyeing the almost empty bottle of whisky.

It was a depressing end to an exciting day. Before Bill left, he and Olivia kissed fondly in the manner of an engaged couple that had recently made a mutual decision not to sleep together again until after their marriage. "Too risky," said Bill sensibly. He had no faith in Olivia's preventative measures.

In the morning, Olivia was roused from sleep by the urgent hand of Hilda, shaking her. "It's Pat. I can't wake her!"

The girl was filled with terror. Her body turned to ice as she dragged herself out of bed. As she struggled into her dressing-gown she wondered what she would see in Pat's bedroom.

Pat lay in her dishevelled bed, surrounded by empty pill bottles and scattered tablets. The whisky bottle was empty. It was impossible to tell what she had taken, but her terrible stentorian breathing struck dread into Olivia's heart.

"What shall we do?" she gasped. One look at Hilda's anguished face made her realise that she would be no help. It meant that she, Olivia, would have to deal with the situation and she did not know if she was up to it.

"I must telephone for an ambulance." Olivia raced to

the telephone that was downstairs in the hall. With trembling fingers she dialled nine three times. Never in her wildest dreams had she imagined herself dialling those particular numbers. She wondered whether she would be able to utter any words when the call was answered, and was surprised that her voice sounded so normal when she asked for the ambulance service.

When a voice said "Ambulance service. Can I help you?" she tried to describe Pat's condition, and she spoke of an 'overdose' and, naively, 'heavy breathing'.

On the way back to Hilda she heard the workmen hammering and sawing as usual. They were in the room that was slowly being turned into a bathroom. Olivia spoke to the foreman, "I'm sorry, but Lady Lucas is ill. The ambulance is on its way, and I must ask you to leave."

"Now, miss?"

"Yes, please."

"Do you want us to come tomorrow? The lady said she wanted the job done as quickly as possible."

"I don't know. Yes, I think you should come tomorrow."

"We'll do that, miss." The other men stopped working, and Olivia was aware of their sympathetic faces. "I hope the lady will be better soon," said the foreman.

Olivia flew back to Hilda, and was dismayed to find that the poor woman had scooped up all the pills and empty bottles, and put them in the wastepaper basket.

"No, no," cried Olivia, remembering something her

father had once told her in the distant past, "they will want to see them." They put the pills, phials and the empty whisky bottle on Pat's bedside table.

"Can I tidy her up a bit, dear?" asked Hilda.

"Yes, of course."

Hilda gently wiped Pat's face with a damp flannel, and then she brushed her beautiful hair. "There, there, my lovely," she murmured, but there was no response from the unconscious woman. She did not stir or speak when Hilda tenderly lifted her head so that she could brush her hair away from her face.

"Now we must wait until the ambulance comes," said Olivia, trying to appear calm. "There is nothing we can do but wait."

Would Pat die while they were waiting? The rasping sound of her breathing, in and out, in and out, became horribly important to the anxious listeners. The possibility of it suddenly stopping was too terrible to contemplate. No doubt Hilda was silently praying, and Olivia joined her in her thoughts. Dear God, don't let her die, and then appealing to Pat herself, please, don't die.

It seemed an eternity before the ambulance men arrived, brisk, efficient and so welcome. They lost no time in gathering up the pills and bottles and putting them in a paper bag, and then rolling Pat's inert body on to a canvas stretcher. Olivia heard her give a little moaning sound as they did this.

"Are you staying here, Miss, or coming with us?"

"We're both coming," said Olivia firmly.

They had to sit in the hospital waiting room for three hours while Pat had the poisons washed out of her stomach. At the end of that time, a nurse appeared and told them they could see her for a few minutes.

They found she had been put into a room on her own. Her face was the colour of the hospital sheet folded beneath her chin. She looked at Olivia and said simply, "I don't want to live without him."

Close to tears, Olivia asked, "What happened?"

"I'm so tired, darling. Do you mind if I don't talk now?" Something strange had happened to Pat's voice, and it was like a croak.

Olivia brushed away a tear, and begged, "Please, don't say anything more."

But Pat indicated for her to lean over the bed. "There is a letter in my bedroom," she whispered. "Read it. I mean it, please read it. I want you to, promise me you will."

Olivia promised, and said, "I'll be back to see you again soon. In the meantime, dear Pat, please, please rest, and try not to think of anything bad."

There were convulsive sobs from Hilda standing on the other side of the bed. "Don't cry," Pat managed to say to her.

Olivia took Pat's hand, and it lay limp in hers, as if all Pat's old vitality had ebbed away. She turned her face to the pillow and was instantly asleep.

They managed to get a taxi outside the hospital, and Hilda wept noisily throughout the journey to Queen's

Gate. The taxi driver refused to take the fare, saying, "I can see you're in trouble." Olivia pressed a big tip in his hand and thanked him for his kindness. People are wonderful, she thought, the ambulance men, so comforting, the nurse at the hospital who spoke encouraging words to them, and now this sympathetic cabby.

In the kitchen, Olivia said to Hilda, "We'll have a nice cup of tea and that will make us feel better."

"I'll do it, dear." Hilda carried the kettle to the tap; glad to do something that was normal and routine. When the tea was made they sat very close to the stove, warming their hands on the cups.

"You know, dear," said Hilda, now almost recovered and eager to seek an explanation for the events of the morning, "the Captain hasn't been around lately. Pat has been depressed, missing him."

"I did not notice it. I wish I had noticed more." Olivia was wretched.

"Don't blame yourself, dear. You have had a lot to think about, with your young man and all."

Bill! She must telephone him and tell him what had happened. It seemed an age ago, the Bedlington Hotel and, only yesterday, choosing the ring. She looked at it now, new and shining on her finger, the first time she had been aware of it on that extraordinary day. Now, suddenly brought back to reality, all she wanted to hear was the sound of Bill's voice.

But first she went to Pat's room to look for the letter.

It was not on the dressing table or on the bedside table or hidden in the rumpled bedclothes. Eventually she discovered it under the bed.

Feeling intrusive, she read:

Dearest Pat, for you are and always will be my dearest, after all the happy years we have spent together. Please never imagine I am not grateful for them. Perhaps it is because I am getting old but suddenly I want a more solid relationship, marriage in fact, a concept that, I know, fills you with misgiving. However, I find I am of a different view and look upon it as a challenge and a commitment I want to experience before it is too late.

I have met someone who shares my hopes for the future, and whom I love dearly. You will be surprised to learn I intend to marry Alice Mountjoy, Olivia's friend.

My blessings on you,

Nigel.

Olivia was stunned. She read and reread the letter so that the full meaning became clear to her. It was the culmination of an emotional day. She was sitting on the edge of Pat's bed, the letter in her hand, when Hilda came into the room. Without saying a word, Olivia handed the letter to Hilda, dear loyal Hilda who had played a part in the drama and was so close to Pat.

"No, dear. I would not like to read her private mail. She wanted you to see it."

Olivia nodded.

"But you can tell me what's in it," said Hilda hopefully.

"It's as we thought, Captain Nigel has left Pat. He is

going to marry Alice. You remember Alice, my friend from the secretarial college?"

"Oh, my goodness, a young lady like that, no wonder Pat has taken it badly! Well, dear, I came to tidy her room, and that is what I will do, if you don't mind, so that it is ready for her when she comes home."

And I will telephone Bill, thought Olivia.

He came with all possible speed, and listened carefully to all she had to tell him. She had no hesitation in showing him the letter Nigel had written to Pat.

"It doesn't surprise me in the least," he said when he had read it. "I've always told you that girl is bad news. Now perhaps you will believe me. Nigel is getting all he deserves. I think we should try and get hold of him to tell him what has happened here today."

"Do you think Pat would want us to do that?" Olivia was fairly certain she would not, although she thought every decision made by Bill was the right one.

He brushed aside her doubts, and immediately started telephoning Nigel's flat, Alice's flat, Nigel's club, but Captain Nigel was not in any of these places. Bill then telephoned his father to see if he knew the whereabouts of Alice. Up to the moment, Olivia had almost forgotten Bill's familial link with the person she had once regarded as her closest friend.

George always shouted when he was on the telephone, and Olivia could hear what he said quite clearly. No, they had not seen or heard from Alice for weeks. Had something happened? Bill avoided complicated explanations by telling his father of his intention to get married. Olivia was astonished that Bill had not already notified his family of his engagement; after all she had wasted no time in calling her parents to tell them the momentous news.

"Amazing!" George yelled. "Very pleased. I'll tell Maureen at once. Give our best to the girl . . . Olivia? Yes, of course, Olivia. Goodbye."

Later that evening Bill and Olivia went to the hospital to see Pat, without Hilda who wanted to stay at home and cook the supper.

They were told that Pat had been moved to the general ward, and Bill sat in the waiting room while Olivia went in to see her. Pat was sitting in a chair by a bed, wearing her nightdress and a hospital dressing-gown. Hilda had packed a little case for her containing clothes and a wash-bag, and Olivia put these into a locker. Then she sat down in the other chair, relieved to see that Pat looked almost normal.

"I'll be out of here tomorrow," she said. "The sooner the better. I've made such a bloody fool of myself."

At least, thought Olivia, it doesn't sound as if she will try to repeat the performance. She felt she should admit straight away, before Pat found out, that Bill had tried to contact Nigel, and failed. As she expected, Pat was not pleased and became quite animated. "Bill should not have done that," she protested. "Please tell him to leave it alone. It's over. Nothing to be done." She put her head against the back of the chair as if the sudden burst of energy had exhausted her.

Presently, she revived and asked, "Did you read the letter?"

"Yes."

"Have you ever read such sanctimonious claptrap? 'I have met someone who shares my hopes for the future.' I can't believe that Nigel wrote those words to me. That smarmy little tart! I disliked her from the beginning."

"I wish I had never brought her to the house," said Olivia miserably.

"You must not blame yourself," said Pat, echoing Hilda's words. "How could you know that sweet little Alice was a scheming bitch?" Grief seemed to take over anger, and she started to cry. Her rather heavy body heaved, and her sobs became louder and louder. Olivia became acutely aware that a silence had descended on the other patients and their visitors, and all eyes were focussed on them, concerned faces reflecting a mixture of sympathy and curiosity.

Olivia patted an agitated shoulder, and then produced a handkerchief that she handed to Pat, who blew her nose vigorously. The people in the ward resumed talking, sensing the crisis had passed.

"I could ask Mummy to come to Queen's Gate, if that would help. She could come at once, so she would be there when you come home. What do you think?"

"You know, darling," said Pat, "I think I would rather go and stay with Joan for a few days when I leave here. I know how she and Kenneth hate being parted, and a little break in that peaceful house may be just what I need."

So, later that evening, Olivia telephoned her mother and had the difficult task of explaining to her what had happened to Pat. There was no way of making light of the truth: Pat had tried to kill herself, and it was a miracle she had not succeeded. Joan was shocked – she had always thought the realistic side of her sister's character was stronger than the romantic side, and yet now she was being told that in middle age she had tried to kill herself because a man had left her. Olivia did not mention Alice by name, and just said that Nigel had met 'someone else'. If Pat felt inclined (and Olivia felt sure she would feel inclined in time) she would fill in all the details when confiding to Joan.

"Of course she must come here, as soon as she is well enough," said Joan.

After supper, and after Hilda had retired to bed telling them she wanted an early night, Olivia and Bill found themselves alone. Olivia gave a little sigh of exhaustion and happiness, and encircled Bill's waist with her arms and laid her aching head on his chest. "It's been quite a day," she said.

He made her sit down on the sofa while he lit the gas fire with a match. Then he sat close to her. The hissing fire gave off a comforting glow in the cold room, and Bill bent his handsome head to kiss her. Suddenly, the house vibrated with the sound of the front door bell.

"Leave it," said Bill before he pressed his lips against hers.

She moved away from him. The bell pealed again, and

she feared the noise would bring Hilda down from her bedroom under the roof. "I must answer it."

"Leave it!" he said again.

"I can't do that," She disentangled herself from his embrace, and he made a little exclamation of annoyance.

Olivia walked through the chilly hall, her shoes clattering on the bare boards. Hilda had removed the rugs because of the workmen trampling through that part of the house. She pulled back the chain, and unlocked the door.

She peered into the darkness, and in the beam from the streetlight, she saw a familiar figure.

It was Alice.

Chapter 10

"I was beginning to think you must be out," Alice said as she stepped into the hall. She shivered. "It's freezing."

Olivia led the way to the sitting room. She did not know what to say so she said nothing. As they entered, Bill rose to his feet.

"Oh," cried Alice, "you are both here. I am lucky!"

There was an awkward little silence before Alice grabbed Olivia's hand, and examined the modest ring. "I've been hearing about you two."

Olivia wondered – how could she have heard about them?

"What a sweet ring! Just think, Livvy, you and I will be related."

Olivia glanced at Alice's left hand, but there was no ring there. No, she thought, Captain Nigel would not commit himself to that extent until he had sorted things out with Pat. After all, he must have written that letter very recently.

So far, neither Bill nor Olivia had uttered a word, but she managed to pull herself together and said, "Sit down, Alice. Would you like a drink?"

"Yes, I'd love a glass of wine, if that is possible. What a pity we haven't got champagne to celebrate your engagement."

Of course there was champagne in the house, but Olivia had no intention of opening one of Pat's bottles. She went to the kitchen to find the white wine that she knew would be cooling in the refrigerator. By the time she had opened the bottle and set it on a tray with three glasses, she hoped that some sort of conversation would be under way in the next room.

"Bill is cross with me," said Alice. She was sitting in the place on the sofa Olivia had vacated, and Bill had moved to the armchair opposite her. "I hope you are more understanding, Livvy."

"It's hard to be understanding after such a terrible day," said Olivia, pouring wine into the glasses.

"As you seem to know so much," said Bill, "perhaps you have heard that Pat is in hospital after an attempted suicide?"

"Yes, I have heard that," replied Alice quietly. "I'm very sorry."

"It's too late to say that now," Bill said.

"I have not come between a married couple," Alice

argued. "I would never break up a marriage. It is not my style."

Olivia felt moved to say something. "They were together for six years," she reasoned, "and it was a good relationship. As good as any marriage."

Alice took a sip of wine. "She is much older than he is," she said. "She could not expect to keep him."

"And you will make him happy?" asked Bill sarcastically.

"I hope to make him happy. I want to very much." Alice paused. "Neither of you seems to have grasped what has happened here. Nigel and I have fallen in love. Surely you two, at this time, must understand about two people loving each other? Loving each other so much that nothing can stand in the way. If we have caused grief we are truly sorry, but what can we do about it? We cannot deny our love because of someone Nigel no longer cares for. That would not benefit anyone. We must go forward." She looked at Olivia as if she hoped to get support from that direction, but Olivia could not meet her eyes, and looked at Bill instead.

"I love him," Alice said, "I shall always love him." Her voice broke. "I love him," she said again.

Olivia felt her throat tighten. If Bill had not been there, glowering, she would have put out her hand to touch her friend who sat, head bowed, fighting back tears.

Eventually Alice looked up, eyes brimming, and said, "I don't want us to quarrel. I did not come here to defend myself. I came to tell you that Nigel and I are getting married in three weeks' time at Chelsea Registry Office. I would have liked a white wedding, like you will have, Livvy, but Nigel wants it this way. I will send you the details."

"Don't bother," said Bill shortly. "Olivia and I will not be coming."

Alice opened her eyes very wide. "You can't mean that! You are my brother!"

"I am not your brother."

She turned to Olivia. "You will come to my wedding, won't you, Livvy?"

Olivia took a deep breath. "As Pat is so upset I think it would be disloyal of me to come. Of course I will think about you on the day, Bill and I will, I mean, but I hope you understand why we can't be there."

"No," said Alice, "I do not understand."

Olivia's headache was getting worse. She wished the day could come to an end, that she could go to bed and sleep, and think about all these problems tomorrow. She said wearily, "I can see it is difficult for you, and it is unfortunate that Pat has taken it so badly."

Alice stood up, and slammed her half-empty glass on a small antique table by the sofa.

She smoothed her tight skirt over her hips, a characteristic gesture, and tossed her head so that her amazing mane of straight hair fell over one shoulder. "I suppose this means that you will not be inviting Nigel and me to your wedding either?"

"That's right," said Bill.

"Pat will be there," Olivia explained. "She is my godmother as well as my aunt, so of course she will be invited. You must see how awkward it would be if you and Nigel were there as well. That's what Bill means."

"I'll tell you what I mean," said Bill decidedly. "I mean that although I shall probably have little say in the wedding arrangements, I would like to make it clear now that I do not want you there, or Nigel, the poor sod. And if you are about to say, Alice, that your mother will stay away if you are not invited, then that is just fine by me."

With that, Alice began to cry in earnest. Olivia accompanied her to the front door. Nothing but tears all day long, she thought. "Bill didn't . . ." she began.

Alice wept uncontrollably. Still weeping, she pressed Olivia's hand, and then kissed her cheek. Olivia felt her wet face against hers, and was inexpressibly moved. Neither girl could speak. Olivia stood in the doorway and watched Alice walk away from her, head down, her bent figure silhouetted against the streetlight.

When she returned to the sitting room, she found that Bill had resumed his seat on the sofa. "She was crying her eyes out," she told him.

"All put on," he replied coolly, and he leaned forward for the bottle of wine and replenished his glass.

Part Two

Chapter 11

Ten years had passed, and Kenneth was in the garden when he heard the telephone ringing. Its persistence annoyed him because he did not want to take his boots off, which he would have to do if he went into the house to answer it.

It could not be ignored and when he got to the telephone in the main house he was out of breath. "Hello?" he gasped.

He heard the light crisp tones of a woman, a pleasing voice, though rather affected. "This is Alice Benton."

The name meant nothing to him, and he said, "I'm afraid Olivia and Bill are not here at present. Can I give them a message?"

"It's Dr Anderson, isn't it? I've heard so much about you from Livvy. I was her friend at the secretarial college in London."

"Well, I'm not sure . . ."

She asked politely, "Are you visiting?"

"No, I live here. Rather I live in part of this house, their house." Further explanation was needed. "I live in a flat attached to the house, a granny flat, but in my case a granddad flat." It was a mildly humorous comment he had made many times.

"And your wife . . .?"

"My wife died five years ago." He still found the statement difficult to say.

Over the telephone he could hear the sharp intake of her breath. "I'm so sorry."

In that rapid exchange of words he felt as if he had bared his soul to a stranger, said more than he intended. He did not know how to continue the conversation, but she took it up again with brisk efficiency. "My husband, Nigel, and I have moved recently to Pennel Bridge. I don't know whether you know this, Dr. Anderson, but Bill is my stepbrother, so of course we are delighted to be so near. Nigel and I hope that Bill and Livvy will come to dinner with us next Friday the fourteenth, and please say you will come too."

Halfway through her spiel Kenneth anticipated what she was going to say, so he was prepared. He did not like going out to dine and it was his custom to refuse any invitations that came his way, not because he was unfriendly but because he preferred to stay at home. Most of the locals understood that by now. He explained this in his usual courteous way, but he did not know then how impossible it was to overrule Alice.

"I insist. It is very important to me that you come."

"Look here," he said desperately, beginning to lose patience, "you don't know yet whether Olivia and Bill are free on that evening. Leave it until you hear from them." He hoped she would not take this as a half acceptance. "I'll give them your message."

After replacing the receiver, he padded back to a chair by the back door and, sitting down, laboriously put on his stout boots over the thick socks he wore in the garden.

His old dog lay with his nose resting on his front paws, filmy brown eyes watching him, loving him. Kenneth spoke to the dog, as he often did when they were alone. "Inconsiderate, ringing in the afternoon."

Who was that woman? Evidently she knew who he was. 'Alice', he repeated the name several times in his head, searching his mind for clues. He knew the name was vaguely familiar. "*Alice, where art thou?*" he asked the dog.

People of Kenneth's age have so many memories, they unfold gradually when bidden. It came to him; ten, or perhaps eleven, years ago, a haggard Patience had come to stay with them at the old house. It must have been the year before Olivia's wedding. She had waited to finish the secretarial course before marrying Bill. Kenneth remembered that during the visit the name Alice had been bandied back and forth between the two sisters. He had been sorry for Patience, but the endless discussion about the end of an affair had become wearisome. That is why he had put it at the back of his mind until now, but the memory came back sharply, and there was no doubt Alice was the villain of the piece.

He stepped outside into the cool fresh air of the garden. For some reason, the air felt more clean and pure now than it had before he went inside to answer the telephone. He took a deep appreciative gulp of it, before picking up his little fork and kneeling-pad to do some weeding.

He remembered how concerned Joan had been about her sister. She was worried that she might try again to kill herself, and appealed to her husband as a medical man to give an opinion as to the likelihood of this happening. Kenneth was certain that Patience had acted under great duress and later regretted it. He listened to the two sisters talking animatedly about Olivia's forthcoming marriage, and he commented to Joan that the prospect of a wedding in the family must be the best deterrent for a suicidal woman.

How happy they had all been on the day of Olivia's wedding! Olivia was radiant, and Kenneth could hardly recognise his beautiful daughter. Joan was by his side, and he envisaged many years ahead when they would be together. Patience was her former exuberant self, and he was relieved that she made no mention of the incident of the previous year. The house in Annesley was full of people staying for the wedding, including George and Maureen. Joan and Kenneth had liked George right away, he was such an open uncomplicated character, but

Maureen was hard work. "She really does wring her hands," Kenneth whispered to Joan. Before they returned to Cornwall, the Andersons pressed them to come again soon, but it was an invitation made out of politeness, and they did not expect them to take it up. The two families could not have been more different.

As he dug into the chalky soil and pulled up the weeds, careful to bring the roots with them, his thoughts turned from the past to the present, and the invitation to dinner. What a waste of time that would be! He sat on his heels and looked up at the sky – an English day, a little warm breeze and a few clouds moving slowly across the blueness – and he remembered a line from Keats, something about '*the sailing cloudlets bright career*' and, as ever, he thought of Joan and how much she would have liked the day.

Kenneth had been instrumental in buying the beautiful house behind him. It was called Carpenters and had a big garden, two fields and even a small wood. Four years after Olivia and Bill were married several things happened. Kenneth retired, Joan became ill and Bill accepted a partnership with a firm of Solicitors in Melbury, a market town in Oxfordshire.

Before they moved to the country, Olivia and Bill lived in a flat in the Fulham Road. She wanted a child, but Bill persuaded her it was impractical while he was still working at Abbott and Cunliffe on a fairly low salary. The money Olivia earned from working for an Estate Agent, typing details of houses, was useful to them.

In the midst of Bill starting his new job and looking for a house near Melbury that they could afford, Olivia found she was pregnant. She did not know how this had happened, as she had been careful since her first lessons in birth control. Perhaps her longing to have a baby made her careless. Bill accused her of bad timing, and she wept. Her happiness was marred by the knowledge that in some way she had let him down.

Kenneth, on the other hand, thought the timing was perfect. If he had been a praying man he would have thought it the answer to his prayers. It turned Joan's mind away from her illness She had cancer and they both knew what the outcome would be. Olivia's pregnancy gave her a reason to look forward to the future.

As they had shared everything during their marriage, Kenneth and Joan now shared the inevitability of her death. She accepted it in her usual practical way. "I don't want you to live here on your own," she told him. "You must sell this house when . . ."

He accepted her reasoning, but he found her sensible planning almost unbearable.

Her idea was that Kenneth should help Olivia and Bill to buy a house, a house with a flat attached or a cottage nearby, where Kenneth could live on his own, and yet be near his daughter and family. Joan and Kenneth were painfully aware of their son-in-law's irritation with his present domestic set-up. Bill hated the rented house they had been forced to move into while they were looking for a more permanent place to live, and Olivia was, in his eyes, unattractively large, and constantly worrying about her mother. When it was revealed that she was carrying twins, that alarming prospect put Bill into an even worse humour. His mouth turned down, and his robust laugh was seldom heard.

The babies, a boy and a girl, were shown to their grandmother a week before she died. Kenneth tried hard to disguise the emotion her felt on seeing Joan's joy when the two little bundles were presented to her. He wanted the girl to be named after her, but his wife summoned up enough strength to register her disapproval of the name. "Joan is old-fashioned," she said. "No one under forty is called Joan."

"We'll give her any name you choose, Mummy," said Olivia brokenly.

"If I'd had another daughter I think I would have liked her to be called Claire." So Claire it was, and her twin brother was called George.

Olivia and Bill were surprised when a week after Joan's funeral Kenneth put his house on the market. They were even more surprised when he told them of the plan to contribute towards a house for them. Instantly, they forgot about buying a modern house on an estate, and set their sights on grander things. Very soon Carpenters became the object of their desire.

"It is an interesting name," said Kenneth when they told him of their find. "Is it a cottage that once belonged to the village chippy?"

"Well, no," said Bill, "I don't think you could describe

it as a cottage, and I have no idea how it came by that name. We can't wait for you to see it."

They drove there one sunny afternoon, and Kenneth was dismayed and astonished. Even taking into account that he would get a good price for his house, with its unique position in the New Forest, the asking price for Carpenters was much more than he expected to pay. What would Joan have thought of such a venture?

He was used to living in a rambling old house, but this seemed more like a mansion, with seven bedrooms, several other larger rooms with high ceilings, a nursery and a playroom. There were stables and outhouses, and a beautiful garden; Kenneth thought he would find pleasure in the garden. The remaining dog was too old to walk far, and the garden of the house in Annesley was too small to be a challenge. He could abandon the long walks, and take an interest in gardening instead. Also, he had to admit Carpenters had the advantage of a separate flat, facing south, with everything he needed.

Bill took out a substantial mortgage, which meant that his name was on the deeds. Kenneth found the initial payment, and began to have serious doubts. He had pictured an investment for his daughter, but now he found he was investing for both Olivia and Bill, and his own name did not appear on anything. He would have liked to consult his own lawyer, but that was awkward.

"Bill is a solicitor, Daddy," said Olivia, "and you must let him do what he thinks best. He does understand these things." Kenneth had the uneasy feeling that Joan would have thought otherwise, but Joan was no longer there and he took the easy way, which was to sign, without argument, every document that was put in front of him.

Thinking about it, five years later, on a sunny afternoon, Kenneth decided everything had worked out for the best. He was very happy in his flat, which was warm and comfortable, and a cheerful lady from the village cleaned for him on Wednesdays and Fridays. She worked in the main house on the other weekdays. Her son, an obliging but slightly retarded man in his forties, helped Kenneth in the garden. He did all the mowing, and tackled any task that was given to him. His mother's name was Mrs Bracegirdle, a name that afforded Kenneth much amusement. She liked him because he was a man on his own and, without being asked, she cooked an occasional meal for him.

Yes, he thought he was lucky and his initial misgivings were unfounded. He had the garden, and the additional interest of a book he was writing, a biography of Dr Edward Jenner, a man he revered. His grandchildren ran in and out of his flat, as they did in their own house, and his love for them was overwhelming. He was constantly enchanted by the variance of their characters, the thoughtful boy and the stubborn girl, so different and yet, in many ways, so alike. Their closeness interested him, and he thought it similar to his relationship with Joan. They had been like twins, and he did not think his daughter had the same bond with her husband.

When the day became chilly, he went indoors. He heard a car in the drive, and he knew it was Olivia and the children. He could hear the childish voices of the twins, Olivia's distinctive quick voice, and then the high-pitched tone of her friend, Mary Chalmers. The car door slammed and the front door banged. Presently, he heard the arrival of a second car, Bill, home from the office. Kenneth decided to wait until Mary left; she lived nearby and would walk home. He knew she would not stay long after Bill's return. She maintained that she got on splendidly with Olivia, but Bill she found difficult and moody. The truth was that he could not be bothered to be charming to her, and she sensed his disinterest and retreated. Kenneth peeked through the curtains, and watched her stride away on her stout legs. When he thought the moment was right, he strolled over to the house to deliver the message from Alice Benton.

As he entered the front door Kenneth was struck, as he had been many times before, by the friendly feel of the old house. Some of the furniture had a comfortably familiar look; the dresser standing in the hall was the one he and Joan had acquired for eight guineas, and it looked very much at home.

The twins clattered towards him, slithering on the bare oak boards, throwing their arms around him, clasping his legs and almost pulling him down. He loved their exuberant welcome. When he had disentangled himself from their hugs, or rather when Bill had reprimanded them sharply, he accepted the offer of a drink. By this time, Olivia had joined them and, when they were all seated in the room they called the parlour (they seldom used the grand drawing room), he told them about the telephone call he had taken that afternoon.

"Alice!" cried his astonished daughter. "After all this time!"

"She wants you both to go to dinner with them next Friday the fourteenth. She asked me as well, but of course I shall not go."

"Why not, Daddy? It would do you good. You ought to go out more often. We'll all go." She sounded quite excited about it.

"You can count me out," Bill growled. "I have no intention of going."

Olivia looked unhappy. "You can't keep this feud up for ever and ever. Alice and Nigel are our neighbours now; we must not start by being hostile towards them. Besides Alice is your stepsister."

"Why do you always remind me of that?" asked Bill. "I would rather forget it. Anyway, I thought we decided to remain loyal to Pat. It is not exactly loyal to have dinner with her arch enemy."

"Alice is not that any more. You know that Pat never mentions either of them these days. She is a perfectly happy woman."

"She does not appear to have become involved with another man since it happened."

"Darling, that is because she is getting old. She told me that sort of thing does not worry her any more. She is always saying how awful it would be to have a difficult man around all the time."

"I don't believe a word of it."

"Bill, it's more than ten years ago! Surely we can forget what happened all that time ago?"

"As far as I am concerned, it happened, and it damned nearly spoilt our wedding."

"It did not."

"There was a feeling of tension before the wedding, you must admit. When Pat went to stay with your parents, and the two sisters were continually yapping about Alice and her behaviour, and about Nigel and his behaviour."

"Our wedding was not spoilt," said Olivia obstinately. "It was the most wonderful day of our lives, and long after Pat's visit."

And so they went on, as was their custom, backwards and forwards, like tennis players in a rally. One player would eventually win the point, and it was usually Bill.

This time, however, Olivia still had something to say. "Alice was my friend. I liked her. I still like her, even though I have not seen her for so long." She ended on a defiant note. "The trouble is that you do not like any of my friends."

"If you are talking about Mary Chalmers, and I suppose you are, I do not dislike her. What is there to dislike about her? She is the dullest woman in the world."

"She is a good friend," Olivia retorted, "in fact, the best friend I have around here."

"And yet you are always saying things about her," Bill

persisted. "That she is always coming here without warning, that nothing ever goes wrong with her life, perfect husband, perfect children, that they just go along in their self-satisfied boring way."

"You never understand how it is possible to criticise people, and still like them. Everything is black or white for you. It is the same with Alice. I know she has faults, but I like her in spite of them. She is a more interesting person than Mary, and I can't understand why you are not pleased for me to know someone like her."

Bill gave a big sigh. "Olivia, you have always known how I feel about Alice."

Kenneth wondered – what did he really feel about Alice? It seemed unlike Bill to persevere with a vendetta. He was too lazy a character to nurse a grievance for so many years, it was more his style to allow relationships to lapse when they no longer interested him. Bill never went to Cornwall, and on rare occasions George came alone to visit his son. Maureen, like Alice, was out of the picture. Bill liked Patience, but not to the extent of taking a stand for her for so long. Why did he bother?

Kenneth thought he should intervene. Up to that moment he had been quite content, sitting in an armchair that had once belonged to him, with George on the floor by his knee, and Claire sitting on his lap with her head against his chest. Suddenly, he decided that there could be no real reason why they should not accept the invitation.

"Children, children," he said, "for God's sake, let us go

– one evening will not disrupt our lives too much, and can do us no harm."

He agreed to go as well, believing that his presence might prevent Olivia receiving any crossfire from Bill during the journey there. Also, Kenneth wondered if Alice had detected a note of hostility in his voice when he was talking to her, as he had been anxious not to become involved. Now he was involved, and having heard evidence of his son-in-law's antagonism towards Alice, perversely he was on her side.

Bill looked furious, but Olivia caught his hand and pressed it to her cheek. "Daddy is right, darling. Don't let's quarrel about them. We'll just go." She repeated her father's words, "It can do us no harm."

Chapter 12

Kenneth usually assumed the role of baby-sitter when Olivia and Bill went out to dinner, so on the evening the three of them went to the Bentons they had to engage the services of a girl from the village.

The girl stood in a window with a twin on each side of her, waving to them as they walked to the car. The children were attired in fluffy sleeping suits, one yellow and one blue, and when they wrapped their arms around Kenneth before he left they smelled of soap, and their recently washed hair clung damply to their heads. He could not imagine why he was leaving two such enchanting creatures, especially as he was convinced he would not enjoy the evening that lay ahead of him. He must have been mad to say he would go. He thought regretfully of the alternative, reading them a story and tucking them into bed long after their usual bedtime –

coping with all the delaying tactics they employed before they finally fell asleep.

"That girl seems very young," he said plaintively. "Is she a responsible person?"

They ignored this remark, and Olivia said, "Why don't you sit in front, Daddy?"

It was a ritual they went through every time the three of them were in the car together. Olivia always offered to sit in the back seat and Kenneth always refused. He felt his position in the family was a sensitive one, and he was afraid of being an interloper.

During the journey to Pennel Bridge, Olivia and Bill had little to say to each other. Bill was sulking because, like Kenneth, he did not want to go, and Olivia was fretting because he was not happy and, more than anything else in the world, she desired his happiness. The fields, squares of different hues, brown, blue and brilliant yellow, with the gentle green downs behind, flashed by unnoticed, except by Kenneth in the back who marvelled at the beauty of the countryside.

The Bentons house looked as if it had been plucked from Hampstead Garden Suburb and deposited in a picturesque village. Kenneth wondered how planning permission had ever been granted to build this house amongst all its seasoned neighbours. It stood out, brash and new, flanked on either side by thatched cottages, like a youngster at a pensioner's tea party. It was of solid construction, however, and although the front garden was only a small area of lawn, circled by a drive and a high hedge of the dreaded Leyland cypress, as they approached they could see there was undoubtedly a large garden at the back and they caught a glimpse of a swimming pool.

Bill rang the bell, and almost immediately the door was opened by Nigel Benton – a slightly older looking and much balder Captain Nigel. His hand in Olivia's was warm and dry, and he bent down from his great height to kiss her cheek with the words, "How wonderful to see you!"

As they were removing their coats in the hall, Alice came skipping down the stairs. Olivia looked up with a mixture of eagerness and curiosity, and was at first taken aback by her old friend's appearance. Alice was wearing a diaphanous pink dress with a long skirt, the bodice hugging her figure to the hips, around her neck a choker of pearls. The fashion for wearing 'something long' at dinner parties had been revived recently, and Olivia in an ankle-length brown velvet skirt and a white blouse with a high collar wondered if she was underdressed, or whether Alice was overdressed. She decided on the latter.

Alice hugged her, and seemed genuinely pleased to see her and Bill again, and to meet Kenneth. The years had altered her more than they had Olivia. She had filled out, making her look even sexier, and the magnificent mane of hair was gone, replaced by the popular bouffant style. Olivia's heart sank when she saw the colour, very light ash blonde. Bill detested dyed hair.

Kenneth's first impression of Alice was of a great deal

of tanned skin, no doubt acquired under a lamp or by sunning herself abroad. Few people managed to get a tan like that in an English garden. He was surprised to notice that when she smiled the flash of her large white teeth made her look like an ingenuous schoolgirl. During the evening he was to discover that her whole manner reflected the schoolgirl image, her dormitory-style humour and her constant showing off by making facetious comments about people known to the Bentons. He supposed this mixture of childishness and adult sophistication must go down well in some quarters, and she had perfected the technique.

She introduced them to the other couple at the dinner party. "Rachel Preston, and Edward Preston who is our MP for Melbury. My dearest friend, Olivia, and her husband, Bill Randall who is my stepbrother. And this is Olivia's father, Dr Anderson."

Edward Preston impressed Bill as they had interests in common – golf, fishing and the law. Edward was a barrister. Olivia breathed a small sigh of relief when she saw the two men deep in conversation. Kenneth observed them with amusement; his son-in-law was so transparent, with a reserve of charm to call upon when it was worth his while.

Rachel Preston was a faded beauty with a haunted look. It appeared there was an explanation for the worried expression and, as they moved into the dining room, Alice hung back until she was alongside Kenneth, then she took his arm and pressing her mouth very close to his ear, whispered: "Rachel is a reformed alcoholic." He could not understand why she had singled him out for this piece of information; perhaps because he was medical she thought it would interest him. He could only grunt in reply, and hope that no one else had heard her.

The Prestons knew the people Alice talked about during dinner, whereas Olivia, Bill and Kenneth did not, so the witticisms were lost on them although they understood their meaning. Edward Preston chortled with delight, but his wife looked uneasy. Olivia sensed a feeling of deep disappointment that what had once seemed like youthful high spirits in Alice now appeared plainly vulgar. It was a relief to talk to Nigel who was comfortably familiar, and yet, when she thought about it, not so familiar. He was much quieter than she remembered, almost withdrawn. Perhaps if she had known him and Alice over the years the changes would not have been so apparent.

"Do you still search for fossils?" she asked him.

His sad face lit up for a moment. "You remember! I used to go to Lyme Regis and hack away at the rocks with my little hammer. Alice and I went there a few times before we were married."

"Not any more?"

"No, I gave up that hobby years ago. Gardening is my main interest now. I bought this house because of the garden. The soil is right, you see." Rhododendrons were Nigel's speciality. "You will not be able to grow them at Carpenters," he stated. "Too alkaline."

"I'm afraid neither Bill nor I know much about gardening. We leave that to my father who is very keen. He spends hours in the garden." As she spoke she glanced down the table and she and Kenneth exchanged a little smile.

In his capacity as the oldest person there, he was sitting on Alice's right hand and Rachel Preston was on his other side. He had been trying to make conversation with Rachel but it was hard going. Because of the uneven numbers Alice had two men on her left, Edward and Bill, consequently she monopolised that side of the table. She abandoned Kenneth to Rachel. He was glad to see that his daughter was talking to Nigel who seemed a likable fellow. He thought she looked very sweet, with her listening face on, and no one would guess she was the mother of two children.

"Yes, well, that is my project for the future," said Nigel, "to make something of this garden. I can't wait to get started on it."

She thought, I wonder why they have no children? It occurred to her that neither Alice nor Nigel had questioned her about her children. Most people were polite enough to show an interest in the twins. However, she felt safe talking to Nigel, and she listened happily to him speaking lovingly of yakishimanum, racemosum and falconeri. He knew the species like a surgeon knows the parts of the body. Listening to him droning on about flowering shrubs was preferable to listening to his wife expound about who slept with whom, and who indulged in unusual sexual practices.

Then he leaned forward, and spoke in a lowered voice, "How is Pat?"

She tried not to appear startled. "Very well. She's absolutely fine."

"Unchanged, I imagine?"

"Still the same Pat. Always busy." Of course she did not mention that Pat had changed in one respect: she was much fatter. Her weight had increased steadily over the years, and she now wore voluminous clothes to disguise her size. She still managed to look good though.

The food was superb, prepared by their hostess who did everything – carried in the dishes and, when the guests had eaten, whisked away the plates with effortless ease. They all murmured words of praise about the cooking, but Alice brushed their compliments to one side as if she was intent on moving on to more entertaining topics.

At last dinner was over and they all trooped into the sitting room. Olivia thought, I know they have recently moved in, but Alice must have brought that ghastly shiny sofa with her, and didn't it look as if the room was newly decorated? Incongruous in such a setting were some beautiful pieces of antique furniture, and a Morland hung unhappily on the elaborate wallpaper. On a narrow shelf, the height of a picture rail, were plates, side by side, each with a coat of arms in the centre.

"Yours, Nigel?" Bill asked.

"No, Alice is the collector. She loves auction sales, and she has an eye for antiques. I expect that's why she married me."

Alice retired to the kitchen, and they heard the clatter of coffee cups. Now she was gone, they became quiet, and the room seem to echo with the sound of her voice. Olivia gave her father a fleeting smile, and Bill sat on the edge of his chair, head bent, gazing at the carpet beneath his feet. Edward Preston puffed at a cigar, and his wife looked as if she could fall asleep.

Suddenly there was a little scream from the kitchen, and "Oh, my God!"

Bill jumped up, and went to help Alice. They could hear the murmur of their voices.

Nigel gave a small sigh and said, "I expect she has dropped the tray."

Presently Bill reappeared with the laden tray that he placed on a low table. "No damage done!" he said quite cheerily.

Alice was just behind him with a steaming jug of coffee and, as she bent forward to fill the cups, Kenneth saw the curve of her white breasts and the line where the tan took over. Old as he was, he was aware of her attraction. Wearily he turned to Rachel, but they had exhausted all conversation by now, and he was grateful when his daughter crossed the room and took over from him. He relinquished his chair to her, and moved to another chair, apart from the rest of the party, where he could sit and watch them as if from a distance. It was at this moment that he decided that Olivia and Bill could do without the friendship of the Bentons. It was a mixture that would not work, and reluctantly he had to admit to himself that Bill had been right.

While they were drinking their coffee, Alice decided

to focus all her attention on Kenneth. Perhaps she thought that she had neglected him, that he looked isolated, but now it was as if she dismissed everyone else in the room. She threw a cushion on the floor by his chair, and lowered herself down on it so that she was sitting very close to him. She insisted that she was comfortable, with her shoulder touching his knee. He had noticed that she was a tactile woman, a hand laid lightly on the arm and then withdrawn.

"Livvy tells me that you are writing a book," she said.

Why had Olivia mentioned that to her? In the short exchange the two women had at the beginning of the evening when they should have been talking of babies and marriages, somehow the conversation had turned to his book.

"I don't think it would interest you," he said shortly.

"Try me."

"It is about a man called Edward Jenner. He was a country doctor, like me, but he discovered the vaccine against smallpox. He brought about great changes in England where hardly a family was not affected by the disease. He has always been a hero of mine."

Kenneth was aware, as he spoke, that Edward Preston was eyeing him with an expression almost akin to interest. He wished Alice had not mentioned the wretched book, and he had not been seduced into talking about it. His leg stiffened against Alice's compliant body. Although there was no fire in the grate, the room was unbearably stuffy, and made him feel faint for a moment. It was as if the hideous wallpaper was closing in on him. The upturned face of Alice was so close he could have put out his hand and covered her mouth with his palm.

Of course she knew about Dr Jenner. Triumphantly she said, "He was the man who found out that cuckoos lay their eggs in other birds' nests!"

He was amazed. It was as if she had done her research before he came. He was pleased to see that Edward Preston had turned his attention to Bill. Talk of cuckoos held no interest for him.

Kenneth relaxed, and flattered by her interest talked more about the book. Then they were silent, and she sat very still, leaning against his knee. He began to feel at ease with her there, as if it was the right place for her to be, like Claire snuggling up to her grandfather.

He saw that her eyes were fixed on her husband. No one was listening to them now; it was as if they were alone in the room. She said quite simply, "I love him so much."

"I'm glad."

"It is such a happy marriage."

"Good."

She laughed, and said, "You wouldn't think he raped me every night, would you?"

No, he would not. Kenneth's eyes swivelled round to the inscrutable countenance of the bald middle-aged husband. For some reason, when she made that crude senseless remark, he almost hated him. Perhaps he disliked him for characteristics he had not discerned before. He wondered whether Olivia found Nigel attractive, but she would not have noticed him in that way. Bill was her choice and an uncertain joy he had turned out to be.

Alice sensed Kenneth's discomfort, and immediately changed the subject. She talked about his grandchildren, so that he was on safe and familiar ground. "The twins go to proper school in the autumn," he said, "and they are very excited about it." He described the personality of Claire, her whims and sudden changes of mood. "All little girls are little women," he said. As he spoke he visualised her lying in her bed, thumb in mouth. The baby-sitter would be downstairs watching the television. It seemed very remote from this strange room and this strange woman.

"I understand why you were so reluctant to come this evening," said Alice. "You would so much rather be with them." She paused. "I love children," she went on, "it is a great sadness to me that I have none of my own."

It was time to leave; Kenneth pressed Rachel's hand, and thought that her face reflected relief that she had got through the evening on mineral water, thoughtfully provided by Alice. Her husband boomed out his thanks. Alice kissed all her guests, and when it came to Kenneth's turn, she wound her soft arms around his neck and, with her cheek against his, he suddenly felt overwhelmingly tired and old. What an evening! Worse than he had expected.

At last they were in the car and heading for home. Olivia, almost asleep, managed to throw out a remark about the unsuitability of Alice's dress. "As if she was going to a ball!" Then she felt sorry for what she considered an unkind comment, and countered it by saying, "She went to so much trouble, and the dinner was delicious." She imagined at that moment Alice would be stacking dishes into the dishwasher, and donning rubber gloves to wash the pots and pans. No doubt Nigel would be helping her by putting things away – the table mats into a drawer and emptying the salt cellars. She remembered how domesticated he had been at the house in Queen's Gate.

Olivia had to admit to herself that, as usual, Bill had been right about Alice. The years had not improved her, and there was a grossness about her that must have been there before, but she had not noticed it. Again she felt the deep sense of disappointment and, glancing at her husband's profile, she detected a little smile of self-satisfaction on his face. Oh well, she thought, let him feel smug, bless him.

The rest of the journey passed in contemplative silence, except for Olivia's kindly, "All right, Daddy?" and Bill saying, "God! What a woman! How can a chap wake up to that every day of his life?"

Chapter 13

It did not take Mrs Bracegirdle long to clean Kenneth's flat. It was small, uncluttered and he was a tidy man. His typewriter, papers and notes connected with the book he was writing were on a table overlooking the front garden. At his request, she did not touch them.

He would not have admitted it, but he welcomed her twice-weekly visits. Her chatter was a diversion; sometimes he felt lonely despite the family being on the other side of the wall. They sat at the kitchen table with their mugs of coffee and a tin of biscuits, and she recounted what was happening next door. George had been sick; Claire was rude to her mother, that sort of thing, interspersed with the typical comment about how hard Olivia worked. "Looking after the house and the children, and looking after other people as well, I don't know how she does it."

Kenneth said, "When the twins go to school she will have more time to herself." Privately, he thought Olivia ought to be able to cope; many women in her position had no help in the house at all. Except for a brief period before the war Joan had managed on her own.

"She needs a holiday. Why doesn't Mr Randall take her away for a few days?" Kenneth realised that this remark could be interpreted as meaning 'Mr Randall is a selfish brute who does not consider his wife'.

"It's difficult to organise," he said a little coldly, wishing to convey to Mrs Bracegirdle that she was coming close to overstepping the bounds of loyalty to her employer. Olivia and Bill did take a family holiday once a year to a seaside house in Scotland. It was not exactly a rest for Olivia, just switching her day-to-day activities to another venue, with the additional burden of having to clean the place from top to bottom before they left.

Bill was not a beach man, and he spent most of the holiday at the local golf course playing with an acquaintance he had made there, while his wife spent each day on the sands with the children, and then humping all the gear back to the house. Olivia was often more exhausted at the end of the holiday than she had been at the beginning.

"She looks really tired sometimes," was the opinion of her cleaning lady.

She was right. Olivia became easily harassed, and she was too easy-going with the children who played her up. There were times when Kenneth thought she had no spirit left to discipline them. He blamed Bill for the fine lines he noticed appearing on her girlish face. It was a very English face with a pale flawless skin, apt to burn in the sun. She had lost weight since the birth of the twins, and Kenneth though she was too thin, but she moved gracefully, as her mother had done.

Kenneth acknowledged that Olivia had always lacked self-confidence, and he felt since her marriage her self-esteem had lessened. Bill had a stock of phrases he used in downgrading his wife. He would interrupt her by saying, "Do you mind if I tell this, as I don't think you have got it right?" When she did speak up for herself, he would stop her and say, "Sorry, but I didn't understand a word of that." Olivia allowed these little barbs to pass unnoticed, as if they were her due, but Kenneth did not like anyone to be critical of her. His love for her was unconditional, and he did not think Bill capable of such love.

He had to be careful, knowing that revealing his true feelings could do untold damage. In a sense, he was a guest in his own house, and must stick to the rules. He counted his blessings: a home, and a garden which was his kingdom, and a son-in-law who was not there a great deal of the time, when he had Olivia and the children to himself.

Olivia had not thought of Alice again until Mary Chalmers mentioned her name. Mary and her husband,

Alan, were staunch members of the Conservative party, and Mary served on the council and attended political meetings. She told Olivia, "A rumour is floating around that our Member of Parliament, Edward Preston, is having an affair with your friend, Alice Benton. Do you think there is any truth in it?"

"No, I do not," said Olivia firmly. "We met the Prestons at Alice's house, and there was no suspicion of anything going on between them. Besides, Nigel and Alice are very happy together." After she had spoken, she remembered the anguished face of Rachel Preston, and she decided not to mention Mary's comments to Bill.

However, she did express a view that the Bentons should be invited back. She mentioned it one evening when she, Bill and her father were sitting on the terrace at Carpenters, watching the sun sink behind the trees and the bats circling in a darkening sky. Kenneth had been asked to join them for a drink, and Bill was lying on a long deck chair, feet up, hands behind his head. "But why?" he said.

"Why indeed?" asked Kenneth.

"If we do not ask them back," said Olivia, "it looks as if we do not like them."

"Well, as you know, I do not," replied Bill. "I never have, and never will like either of them. Oh, I grant you, Nigel is harmless enough, but he lowered himself, in my view, by marrying Alice. Ten years have done nothing for her, and I do not care for ageing dyed blondes who try to impress by shock treatment."

"That seems clear enough," said Kenneth. He was glad that Bill had taken this view. If the Bentons were asked to Carpenters then the Randalls would be asked back, and so it would go on. Better to cut off the acquaintanceship before it was renewed.

Olivia laughed happily. She loved Bill in this sort of truculent mood. With no criticism levelled at her she felt secure. It was a moment to cherish, the perfect evening, her children sleeping sweetly in the house, and the two men she loved most by her side. "All right, darling," she said, "let's forget about them."

He scowled, and went on rumbling like the last echoes of a thunderstorm. "I wish I could believe you will forget about them. I don't want to hear their bloody names mentioned again."

"All right, all right."

"I see no reason why we should stick to these absurd social conventions."

"I've promised, haven't I?"

A week later Alice telephoned Kenneth. "May I come and see you?" She sounded reproachful, as if she had overheard their conversation about her.

The unexpectedness of her call put him at a disadvantage, and no excuse came to mind. He found himself saying, "When would you like to come?"

She had decided that before she telephoned. "I have to do some shopping, but I'll be with you after that, about noon." She was such a well-organised person, he knew instinctively she would arrive at the time she said she would. When he put the telephone down he cursed himself for being such a fool. He hoped Bill would never find out about it.

At twelve o'clock her little car turned into the drive. There had been weeks of sunshine since their last meeting and Kenneth noticed, when he went outside to greet her, that she looked even more tanned. She was dressed in a pale blue trouser suit, the top buttons of the jacket, he observed, undone as if by accident. She looked young, but not too young. Brown skins gather wrinkles, and the lines showed around her blue eyes when she smiled.

He poured her a glass of cold white wine, and one for himself, and they sat on two very comfortable wicker chairs under a Catalpa tree. The tree cast gentle shadows with the sun filtering through the large leaves. The sky was an unblemished blue dome, so unusual for England.

"I'm lucky to have this tree in my bit," Kenneth said. It made no difference, the whole garden was his responsibility, but this favourite tree was in front of his window so he regarded it as his own.

She asked him about the garden. "Do you do it all yourself?"

"No, I have help from a chap called Brian Bracegirdle. He has a very humble brain but he makes up for it with brawn and good humour. He is a hard worker,"

"You need him in a garden of this size," she said.

He wondered if it was going to be difficult to find things to say to each other. "Well, what have you been up to?" he heard himself asking in an absurdly paternal tone.

"Nothing much. Just sitting by the pool." The reply sounded rather forlorn, and he decided she did not have enough to do. That would account for her visiting him like this, on the spur of the moment. He recalled the meal she had prepared and presented with such skill. A woman like that needed something to occupy her every hour of the day. It was a pity she had no children.

"Livvy is lucky. If only I had children . . ." She seemed to have an almost uncanny aptitude for reading people's thoughts.

"Surely there is lots of time. Is there any real reason . . .?" He thought how he and Joan had given up the idea of having a child, and then Olivia had been conceived and their lives had taken on new meaning.

"It's not me, it's Nigel. He's had all the tests and he can never have children. He had chicken pox when he was young and, as a result, the sperms are no good . . . or something."

"I see." In a very short time she had told him one of the most intimate details of their marriage. "Have you thought of adoption?" he asked

"Thought about it, but Nigel is not keen. He is not as unhappy about the situation as I am. He thinks we have such a marvellous marriage we don't need anything else." She looked sad, and then brightened. "I suppose you wouldn't talk to him? About adoption, I mean."

"I'm afraid I could not do that," replied Kenneth slowly. "I don't know him well enough."

"You are a doctor though."

"No longer. I'm retired. Anyway, adoption is something I know nothing about, but I'm quite sure your own doctor could advise you about it."

She changed the subject. "Are you happy living alone? Do you like your granddad flat?" She had remembered his little joke then. Kenneth told her it was an ideal solution; he could never really feel alone with the family so close.

"I remember Livvy telling me that she was an only child, like me. Although I do have a stepbrother, as you know, but it is not quite the same as a real brother or sister."

"Yes, I've often wished Joan and I could have had another child, but it was not to be."

"Do you miss your wife very much?"

"Yes, I do." The conversation seemed to have turned from her personal life to his, and he took a small cigar from his pocket, in the hope that in the business of lighting it he would avoid any more questions about Joan.

Alice persisted, "Do you miss her because you are lonely without her, or because you loved her so much you can hardly bear life without her?"

It was the limit, and he felt the private areas of his life were being invaded. Nevertheless, he found himself answering a question that had never been put to him before. "We had a very happy marriage," he said, "and I would give anything to have her back with me. I have no faith, so I fear I have lost her for good. Her death was an agony, and I wish I could remember our life together without the ending. The finish spoilt the story for me." It was the truth, and he had never said it to anyone. He wished he had not said it now, and he felt, in some strange way, he had been disloyal to Joan.

"Oh, I know how you feel!" cried Alice, as if suddenly stricken with a common grief. "My father died when I was a little girl, and I remember so well the sadness of his last illness, how he changed every day so that my mother and I could hardly believe it was the same person. I used to pray that I could hold on to the memory of him as he was, and that one image would not take over the other."

"Did you manage it?" asked Kenneth, interested. "How do you think of him now?"

"Mostly how he was just before he died," Alice admitted. "I'm afraid it is like a love affair that ends on a bitter note. All the lovely moments are wiped out by the bad ones at the end."

"I wouldn't know about that!"

A little silence fell between them until she said, "I'm so glad to be here. I was sure you would make an excuse not to see me."

"I'm delighted you came."

"I don't suppose Livvy and Bill will want to see me again. Bill especially is not at all keen, I can tell that. You know why we fell out, don't you?"

"I know a bit about it."

"It's so unfair!" She was impassioned. "I would never

come between a man and his wife, but Nigel was not married to Pat. Bill made it sound so sordid, and it was not that way at all."

"I don't know the details," lied Kenneth who recalled Pat's version of the affair very well.

"She tried to kill herself, and it looked as if it was my fault." She gazed at Kenneth very earnestly. "I would so love to be friends with Livvy again. Do you think that is possible?"

"I think Olivia would like it," said Kenneth thoughtfully. "She needs a friend at present. Her closest friend in the neighbourhood is Mary Chalmers, but Mary, nice as she is, has limitations."

Alice's bright blue eyes opened very wide, staring straight ahead as if fixed on an objective. "We must try and put things right between us. When we were in London we were the dearest of friends. The dearest! Please, dear Kenneth, will you help me to overcome Bill's reservations about me?"

"I'll try," he promised, "but I think you should understand that I do not have any influence with my son-in-law."

They continued to talk quietly about more trivial matters. The hot sun slanted through the branches of the old tree and warmed them. Between them they had managed to finish the bottle of wine. She did not seem to be a bit concerned about drinking and driving. She gave him a sweet wide smile, and he suddenly remembered the strident voice at the dinner party, the schoolgirl humour and the vulgarity. "You are different," he said.

She gave him a quick discerning glance. "I know," she replied. "I am well aware how awful I can be. It's a form of shyness, I suppose."

"Surely not."

"I don't know what makes me behave so stupidly. I know Nigel often feels ashamed of me. I don't know how he puts up with my behaviour." She looked down at her hands folded in her lap. "What must you think of me?"

"You are charming," said Kenneth reassuringly, "not in the least awful, as you describe yourself."

"I want you to like me," she said, looking up. "It is important to me,"

"I can't believe you value the approbation of an old man."

"You understand me," she said, "and you are not as old as all that. I find you attractive, all that lovely white hair and your beautiful hands." She took one of his beautiful hands in her own, and Kenneth decided they had both had enough to drink. The combination of sunshine and wine was beginning to take effect, and he released his hand hastily and told her sharply that he was not in the habit of drinking with fascinating ladies in the early afternoon. She said she was not used to drinking at that hour either, but she was enjoying it.

"Here come the children!" cried Kenneth, relieved.

They came running across the lawn, dressed in shorts

and Aertex shirts and looking delightfully summery. Claire put her plump arms around Kenneth's neck and pressed her sweet-smelling face against his cheek. Her skin exuded a delicious mixture of moisture, sunshine and fresh air. He was overwhelmed with love and pride. "George, Claire, this is Mrs –"

"No! I want to be called Alice, please."

They were enchanted, especially the little girl who loved the polish on Alice's nails and the pale hair, like candyfloss, so fine and brittle. Kenneth thought, '*within the little children's eyes*' . . . they did not consider Alice an ageing dyed blonde. How unreasonable his son-in-law could be at times! Why, she was only a few years older than his wife.

George had brought with him a game called 'Sorry!' which he had lately acquired, and longed to play. Alice consented to sit on the ground under the tree and listen to his laborious instructions. Kenneth marvelled at her patience, and when they eventually started to play the game her laughter rang out, spontaneous and uninhibited, as if she was really enjoying herself. When she won she was transported with childish glee, and Kenneth was glad to see that she did not let George win. When she lost she pretended to be envious of his skill. "You little horror, you've beaten me again!"

Claire was left out, and began to be cross. "Why can't I play too?"

"Because it is a game for two people," said Alice. "But never mind, darling, I'll bring you a game we can all play.

Even grandpa. It is called the Peter Rabbit Race Game, and I used to play it when I was a little girl."

When they had played the last game of 'Sorry!' and George had won, Alice got up to leave. She sprang to her feet, like a young girl, the blue trousers tight across her flat stomach, the short jacket nipped in beneath her breasts. Kenneth could not imagine her wearing anything that did not emphasise those perfectly formed firm breasts. The four of them walked to her car, Claire clinging to Alice's hand, pleading, "You will come again, won't you?" Kenneth was astonished. The twins did not usually respond to strangers. It was as if Alice had worked some spell on them.

"I'd love to do that." She looked at Kenneth. "May I?"

"Of course," he replied rather stiffly. "Thank you for coming today."

She drove off much too quickly, waving her hand through the open window on the driver's side. The car disappeared from view in a little cloud of dust. It was a ramshackle affair, not the sort of car Kenneth would have expected her to have. But, by now, he thought everything about her was unexpected. After she had gone, it seemed very still, just the buzzings and distant cooings of the sunlit garden. With a twin dragging on each arm, he walked back to the house.

"She is a very lovely lady," said Claire.

Chapter 14

Kenneth wondered whether he would see Alice again. He thought it unlikely, and as the weeks passed did not think of her. He was relieved when she did not telephone him again. If she had, this time he would have been ready with an excuse. No one in the family was aware of her visit, and that too was reason for relief.

There came a break in the seemingly endless summer and, when the welcome rain stopped, a cool drying wind took its place. Early one afternoon Kenneth decided to have a bonfire, and he was stoking it with his garden fork when he noticed Alice's little car parked in the drive of the big house. He had not heard it arrive. Perhaps I am getting deaf, he thought. Backwards and forwards he went, trundling the garden rubbish in a wheelbarrow, and on each trip he glanced in the direction of Alice's car and noticed it was still there.

Then he went into his kitchen and exchanged his boots for shoes, and put on the kettle for a cup of tea. After he had finished drinking it, he went to his desk in the window where he had a good view of the drive; he attempted to work but found he was looking up, from time to time, to see if her car was still there. At exactly six o'clock he pottered back into the kitchen and poured himself a whisky. When he returned with it to his seat in the window, he saw the car had gone. She must have timed it so that she left before Bill came home.

Kenneth admitted to himself that the little stab of disappointment he felt was absurd and illogical; there was no reason for Alice to call on him –, she had done that already. He considered the fact that when one lives alone everything is magnified in importance. The ringing of the doorbell or the telephone has a special significance, for it is a summons from the outside world – someone out there is holding out a hand to pull one back into the circle. The invitation may not be welcome, but it cannot be ignored. The isolation of old age contributed to these feelings of insecurity. Olivia did not understand, and had a habit of saying, "I'll come and see you tomorrow, Daddy."

"What time will that be?" he wanted to know, as if he had to fit an appointment into a busy schedule.

"Well . . . I'll try and make it by ten o'clock."

When ten o'clock came he was eagerly awaiting her arrival, by half past ten he was beginning to feel restless and by eleven o'clock he was unreasonably anxious. It was likely she had forgotten her promise, and it was certain she had no idea how fussed he became when she did not appear. Kenneth valued his solitude, but the forces outside still had power to draw him. On that late summer evening, sitting at the table with a glass of whisky in his hand, watching the place where Alice's car had stood, he felt curiously deflated.

On the following morning Kenneth called in to see his daughter. She was cooking, and he perched on the edge of the big pine table and watched her. Olivia was a good cook. She had observed Hilda during the last months she stayed in London with Pat, and she learnt from her. She had acquired knowledge of basic cookery from her mother, but Hilda's skill was unique.

She began to talk about Alice straight away without prompting from her father. "Her visit was a complete surprise," she told him. "I think we may have misjudged her. Yesterday she was so nice, just like the old days."

She was stirring a stew in a big pot on the top of the stove. "And the children adored her," she continued. "She brought a present for them, a game, and they were thrilled."

She opened the oven door and carefully lifted the pot, her hands encased in thick gloves, talking all the time. "I must say I was glad Bill was not here when she called. She stayed so long I was afraid he would turn up any moment."

"Surely you can choose your own friends as long as you do not inflict them on him if he does not like them?"

"Of course, but you know what he's like, bless him – he would have made some disparaging remark." She shut the oven door with a bang. "I shall have to tell Bill that I am seeing Alice next Thursday – we are going to an auction sale together. It should be fun." She sounded quite cheerful for a change.

That evening Alice telephoned Kenneth, and that call started an evening ritual that was to continue, with a few breaks, for many months to come. Thereafter, at a quarter past seven Alice telephoned. He never had to wait for it to happen, for at that precise time the telephone rang. The miraculous regularity of the event meant that it was possible for him to be there, telephone at his elbow, drink by his side, waiting for her call.

That first evening set the pattern for the future: light easy conversation. "How are you? I'm sorry I did not come to see you, but there was no time. I had to get home to cook Nigel's dinner or he would have been hungry, poor darling. I had a lovely time with Livvy and saw your heavenly twins. What a lucky old thing you are to have them!"

On the evening before she and Olivia were going out together she telephoned to say she would come and see him after they returned. "That will be at five o'clock," she said. Even after such a short acquaintance he knew she was completely reliable when it came to time. At five o'clock on the following day they would be together. When he turned off his bedside light that night, the thought comforted him.

He was right: she and Olivia walked over to his flat from the big house as his old clock in the hall was striking five. Kenneth had a glimpse of his daughter's face before she hurried off to relieve Mary Chalmers who was looking after the twins. He thought she looked almost happy.

Alice marched into his kitchen, filled the kettle and reached into a high cupboard for the tea caddy. "How did you know it was there?" he asked.

"Because I am a witch," she answered lightly. "Didn't you guess?" She went on, "I suppose we must have tea, as it would not be proper to have a drink at this hour, and I don't want to do anything improper."

They sat facing each other at the kitchen table, drinking their cups of tea, and Kenneth fetched the biscuit tin which was usually only produced for Mrs Bracegirdle's benefit.

"It's bloody cold in here," Alice complained. "You're a bit mean with heating, aren't you?"

Flustered, Kenneth started mumbling apologies, "The heating is not on, and I don't light the sitting-room fire in the summer."

"Summer is over now."

"Would you like me to . . .?"

"No, let's wait a while." She smiled at him. "Don't take any notice of me. I feel I can say anything to you."

She went on to tell him about her afternoon with Olivia. It appeared that Alice attended nearly all the local auctions, and sometimes picked up a bargain, which she would sell for a small profit. "My money," she said, "so I can spend it as I like." It gave her an interest, and she thought it would give Olivia an interest too. "I shall drag her along with me, and it may cheer her up."

He commented, "She looked as if she had enjoyed herself."

"She did, didn't she?" replied Alice eagerly. "Do you think we noticed that particularly because she is not happy at other times?"

"I don't know."

"And why is she not completely happy, I wonder?"

"I suppose she does not lead a very exhilarating life." It was a feeble explanation, as he well knew, but he could not think of another reason to offer.

Alice was thoughtful. "I don't agree with you," she said quietly, "life cannot be dull with George and Claire around – it must be full of surprises and challenges. No, I think she has something else on her mind."

"Have you any idea what that might be?" asked Kenneth, suddenly on his guard.

"Yes, I have," she answered frankly. "A creature by the name of Emily Frobisher."

Kenneth stared at her in disbelief, and she met his gaze steadily. "Olivia told you?" he said.

"Yes, she told me."

"When?"

"Today, in the car, on the way home. People tell me things, it's a special knack I have. I don't nose around for secrets – they just come my way. I suppose I must be a good listener."

"It's incredible," said Kenneth. "Olivia is usually so reserved. Are you sure you didn't hear it from another source?"

Alice looked stricken. "Do you think I am lying?" She almost shouted the words. "What would be the point?"

"No," said Kenneth humbly, "what would be the point? Anyway, I'm sure only the people involved know about it."

Alice put her teacup down on the saucer. "Let's go into the other room. It is freezing in here, and depressing."

He could hear the resentment in her voice; with a few words he had managed to cast her down completely.

He managed to get the fire going fairly quickly; he felt there was an urgency to restore her spirits and vitality. She huddled in an armchair, with her legs curled under her, watching him blow the flames with bellows.

As he knelt in front of the fireplace, he wondered how much Alice knew about Emily Frobisher. The subject was wide open now, but there was still time, if he chose, to close the gap. The words were as yet unspoken, and they could remain that way. Somewhere at the back of his mind lingered the echo of the gossip at the dinner table, the first time he met Alice, but instantly the memory was wiped out like a chalk mark on a blackboard.

Kenneth felt the moment had come to pour out drinks for them both, which he did.

"I can only stay a short time," she warned him.

Despite the crackling fire, she had not lost the rather woeful expression, and he found this slightly irritating.

He said sharply, "Please do not make heavy weather of this. I think it best that I tell you the whole story, as Olivia has talked to you about it."

Alice unwound her legs, and sat rather primly on her chair, waiting for him to begin. Kenneth knew that this calm demeanour hid an intense excitement, which communicated itself to him.

"The Frobishers live about three miles from here. They are a very ordinary young couple with two children, a boy and a girl, one slightly older and one slightly younger than the twins. I have no idea where Olivia and Bill met the family, probably about two years ago." He thought for a moment, "Yes, I think it was two years ago when they moved in . . ."

"Moved in?"

"Yes, they moved in. Although a furniture van did not arrive with all their belongings, in all other respects Carpenters became their home. Rather, it became Emily's second home. I don't think Bruce, her husband, was enraptured by the general trend of events. He, poor fellow, seemed incapable of taking a stand about anything – she was the boss in that household, a small feisty little person, in my view not especially attractive.

Whenever I went to see Olivia and Bill the Frobishers were almost certain to be there. Their children played and fought with George and Claire, and the two wives shared the cooking. On some evenings Emily arrived with the food, and Bruce followed behind her with a bag containing the children's nightclothes, so that they could be 'bedded down' while their parents enjoyed each other's company. To start with, there was harmony between the two families, and a real friendship between Olivia and Emily. Later, this constant intermingling began to take on a sinister tone."

"When did you notice that?" Alice's voice was eager, and she hung on to every word Kenneth uttered.

"Well, I remember arriving one evening just as Emily was about to depart. She was alone; perhaps she was on her way home to fetch Bruce and the children, I don't know. It was getting dark as I walked over to the house, but I could see her sitting at the wheel of her car, ready to move off. Bill was standing by the car, and holding her hand through the open window. I could just hear the murmur of their voices and, when they saw me, they unclasped their hands and stopped talking. It was a trivial incident, but I sensed a feeling of embarrassment that made me suspicious. I started visiting the house more frequently – I suppose you could say in order to spy on them."

"They asked for it," said Alice.

"I watched Bill and Emily when they were together, and there was no doubt she was in love with him. I don't think he is capable of real love, but he was flattered by her adoration that soon became apparent for all to see, including Bruce who seemed at a loss to know how to deal with the situation. I came to the conclusion he thought it safer to do nothing.

I was certain Bill was seeing Emily in secret, and there were opportunities for this. Bill was working all day in Melbury and Bruce commuted to London, so when Bill drove his car out of the drive and Bruce stepped on the train, there were many hours during the day when they could have been together."

"And Livvy, didn't she notice?" asked Alice.

"Not at first. She enjoyed the friendship, although she did seem to be the working horse for all of them. It annoyed me the number of times she was left to look after those wild Frobisher children, more often than Emily looked after George and Claire. It was unfair all round."

"And you could see that Livvy was going to be the loser?"

"That's right." Kenneth got up and gave one of the logs in the fire a push with his foot, sending up a little shower of sparks. "I observed the starry-eyed wonder of Emily Frobisher gradually change, over the months, into a sort of neurotic despair. I imagine she realised Bill was not prepared to relinquish his home and family and, I may add, his financial assets, just like that. At the same time, I noticed a weariness of mind and spirit in my daughter that has, I'm sorry to say, never left her. As for Bill, he just became more irrational and irritable, and I think part of Olivia's unhappiness was that she could never please him."

"I expect their sex life was pretty non-existent by that time too," said Alice, as if she was an expert on such matters.

"That may be true, although it is something I could never discuss with Olivia. We are close, but not that close. Sometimes I find it hard to communicate."

"You seem to be doing very well at present," she said. She got up, and sat in her favourite position, on a cushion on the floor in front of his armchair. She took Kenneth's hand and stroked his fingers while he was talking.

"I thought one of these people was going to break first, and I could not decide which one it was going to be. I did not want it to be Olivia, for that would be undignified and degrading for us all. I could imagine Bill denying any charge put to him by painting his wife as a jealous unbalanced woman, prey to unfounded suspicions. Emily began to show more and more signs of emotional strain and Bill, seeing the danger signals, tried to calm her down, but it was no use. She began to pick quarrels with Olivia over unimportant issues, and spat out remarks in her direction, like, 'How can Bill put up with you?' and 'I feel sorry for him, you make his life a misery.'"

"What was Livvy's reaction?"

"She knew the reason, of course, but she did not want to acknowledge it. She turned to me for reassurance, and I gave it to her. I told her that Emily, by filling her mind with doubts about her marriage, was using the strongest weapon she had to hurt her."

"I expect by the time you said all that, you almost believed it yourself," said Alice. She still held Kenneth's hand lightly clasped in her own, fingers interlocking.

Kenneth loved the closeness of her. Since Joan's death he had missed the touch of a woman's hand in his. He felt it right that it should be Alice's hand he held. He knew he had all her attention.

"No, I did not believe it," he told her, "and I'm sure she did not either, but she pretended she did, and it gave me a breathing space to do something about the sorry situation. I told Olivia to behave as if everything was normal, and that evening I heard the Frobisher gang arriving as usual, and Emily and Bruce departing well after midnight, each carrying a sleeping child to the car."

Kenneth bent to refill Alice's glass and then his own.

"The following day I hired a car from the local garage. I had the use of it for one day. I drove it into Melbury, and parked it outside Bill's office. It seemed a long wait before he emerged through the swing door at about noon. By that time I had read every item in the newspaper, completed two crosswords and decided many times I was acting foolishly. Then I saw Bill come out and head for the car park adjacent to his office. Very soon his car nosed out into the main road, and he set off with me fairly close behind him."

"How thrilling!" cried Alice. "You, of all people, playing detective. It is so out of character."

"Some things are necessary. I followed him for some distance until he turned into the drive of a country hotel. At this stage I was convinced I was on a wild-goose chase and that Bill was probably going to meet a business colleague for lunch. I parked my hired car near to his car, and he did not glance in my direction. I walked some distance behind him, collar up, hat over my eyes. As I came in the door, he was standing at the reception desk and I heard him confirm a room reservation for the afternoon."

"I did not know you could do such a thing," said Alice.

"Bill bounded up the stairs, and I sat in the foyer, waiting for Emily. This time I did not have to wait long. She is not a pretty woman, but on that day she looked radiant. Happy and expectant, going to meet her lover."

"I envy her," cried Alice.

"Yes," replied Kenneth, "I must say I envied them both at that moment. I ordered a drink and a plate of sandwiches, and I sat down to wait for them to reappear. I was alone except for the desk clerk, and he gave me a few odd looks. I think he suspected I was a bona fide private investigator. I toyed with the idea of asking for their room number, and going up and hammering on their door, but my courage failed me.

I sat there for four and a half hours before I observed them coming down the stairs together. They both had expressions of studied composure that rapidly changed to acute discomfiture when they saw me. The hotel lounge was next to where I had been sitting, and I indicated that we should go in there. We sat at a little table where there were three chairs – heads down, like criminals. My hands and feet were like ice, and my head was swimming. Bill began to protest that it was not as I imagined, but Emily broke down and sobbed. I was glad the place was deserted.

"How like Bill to try and wriggle out of it," said Alice.

"He floundered with words, and it soon became apparent to me, and to her, that he had no intention of doing anything drastic. I was relieved that he took this line; if he had sworn unswerving loyalty to Emily it would have put me in a dilemma. As it was, I realised that I had these two people under my control, and it was a new experience for me. Never, in all my years as a doctor, had I possessed such power, and it was gratifying to realise that I could dictate to them what they must do next. Emily was to play a passive role, and Bill was to go and see Bruce and tell him that the two families must stop seeing each other, as he felt a dangerous situation might develop between him and Emily. I was certain Bruce would accept this explanation without asking awkward questions; it was not in his best interests to dig for the truth. Bill had to tell Olivia the same story, and try to convince her that he had withdrawn from a liaison before any damage was done. I think he did his part, and the main thing is that it achieved a complete break from the Frobishers, and we have not seen them since, thank God."

"When did all this happen?"

"Fairly recently. Just before we met you."

Alice looked at the clock, and told Kenneth it was time for her to leave. She got to her feet, and went through the usual smoothing and tucking-in routine. "Olivia is not quite satisfied that it is over," she said, "but in time she will be. She needs help to put the whole thing out of her mind. It was only an incident, after all, a silly vain man fancying another woman. It happens all the time, and it meant nothing to him, that is obvious. Bill could have put things right with Livvy, but his pride would not let him say that he was sorry and ask for her forgiveness. If he had shown any sensitivity, he could have saved her from so much unhappiness."

Alice left then, and he wondered if she would telephone that evening, and was glad when she did.

"I'm home!" Her voice sounded bright and cheerful. "There is nothing left to say is there? Except that Livvy has a bastard for a husband and a fantastic father! I love you. Goodnight."

Chapter 15

Kenneth was pleased when Olivia and Alice renewed their friendship. The companionship between his wife and their daughter sadly came to an end with Joan's death. He knew that Olivia missed her mother dreadfully. When she moved from Annesley and went to London she left friends behind; then there was the move to Carpenters, and it happened again. The Frobishers came into her life and a bond was formed between Olivia and Emily, but that no longer existed. Alice had taken Emily's place, and Kenneth's heart lifted when he saw Alice's little car chugging up the drive to collect Olivia for one of their many excursions. Sometimes Mary Chalmers joined them, as Alice expressed anxiety that she should not be left out. Alice had a talent for gathering people around her. Kenneth breathed a sigh of relief as he observed this happy state of affairs. He felt his daughter was in safe and caring hands.

Although she never failed to telephone him every evening, Kenneth did not see as much of Alice as he would have liked. When his old dog died, she arrived with a ridiculously large bunch of flowers that she arranged in a vase for him. He was touched by the gesture, particularly as he knew she did not like dogs.

He was pathetically pleased when she was next door and came over to his side, often with a child clinging to each arm. George and Claire were devoted to her, and it was a joy to see the three of them together. They were good with her, charming and well behaved. She gave them presents, too many presents in Kenneth's view.

"Every day is Christmas Day with you," he grumbled.

"It is good to be happy," she said. "Why must we always justify everything we do? We are all happier people now. Don't you think Olivia is a different person?"

Yes, he did, and they often spoke of her during their evening telephone conversations and agreed she looked less strained and anxious.

Bill had grudgingly resigned himself to the fact that Alice and Nigel had become part of their lives. When Olivia told him that she was seeing Alice again, he was surprisingly nice about it. Perhaps, like Kenneth, he thought something had to be done to pull his wife out of depression.

"She's always there," said Mrs Bracegirdle to Kenneth during one of their coffee breaks, "but she keeps Mrs Randall amused, I'll say that for her." For some reason, hard to understand, she did not like Alice.

The Bentons had a dinner party and asked Olivia, Bill, Edward and Rachel Preston and Mary Chalmers and her husband, Alan. Mary, completely under Alice's spell, regretted she had ever listened to rumours about her and Edward Preston that were patently untrue. Alan Chalmers was an odd character, very rich and with no occupation other than overseeing his estate and keeping an eye on his wife. He was a fish out of water at that gathering, and very soon resigned himself to taking no part, and was content to watch his wife making futile efforts to join in.

As usual the food was perfect, and Alice in sparkling form. Nigel was the courteous more reserved host. Olivia felt differently towards Alice, now firmly reinstated as her friend, and forgave her for her silly chatter. She reverted to her old way of thinking, that it was foolish talk, but harmless. She was almost amused listening to Alice getting dangerously near the knuckle, at the same time aware of Alan Chalmers' closed-up face on her right. Bill enjoyed it, and his loud laugh testified to this. Olivia loved to hear his laugh.

Rachel sipped the mineral water that had been put into a small carafe in front of her, but shortly after dinner, when the women were on their own in the sitting room, Alice persuaded her to have a glass of red wine. "Go on, one glass won't hurt you."

But one glass was not enough for Rachel, and she had another, and another and then commandeered the bottle so that she could replenish the glass herself. Sadly, the other guests watched Edward support his wife to the car. It was a strange evening, thought Olivia, and perhaps just as well her father had not been invited.

A tremendous change had taken place in Olivia's life, and her friendship with Alice had given it a new dimension. At last she was able to talk openly to another woman about her problems, and it was a relief to talk to someone about Bill, especially Alice who understood so well, and had never really liked Bill. Olivia found herself defending her husband. "He doesn't mean to be unkind, he is just thoughtless."

"He is two-timing you," replied Alice, "and I cannot bear to stand by and watch it happen." She was driving Olivia to Mary's house, and the three women were going to the cinema together.

It was not the answer Olivia was expecting, and it frightened her. "What do you mean?" she whispered.

"He is still seeing Emily Frobisher."

"Are you sure?"

"I'm quite sure. They meet about twice a week. He has tried to forget her, but he can't. She is the love of his life."

"Who told you this?"

"As a matter of fact, Bill did. I have this knack of getting people to talk to me because I'm a good listener. You may have noticed that Bill is not as against me as he used to be – he tells me things."

"Oh God," cried Olivia in anguish, "I thought it was all over."

"Say nothing," advised Alice. "Don't mention it to anyone, not even your father. It will burn itself out."

Alice came to see Kenneth one late afternoon. It had been raining, and he had not been able to work in the garden that day. She stepped into his flat, shaking the water out of her hair.

"You're soaked!"

"Your family take up so much of my life," she told him, "I thought it was about time I came to seduce Grandpa."

He was delighted to see her, and she came like a draught of pure fresh air into his rather drab existence. She looked radiant, vibrant, and energy seemed to emanate from her. Sometimes he teased her by saying she had days when to touch her might produce an electric shock. This was one of those days. She liked to boast she had explosive qualities, and that one day she would disappear as a result of her own internal combustion. The twins heard her make this absurd statement, and George asked her what she meant.

"When I die," she explained to him, "I will leave a puff of smoke behind me, or perhaps just a puddle seeping into the ground."

George was interested, "Like the Wicked Witch of the West?" he asked.

"Yes, like her, but I am a good witch."

Now, she kissed Kenneth on the cheek, and he

shuffled off to get drinks for them both. He usually waited for six o'clock to strike before having a drink, but he waived the rules because she was with him. He felt excited that on the spur of the moment she had decided to call on him.

They sat and talked, mostly about Mary Chalmers and her terrible husband. It was a relief to get off the subject of Olivia and Bill, and discuss someone else's marriage.

Alice said, "Mary must have a miserable time with him. When I look around at all these disasters, I can't help thinking how lucky I am to have my marvellous Nigel."

She got up and stood with her back to the fire. He had drawn the curtains as darkness came early on such a grey day. "When I said I had come to seduce Grandpa," she said, "I was not joking."

His mouth went dry and his heart thudded in his chest. "My dear," he said at last, "it is very flattering, but I'm afraid I am too old for that sort of thing."

"You are always harping on about your age," she answered impatiently. "I wish you wouldn't. I love you. You know I love you."

"You love Nigel. You have just said so."

"Of course I do, but I love you as well. I want to be with you. Is that so wrong?"

She came close to him and started to undo his tie. He was old-fashioned enough to wear a tie even in his own home. She was very deft, as if she had done this many times before. She unbuttoned his shirt. Then she started to remove her own clothes; one by one she peeled them off until she was standing in a flimsy pants and a lacy bra.

With the blood surging in his ears, Kenneth's hand went out to unfasten the bra. "I can't," he moaned, "I shall disappoint you."

She took his hand and led him quietly to the bedroom. They lay on the bed with their arms around each other. The light was on, a very bright lamp on the bedside table because Kenneth's sight was failing and he liked to read in bed. He was completely baffled; it was a situation he had never envisaged even in his wildest imaginings. Presently she got up, and he saw her standing by the bed. She looked so beautiful he longed for her to stay there so that he could just look at her. But she tiptoed out of the room, and he heard her turning the key of the front door. How sensible she was, even at such a moment!

When she returned she had a glass in her hand, and she handed it to him.

"What is it?" he asked.

"Brandy."

"An aphrodisiac?" His sense of the ridiculous nearly brought him back to reality and the absurdity of his position. But then he found himself swallowing the stuff, to please her. The fiery liquid coursed through his body. He clasped her to him, and she was so soft, so pliant, he felt the old feeling of desire return to him.

"Turn off the light," he demanded. He did not want that damned light.

She obeyed at once, leaning over him to switch of the lamp on his side, her breasts brushing against him. Then she rained kisses on him, her hands exploring his body while she whispered words of love and obscenity in his ear. He was lost.

Later from home she telephoned as usual, "You were wonderful," she said.

He was horrified. Supposing Nigel was listening to what they said?

"Don't worry," she said. "Everything will be all right."

Kenneth got into bed that night and lay between sheets that still smelled of Alice. His usual routine of reading for an hour before going to sleep was disrupted. He felt nothing would ever be the same again. He lay on his back, wakeful, staring into the darkness, thinking of Joan.

Alice did not visit Kenneth for several days and he was glad she did not come. An experience that might have made him feel youthful had the opposite effect; old age dragged his feet and depressed his spirits. He no longer looked forward to the nightly telephone call; the old eager expectation was gone. His words, when he spoke them, sounded stilted and unnatural to his ears and, she, no doubt sensing his unease, uttered a few pleasantries and then cut off abruptly.

When she did arrive, one afternoon a few weeks later, he had a moment of panic, but it was dispelled at once when she said that she had come for one reason only, to impart important news. She looked distraught, rushed into the sitting room and flopped into an armchair. He hovered around her, offering refreshment that she refused.

She told him that on the previous morning her car had broken down in Melbury High Street. She had abandoned it and walked to the nearest garage. They agreed to get it going, and then take it to their workshop where they would try and pinpoint the trouble. All this would take an hour or two, so Alice decided she would get lunch in a nearby pub and return to the garage in the afternoon.

She went to a place called the Queen's Head because she had heard Bill talk about it in favourable terms. She found herself a seat in a dark corner of the saloon bar. She ordered a glass of dry white wine and a plate of sandwiches. She had nothing to read, so she passed the time by looking at the people sitting at adjacent tables or coming in and out. That is why she saw Bill and Emily at once when they entered. She lowered her head in case they should see her, but they sat at a table on the other side of the room. They were deep in conversation, and she noticed their hands were often under the table as if they were touching.

"In love," said Alice dolefully, "so obviously in love."

Kenneth wished she would not fantasise about love all the time. She was always saying that she and Nigel were 'madly in love' or that Bill and Olivia were 'no longer in love'. She sounds like a cheap romantic novel, he thought irritably.

But it was bad news she had brought, and Alice was devastated. "How wrong we were when we thought it was all over," she said.

Kenneth admitted, "I'm surprised to hear they are still meeting."

"Can't you see what this means?" she cried. She was pulsating with excitement.

To calm her, Kenneth said, "Things may change when they go to Scotland."

"What do you mean?"

"They go to Macrihanish every year for a holiday, taking the twins with them of course. I wonder you haven't heard about it from Olivia."

"She may have mentioned it to me sometime and I didn't take it in. Won't it be very cold?"

"Probably not. Scotland can be lovely at this time of the year. They take a rented house near the beach, and Bill plays golf with a retired solicitor from Campbeltown."

"How long do they stay there?"

"Two weeks."

"I see," said Alice thoughtfully. "What a wonderful holiday it sounds!"

"I don't think it would be to your liking," answered Kenneth dryly. "I imagine you would prefer a beach in the south of France. But Olivia and Bill seem to enjoy it, and I have great hopes that it will resolve their difficulties. They need to get away together, and Emily Frobisher will not be able to do any damage from that distance."

When she left she leaned forward and kissed him on the lips, very quickly, a chaste kiss.

Later, she telephoned to say she would be seeing Olivia on the following day.

"Don't mention —" he began.

She cut him short. "Of course not. What do you take me for? I wish I could come and see you too, but Nigel wants me home early."

Instead, it was Olivia who called to see her father. "Alice came today," she told him, "and she is very keen to come to Scotland with us. There is plenty of room in the house for another couple, and of course it would be absolutely wonderful for me to have Alice there. She is so good with the children, and they would love it. What fun we could all have together!"

But it was not to be, for the usually accommodating Nigel put his foot down on this occasion. Scotland held no charms for him, and he did not play golf.

"Of course I am disappointed," said Alice on the telephone to Kenneth, "but you know me, I never argue with Nigel. If he doesn't want to go, that's good enough for me. He has promised to take me abroad later on."

Chapter 16

The long drive to Macrihanish was the same as other years, the children bored and restless in the back, and Olivia trying to keep them quiet so that they would not annoy Bill. Eventually, they slept, and Olivia took over the driving for the last lap, with Bill dozing by her side. It was all she could do to keep awake on the long road winding northwards to the Mull of Kintyre.

The weather was not good during the two weeks, but if there was not much sun there was not much rain either. The twins, wrapped up well, were happy on the sandy beach, playing with friends they had made from other years. And Olivia and Bill were happy too. The wife of the solicitor in Campbeltown was not well, and her husband restricted his golf playing to twice a week. Bill took George on an expedition to the town and they purchased a cricket bat and stumps. He set about teaching his son to play cricket. Olivia sat in a deckchair on the beach, watching them and providing food and drinks when needed. Claire took part in the game. Bill was proud of George's progress. If he had been a duffer he would have soon lost interest, but George was not a duffer and his enthusiasm was boundless. They played until they were exhausted and, tired and hungry, they gathered all their belongings and made their way back to their rented accommodation.

Every year they expected some changes would have been made to the house, but every year it was exactly as it had always been, the same lumpy sofa, the same cooker in the kitchen with one burner that did not work. The double bed in the main bedroom was an annual joke. It creaked with every movement, and they were afraid the children would hear them through the thin walls.

"It's worse than ever," giggled Olivia. They put an eiderdown on the floor when they made love. There was something rather daring and different about this, the close proximity of the sandy floor and the big area in which to manoeuvre – it gave a spice to what had become rather an undistinguished event over the years.

Alice telephoned. "Are you all right?"

"We are having a wonderful time."

"Really?"

Olivia made sure that Bill was out of earshot. "I'm very, very happy."

There was a silence on the other end of the line.

Olivia asked, "How is Daddy? Have you seen him?"

"No, I haven't been able to get over to see him, but I keep in touch by telephoning every evening."

"Thank you so much. You are a marvellous friend."

Alice proved to be a marvellous friend in more ways than one when they got home and found she had filled every one of Olivia's vases with flowers, and stacked the refrigerator with food. Even Bill was impressed. "She has tried," he said.

As for Kenneth, he rejoiced when he saw his healthy looking daughter, restored and contented. There was a bloom about her that he had not seen for years. He had been right, the holiday was a turning point in their relationship. From now on the marriage would sail ahead in untroubled waters, he was sure of it. From his window, he watched Alice arrive in her little car to take Olivia out on one of their jaunts. In the crisp darkening days of autumn he spent more and more time in the garden, preparing it for the fast approaching winter.

Olivia confided in Alice, "Everything is going to be fine now. I am no longer worried about Emily Frobisher. I know that is all in the past."

"Did Bill tell you that?"

"No, of course not."

"It was not in the past before you went to Scotland," Alice said, "so how can you be so trusting? I can't bear the idea of your being hurt again." She told Olivia about seeing Bill and Emily in the Queen's Arms.

"You saw them together?" said Olivia wonderingly. She felt sick as she recognised the name of the pub – it was a place Bill often mentioned. She and Alice were in the kitchen at Carpenters. The wooden table was covered with a jumble of cooking utensils and packets of sugar, raisins and flour. Olivia was in the process of making a cake; Bill was very partial to rich fruitcake.

"I'm so miserable," said Alice, and it was true she had not been her usual carefree self since their return from Scotland three weeks earlier. Her appearance had altered too, and her hair looked brassy and unkempt. Her eyes were buried in black shadows and darted from side to side in a strange wild way. It occurred to Olivia that her friend might be heading for a nervous breakdown.

"I look awful because I am so worried about you," explained Alice. "Your troubles have taken me over and I'm sleeping badly. I'm not used to this sort of drama, and it is making me ill. Nigel and I lead such peaceful ordinary lives."

Olivia felt slightly irritated. "I did not ask you to take an interest," she said coldly. How had it begun – this muddle? Oh, the Frobishers, of course, long before poor Alice had come on the scene, so it was unfair to blame any part of it on her. Alice had just wanted to help, and now she was suffering for it.

Olivia asked, "Surely they saw you in the pub?"

"No, I was sitting in a dark corner, not in their view." She paused with a worried expression on her face. "Perhaps I should not have told you, kept it to myself."

"No," said Olivia, "you did right to tell me."

She was leaning against the side of the kitchen table,

watching with a detached interest the walls closing in on her, with dark areas beyond. "I think I'm going to faint," she murmured.

Alice fetched a chair, and Olivia sat on it and put her head down. The feeling passed. Alice stared at her aghast; she hated illness of any sort. "What is wrong with you?"

"I'm pregnant."

The effect of this statement on Alice was extraordinary; the colour drained from her face and she looked as if she might faint herself. She did not speak, and the silence hung between the two women like an invisible barrier.

"You don't seem very pleased for me," said Olivia at last.

Alice's voice rose. "How can I be pleased for you? With your marriage falling to pieces around you, how can I be pleased that you are having a baby by a man who does not love you? You know, as well as I do, that Emily is —"

"The love of his life," Olivia wearily finished the sentence. "I know, you have told me before."

"No, I am not pleased," said Alice. "Envious, but not pleased."

Then something happened that was so unexpected, so unreal it could only have happened in a true-to-life situation. The front door rang, and when Olivia went to answer it, she saw, standing there, Bruce Frobisher.

"Bruce!" she hoped her greeting sounded genuine. It was some time since she had seen him. He was unsmiling, but he stepped inside when she invited him and followed her into the kitchen. "I'm afraid it's an awful mess," she said.

He glanced in Alice's direction, and said, "I was hoping we would be alone. Shall I come another time?"

Olivia felt she wanted Alice to be there, and she motioned her to stay. "This is my great friend, Alice Benton," she said. "Alice, Bruce Frobisher."

"I have met Mrs Benton," he said.

"Oh?"

"We met about three weeks ago at a drinks party in Pennel Bridge."

"You can say anything you like in front of Alice," said Olivia.

He seemed satisfied. He was offered a chair, but he preferred to stand. What he had to say was that a rumour had reached his ears that she, Olivia, thought that something irregular was going on between his wife and Bill.

Olivia felt her hands begin to tremble and she clasped them behind her back so that he would not see. She tried to look straight into his familiar face. He was a pale man in every respect, light fair skin, slightly freckled, sandy hair and a stooped body. His wife had stopped finding him attractive years ago. He was aware of that fact, but he clung to the remains of his marriage as a drowning man clings to a raft. He had known of her relationship with Bill, that she was besotted with the man, but he had thought it best to turn a blind eye. Now, if it was still going on he felt the time had come to take decisive action.

If Olivia had any doubts about what Alice had told

her about Bill and Emily, they were instantly dispelled. There, standing before her, trying to look defiant and only succeeding in looking foolish, was the living proof of the truth of Alice's assertions.

Olivia thought for a moment, "Shouldn't you have talked to Bill about this, before coming to me?" she managed to say.

He had the decency to look a little shamefaced. Perhaps the domestic scene, the evidence of cooking, made him wonder if he had misjudged the position. For once, Alice had nothing to say. She sat, watching them both carefully, not uttering a word.

"Well, I understood the rumour came from your direction," he said, "and I did not want to embarrass Bill if there is no truth in it."

He had handed her the means of escape from an awkward situation, and she grasped it at once. "Have you asked Emily about this?" Her voice was getting stronger. She unclasped her trembling hands and put them by her sides. He had, and Emily had denied everything.

"Surely that is good enough for you? A marriage is impossible without trust. You asked Emily to tell you the truth, and now you must believe her." Olivia warmed to her theme. "I trust Bill. We love each other very much. On second thoughts, I think you were right not to speak to him about this. It would have upset him dreadfully."

Bruce's expression did not change. His face was wooden. "Then you would think it absurd if I suggested they are planning to go away together?"

"I would," said Olivia firmly.

He looked immeasurably relieved. He had completed an unpleasant task, and the result was encouraging. "I hope you are right," he said.

He got up to go. He nodded at Alice. "Please don't let this go any further, Mrs Benton," he said.

Olivia accompanied him to the front door. Standing under the light in the porch, she watched him walk away. "I'm sorry," had been his last words to her. They had all been such good friends before things got complicated.

"You were amazing!" Alice was full of praise. "So calm and dignified."

"I did not feel calm and dignified," said Olivia.

"What are you going to do now?"

"Well, the first thing I must do is to tell Bill about the baby. I'm not sure how he will take it, but I hope he will be pleased."

"Not when he is planning to go off with another woman," said Alice.

"Do you really think there is any truth in that?" asked Olivia thoughtfully. "Bruce said it was a rumour, and perhaps that is all it is. I saw Emily the other day in the grocer's shop, studying her shopping list. She did not see me, as I hid behind one of the shelves, but I had a good look at her, and she did not look like someone in the middle of a violent love affair. Quite the reverse, in fact."

"How can you talk such nonsense? Of course she has to be careful. They both have to be careful. Please, please do not mention the baby to Bill just yet. I fear for you."

"I am sorry you are so worried about all this," said Olivia, who seemed to have acquired a new strength. "I think you should retire from the fray and leave it for Bill and me to sort out. I know you have tried to help, and I am grateful for your support, but I can see it is taking it out of you."

"That's true," Alice admitted. "I feel terrible, and I know I look it. So much so that my dear old Nigel has noticed, and he has suggested we go away for a while. We are going to Madeira to get some sun. That's one of the reasons I came to see you today, to tell you the tickets are booked, but so much has happened I forgot to mention it. We leave the day after tomorrow."

For a moment Olivia wondered how she could possibly manage without her, but then she had a further thought that perhaps she could manage better without her help.

"I'm delighted for you," she told her, "a holiday is just what you need. I wish I could persuade Bill to go abroad, but he never will."

"What are you going to do with all this bloody stuff?" said Alice looking at the table. "Put it all in the bin?"

"No," said Olivia, washing her hands under the kitchen tap, "I'm going to make a cake with it."

"For Bill, I suppose," said Alice scathingly, "everything is for Bill."

"I love him, you know, Alice. I shall always love him."

"He does not deserve you," was Alice's reply.

Chapter 17

After the Bentons went abroad Olivia hoped that life would settle down to some sort of normality, but this did not happen. It was as if the happiness of the holiday in Scotland had no substance, and she had imagined it. It was the last twitch of life in their marriage. She tried to convince herself that the child conceived during that happy time was a proof of their love, but it was hard to believe when discontent hung over them like a dark cloud.

Only the twins were their usual ebullient selves. Being driven to school every morning was still a novelty for them, and being young they did not notice how ill their mother looked. Bill went to work first, and after he had gone (he had given up having breakfast) she went to the bathroom and was sick. It became a routine, and after it was over she washed her face in cold water and then went downstairs to bustle the children into the car. On the mornings Mrs Bracegirdle was there she wondered if the woman suspected the truth, but nothing was said. On her return from the school trip there was always a cup of tea waiting, which was welcome.

There was no chance to talk to Bill who had sunk into a state of sullen despondency. Something was on his mind, haunting him, and as soon as he came home he escaped to his study, locking the door. Olivia knew that he spent a long time on the telephone, but, being Olivia, she did not lift the receiver downstairs to listen in to what he was saying. The idea that he might be making plans filled her with terror. He hardly spoke to her, although sometimes she caught him looking at her in a speculative way. Although they shared the big double bed, as soon as he got into it he turned his broad back away from her.

In the afternoons Olivia usually took the twins to the local park where there were slides and swings. She felt she had to get away from the house when the utter desolation of her position became almost too much to bear. Carpenters was a family house, and Olivia felt the family was disintegrating before her eyes. She sat on a damp bench in the cold bleak playground, watching the children play and feeling completely alone. There was no one she could talk to, she could not be sure of Mary's discretion and lately her father had become a querulous old man whom she could not burden with her problems. She longed for Alice to return. A brightly coloured postcard had arrived from her, addressed to them both, saying that she and Nigel were having a fabulous time.

Olivia had handed it over to Bill, but he had put it on one side without even glancing at it.

"Don't you want to read it?" she asked.

"I'm not interested."

Then one evening Bill did not return at the usual time, and Olivia became anxious. Her heart felt cold and heavy as she watched the clock. She wondered what she would do if he did not come home at all. People did not call the police to report a missing husband – that would be a laughable situation, but one that Olivia had never experienced before. Bill had always been so reliable when it came to matters of routine, returning home from work at the same time every day, never late for an appointment.

She was walking listlessly up the stairs shortly after midnight when she heard his key in the lock. She stood on the landing, and switched on the light in the hall. He was drunk. Olivia had never seen Bill really drunk, and it frightened her. He was slumped against the inner door, one hand holding the handle for support.

"What is it?" breathed Olivia. "Why?" They were questions she had wanted to ask him for weeks now, but had been fearful of his reply.

"I'm so unhappy," he said, tears of self-pity rolling down his cheeks. He looked straight at her. "I can't go on like this."

She was weeping too, but she put her arms around his waist and helped him up the stairs. He was heavy and it was difficult for her. Halfway up the stairs they had to stop for a rest. He hung on to the banister. "We should never have bought this house," he said. "It was a big mistake."

Somehow she managed to support him to the bed. He lay, his face pressed into the pillow, not moving. Gently, she moved his head so that he was breathing freely. Then she gathered up her nightdress, slippers and dressing-gown and went to the spare room.

Sleep was impossible. She sobbed, and when she could sob no longer, she began to form a plan. She watched the morning light coming through the curtains, and she thought of that first night in the Bedlington Hotel, and the tears began to flow again.

Bill did not get up until noon, but it was Saturday so it did not matter. When he did finally heave himself out of bed he dressed quickly, and then went to his study and shut the door.

Olivia knocked on the door, but he did not answer. She tried the handle, but the door was locked. She called out, "Please let me in. I must speak to you." Nothing happened, so she called out again, "Please, Bill, you must let me in."

He opened the door, and she entered the room. It was very untidy, which was not surprising, as Bill had not allowed anyone in for weeks. Mrs Bracegirdle had protested about not being able to get in to clean and tidy, but he had taken no notice. He was sprawled in his chair behind the desk and, for the first time, Olivia noticed how his body had thickened and that his old youthful expression had gone. Perhaps it was the hangover that had aged him overnight.

She stood in front of him as if she was being interviewed for a job.

"I'm sorry, darling," she said boldly, "but I can't bear to think of you being so unhappy living here, in this house, with me."

He said nothing.

"If you are as unhappy as all that, I think we should separate. Is that what you would like?"

"Yes," he said, and she thought she heard relief in his voice, "it is the only thing to do." He stopped looking at her, and his eyes focussed on a picture on the wall behind her head.

It was all amazingly easy, a few words and their future was settled, and their past life together annihilated with a single blow. Olivia and Bill had never discussed anything in depth, and they did not do so now. She thought there is no need to tell him about the baby or about Bruce's visit. What was important was the indisputable fact that he did not love her, perhaps had never loved her. With that knowledge, she would have to face life as best she could.

"Will you tell the children, or shall I?" she said quite briskly.

"I think we should do it together," said Bill. He went to the door, opened it, and called very loudly, "George! Claire! Come here a moment, will you?"

They came running. Because it was the weekend they were dressed for playing. George's shirt was not clean, his knees were grubby and his socks hung over his shoes. Claire was wearing an old pullover over a faded cotton dress, and her straggly hair was held in a ponytail with an elastic band. They look a mess, thought Olivia wearily, and no credit to the person looking after them. As well as being an inadequate wife she was a bad mother. They stood restlessly, shifting from one foot to the other, longing to get away.

Bill said, "Mummy and I have not been getting on very well, and it has caused a lot of tension. We have decided to separate so that we can see how we get on living apart from one another." It sounded so pat, as if he had read it in a manual for parting couples (the chapter on how to break the news to the children).

"You mean that you and Mummy do not love each other any more," said George. It was typical of him to have grasped the facts so quickly. Olivia saw him glance at his twin, as if protecting her. He was the spokesman. "Where shall we live?" he asked.

"Well, not in this house," replied his father, "it would be too expensive. I think we shall have to start looking for a house where you two can live with Mummy." Olivia marvelled that he had planned it so well. He and Emily must have talked about it for hours.

"What about Grandpa?" George wanted to know. "Will Grandpa live with us?"

"I don't see why not," said Bill, "if that is what Mummy wants."

"When Philip Grant's parents got a divorce," went on

George, who then explained, "Philip is a boy we know at school – when his parents got a divorce Mr Grant went to live with another lady. Are you going to live with another lady?"

Olivia held her breath, but Bill looked affronted and said, "Of course not. I have already explained to you it is a separation, not a divorce."

George took Claire's hand. The little girl had not said a word. A frown furrowed her gossamer brows, and the look she levelled at her parents with steely blue eyes was distinctly belligerent.

"Me and Claire are going out to play now," announced her brother, and, still holding hands, they left.

In a thoughtful mood, Olivia walked to her father's flat. He was not there. She looked for him in the garden, his garden; the colours, which had been so bright in the summer and early autumn, were beginning to fade, the garden was withdrawing for the winter. She thought, next year I shall be away from all this. The unknown future was very frightening.

She could hear the children shouting somewhere in the garden, and there was laughter as well, as if nothing had happened. She wondered if they would talk together about the changes that were going to take place in their lives. Perhaps even George was not mature enough for that sort of discussion. She thought that he had probably found out all he needed from Bill, and he would leave it at that. She was glad they had each other and, not for the first time, she envied their closeness.

She did not dread telling her father the news as much as she expected. She was so emotionally and physically drained there was no pity left over for him. He must accept the inevitable, as she had done.

She found him in the greenhouse, surrounded by pots of geraniums which he had brought in before the first frost of the winter. Olivia loved the greenhouse, set in the corner of the garden. It went back a long way and was beginning to show signs of age. The door stuck and the glass was bleary and covered with green marks. It had a delightful cool but stuffy atmosphere, and now was heady with the distinctive scent of the geraniums.

"Bill and I are parting, Daddy," she said.

He looked stricken. "Oh, God," he said. "I hoped this would never happen."

She did not want to break down, so she spoke abruptly, "Well, it has happened, so we must face it in a practical way."

"My darling," he said, putting his arms around her. She laid her head against his chest, as she had done when she was a little girl and something bad had happened, like the death of a dog.

He stroked her hair. He could find no words to comfort her. "You are so alone," he said. "What a godsend it will be when Alice returns."

Chapter 18

When Alice returned she looked refreshed, and was feverishly eager to embark on a crusade to help Olivia in her plight. Alice, her blue eyes startling in a face the colour of mahogany, was shocked by her friend's appearance. She could not believe that Bill had not been told about the baby.

"You said I should not tell him," Olivia reminded her.

"Yes, but that was then, not now!"

"I do not want him to stay with me because of duty," explained Olivia, her eyes filling with tears. The tears were always there; ready to spring to her eyes, and the effort she made to hold them back, especially in front of the children, only added to her grief.

"Please do not tell Bill," she pleaded, and Alice reluctantly agreed to take part in the deception.

"Oh, it's so good to see you!" cried Olivia. "I can't tell

you how much I missed you." She went on, "However, I do not want you to be worried by all this. The last thing I want is for you to get upset."

"I did feel a bit overwhelmed before I went away," Alice admitted, "but I'm fine now, and all I want to do is to help in any way I can."

"What about Nigel? He may not like the idea of you being involved."

"Nigel doesn't worry about what I do," Alice assured her. "He's just sorry that this has happened."

Carpenters was in turmoil, with people coming every day to view it, tramping from room to room, peering into cupboards and asking endless questions. Olivia had to escort them around the outhouses and show them over her father's flat.

It had been hard explaining the situation to Mrs Bracegirdle who, while listening sympathetically, realised that she was being dismissed. Also the services of her son would no longer be required. "We will not be able to afford you," said Olivia sadly.

"I'm sorry," said Mrs Bracegirdle. "You have always been good to me, and I will miss you and your father. It's a pity," she said darkly, "that some people can't keep their sticky hands to themselves."

Now, she was busy scrubbing shelves and helping Olivia with the onerous task of sorting out possessions. Olivia put a small sticker on each reminder of their married life, a red one for Bill and a blue one for herself and her father. Alice, although amazed by the way Olivia was tackling everything, told her frankly that this frenetic behaviour must stop. Olivia was exhausted and irritable which was bad for the morale of her children.

"Their world is falling apart," Alice reminded her. "You must think of them."

"What can I do?"

"Well, the first thing we must do is to find somewhere for you all to live."

She invented a game called 'Looking at Houses' and the twins adored it. On most days the four of them set out in Alice's car to view as many houses as possible. Alice maintained it took their minds off leaving their own home, and she was right. Prying into other people's houses was fun, and George and Claire enjoyed announcing the verdict as soon as they left.

"That house was *disgusting*," pronounced George or "I didn't like the lady," from Claire.

On the whole the properties were disappointing, and there came a day when there were no more to view. Alice marched into the local estate agent's office and told the young man sitting behind the desk to 'get your arse into gear'. Startled, he began to leaf through particulars until he found a house in the nearby village of Tapworth.

Laughing, they all piled into the young man's big car (intrigued by Alice, he was enjoying it as much as they were) and he took them to see a tall modern house in the centre of the village. It was one of a terrace of similar houses, all with steps at the front flanked with pillars. It needed painting, but it was light and airy and had a certain charm. There was one village shop and, down the lane, the primary school.

"You would not be lonely here," said Alice who was determined they should not live in an isolated place. The house was empty, so the children ran from room to room, their feet echoing on the bare boards.

"This is my room!" shouted George.

"I want this dear little room," pleaded Claire.

"You are a marvel," said Kenneth to Alice on the telephone, when she called to tell him she had found a house they all liked.

Their relationship was on an easy footing again, and it was as if the events of that strange afternoon had never happened. Kenneth supposed she was sensitive enough to understand he had been tortured by feelings of remorse and guilt, and had decided not to torment him any further.

Also, his mind was occupied with other matters. He felt aggrieved that the division of the property did not take into account his initial contribution to the purchase of Carpenters. It was in the joint names of Olivia and Bill, and a house for herself and the children would come out of her share, after the payment of the mortgage. Kenneth, who had put up a large sum when the house was bought, did not feature in the scheme at all. He tried to talk to Bill about it, but Bill was hard to corner – he was either at work or out somewhere. When he did come home, he closeted himself in his study with the door locked.

"It is unfair," Alice agreed when he complained about his treatment. She had heard it before, but was always sympathetic. "I'm afraid Bill has pulled a fast one on you, as he has with your daughter."

"I am an old man on the scrap heap," said Kenneth bitterly. "Where am I going to live?"

"With Livvy and the children, of course," Alice told him. "They need you, and this house I have found for them is ideal. There is an enormous room on the ground floor which will be perfect for you, with lots of room for your books."

"No garden, I suppose?"

"No garden," she replied sadly.

An offer was made for Carpenters, and accepted. Arrangements were made for the purchase of the house in Tapworth. Settlements were drawn up, maintenance agreed, and, in the midst of all the legal mumbo jumbo, relentlessly riding roughshod over family breakdowns and private heartbreak came Christmas.

Alone, in the spare room, Olivia considered the problem of Christmas. She decided there was only one course open for her, to turn to Pat for help. She had not seen her for some time, mainly due to a slight feeling of uneasiness because of her renewed friendship with Alice, of which Pat knew nothing.

She wrote in her letter that her lovely marriage was over; she was in the throes of moving house and, with the best will in the world, she could not supply the magic of Christmas for George and Claire. Pat replied at once, she was only too happy to take over the role of magician.

What about Bill? Even at such a time, Olivia wondered what he would do that year.

"Oh, for heaven's sake, don't worry about him," said Alice impatiently. "He can spend Christmas with Nigel and me. We'll put up with the gloom." It seemed a lot to ask of them.

Kenneth refused to be catered for; he desired to spend Christmas alone, his last in the flat. Alice promised Olivia that she would visit him on Christmas Day.

Very little had changed at the house in Queen's Gate, and to Olivia it was like coming home. Standing in the little hall, surrounded by suitcases, the children silenced by the strangeness, she felt like bursting into tears. But the very old Hilda, white-haired and lame, with legs bowed like those of an elderly jockey, whisked the twins off to the kitchen, saying, "Come along, dears, I have something to show you."

It was a Christmas tree, somehow looking more artistic than any Christmas tree they had ever seen. The whole house was decorated with sprays of holly and gold-painted branches, and Pat excitedly took Olivia on one side and showed her stockings bulging with presents, ready to put at the end of the children's beds.

"You have taken so much trouble," said her niece.

"It was time Hilda and I had a proper Christmas," Pat replied. "We have been too lazy to do anything about it for the last few years. The thought of having the children here spurred us on to make an effort. I hope we will all have a happy time." The look she gave Olivia was full of concern.

Pat had become a very large woman, but she had decided not to give a damn about being fat. She knew that her increased girth had given her a majesty and dignity she had not possessed before. She was shocked to see that Olivia had got so thin, the cheekbones emphasising the narrowness of her face. An anxious young woman, who looked old for her years, replaced the sweet naïve girl Pat had known in the past. She longed to tell her to take off the shapeless cardigan she wore all the time, and to do something about her hair which was lank and straight, and which she nervously kept pushing behind her ears.

On the first evening of the visit, after the twins had gone to bed, Pat cautiously asked the question, "Is there another woman?"

Olivia told her about Emily Frobisher who, at a distance, seemed curiously unimportant.

"Are you absolutely certain?" Pat asked. "Are you sure you are not mistaken? Why don't you confront these people so you know exactly what is going on?"

"It doesn't matter," Olivia told her wearily, "all that matters is that Bill does not love me. He has told me that he is terribly unhappy living with me."

Pat remembered herself, years before, swilling down pills with whisky because a man no longer loved her. Olivia could not indulge in that sort of selfishness because she had two children to consider. What right had Pat to advise? She decided to probe no longer.

A new light on the affair was revealed when Pat's favourite twin, George, started to tell her about the new house they were moving into after Christmas. "Me and Claire, Mummy and Grandpa are all going to live in the house Alice found for us."

The moment Olivia had dreaded had arrived. "Nigel and Alice came to live near us," she explained, trying to make her voice sound as natural as possible. "Alice has been very helpful."

"Good," said Pat lightly. "You don't need to worry about mentioning Alice to me. That business is all in the past, and I never think about it". She paused. "How is Nigel? Has he changed?"

"Hardly at all. Even less hair, that is the only difference." Nigel had changed, but the change was so subtle, so difficult to analyse that Olivia did not attempt to try.

Pat still did her illustrations for cards and calendars, and painted panels and screens which were now more popular than ever. They were much sought after for wedding presents. Her studio was just as Olivia remembered it, the same broken jug holding the paintbrushes, the smell of turpentine pervading the room.

The kitchen had not altered either, but it was no longer the only warm room in the house. Central heating had been installed, and there were radiators in the bedrooms and the passages. Pat did most of the cooking now, although Hilda was always at her side, making the gravy or peeling vegetables, issuing instructions. The crippling arthritis had slowed her down. She and Pat bickered in a companionable way, Pat complaining that Hilda got under feet.

On Christmas morning when the frenzy of opening stockings was over, Pat told the twins that their main present from Hilda and herself was in the studio. In a state of high excitement, they clattered into the room to find, in the middle of the floor, a wicker laundry basket tied up with blue satin ribbon. They fell upon it, and when they undid the ribbon and lifted the lid, out scrambled a small Jack Russell puppy.

Olivia was taken aback; a puppy did not seem appropriate at such a chaotic time in their lives.

"I remembered how much you loved Rufus and Rusty," said Pat. "This one came from Harrods, so it must be all right."

The children were in transports of delight. They gave the puppy a name at once, Spot. He had a black patch over one eye that gave him a rakish piratical look. They soon discovered he had a manic streak in him – he tore around the house, slithering on the rugs, barking furiously at imaginary foes, snarling in a playful way, biting at fingers with his little sharp teeth. There were squeals of joy when the twins rolled with him on the floor. They took it in turns to have him on the bed, and they dragged him around Kensington Gardens on a lead, which he resented. They mopped up his puddles and scooped up his messes. George took command with strict orders about the disposal of the soiled newspapers and the importance of washing hands afterwards. Spot chewed up shoes and bit holes in the cushions; he even mangled the bottoms of the curtains. Pat and Hilda did not seem to mind what he did – they were just pleased that the twins were so happily occupied every hour of the day. It was their idea, thought Olivia, when she felt a twinge of mortification at the puppy's misdemeanours.

At last it was time to go home, to face the reality of the move and a new existence. Pat had one last message for Olivia before she stepped on the train, "Make a success of the children. You have made a good start – they are a splendid pair."

She turned to George. "Look after your mother and sister – they can't go wrong with you around."

The train journey home was a nightmare. Spot refused to sit. He yanked at his lead and slipped his collar, scratching on the door to try and get out. He whined all the time, and finally disgraced himself by making a mess on the floor of the carriage.

A harassed Olivia was thankful to see Alice at Melbury Station to meet them when they all tumbled out of the train.

"My God," cried Alice, "as if you haven't enough troubles, without a dog! It's typical of that woman to be so short-sighted."

"We love him," said George defiantly.

"In that case, darling," she said, "I shall love him too."

Carpenters was sold, and completion dates were fixed

for both properties. As the house in Tapworth was empty, Olivia was able to go there most days to paint the walls and ceilings. The children were safely in school, and it was strangely peaceful in the empty rooms, a radio on top of a cardboard box, sloshing on paint with a roller. Even Spot settled on a piece of sacking in a corner, and slept. Olivia wore one of Bill's old shirts, for by now she was beginning to thicken around the waist. Privately, she did not think the baby would survive; there had been specks of blood that seemed to her to be ominous.

Then Alice told her that she too was pregnant. She had been to a doctor who had confirmed it. "After all this time," she said, "it is a miracle." Apparently Nigel was over the moon. She was so full of joy that it made Olivia even more aware of her less joyous situation.

"Do you know that Alice is expecting a baby?" she asked Bill on one of the rare occasions when she saw him.

"The whole world knows it," he said dryly.

Alice's comforting words were, "It will all work out, Livvy, you'll see. When you and the twins are in your new home and we both have our babies, just think what friends they will be!"

While Olivia coped with the move Alice was busy with the children. She made herself indispensable, taking them to school and fetching them, giving them treats. She gave George an expensive watch and Claire a flouncy frock. She tied Claire's hair back with a gold ribbon and painted her stubby nails scarlet.

She was helping Bill too, and had found him a place

to live, Number Fifteen, Mulgrave Terrace in Melbury. Olivia could not bring herself to go and look at it, but she knew the area. "It is very grand," she said.

"It is not at all grand," said Alice decidedly. She had come over to see Olivia one afternoon , and they were sitting in what had once been a charming drawing room. Only two armchairs had been left in place, and they were surrounded by huge packing cases marked with red or blue stickers. The move was two days away.

Alice was drinking lemonade in deference to her condition, and Olivia was drinking a large gin and tonic in the belief that if the baby had survived so far it could survive the onslaught of alcohol. In fact, Olivia had been drinking quite a lot of spirits lately.

In a rather giggly mood she was telling Alice of her recent encounter with Mary Chalmers. Mary had come to see her in order to tell her that Bill did not want a separation, that it was a mistake and a figment of Olivia's deranged imagination. Mary had gone on to say that Alan was extremely annoyed by something that Olivia was supposed to have said.

"Alan!" interrupted Alice. "What has he to do with anything?"

It appeared that a rumour had reached Alan's ears that his wife was having an affair with Bill. He was very angry and Mary accused Olivia of spreading the rumour.

"Have you ever heard of anything so funny?" moaned Olivia, overcome with laughter. "Mary, of all people! Bill can't stand her."

"It's crazy," agreed Alice.

"Someone is spreading these rumours," Olivia said. "Perhaps it is the same person who told Bruce that Bill and Emily are going to run away together. Who do you think that could be . . .?" She stopped and stared at Alice.

"I'm glad Alan Chalmers has had a fright. It's all he deserves." She started to laugh helplessly, and Olivia laughed with her until the tears stood in her eyes. Tears of bewilderment at the way things were going in her life.

In her half drunken state she had reached the point of despair.

Chapter 19

The next day Olivia had a headache but she was determined to return to the painting of what was to be her home for the next eighteen years. It was the day before the move, and it was imperative she finish the ceiling in one of the bedrooms. That was her aim, to get it done before the place was cluttered with furniture and boxes. The house had a hollow unlived-in feel about it which, anticipating the chaotic muddle that lay ahead, she found rather satisfying. She welcomed the solitude because it was a temporary separation from all the unpleasant happenings in her life.

With the tray of paint on the top of the stepladder, her feet firmly on the step below, she drew the roller backwards and forwards across the ceiling. Little flakes of emulsion settled on her hair and fell on Bill's old shirt. The action made her back ache and her neck stiff. The foetus inside her made a little plopping movement, as if in protest against the upward pull of her body. She had felt a bond with the twins before they were born, but with this child she felt hostility. It represented another problem in a sea of troubles.

Suddenly, she heard steps on the uncarpeted stairs. There were two flights to the top floor where she was painting, and someone had walked into the house without hammering on the door or ringing the bell. She remembered that she had closed the door, but left it on the latch. She had thought at the time no one would want to burgle an empty house.

She remained quite still, the roller poised in her hand, perfectly calm. So much had happened to her lately she had become impervious to fear or alarm. Spot, lying asleep on the piece of sacking in the corner, leapt to his feet, instantly awake, and made little growling noises at the back of his throat that rapidly turned into a crescendo of barking.

"Hello, Olivia." It was Captain Nigel, standing at the foot of the ladder. Tall and elegant, looking up at her and no doubt observing the swollen stomach beneath the paint-spattered shirt. "You should not be doing that."

She descended the ladder slowly and carefully, leaving the tray of paint and the roller at the top. "I'm so glad you interrupted me. I was getting very tired of that ceiling."

It was awkward, and she apologised for the lack of chairs. "The electricity hasn't been turned on yet," she told him, "so I can't even offer you a cup of tea." She quietened the dog, and turned off the little battery radio.

He must have come for a reason and it was obvious that he intended to stay, so there was nothing for it but to sit side by side, backs against the wall, on the dusty floor. "I'm so worried about your suit," she said. Like all tall people he sat on the floor in an ungainly way, all hands and feet.

"Don't worry."

He told her at once why he had come. To inform her that Alice was leaving him.

"Oh!" was all she could find to say.

"Tomorrow, in fact. She is moving in with Bill. They are lovers."

Olivia wondered if this was the way people usually broke bad news, quickly, without any preamble or unnecessary preparations. The strange thing was that it did not come as a shock to her; she had almost expected it. Had she known all along, but had been too tired or too dazed to grasp it? There had been a moment during the previous evening when she had a shaft of realisation, but she had been too befuddled, too weary in spirit to follow it up. There was no room in her life for further suspicions; she had to have faith in someone.

"Emily Frobisher has not been in the picture for a long time," went on Nigel. "Alice just kept it going. That is her method – she pounces on the truth, and then bleeds it to death. Bill has always been a challenge to her because she knew he did not like her, and, above all things, she wants to be liked."

"But he is her stepbrother!"

"That fact did not worry Alice – it just made the deception easier."

"I thought she was my friend!" cried Olivia, and at that moment the loss of the friendship seemed very hard to bear.

"She believes she is your friend," Nigel told her. "She honestly believes that you will move into this house with your children and she will move into the house in Melbury with Bill, and everyone will be happy. She cannot see a reason why you should not remain her friend. She has paved the way for this situation, and is too naïve to understand it will not work."

"Couldn't you have stopped it happening?" asked Olivia.

"I tried. I prevented her from going to Scotland where I thought you and Bill might have a chance to sort things out. I took her away to Madeira, but by that time I was too late. Bill was committed. I did my best."

"You should not be telling me this," cried Olivia in anguish. "Bill should have told me the truth ages ago!"

"I know," he said sadly.

Olivia thought of the twins, and how Alice had plied them with gifts and treats. "She manipulated the children?"

"Oh, yes. They were part of the complicated pattern she was weaving. If she was to be with Bill, she must have the love of his children as well."

There was a pause while Olivia tried to get her mind around the idea of Bill and Alice. Not Bill and Emily, but

Bill and Alice. She recalled seeing the forlorn figure of Emily Frobisher in the grocer's shop, and how she had thought she did not look like a woman in the middle of a torrid love affair. Out of the picture for a long time, according to Nigel.

Nigel continued, "Alice is a very unusual woman. I do not understand her fully myself so it is hard for me to try and explain her character to you. She has tremendous energy, much more than the ordinary person. Have you noticed that about her? It fills her being, and she uses that power in the wrong way, in stirring up trouble, in destroying relationships and in getting people to confide in her so that she can then betray their confidences. With her it is a drive stronger than the sex drive. Sex is of secondary importance to the success of her schemes, but because she is still young and attractive that weapon is available to her as well, and she uses it. God, how she uses it!"

Yes, Olivia thought, she used that weapon when she persuaded Nigel to leave Pat.

"Before we moved here," he went on, "she had an affair with the local doctor. He was in danger of being struck off, poor chap, for she was one of his patients. I insisted that we move away, leaving behind us the tangled mess of a broken marriage, unhappy children and an uncertain career. Alice was happy to leave, the affair was beginning to pall and she wanted to distance herself from it. She chose Pennel Bridge, and now I understand why."

"You are saying that Bill was her next objective?"

"That is what I am saying. Every presentable man is her target. For instance she set her sights on Edward Preston, but he is a Member of Parliament, and we all know what happens to them if they overstep the mark. His ambition saved him, and when she realised he was not prepared to take the risk, she contented herself with ensuring that his wife remained a complete alcoholic."

Olivia was shocked. "That poor woman!"

"Oh, it was not all Alice's doing. Rachel was drinking before we met the Prestons, but she was trying to give it up, and Alice made sure she did not succeed. She contents herself with little games until something bigger comes her way. That silly nonsense about Mary Chalmers and her jealous husband suspecting Bill. You may be sure that Alice planted that seed of doubt into Alan's mind. It has her stamp. A small diversion that amused her for a while."

Why did Olivia suddenly think of Marcia Drake? She had a sudden picture in her mind of that sad plain woman weeping into her teacup because someone had made a complaint about her, a complaint which had resulted in her losing her job.

"Your father," said Nigel. "Alice had a love affair with your father. He might have guessed what was going on with her and Bill, so she clouded his judgement by sleeping with him."

For the first time during the conversation Olivia had doubts. With so many lies and deceptions, how could she be sure of Nigel's integrity? "How do you know that?"

she demanded. "How do I know you are speaking the truth?"

"I know because Alice told me," he replied. "that is the strange part of all this. I am the father confessor to my wife. I knew about Bill months ago."

"You should have told me," she said.

"If I had, you would not have believed me. You were too much under Alice's spell. As for believing me now, Olivia, you have known me for a long time and by now you must realise I am not a liar. I have many faults, but lying is not one of them."

She knew he was right, but she still said, "I can't believe what you tell me about my father."

"Alice enjoyed that. She gave Kenneth a brandy to improve his performance. It was a big joke. I am sure Edward Preston heard the story, and it went the rounds. Alice is ruthless when it comes to spreading gossip, it is the breath of life to her, and you would be surprised how many people want to listen to that sort of stuff."

"It is so cruel," said Olivia wretchedly. "He must never find out that we know about it, or that anyone knows. It would kill him."

"Yes," agreed Nigel, "he must never find out that he was betrayed."

He shifted his position a little on the hard floor. "I am telling you this," he said, "because I think you should know the facts. Alice will move in with Bill tomorrow, but it won't last. When she loses interest she will come back to me."

"And the baby?" Olivia suddenly remembered the child Alice was carrying. She looked into Nigel's face, but it was impossible to read his expression. She wanted to know more. It was vital to get to the truth, but, being Olivia, she allowed the moment to pass. It was her great virtue, or her fault, that she was so well brought up, so polite, she could not intrude on a personal grief. She sensed there was real grief here, and to question him would hurt him deeply.

"She always wanted a child," he said shortly, and his stony face forbade her to say anything more.

Kenneth and Joan had not taught her how to behave in a scenario like this, or how to deal with someone like Alice. Such a person did not enter their orderly lives. Olivia thought their gentle influence had made her too gullible and trusting.

"I have been through so much," she said brokenly. "I can't take any more."

"You are strong, Olivia," Nigel told her. "A lesser person would have gone down long ago, but you have a sliver of steel in your backbone which nobody knows about. This house is fine. Come here tomorrow with your children and create a new life for yourselves. I envy you and I wish I had your strength."

He managed to pull himself to his feet, and help her to rise. He brushed the dust from his well-cut suit.

She asked, "Where are you going now?"

"Home, but not for long. I intend to make myself scarce before the momentous move. What about you?"

"I can't finish the painting," she told him, "as it is nearly time for me to pick the children up from school. I have to clear up here, and then I'll go."

He insisted on helping her. He washed the roller under the tap, and together they carried the stepladder and the pots of paint to the empty garage. She locked the front door of her new house, and they walked along the road to the place where she had parked her car. His car was parked behind hers.

He is a nice man, she thought, as she watched him shove the wriggling puppy into the back seat.

He took her hand and looked into her face. "I'm so sorry," he said.

The children came rushing out of school as if they did not have a care in the world. Their happy chatter comforted her, and turned her mind to the real things in life, the things that mattered.

She drove them straight to Mary's house. Olivia had swallowed her pride and asked Mary to have them for the night so that they would not be at Carpenters for the upheaval the next morning. Mary was pleased to be asked as she was beginning to suspect she had reached the wrong conclusion. She tried to convey this in a roundabout way by being particularly affectionate with Olivia, and very welcoming to the twins.

"Don't worry about anything," she said to Olivia. "They will be fine with me, and we will have a lovely time together."

After leaving them Olivia drove to the old house. It

did not seem like home any more, and she shut the door on the emptiness and went next door to see her father.

Kenneth was sitting in his usual chair, surrounded by boxes marked with blue stickers. The furniture removers had left a few essentials, the chair he was sitting in, a small table and a reading lamp, perched haphazardly on top of one of the packing cases. The other furniture was stored in a van parked in the drive, and the men would arrive first thing in the morning to pack up the rest and drive to Tapworth. Another van was parked nearby, ready to go to Mulgrave Terrace in Melbury.

It smote Olivia's heart to see her father looking so listless, his typewriter and papers bundled away somewhere, all the work he had done in his beloved garden to be passed on to strangers.

"Would you like to sleep in the house tonight, Daddy?" she asked gently.

He took her hand. "No, my dear. They have left me my bed, and I would rather sleep in that."

"All right, darling." She leant down and kissed his forehead. Understanding so much more now, she longed to say, don't worry, forget it. Mother would understand.

She knew that Kenneth, who did not believe in God and had no conviction other than that life was valuable and worth saving, was consumed with guilt because he had betrayed Joan. That betrayal had made an old man of him.

Chapter 20

Alone in a house empty of belongings and people, Olivia thought about Alice. At last, after a busy day, she was on her own and able to consider everything Nigel had told her. It was so straightforward and simple; she wondered how she could have been so blind.

She remembered a time when Alice had laughingly said to her, "I am an evil woman." She had spoken the truth then – she was evil. She had beguiled Bill into cheating his wife and sacrificing his children. She had hoodwinked Olivia and Kenneth into believing that he was in love with Emily Frobisher, long after he had finished with her for good. How could Bill have gone along with such a terrible deception? Then she had worked her charms on Kenneth. Olivia shuddered when she thought of her poor misguided father. It was disgusting!

The houses in Mulgrave Terrace swam into her confused mind, imposing houses with gardens. From tomorrow one of them was to be the home of Bill and Alice, a place where they would entertain their friends, a place George and Claire would be happy to visit. Together with the Order for Maintenance and the Property Settlement had come a list of rules for access to the children. Olivia had been appalled when she read about alternate weekends, every other Christmas and a holiday spent with the father once a year. She had thought that she and Bill could arrange these matters between them in an amicable way, that he would see his children whenever he chose, and it was partly for this reason she had decided they should live fairly near him. Dispassionately, the lawyers had set out the plans for the future, and they did not include any mutual concessions or compromises between the parties.

The more Olivia thought of her pseudo-Georgian house in Tapworth the less she liked it. The cheap hollow doors, lack of space and tiny strip of garden at the back. Her father would have to live in a basement room, probably for the rest of his life. Why should he be made to suffer because of Alice's total disregard for human feelings? Every word she had spoken to her, every overture of friendship had been a mockery. Olivia, on her last day at Carpenters, with the shadows lengthening across the bare boards, imagined herself surrounded by Alice's derisory laughter.

By evening, it was bucketing rain, smacking against

the uncurtained windows. Olivia flooded the rooms with harsh electric light. Looking around her at the empty bleakness, she came to a decision. She must speak to Alice. Before the blackness of the night, before the advent of her new existence, Alice must be confronted.

The telephone was in the bedroom she and Bill had once shared. The removal men had left her the matrimonial bed. On the floor beside it was the telephone. She dialled the Benton's number, and at once heard the engaged tone. She leaned back on the bed, and Spot snuggled up to her. She was glad of his company. After ten minutes she dialled again but it was still engaged. Another ten minutes, and the same result.

There was a cardboard container in the room holding her clothes. She rummaged around in it until she found a coat. She put it on and went downstairs. She kept the lights blazing when she opened the front door and made a dash for the car. She wriggled into the driving seat with a sideways crab-like movement, to protect the small bump from the impact of the steering wheel.

It was not pleasant driving with the windscreen wipers battling against torrential rain, peering into the darkness, the lights from the other cars making pools of brightness on the wet road. Olivia drove carefully, aware that she was important to her children and must not take risks.

When she arrived at the Benton's house in Pennel Bridge she parked the car on the opposite side of the road. There was a high hedge in font of the house, so she could not see if Nigel's car was parked in the drive. Then she remembered that he had told her that he was going to make himself scarce during the 'momentous move'.

There were narrow strips of light edging most of the windows, including the one upstairs which she knew to be the room where Alice and Nigel slept, an extravagant affair with a giant four-poster bed bedecked with flowery chintz.

Olivia sat in the car for a long time, at least it seemed to her a long time, and she wished she had brought Spot with her, for he would have been company. Her intention was to get out of the car, cross the road and ring the front door bell of the Benton's house.

What happened next was in her imagination. Alice would answer the door, and would be surprised to see Olivia standing there in the rain. 'What do you want?' she would ask.

Olivia would march into the house, leaving wet marks on the carpet, and she would say, 'I have come to talk to you'.

But none of this happened. She just stayed in the car, gazing through the rain-spattered window at the house opposite. A policeman, wearing a waterproof cape, walked past, glanced in the direction of the car and then walked on. The water beat on the top of the car and sounded like hammers in her brain. She longed for them to stop. She switched on the ignition, and turned the car in someone's drive. She wanted to go home.

When she got to the house, Spot greeted her with

vociferous delight, jumping up, barking, so pleased to see her again. She peered into the packing cases until she found the one containing glasses. She unwrapped a glass from its casing of newspaper, and found a bottle of whisky in another box. She poured herself a good stiff drink and took it upstairs with her.

The bedroom was as she had left it, denuded of comfort, chilly and unfriendly. She experienced an overwhelming sense of failure. As usual, she had not done what she had set out to do. She sat on the edge of the bed, drink in hand, and Spot snuffled at her legs.

She dialled the Benton's number. This time Alice answered, and Olivia heard that light familiar voice with its rather too perfect enunciation. "Hello?"

"It's Olivia."

The time was half past midnight. "Is anything wrong?" asked Alice.

Olivia took a deep breath. "Alice, Bill has had a heart attack. At least, I think that is what it must be. He is lying on the floor . . . he is unconscious. I have tried to rouse him, but I can't . . ." The night had turned into make-believe, and this was the continuation of her recent fantasy of ringing the door-bell and Alice letting her into the house. Olivia looked at the space beside the bed, and in her mind she saw Bill spread-eagled on the floor, face down.

"Oh, God!" It was a cry of pain from Alice.

Olivia said calmly, "I have rung nine-nine-nine and an ambulance will come as soon as possible. I wondered . . ."

There was no need to continue. "I'll come right away," Alice assured her. There was a short pause, and then she spoke urgently, "Livvy, don't wait for me. If the ambulance comes before I get there, you go with Bill. I'll catch you up at the hospital."

"Yes, I understand." As usual, she was following Alice's instructions.

"Don't touch him. They always say that, don't they?"

"I don't know."

"Christ!" Alice's voice on the other end sounded frantic. "I can't believe this is happening. I'll be with you as soon as I can."

There was a click and then the dialling tone. Olivia listened for a moment before replacing the receiver, and then she put the telephone down on the floor.

She felt triumphant; she had never envisaged that Alice would respond in this way. She had imagined her saying, "Come on, Livvy, what do you think you are doing?" Instead she had sounded genuinely shocked. Other people can play games as well, thought Olivia, as she prepared to wait for the arrival of Alice. She propped herself up with pillows. Spot slept the quiet sleep of a baby, curled up against the bump, warm and safe.

When she had finished her drink, she dozed, and then awoke and wondered why Alice had not come. She had been asleep longer than she thought and the time for Alice's car journey, even accounting for delays, had long since gone. She is not coming, thought Olivia, and perhaps it is just as well. Instinctively, her eyes went to the place on the floor where, in her mind, she had seen Bill in the throes of a heart attack. It was just an area of bare boards, as she knew it would be. Alice must have realised that she was being deceived, and in the sobering light of the early morning Olivia was relieved that she had guessed. It was not in her nature to tell lies, especially when they involved her husband. She closed her eyes and slept.

She was awoken by the sound of Bill's key in the front door. So he had decided to spend the last hours in his old home. His heavy step was on the stairs, and he switched on the light in the bedroom. Standing in the doorway, he took in the whole scene: the bare room, his wife sprawled on the bed, the dog and the empty glass.

Bill looked strange, dishevelled, almost ill. "Come with me," he said.

Olivia got off the bed. He picked up the coat, which she had flung over the top of a cardboard box, and abruptly ordered her to put it on. As he held it out to her, he started, then recoiled in disbelief as she huddled into the coat, too late to hide what he had seen in that moment of realisation. For weeks he had been avoiding her, retreating to his study, he had purposefully kept his distance from the family. This was the first time since she moved into the spare room that he had been in close contact with his wife.

He led the way to his car, which was parked in the drive. They got in, Bill in the driving seat. She wondered if he had been drinking, but he seemed terribly sober.

He started the engine and the windscreen wipers, it was still pouring with rain.

He drove through the silent village and on to the main road. He did not speak. They reached the place where the road met a side turning, signposted to Pennel Bridge.

There were a great many dazzling lights, ambulances, police cars, people darting about in the inky wetness. Through the driving rain Olivia could see the silhouette of a giant crane, like a predatory primeval monster, filling the sky between the waving trees. It was lifting the main body of a car from of a tangled heap of wreckage spewed across the road. It was Alice's car they were hauling into the air – Olivia recognised it at once, even though the searchlights only showed mangled wheels and a bonnet stove in like a concertina.

"Alice was somewhere in there," said Bill at last. "I wonder if Nigel has been told?"

They got out of the car and walked about between all the busy efficient people and the machines. A group of people, wrapped in blankets, were being helped into one of the ambulances, the occupants of the other car involved in the accident. Standing stolidly was their car, a Land Rover, showing signs of damage and surrounded by sparkling globules of shattered glass. Alice's flimsy little car would have had no chance against that impregnable lump of metal.

Bill was still looking around for Nigel. Olivia knew that he would not be there, but she said nothing. Then they both saw that the ambulance men were lifting something on a stretcher into one of the ambulances. A form covered in a red blanket. Olivia hid her face against Bill's shoulder. He stared straight ahead, then took her arm in a vice-like grip, and steered her back to his car. They followed the ambulance and, when it stopped outside the hospital, Bill drew up behind it but a porter came to the window and asked them to park in the Visitors' Car Park. By the time they had done that, Alice had been taken into the hospital

They sat in a small empty waiting room. From time to time, Bill got up and prowled around the room, examining the pictures on the walls and then sitting down again. Neither of them said a word.

After what seemed like an eternity a man appeared, white coat flapping, looking harassed. He was very young, almost school-boyish with a mass of tight blond curls and a spotty complexion. He asked them if they were related to Alice.

"Friends," said Bill laconically.

Then the doctor told them he was sorry; he stumbled over the words as if he wanted to get them out of the way as quickly as possible. What he had to convey to them was that Alice had been alive when they got her out of the car, but she had died on the way to the hospital.

Chapter 21

Olivia asked Mrs Bracegirdle to look after the twins while she went to the funeral. She did not ask Mary Chalmers, with whom she was now on very amicable terms, because she knew Mary, as Alice's friend, wanted to be there herself, with her husband.

Mary, who was in touch with local affairs, had managed to get information about the inquest, and she was anxious to impart it to Olivia.

"The people in the other car only received slight injuries," she said. "They were in a Land Rover, and I suppose the sheer strength of it saved their lives. Alice in her little car hadn't a hope. Apparently, she came out that side turning and went straight into them. She had been drinking and was driving too fast." Mary dabbed her eyes with a handkerchief. "I can't imagine what she was doing in the early hours of the morning, driving after drinking all evening. Where on earth was she going?"

Olivia thought, of course she had been drinking. It was perfectly reasonable to drink on an evening when you did not expect to have to take the car out. Of course she was driving too fast, she wanted to get to the side of the man she loved because she had been told he was ill, probably dying.

The memory of the dreadful day of the accident would stay with Olivia for as long as she lived but, in the meantime, she had to get on with the business of moving house. Removal men take no notice of human tragedy; they just want to get on with the job. She and Bill were so tired they could hardly take in what was going on. Somehow the cartons with red stickers were delivered to Mulgrave Terrace, and the ones with the blue stickers to the house in Tapworth. Bill went off to his lonely house, and Olivia collected the children from a tearful Mary.

On the Saturday following this dreadful day, Bill telephoned Olivia.

"I'd like to come and see you."

"Of course."

She was sure that the only reason for him wanting to come and see her was to tell her about his relationship with Alice. As far as he knew she had no knowledge of it. His life had been turned upside down and she grieved for him. She could not harden her heart against someone who had been delivered such a cruel blow. She remembered his stricken face when the doctor had told them that Alice was dead. Now the time had come for him to be open with her and she wondered how she would feel when he told her the truth at last. She hoped she would be as truthful with him.

He arrived and immediately she was struck by his haggard appearance. He looked as if he had not slept for days. He asked her if he could have the children for the weekend. This first weekend of their separation was hers.

She agreed at once, and explained that they had gone to play at the house of newly found friends they had made at their new school. She would pack a few clothes and toothbrushes into a case, and then take him to the place where they were, and he could take them to his house from there.

"It's a terrible mess," he said. "I haven't even begun to unpack the cases yet."

"It can't be worse than this," she said, looking around her. She thought she would help him along a little. "This has been such a nightmare," she said, "even worse for you than for me, if that is possible."

"Yes," he agreed, "it is very sad."

"I'm sorry," she said.

A look passed over his face, a look she knew very well. He was anxious to get going, to bring the conversation to a close.

"Are you ready?" he said.

She scurried around getting the things for the children packed into their little cases, while he waited impatiently.

Then she followed him to his car. It was not far to go, and she thought, this is my last chance to get him to speak.

"Alice was very close to you," she said. "I know how awful you must be feeling."

His face was expressionless, stonily staring straight ahead. His reply, when he made it after what seemed a long pause, astounded her. "She was not a blood relation," he said. "You always forget that fact."

She went to the front door of the house and rang the bell. The mother of the children who had befriended the twins came to the door. The situation was explained to her. She nodded, understanding the sad circumstances that were the result of a broken marriage. It was Olivia's first experience of this sort of response. The twins were bustled out and into their father's car.

"Don't worry about me," she said, "I'll walk home. It's no distance." There was no question of any of them worrying about her, they were gone before she had time to say goodbye to George and Claire. She walked home thinking how different her life had become, in the space of a few days it had changed completely.

Although Olivia had made a few attempts to make their new home habitable, when she went down to the basement on the day of Alice's funeral she found that her father had made no effort. His chair was in place and his bed had been made, but the packing cases were stacked against the wall, just as the removal men had left them. She resolved to make a start on unpacking them as soon as possible.

Kenneth had managed to salvage his dark suit and a black tie from a suitcase, and he was sitting, suitably attired for a funeral, waiting for her.

"How have the children taken this?" he wanted to know.

"They will be fine," she assured him. When she told them about Alice's death she wondered if they would break down, but they did not. Children have a fearful and fascinated interest in death.

"Did she turn into a puddle, like she said she would?" asked George. It was unworthy of him, and he asked this foolish question as a way to cover up his true feelings.

"She was joking when she said that," replied Olivia.

"How did she die then?"

"She was killed in a car accident," his mother stated.

"Where?"

"You know the sharp corner on the main road, where we turn off to go to Alice's house? There."

"Was she going too fast?" It was Claire who asked the question this time.

"Maybe."

"In a hurry to get somewhere?"

"Perhaps."

Olivia drove her father to Pennel Bridge. He sat beside her in the car; head lowered and chin on chest. He wore an overcoat because it was bitterly cold, and a muffler wound around his neck, which made him look very old. He spoke once during the journey, and that was when he said, "She did not deserve this."

Nigel was standing at the door of the church, immaculate in a long black coat. As soon as he saw Olivia, he took her arm. He turned to Kenneth, "Do you mind, Kenneth? I want to have a word with Olivia."

"You go on in, Daddy," she told her father.

Nigel guided her along the narrow path encircling the church, away from the people slowly filing into the building. He kept a tight grip on her arm, and she was glad of his support for she felt as if she could hardly put one foot in front of the other. The air was so cold it caught in her throat and made her short of breath. He must have felt her trembling beneath his firm hand. What was he going to say to her? Did he know what had happened, and was he going to make an accusation, and, if he did, what would be her response?

What he did say was, "Please forget everything I told you the day I came to see you in your new house." He set out his requirement so precisely, as if he wanted to be certain that there was no mistake about the time or the situation.

Olivia knew that if she made a promise she would keep it, and a part of her reasoned that it was wrong to make an undertaking of that kind.

Nigel said, a note of desperation in his voice, "Olivia, what happened is irrelevant now in view of the recent event."

She heard herself saying, "Of course. I give you my word."

He did not leave it at that though, he wished to go on to explain his actions and to convince himself that she meant what she said. "It was wrong of me to say all those things. I want the whole conversation blotted out, as if it never took place. Do you understand me?"

"I have given my word." She longed to be free of the whole hateful business, at the same time knowing that she would never be free.

He looked harassed. "I have to go back. People are arriving all the time."

"Go," she told him, "and please do not worry any more."

With these words she absolved him, taking upon herself the burden of secrecy and remorse. It was a lonely decision she had made. Nigel strode ahead, intent on dealing with the awful present, confident that he had dealt with the complications of the past.

Olivia lagged behind him, entering the cool dimness of the church. She slid into the seat beside her father. Bill was on the other side of Kenneth. George and Maureen sat in the pew in front of them, Maureen was weeping. Before the service began Nigel, looking about him to see that all the arrangements were going smoothly, joined them. He is like old Captain Nigel, thought Olivia, positive and assured, as he had been when he was living with Pat.

In his short address the vicar mentioned that Alice

was expecting a child. A long awaited baby after years of marriage, when she and her husband had long given up hope of ever being parents. This made it a double tragedy. He did not say any more because he had not met Alice. St Peter's Church, Pennel Bridge was not a place she and Nigel had visited.

The sobs from Maureen were audible, and George put an arm around her in a comforting gesture. Olivia glanced sideways at the two men beside her in the pew. Her men. She knelt on the hard hassock and covered her face with her fingers, so that she could not see their faces.

Part Three

Chapter 22

"I think I should leave tomorrow," said Stephen France to his hostess, Marigold Armitage.

"Oh, please stay longer," she pleaded, "I don't want you to leave – you are the perfect guest. Do you remember the old rhymes 'The Perfect Guest' and 'The Perfect Pest'? The perfect pest left the soap on the bathroom floor."

No, he had never heard of them. "You are too young," she said comfortably. She was in her seventies, he in his fifties. "I adore having you here," she went on. "You fetch the logs, exercise the dog and, above all, keep Bernard amused."

Bernard was her husband. He had been a housemaster at a public school of which Stephen was now the headmaster. Bernard had been retired for seven years, and Marigold was still not used to having him around all the time. She was sharper than he was, and able to outwit him in any argument although he did his best to compete. Always being the winner had its drawbacks, and Marigold was sometimes irritated by her husband's feeble attempts to express an opinion. She did not suffer fools gladly, and although Bernard was by no means a fool he had his limitations. "I love him dearly," she said, "but . . ."

It was that 'but' that prompted her to write detective novels. Writing stimulated her lively mind at a stage in her life when her children were married, and she only saw her grandchildren at infrequent intervals.

She invented a character called Dominic Platt. In time he became so real to her she felt she knew him intimately. A television series was made about him, and Marigold could not identify her image of Dominic with the person who took the part. She watched the first episode but none of the succeeding ones. It was a near thing; her beloved Dominic was nearly wiped out forever in her mind by a well-meaning actor. She managed to rescue him from a terrible death, and went on to write several more books about him. Platt Cottage, the name of the house Bernard and Marigold bought in Tapworth on Bernard's retirement, inspired Dominic's surname. He lived with his disabled son, Francis, and together they solved a number of crimes, for murder was a commonplace occurrence in their neighbourhood. To date Marigold had written eight books about him, and she was working on the ninth.

Dominic was very tall, with grey hair curling

delectably at the nape of his neck, and the pale blue eyes associated with the typical English gentleman. He was particularly popular in the States where the books were continually being reprinted. He looked young for his age – he was fifty-two. His disposition was a mixture of kindness (with his son he was as gentle as a woman) and a ruthless determination when it came to solving the crimes that fell into his lap.

The formula worked, and Marigold was able to put money aside for each of her grandchildren, and although she and Bernard did not alter their life style they could afford holidays abroad. Not long holidays, however, because Marigold was always anxious to get back to Platt Cottage and, of course, Dominic.

Marigold spoke the truth when she said she enjoyed having Stephen to stay. He appreciated her acerbic sense of humour, although his own was more scholarly and gentle. His jokes were always fit for the ears of schoolboys.

Stephen did not realise it but he was the model for Dominic Platt. Marigold often thought he might suspect, but he never did. The possibility simply did not occur to him. Perhaps the disabled son put him off the track, for he had two able-bodied daughters, one married with two children, the other a career woman living in New York. He was a widower, his wife having died five years earlier. It had not been a successful marriage, although he never admitted its shortcomings to anyone. Sheila, his wife, had disliked being a schoolmaster's wife, and when Stephen became a headmaster it made matters worse, as she could never adapt to being polite with parents or interested in the boys. She had not helped her husband get to high office, and some people, Marigold included, thought he had got there in spite of her.

"I'm sure you will be pleased to get the smell of cigar smoke out of your house," said Stephen in answer to her pleas for him to stay longer. He was smoking small cigars in an attempt to give up smoking. He had started smoking as a fourteen-year-old midshipman, and then continued the habit when serving in the Royal Navy during the war. Now, he found it difficult to stop, although he was trying hard because he did not think a headmaster should smoke when the boys were punished for doing the same thing.

"I like the smell," said Marigold stubbornly. "Anyway, you can't leave yet. I'm having a party tomorrow evening, and I want you to be here to help me. You know how hopeless Bernard is on these occasions. I rely on you staying. That settles it."

A tap on the door interrupted them. Marigold went to see who it was, and returned with a young woman carrying a sheaf of papers.

"I've finished chapter seven," she said and then looked slightly disconcerted when she saw Stephen, who rose to his feet when she entered. "Oh, I'm sorry. I didn't know. . ." She had an attractive quick voice, unsure, hesitant.

"Thank you, my dear," said Marigold warmly, relieving

her of the papers. "What would I do without you? Olivia, I would like you to meet an old friend, Stephen France. Stephen this is Olivia Randall."

She had a firm handshake for such an obviously shy person, and her fingers were slim and cool. Stephen liked people with a degree of shyness; it indicated they were not arrogant or too self-assured, and sometimes it hid an interesting personality.

Marigold urged her to stay and have a cup of coffee with them. "It won't take me a minute to get it ready."

But Olivia murmured something about picking up her children from school, and already she was on her way out, pushing her hair back in a nervous gesture, anxious to be gone.

Stephen could hear them talking in the hall. Marigold was saying, "I owe you," and being assured that "any time will do". Then Marigold's voice again, always an octave higher than anyone else's, "Can you collect a new batch on Thursday?" and then calling after her, "But I shall see you before then. Don't forget you are coming here for drinks tomorrow evening."

"I'm not sure . . ."

"You must come."

"I'm afraid she won't," said Marigold, as she came back into the room.

"Who was that?" Stephen asked – he wanted to know more than just a name.

"Olivia types for me. It's a job she can do at home to make a little extra money. She is divorced, and lives on maintenance paid by her husband, her ex-husband I suppose I should say. It's a godsend for me. She lives nearby, can read my awful writing and is very accurate." She was seized by and idea. "I know, I'll make us some coffee and, while we are drinking it, I'll tell you how I met Olivia."

"Do I want to hear this story?" asked Stephen doubtfully. "Is it going to be as interesting as all that?"

"Yes," replied Marigold firmly. "You know my stories are always interesting, and this one is particularly so. Rather remarkable in fact."

"And I know how your mind works," retorted Stephen. "You are not, by any chance, pairing me off with this young woman, are you? If you are, I can tell you at once it is a waste of time – I am happy as I am." Sometimes he accused her of trying to find a wife for him. She did not think it right that he should live alone in the lovely house that went with the job. He, however, was content with his way of life. Sheila had done nothing to make him believe that marriage was linked to a peaceful existence.

"No, I would not dream of it," answered Marigold. "She is far too young for you."

"Thank you!"

She qualified her statement by saying, "I know you are young for your age, but I do not think Olivia is the right person for you. Very charming, but perhaps a bit limited. Did you notice her sad expression? It is always there. Even when she laughs the sadness does not completely disappear. However, she is a wonderful mother, and her children are a normal happy bunch."

Marigold made coffee in a jug, quickly and efficiently, and carried it and the cups on a tray into the sitting room. They sat on a sofa in a window recess, the tray on a low table in front of them.

The room was a pleasant mixture of old beams, antique furniture and soft materials. It reflected Marigold's excellent taste and liking for comfort. Haphazard flower arrangements filled dark corners, and well-polished little tables were dotted with Bow figurines and photographs in silver frames of babies, children and family groups.

One wall was covered with bookshelves, and halfway up were the hardback first editions of the Dominic Platt novels. Another wall was filled with a huge fireplace, an enormous cavern of stone and old brick where the fire burned brightly, and a pile of ash collected beneath. The room smelled sweetly of furniture polish, wood smoke and, very faintly, Stephen's cigar.

Marigold settled back on the soft cushions and put her legs on a little footstool. Sometimes her bones ached and she felt her age, but she would never admit it.

"It happened four years ago," she began. "Old Colonel Jones asked me to sell flags for the Lifeboats. I haven't time to do such things, what with Dominic, the garden and looking after Bernard . . ."

"In that order?" interrupted Stephen, amused.

"In any order, but it was for such a good cause I did not see how I could refuse."

Marigold went from house to house with the tray slung around her neck, tin in hand. Tapworth was a nice village, and she expected people to be generous and on the whole they were. She was their local celebrity, and they were pleased to see her.

She came to the row of 'town houses' as the estate agents called them, although the villagers still referred to them as the 'new houses'. Each time she rang the bell, it had the echoing 'no-one-in' sound to it. She guessed that young first-time buyers owned these houses, and they were now at work earning a joint income sufficient to pay the mortgage. When they started a family they would think of moving on.

Feeling rather defeated, she rang the bell of the last house. There was no immediate response, so she thought she had struck unlucky again. While she was waiting she examined the Corinthian-styled pillars on either side of the steps; they were made of wood and distinctly rotten at the base. She noticed that the pillars on the other houses had been replaced by ones made of fibreglass, and because it was the sort of trivial detail that interested Marigold she was bending down to examine one of the pillars more closely when the door of the house opened. There stood a large female, or rather a slim young woman with a vast expanse of stomach.

"Will you give something for the Lifeboats?" asked Marigold brightly.

The woman nodded, and Marigold felt guilty as she watched her lumber upstairs to fetch her purse; she knew about the interminable stairs in those houses. A door opened opposite her at the end of the small hall, and an elderly white-haired man emerged.

"The lifeboat men," he said, "such wonderful people." He put some money into the tin, at the same time giving her a gentle smile before going back to his room.

"Thank you," she called out to him, "so kind . . ."

The woman came down the stairs, treading carefully and holding on to the banister.

"Thank you," said Marigold again as the money dropped into the tin.

The woman smiled. In Marigold's eyes she was less of a woman and more of a girl, and she had a very sweet smile.

"How many flags do you want?"

"I'll just take one. It's no good giving them to the children. They will only lose them."

"You have other children?" Marigold was always curious to know more about people.

"Twins, a boy and a girl, nearly seven years old."

"How lovely! I longed for twins. And when is this one due?" Her eyes focussed on the bulge that seemed to fill the doorway, and had gone past the stage when it could be tactfully ignored.

"It is overdue by three days." There was a little sigh of desperation. "I am so big. They tell me it is only one baby, but I was not as enormous as this when I was having two."

Marigold was about to embark on the saga of her

own pregnancies, but managed to refrain as she had a few other houses to visit. As she left, she said in what she hoped was a comforting voice, "It cannot be long now. Good luck, my dear."

She could not get the girl out of her mind and wanted to know more about her. As expected, the lady at the village shop was able to fill her in with some details. Olivia Randall, Marigold was informed, was parted from her husband. They used to live in a house called Carpenters, "You know the one, Mrs Armitage, a big house set back from the road, this side of Melbury." Marigold knew the house she meant, and had often admired it. "She has two children, a boy and a girl, and another on the way. Her old father lives with them, although how they all fit into that house, I can't imagine. He is a very nice gentleman."

On Marigold's next visit to the shop she was told that Mrs Randall's baby had been born. It was a girl, and mother and child were in the Maternity Wing of Melbury General Hospital.

Marigold was an impulsive woman, and it was on impulse that she went to visit Olivia. She had only met her once, and then very briefly, but she told herself it was a neighbourly action to show kindness to someone new in the village. Also, there seemed something tragic about giving birth so soon after the breakdown of a marriage, and she could not help wondering about such a strange sequence of events.

She was surprised to find that Olivia was not in the

general ward but in a private room. As she was directed down the passage she began to have doubts about being there, as private patients usually have a full quota of visitors. Mrs Randall might not welcome a visit from someone who was almost a complete stranger; she might not even remember meeting Marigold.

"She'll be glad to see you, I'm sure," said the nurse guiding her. "She's been feeling a bit low."

Marigold forgot her misgivings when she saw at once the look of recognition. Olivia was in bed. She had a minor infection and had not been allowed to get up yet. Her daughter lay in a crib beside the bed, and Marigold bent over to look. She loved babies, especially at this very new and vulnerable stage. This was a particularly beautiful infant – perfect features, little mouth working although in sleep, one tiny star-like hand curled up by her face.

"Oh!" Marigold whispered. "I must not waken her." She plonked her offering, a small pot of African violets, on the locker. She noticed the room already contained flowers, and very prominent was a vase of red roses. "Mm," she murmured, smelling them and finding they had no scent at all.

"They are from my husband," said Olivia.

"Is he pleased with his lovely new daughter?" asked Marigold, settling herself in the chair by the bed.

Olivia did not answer the question, but instead said, "He brought the twins to see the baby."

"And did they take to her?"

"George was over the moon. He could not get over

how little and sweet she is, and I think he felt protective towards her. Claire, well, I am not so sure about Claire. I think she might be a bit jealous."

"Ah, that is the sex thing," said Marigold wisely. "A rival female. If you had produced a boy she would have been much happier about it."

Marigold was a woman totally in control, able to write books that became bestsellers and be a loving wife, mother and grandmother as well. Olivia could not know these things about her, and she just saw an old woman, bordering on stoutness, with straggly grey hair and a face criss-crossed with lines. Her hands, clutching a large overstuffed handbag, were veined and calloused, due to age and gardening. She wore a baggy tweed suit and sensible brown brogues.

"I'll not stay long," she said. "I don't want to tire you."

"It is so nice of you to come and see me."

"I thought a representative of Tapworth should visit you," explained Marigold. "After all, you are a new resident in our village."

For some reason this simple statement affected the girl deeply, and Marigold was concerned to see tears in her eyes. The tears brimmed over and coursed down her cheeks.

Olivia felt under the pillow for a handkerchief, "I'm sorry," she said in a muffled voice.

"Please don't be sorry," said Marigold laying her hand over Olivia's hand, "it is called baby blues, and the feeling of depression will soon pass."

"Yes, I'm sure it will," replied Olivia, clasping the old woman's hand tightly. "It is just that so many awful things have happened to me lately, as well as the nice one, having the baby. I know I should feel grateful that she is so perfect."

"Have you decided on a name for her?" asked Marigold, thinking it as well to get on to more practical matters.

"No, I haven't."

"Oh, dear me," said Marigold. She had no patience with people who did not have a name for each sex lined up before the child was born. After all, they had nine months to come to a decision, and a child without a name had no identity. "You must decide what to call the little mite."

Olivia paused for a moment as if trying to pull herself together. At last she said, "You see, I had a friend who was killed in a car accident a few months ago. She was having a baby too."

"What was her name?" asked Marigold gently.

"Alice."

"Alice is such a pretty name. Have you thought of calling your baby Alice, after your friend."

Olivia sat up in bed and covered her face with her hands. Terrible sobs wracked her body, and Marigold did not know what to do, except put her arm around the shaking shoulders. They stayed like that, the old woman holding the young one, waiting for the tears to subside.

Presently, Olivia recovered enough to say, "No, I will

not call the baby Alice, but I realise I must choose a name for her. Alice is the reason I have not done so before now."

"Thinking of a name will give you something to think about," said Marigold briskly, and she got to her feet.

"You are not leaving?"

"I am, for you need all the rest you can get. I can come again though – would you like me to do that?"

"Yes, please."

"All right. I'll come tomorrow afternoon, if that suits you."

"I'd like that very much," said Olivia, "and I'm sorry I have been such a bore today. What must you think of me?"

"My dear, you must not worry about it for a moment," said Marigold kindly, "one's emotions run riot at such times. I understand perfectly."

As she reached the door, Olivia stopped her. "Do you mind telling me your name?"

Tapworth was very proud of its famous authoress, and everyone in the village knew her. It had never occurred to her that the girl might not know who she was. She had not thought it necessary to introduce herself. "Marigold Armitage," she told her.

"I see. Thank you." Obviously the name meant nothing to Olivia, and Marigold concluded wryly that she was not a fan of Dominic Platt.

"Marigold," said Olivia thoughtfully, "I would like to call my baby Marigold."

Marigold stepped back into the room, "Are you sure? Isn't that rather a hasty decision?"

"I don't think so, but only if you approve of course."

"And that was that," said Marigold to Stephen with great satisfaction. "The baby was named Marigold. I went to see Olivia several times after that first visit, and it was I who drove her home from the hospital. I met her husband, who is good looking and has a marvellous smile, and I became friends with her father. He was a dear old gentleman who had an allotment in the village, and supplied his family and friends with vegetables. Everyone in Tapworth was sorry when he died three months ago. I became very fond of Olivia, and when I found out she had been to a secretarial college I asked her to work for me. The arrangement has been very successful for nearly four years."

"It is a touching story," said Stephen, "one of your best. And little Marigold – she is a good child, worthy of the name?"

"An enchanting creature," she told him, "I love her almost as much as one of my own grandchildren."

Chapter 23

On the day of Marigold Armitage's party, Olivia was alone in the house because her three children were attending the marriage of their father with someone called Philippa Baker. The children and everyone else referred to her as Pippa. Pippa was in her early thirties, had been married before but was childless, and the twin's acceptance of her could be judged by the fact that they did not show their disapproval. Marigold was too young to express an opinion, but she was excited by the event, and told people she was going to be a bridesmaid (she called it a "widesmaid"). Olivia was afraid she was in for a disappointment for it was to be a registry office wedding. She had met Pippa, once, shortly before she and Bill agreed to divorce.

Soon after Olivia, in the first months of pregnancy, moved to Tapworth, Bill embarked on a campaign to get her back. They had lost their old home, but he had a good house to offer her, and he pointed out there was room for the old man as well, and a garden for him to potter in. He could not understand why she refused. The name of Alice did not pass his lips – it was as if she never existed. The house at Pennel Bridge had been sold and Nigel had moved away, so there was nothing to remind him of that unsavoury episode in his life.

It was true that Bill was lonely, living in a house too big for one person, but his conscience did not trouble him during his solitude. He just felt sorry for himself. During his weekends with the children he entreated them to persuade their mother to come to her senses. He managed to convince them that it was her fault they had to live apart. They believed him, but loved her just the same. George sometimes felt the truth about his parents was just within his grasp, but he was too young to think deeply about it.

Sometimes Claire, the more impressionable of the twins, did as her father had asked her, and said, "Daddy wants us to live together as a proper family. Why can't we do that?"

Bill turned to friends, and they came to see Olivia in order to plead his cause. He even approached the old lady she typed for, and asked her to speak to Olivia on his behalf, but Marigold said firmly, "It is her decision. I'm sorry, but there must be a good reason why Olivia does not want to go back to you."

Bill thought he knew the reason, false pride, and he accused Olivia of it. Spiritedly, she retorted that the reason was loss of trust – on both sides she hastened to add. She willed him to speak, to tell her everything; then perhaps she could have told him the terrible truth about the night when Alice died. After all, he was the only person she could have told and, sharing the guilt, they might have been able to face the years ahead, together for the sake of their children.

Little Marigold started going to stay with her father when she was three years old. Although she loved him, and the twins were with her, tears were shed when he arrived in his big car to fetch them.

On that Saturday morning when Marigold was leaving home for the first time, Olivia stood by the upstairs window of the sitting room and watched the departure of her family. It saddened her to see the small figure of Marigold, clutching her little suitcase, stumbling between her brother and sister, and being pushed into the car.

When they returned on Sunday evening, Claire, in particular, was in a truculent mood. At that stage in her development she adored her father, and she flounced around the house in Tapworth, muttering, "You are so mean, Mummy. Daddy is really unhappy. Please, please let's go and live with him in his lovely house. He doesn't want us to live apart."

Marigold snuggled up to her mother, glad to be at home again, and not at all certain she wanted to live anywhere but in this dear familiar place.

George was angry with his sister. "Why don't you leave things alone?" he demanded. "It's not your business You don't know anything."

"I do, so!" They argued, as they often did after being away, finding it difficult to adjust to their usual routine.

When they had all gone to bed, Olivia sat quietly, thinking about them. She was convinced she was letting them down, blighting their childhood when life for them should be happy and uncomplicated. She loved Bill, so what was the matter with her?

She went to the house of the Bairds who lived two doors away. She asked their teenage daughter whether she would bring her homework to the house, for a short time only. The girl agreed readily, she was used to baby-sitting for Mrs Randall. She bundled her schoolbooks together and came at once.

Driving to Melbury, Olivia felt hopeful. She resolved to tell Bill about her involvement with Alice's fatal accident. He would have to listen, perhaps he would understand and they would go on from there.

When she got to Mulgrave Terrace she rang the doorbell, and Bill answered it. He was clearly surprised to see her standing under the porch light. "Come in," he said.

She followed him through the hall and into the elegant drawing room, and immediately saw a woman standing on a stepladder, adjusting a curtain. It was a high window, and the curtain was made of heavy expensive material. She was trying to fix it on to rings on a pole, and she was having difficulties.

"This is Pippa," Bill explained. "She has been very kind and made the curtains for me." Pippa. No other name was mentioned. Did she come from a shop? Not on a Sunday, surely?

Pippa stepped down from the ladder, and the curtain fell to the floor. "You'll have to help me with it, darling," she said.

It was apparent she was a friend, a very good friend, and Olivia understood, and felt herself blushing.

She mumbled that she had to leave, and the other woman said, "Please don't go on my account." She made it sound like an insult.

Pippa had listened sympathetically to Bill's tale of woe – she had known about his problems for months. As she was in love with him she decided his wife must be paranoid, behaving in a completely unreasonable way. Of course, she did not want Olivia to behave any differently, that would have been against her own interests. Seeing her now, for the first time, she thought she did not look a happy woman, very thin, very nervy, in fact just as she had imagined she would be.

"The curtains are lovely," said Olivia, on the way out. "You are clever."

Bewildered, Bill accompanied her to her car. He watched her get into the driving seat and turn on the lights, and then asked, "Why did you come?"

"It's not important," she said hurriedly, the engine running. "I'll speak to you another time."

"That was quick," said the baby-sitter when Olivia got

home. She looked at Olivia's face. "Are you all right, Mrs Randall?"

"Yes, perfectly all right. It was very kind of you to help me out." She paid her and, after she had left, Olivia went upstairs to her children. Marigold slept sweetly, her thick black lashes fanning her plump rosy cheeks. In the bed beside her Claire was completely covered by a duvet, and Olivia tenderly pulled it away from her face so that she had air. In the next room George was awake. He was a light sleeper, and had heard Olivia come in. He was sitting up in bed hugging his knees. "Mother, where have you been?"

"I went to see Daddy."

"And Pippa was there?"

"Yes, how did you know?"

"She arrived as we were leaving."

"I wish you had told me. Do you like her?"

"She's all right."

"And you are all right, all of you?"

"Of course we are," said George. "Don't take any notice of Claire, she was just being silly."

Olivia kissed him, "Goodnight, darling. I love you."

"I love you too, Mummy."

Bill's marriage was a surprise to most of his friends, as he had managed to conceal this new relationship from them, a fact that irked Pippa but she decided to be patient. Bill preferred his friends to picture him in his lonely state, closeted in a big empty house, cooking a meal from a packet and then going off to bed alone. This is how it had been at the beginning, and sometimes it had been difficult having the children on his own, although Claire was a helpful child. When Pippa had appeared on the scene it was easier for Bill, she had been so anxious to make everything work. Claire showed signs of resenting her presence, but George said to her, "For goodness sake remember how awful Daddy was before she came."

Olivia spent the morning of the wedding getting the children ready for it. George wore a grey suit, recently acquired for the new school he was going to next term, and with a white shirt and a tie he looked handsome. His hair was brushed and Olivia made sure his ears were clean. The rather gawky Claire was dressed in a skirt and blouse and her long hair was tied back in a ponytail. Marigold was in her party frock and looked angelic. Olivia was proud of them, and waved from the window as they went off in Bill's new car. He had come to fetch them himself.

After they had gone she decided to do some housework, a task that never appealed to her, and she started to clean the room that had once been Kenneth's room. She intended turning it into a rumpus room for the children, but so far she had not had the heart to begin on the change. Her father's clothes had already been given to the Salvation Army, but when she opened a drawer she found it to be full of his ties that somehow had been forgotten. Finding them tumbling out of the drawer was a shock. She sat on the edge of his bed, holding the ties, and she wept comfortable tears. Not tears of desperation and self-pity as she had in the past, but tears for someone she had loved and who had left her for good. She pressed her nose into the ties and they had his smell. Hastily, she shoved them into a bag, thinking that she would take them to the charity shop in Melbury.

She flicked over his books with a feather duster. Under the bookcase she found a cardboard shoebox containing old snapshots. It was covered with dust, and she reflected that it just proved what a rotten housewife she was. Small black and white photographs taken with a Brownie camera, and she squinted at them under the light. Herself and her father, hand in hand, the dogs, Rufus and Rusty, and the house where she was born and spent all her childhood. There was a photograph of her mother, smiling, standing beside Kenneth in his naval uniform. At the bottom of the box she found a brown envelope containing their wedding pictures. Her mother and father, looking young and very happy, and one of Pat, sister of the bride, looking so different and yet unmistakably herself. Olivia thought of that day, so many years ago, when her parents were married.

She looked around at the rather desolate room where her father had spent his last years. He had never complained, but he must have wondered at the twist of fate that landed him there. Could she have prevented it?

From here he had set off to dig his allotment. From

this basement room he had listened for the twins coming back from the village school. Olivia remembered the meals they had shared together, the evenings watching the television after the children had gone to bed. She missed him so much. She knew that he found great happiness in being so close to them all, and perhaps this made up for all the things he had lost. He adored Marigold, that beautiful loving little girl who had sat on his knee, her face against his chest.

Olivia decided to put aside melancholy thoughts and take Spot for a walk. He was asking with his eyes for that particular pleasure, and her reaching for his lead, hanging on a hook in the hall, put him into a frenzy of excitement.

They walked along the path that reminded her of the Muddy Lane in Annesley. The lane led to a village school, and she had walked along it many times with the twins. The muddy lane of the past had always been empty of people, but this lane was not, and she met other walkers, friends, and greetings were exchanged. When a bicycle came into view she put Spot on his lead, for he had the Jack Russell habit of biting at cyclists' ankles.

When she got home and put the key in the lock, the emptiness of the house struck her at once. She was used to the children being away every other weekend, but this was different. By now they would be assembled in the registry office. What would Pippa be wearing on such an important day in her life? Olivia wondered whether Bill, at some point, would remember his marriage with her. She rejected the thought, and wished she had some typing to do; Dominic would have diverted her mind from disturbing imaginings.

Olivia made herself a mug of tea, and sat on the sofa in the bay window of her second-floor sitting room. The lights were coming on in the houses on the opposite side of the road, and she heard sounds of busy people, cars parking in the road, doors slamming and children's voices.

In her solitude, terrible memories came to torment her, familiar foes, and in her anxiety to be rid of them she came to a sudden decision – to go to Marigold's party.

Chapter 24

Stephen saw her arrive. Without realising it he had been looking out for her, but with no feeling of expectation because Marigold had been so certain she would not come. When Olivia entered the room he watched her moving between the people. He was talking to the elderly Mrs Jones, wife of the colonel, but he managed to keep Olivia in sight while she accepted a drink, and then, out of the corner of his eye, he watched her accept a morsel on toast from a plate being handed around by one of the younger guests. When she sat down on the sofa in the window he crossed the room, and sat down beside her.

The thought passed through his mind that she would not know who he was, but when she said, "Hello," it sounded as if she remembered meeting him.

"I'm glad you decided to come," he said.

"Well, it was easy because my children are away, and so I did not have to worry about a baby-sitter."

"I see. Will they be away long, your children?"

"They return tomorrow." She paused, and then said as if in a burst of confidence, "They have been to my husband's wedding today."

He smiled. "You make him sound like a bigamist."

She smiled back. "I never know what to call him to people who do not know his name is Bill. Ex-husband sounds so awful, doesn't it?"

"I suppose it is slightly better than 'my ex'. If you had lots of husbands you could call them my first and my second, and so on . . ."

"I have had just the one."

"And the day he married again cannot help but feel strange?"

She looked at him. "Yes, it is strange."

He went on, "And my guess is, that is the reason you came to Marigold's party."

It was a very personal statement after such a short acquaintance, and he surprised himself by making it. He felt he had reached out to her across the usual barriers of convention, and instantly regretted it because she closed up on him, and looked at her shoes. He decided it was the Englishness of her that attracted him, for by this time he admitted to himself that he found her attractive. Her voice, the way she did her hair, it was a combination only England could produce. She suited Marigold's drawing room.

In an attempt to put her at ease, he said, "Whatever the reason, I'm glad you decided to come."

Politely she asked him about himself. He told her he was a schoolmaster, that his wife had died and that he had two daughters. "Way beyond the baby-sitting stage – in fact, I am a grandfather."

"You are the headmaster of the school where you work?"

"Yes."

"Does that mean that you don't teach any more? You are too busy, just running the school?"

"Not at all," he replied. "I like to keep my hand in with the teaching. I teach two subjects."

"What are they?"

"History and English Literature. They interest me very much, and I do my best to make them interesting to other people as well." How pompous that sounds, he thought.

"I'm sure you succeed." She paused as if in thought, and then spoke impulsively, "I hope you will not think me very silly, but I would like to ask your advice – you see, I have a problem."

He looked startled. "What sort of problem?"

"I don't read. I never have. I read the newspaper every day, but I never read a book."

"That is a problem."

"I don't know why it is. My father was always trying to get me to read, maybe he tried too hard." Saying this made her look worried. "No, that is unfair. It is just that

I never thought of it before, and it didn't bother me. Now he is dead, I wish I had listened to what he said. I feel I have missed out on something valuable."

"There is no doubt about that," said Stephen. "Have you a house without any books? If so, I don't think I would like it very much."

"There are a great many books in my house," she told him, "and they all belonged to my father. I'm ashamed to say I have not read any of them."

"And your children, do they take after their mother or their grandfather in this respect?"

"My father used to read aloud to them when they were small. Yes, the twins like reading, I'm glad to say." She laughed suddenly. "It doesn't matter. I wish I hadn't mentioned it to you. You must think me quite ridiculous. Forget it."

He knew he had to tread carefully. A hint of mockery would discourage her, and he did not want to do that. He noticed the little lines around her eyes, and the fine hairs lying flat against each other in the line of her eyebrows. In one hand she held a glass of Bernard's special party mixture that she had hardly touched, and her other hand lay quietly in her lap. He wanted to put his hand over hers, to feel the soft coolness of it.

It occurred to him that he might be going through some midlife crisis.

He said very seriously, "I think we should treat this as an academic challenge. If reading had been a pleasure for you it would have become an essential part of your existence. For some reason we do not understand, that did not happen. Now you will have to force yourself to read for a certain time each day, thereby proving you can do it. Like learning a new language, the sense of achievement will compensate for the borings bits. Once you have started on this course you must keep to it or you will be lost. I hope the enjoyment will come later. I think you are under the illusion that someone like me finds all reading easy. It is not true – some of the old philosophers are hard going, but there is a moment of enlightenment which makes the studying worth while."

They became aware of Marigold standing in front of them, jug in hand. She addressed Olivia, "Come with me. There are some people I want you to meet."

With a heavy heart Stephen realised that one of them was being rescued. Was it that Marigold had guessed he was delivering one of his small lectures, and had decided to free the victim?" Olivia gave him a fleeting smile, and stood up obediently. He watched her join a group on the other side of the room. The curve of her cheek was faintly pink; she was sensitive to his regard then and the knowledge pleased him.

When it came time for the guests to disperse, he offered to walk home with her. It was dark, and she was alone.

"The Bairds will take her," said Marigold, in command as usual. "They have a car, and live nearby." The Bairds, whose daughter was the baby-sitter, were delighted to give Olivia a lift.

"It is very kind of you," she said, looking at Stephen. "Thank you."

"It is the sort of thing he would suggest," said Marigold, linking her arm with his. "He is a very special person."

"You didn't want to take her home, did you?" she asked anxiously, later, when he was helping her carry the glasses to the kitchen. Perhaps she sensed she had made an error of judgement.

"Of course not. It just seemed the right thing to do."

"That's what I thought." She sounded relieved. "The Bairds were happy to take her. They are a nice couple. What did you think of Olivia, by the way?"

"Charming."

"Yes, but, as I told you, shy. Very shy."

"There is a charm about shy people."

"You sound as if you were quite taken with her." She was always very discerning about human relationships. He detected the interest in her voice.

"It was a coup de foudre," he said lightly.

She glanced at him sharply. "You are joking, of course?"

"Yes, I am," said Stephen firmly. "You seem to forget, Marigold my dear, I am a fusty old schoolmaster, and please do not give me a romantic image that does not suit me."

"Such things do happen," she pointed out.

"I'm afraid being a writer of fiction has made you fanciful," was Stephen's retort. "Now, where is Bernard? Isn't he going to help with the washing up?"

"He has gone to bed."

"Oh, God! Then we will have to do it on our own."
Half the glasses they stacked in the machine, the rest they
washed by hand.

While he was drying the glasses, he asked her, "What
is your favourite book?"

Her hands in the sudsy water, she thought for a
moment. "The old desert island question: what book
would you take?" It was the sort of game she liked to play.
"I think *Persuasion*. I've always loved it. It is such a gentle
book. I suppose it has not got the wit of *Pride and
Prejudice* but I find the characters in it very endearing.
Sweet Anne Elliot most of all. . ."

"Yes," he said thoughtfully, wiping a plate with a
sodden teacloth. "*Persuasion*. Thank you, Marigold."

When they shut the kitchen door at last, they went
back into the sitting room, and Marigold rattled the
poker at the remains of the fire until she produced a
small blaze. Then she poured out two good glasses of
whisky, one for him and one for herself. "I can't abide
the terrible concoction Bernard makes. We must have a
decent drink before we go to bed."

He settled down in one of the unbelievably
comfortable armchairs – even the threadbare covers were
soft to the touch and there were cushions in all the right
places. He stretched his long legs, and thought, what a
lovely house this is, and how I should love to live here.
He said aloud, "You and Bernard are lucky to have this
place. I envy you very much."

"Well, we can't live for ever," said Marigold practically. She was not sitting down yet, but peering along the bookshelves. "When we die, or move into a home for old folk, perhaps you can buy it. You may have retired by then, and will be looking for somewhere to live."

"I doubt if I could afford it," Stephen replied, but it was a thought to latch on to, a dream.

Marigold found the book she was seeking, and sat in the armchair opposite him, turning the pages. "I have not read it for years. It is like meeting an old friend again. I am looking for a particular passage I like – yes, here it is. Do you remember when Admiral Croft said to Anne Elliot, '*There, take my arm; that's right; I do not feel comfortable unless I have a woman there.*' What a gentleman! There is a lot of Admiral Croft in your make-up, Stephen."

He laughed, "Oh well, I suppose it would be too much to hope that you would think I am like the gallant Captain Wentworth. Here, give me the book, and I will read bits of it before I go to sleep."

"I thought I would!" she said.

"Very well."

She handed him the book. "You have it," she said.

The fire became ashes and they finished their drinks. "It was a splendid party," he told her, "and I enjoyed it immensely. However, tomorrow I return. There is a great deal of work to be done before the beginning of term."

When he was in his room, he opened the window wide and leaned out. He smelled the sweet night scents of Marigold's garden. He was always sorry to leave this peaceful happy house. He was too tired to look at the book and fell asleep immediately, his last thoughts being of the house and garden and what he intended doing on the following day.

After breakfast, during which he and Marigold spent an agreeable time persecuting Bernard for skulking off to bed and avoiding the washing up, Stephen said goodbye to his dear friends. They stood together in front of Platt Cottage, waving to him. Marigold called out, "Come again soon!"

When he got to Melbury he stopped at a bookshop and purchased a copy of *Persuasion* by Jane Austen, a hardback as a paperback copy would not suit his purpose. Then, feeling an absurd sense of guilt, he turned the car and headed back to Tapworth. Driving through the village he hoped he would not see Marigold. He did not. He rang the doorbell of Olivia's house, thinking, she is probably not at home and this is a waste of time. When she came to the door, she looked surprised but pleased to see him.

"Marigold told me you lived in the last house," he explained.

He followed her up narrow stairs which led to the sitting room, From the front windows there was a view of tops of trees and roofs of the houses opposite and, between them in the distance he could see the narrow ribbon of the river.

"It's such a good idea having a sitting room at this level," he said.

"I think so."

The room was unpretentious and cosy, and a dog greeted him with friendly exuberance. Stephen handed over his gift, still in the paper bag, which she accepted with delight.

He assumed his schoolmaster's role. "She writes with great simplicity," he said, turning the pages. "For instance, here on page forty-four: '*Anne walked in a sort of desolate tranquillity to the Lodge*'. Desolate tranquillity! I think I am right in saying that you understand that sentence all too well? Look out for the wonderful phrases. Read the book slowly and carefully."

She promised she would do as he asked. Please, would he write on the flyleaf of the book? She fetched a pen and he wrote in his neat scholarly hand, '*For Olivia Randall from Stephen France*' and the date.

She offered him refreshment — a cup of tea or coffee perhaps? He refused, and told her he was in a hurry. He almost ran down the stairs in front of her, so haunted was he by the feeling that Marigold might appear suddenly.

On the ground floor, to the right of the small hall, Olivia opened a door and said, "This was my father's room."

They walked into the room, and she pointed to the shelves, from floor to ceiling, filling up one wall. "These are the books I was telling you about."

He looked along the shelves and fingered one of them. "*Persuasion*," he said. She noticed his strong hands and blunt fingers.

"I prefer to have my own copy."

He smiled at her.

"It is so sad," she went on, looking around the room. "He was a doctor, the old-fashioned kind, dedicated to his work and loved by everyone. When he retired he started writing a book about Dr Edward Jenner, a person with whom he felt an affinity – he was a country doctor like himself. He spent hours on research and used to type the book on his old typewriter – there it is in the corner. But the manuscript has disappeared. I have searched and searched, and now I am beginning to think he may have destroyed all that work."

"Perhaps he lost heart when you moved," Stephen suggested. "Sometimes old people do not react well to a change in environment." He thought it a very bleak room. Not much sun could penetrate the small ground-level window. He could imagine the weariness of spirit that might afflict the occupant of such a room, which was very different to the cheerful atmosphere of the area above.

"He lived in a flat attached to our house," Olivia told him, "that is, the house where we used to live. It was a nice flat, and Daddy loved the garden. Moving here must have been a terrible wrench for him. I suppose, as you say, he did not have the heart to finish the book, and probably put it on a bonfire on his allotment."

She looked so sorrowful and bewildered he longed to put his arm around her, but of course that was out of the question. Instead he said, "May I drive over one day and take you out, for lunch perhaps?"

"I'd like that very much. It would be best after Bill returns from his honeymoon." She saw the humour of that remark, and gave a little laugh. "I imagine he will have the children to stay the weekend after he returns, so Saturday in three weeks' time would be lovely. If that suits you, of course."

It seemed a long time away, but he had to be content with the arrangement.

She stood in the doorway, waiting for him to drive off. She was far too polite to go in and shut the door before he was gone. She looked at his grey curly head bent over the steering wheel of his car, and then she saw that he was searching for something in the glove compartment, a little box of cigars. He took one out, lit it and then raised his hand in a gesture of farewell.

When Olivia went back into the house it felt different. A man had invaded the structured composed existence she had set up for herself and the children. There was a very faint smell of cigar smoke in the sitting room; it must be on his clothes. She picked up the book he had given her, and read the inscription. She was amazed that a man like him should have gone to so much trouble for her. And he had asked her to have lunch with him!

She sat in the window seat, thinking about what had happened. Soon she would leave to fetch the children from Mulgrave Terrace, as Bill and Pippa were going abroad on an afternoon flight. They would tell her as much as they wanted to about the previous day's activities, and she resolved not to question them closely. Any interest she had in that direction had vanished.

She went into her bedroom, which was on the top floor at the back of the house. Her clothes hung in a built-in cupboard, a cheap affair with sliding doors that were always sticking. She took out all her clothes and flung them on the bed. Then she inspected each garment before putting it back on the rail. She disliked them all, and decided it would be nice to buy something new for a change.

She sat at the dressing table and examined her face in the mirror. Then she experimented with her hair, pinning it up on top of her head, then letting it fall loose again and pushing it behind her ears. She did not like her hair.

When the front door bell rang, startling her, she thought for a moment he had returned, but it was Marigold, bringing with her the handwritten text of the latest chapter of the new Dominic Platt mystery.

Chapter 25

One evening towards the end of the third week Stephen could not resist the impulse to telephone Olivia. She had been much on his mind since their last meeting. He hoped she would answer the telephone herself but the voice, although sounding like hers, was a younger voice, that of her son. "Who is it, please?"

"Stephen France."

He heard a lot of shouting in the background. "Mother! It's for you! Stephen France. Mummy, hurry up, Stee-phen France!"

"Hello, Stephen."

She sounded breathless, but then he remembered that was the way she always sounded. He felt an unreasonable delight in hearing that quick uncertain voice again.

"How are you?" he asked.

"I'm fine, and I have finished the book, so I'm ready for the second lesson."

"Good, but, more important, did you enjoy it?"

"Very much. I've been busy too, working on Dominic Platt. I'm very fond of Dominic."

"He's a delightful fellow," he agreed. "Do you know that one of the books is dedicated to me?"

"Yes, I do know that."

"Of course you do, and I expect Marigold will dedicate the next one to you." He knew it was her intention, so he was safe in saying it.

"Really, do you think so? My name is in the Acknowledgements, and that is exciting."

He thought he should give her a reason for telephoning. "This Saturday is the day we planned to go out. You haven't forgotten?"

"Of course not."

"Well, as you are now so conversant with Jane Austen and *Persuasion*, I thought we could go to Lyme Regis for the day. Does that appeal to you?"

"I'd like that very much," she said, and sounded as if she meant it. "I've never been there, and perhaps we can walk along the Cobb and see where Louisa Musgrove had her fall."

The schoolmaster in him was gratified with her reply as it bore out her statement that she had read the book. However, when he said, "I'm impressed!" he was afraid he sounded patronising. He was conscious of the big gap in their ages, and did not realise that his slightly pedantic manner appealed to her because it reminded her of Kenneth.

He arranged to meet her at her house at ten o'clock on Saturday morning. When he arrived he was momentarily nonplussed to find three children there, and Olivia explained that they were waiting for their father to collect them for the weekend. After the introductions, they sat on the sofa in a row, a small suitcase at the feet of each one, regarding him with silent interest.

Stephen was used to girls (he had two daughters) and to boys (he was the headmaster of a boys' public school) so he felt fairly confident he could deal with the situation. He decided George was his best bet, so he talked to him about cricket.

George played junior village cricket, and very soon Stephen was listening to a long drawn out story about how the opposing team had not played fair. Impatiently Claire interrupted him to ask Stephen if there were any girls at his school.

"No girls at present."

"Why?"

"You may well ask, but it is going to change, you can be sure of that." He felt things were going well, they were talking at least, and he had not given anything away.

Only when the smallest of the three, Marigold, demanded: "Where are you taking my Mummy?" did he condescend to sink to her level, on one knee, and tell her solemnly: "I promise to look after your Mummy."

"I forgot to ask you," said Olivia, "do you mind if Spot comes too?"

"No, I was expecting Spot to come with us."

"Look after Spot," Marigold ordered, fixing him with her large liquid eyes. Stephen remembered his own daughters at a similar early age and how he had thought them delightful, but this child was unique. He wondered whether she would fulfil her promise of beauty when she became a woman. He thought Olivia might have looked like this when she was a child.

They all heard the arrival of the car, and Olivia went downstairs to let Bill in. He was introduced to Stephen who saw a handsome tanned man with an engaging smile. Having just returned from his honeymoon in Portugal he was the picture of good health and spirits. All these jovial characters went clattering down the stairs and into the car, leaving behind them two quiet people and a dog. Stephen could not help thinking how strange it was that he had suddenly been catapulted into a life containing small children and ex-husbands, and the fact that Marigold and Bernard were so close at hand made it even more unreal.

Stephen knew from the outset that the day would be a success. He opened the sunshine roof so that they could see blue sky was above them, and the soft warm air blew into the car. Spot sat on the back seat quivering with excitement. For the first part of the journey he barked at every dog they passed, then he settled down, chin on front paws, and slept.

They talked in a companionable way, about his grown-up daughters, about the loud music children played, about the fact that he was a grandfather and about the advantages and disadvantages of being a headmaster. They talked about Marigold and Bernard, and what special people they were, and about the beauty of England, especially on such a perfect day.

They had their first glimpse of the sea shortly after driving into Dorset. From the top of a steep hill they saw a dappled streak of blue, then through the village of Charmouth, flanked on either side by thatched cottages, and into Lyme. Stephen drove slowly through the narrow town, past the place where it seemed as if the sea would encroach on to the main street, and up the hill to a municipal car park.

Olivia and Stephen took Spot for a walk along the path that leads to the Undercliff, where there were stretches of green grass for him to run. He was in heaven, darting this way and that way, barking at the seagulls, and bounding back from time to time to convey his enjoyment to them. There was a nearly vertical path leading to Monmouth Beach, and Olivia put him on the lead, holding him firmly as they slithered down and then walked the length of the Cobb.

Looking at the precipitous steps known as Granny's Teeth, leading to the lower level, Olivia said: "I can understand Louisa toppling off a place like that, especially wearing a long skirt."

"She was showing off, that was the trouble," said Stephen.

Although it was a sunny day there was a strong wind. A handful of people were walking along the Cobb, and some of them smiled at Spot, straining at the leash and buffeted by the wind, with that indulgent interest in dogs peculiar to the English. When they reached halfway the spray from the waves spotted their faces. They persevered to the end, where there was a pile of great rocks sitting in the water. They looked back at the town with the houses tumbling down the hill, and then to the left, across the sea to the Golden Cap sparkling in the sun.

Stephen took Olivia's arm and held it tightly to his side. It was a luminous moment, and Olivia expressed both their feelings when she said impulsively: "I'm so happy!"

He did not reply. They went back to the car and put Spot into it, opening all the windows a crack so that he had fresh air. Then they walked along the front, past the pink washed thatched cottages and to the hotel, where they were able to get a very late lunch.

They were both hungry, and Stephen watched indulgently as Olivia tucked into a big lunch with obvious pleasure. He could not bear women who picked at their food. She had said she was happy, and she looked it. There was a glow about her that he had not seen before.

"I am so glad to have come to this place," she said. "I have heard about it before." She went on to tell him about Nigel Benton who collected fossils at Lyme Regis. "I don't think he came here very much after he was married," she said. "He married Bill's stepsister, Alice."

Stephen recalled Marigold's story of her first meeting with Olivia. "That was your friend who was killed in a car accident?" As soon as he said the words, he knew he had made a blunder. A strange look passed over her face, almost of fear.

"How do you know about Alice?" she asked.

He knew he must put matters right. "Marigold told me that you were very sad when she visited you in hospital after Marigold was born. She said it was because someone you knew, called Alice, had died in a tragic accident."

Her face cleared. "Of course. I remember talking to Marigold about her. I was surprised when you mentioned her name because I never do – in fact the last time I spoke of her was in the hospital, four years ago."

He said nothing, waiting for her to tell him more, which she did.

"Alice was at a secretarial college in London with me, and it was through her I met Bill. I went to stay at her stepfather's house in Cornwall. The visit was a bit of a disaster because I got 'flu, but Bill being there made all the difference. Alice and I lost touch for over ten years, mainly because Bill did not like her, although there were other complications as well. We met again when she and her husband, Nigel, moved to Pennel Bridge which was only a few miles from where we lived."

"And being good friends you picked up the threads as if there had never been a separation?" suggested Stephen.

Olivia paused. "Well, no . . . as a matter of fact, she was not a good friend at all. She pretended to be, which made it a hundred times worse. So many people were deeply affected by her death, her husband, Bill and my father . . ."

"And you, most of all?"

"I think that's true. I was very fond of her, and it was a long time before I realised what a devious person she was. She gathered people around her, and then manipulated them to do things that were against their nature. It was a frightening talent she possessed."

"It sounds a wicked one to me," said Stephen. "People like that usually have a receptive character to work on, otherwise they cannot succeed in moulding and influencing a life."

"I was that character," Olivia admitted, "although I was not the only one to be drawn into the web."

He could understand her being malleable in such a situation, but her husband and father? He decided that a woman like that would use sex to subjugate a man. "So your sinful friend got her just desserts," he said thoughtfully, "or do you think that is going too far in the scheme of things, presuming there is some divine power which casts down the unworthy in one blow? There are many cases in history which support that theory."

"No, I do not believe in that power," Olivia answered, "nor do I believe that anyone, however, bad, deserves a violent death. We do not burn witches any more, and the law does not condemn people because they destroy relationships and tell lies."

"The law does not," agreed Stephen, "but you are telling me about an accident, a straightforward quirk of fate, not an act of revenge."

She was silent, head bent down, the colour gradually suffusing her face. An idea occurred to him. "She was alone in the car?"

"Yes."

He could see that she was upset, and he chose not to speak of the matter any more. In later years, when he thought about the conversation, he wished he had probed further. The wine she had drunk at lunch and the happiness of the day had given her courage. Even at that stage, she knew she was loved, and she yearned to tell him everything that had happened, so that her troubled mind could be free at last.

But he turned away from what he could see was a sensitive topic, and they talked of other things, until it was time for him to pay the bill, and for them to return to the car.

Chapter 26

They stopped on the way home to climb the steep hill to the Gold Cap. Eventually, very puffed, they reached the summit and were rewarded by a spectacular view. On one side, far below them, was the sea, a stretch of dark blue with little flecks of white on the surface. On the other sides were fields, disappearing into the misty distance with only one small white farmstead to be seen.

By this time the wind had increased in strength and it blew their hair flat against their heads and stung their faces. Olivia pulled Spot away from the edge, beyond which there was a sheer drop to the beach beneath.

Stephen said, "For God's sake hold on to him. I don't want to have to tell little Marigold that he disappeared over that."

The stumbled down the hill in the gathering dusk, and Stephen held Olivia's hand. The drive back to

Tapworth was in darkness. Spot in the back slept the sleep of the exhausted. They were quiet, thinking their own thoughts. Stephen was regretting the day was nearly over, and wondering how he could ask her to go out with him again.

"May we do this again, sometime?" he asked at last, breaking the silence.

"Yes, please."

There was a pause, and then he said, "I suppose I am courting you, and I feel a bloody fool, I can tell you. I am far too old and set in my ways for this sort of thing."

"Courting is a nice old-fashioned word," Olivia replied serenely, "and I like it. And, as no one has taken the slightest interest in me for years, it is a new experience for me too."

"If you want me to stop," went on Stephen, "just say the word. Now is the time to tell me honestly if there are things about me you do not like – then I'll not bother you any more."

"There is nothing, I promise you."

"I smoke," he said, "little cigars. I gave up cigarettes after a hard struggle. In fact, I should very much like one of my little cigars now, if you don't object. I'll open the window."

"Go ahead," she said, "but I'm glad you have given up cigarettes, because they are bad for your health."

When they arrived at her house in Tapworth, she asked him to supper. "I'll cook you an omelette." After a moment's hesitation, he accepted the invitation.

She walked around the little house, clicking on the lights, drawing the curtains across the windows. Then she lit the gas fire encased in an Adam style carved wooden surround. "When we first came to live here," she told him, "the previous owner had removed the gas fire. There was an open grate, so I lit a fire. The room filled with black smoke, and I had to call the fire brigade. Later, I got a letter from the council informing me that the chimneys in these houses are not suitable for real fires. The fireplace, like the rest of the house, is completely phoney!"

He watched her cook the omelettes on the kitchen stove. The kitchen area was a very small space, and there was nowhere to sit. He leaned against the door that he noticed had a hole in it.

"George did that," she explained, "with his foot, when he was in a temper. The doors are so flimsy – egg-box doors."

"If I'm getting in your way standing here," he said, "I'll move, but I'd rather stay."

She smiled at him. "You stay," she said.

He liked her little kitchen; it was so basic – the cheap cupboards crammed with bottles and tins, a small electric stove and a refrigerator, the latter adorned with Marigold's artistic efforts stuck on with blue tack. It reminded him of a flat he had shared when he was a student at university, in the days before kitchens were all stainless steel and shiny surfaces.

"What sort of kitchen has Bill got?" he asked. He had to admit to a feeling of curiosity about Bill.

"Oh, very smart. He had it done up when he moved into the house in Melbury. Pine cupboards, tiled floor and a big pine table."

"His new wife may want to change it," said Stephen wisely.

"I expect so." There was no resentment in her voice.

They sat in front of the fire, eating omelettes, crusty bread and cheese off two trays. Olivia had given him a bottle of red wine to open, and she reached for it to refill their glasses. He stopped her. "Don't give me any more, please. Remember, I have a long drive ahead of me."

"You could stay here," she suggested, "in George's room."

"I don't think that is a good idea. George might not like it."

"He wouldn't mind." But she did not insist.

Afterwards he was to maintain that he never had a chance. "After such a short acquaintance too!" he told her, and she replied, "I did not want to waste any time. Time is so precious."

Now she said to him, "Choose a book for me before you go." So when he got to the bottom of the stairs he turned into what had once been Kenneth's room. He looked along the rows of books, trying to decide which one she should read next. Bronte? Trollope? Hardy? It was a difficult choice and he was not thinking clearly. He was conscious of her hand near his arm, her hair almost brushing his face as he bent to read the titles. Eventually he picked something completely different, touching and humorous – Nancy Mitford's *The Pursuit of Love*.

When they reached the front door she struggled with the latch, he attempted to help her but she stopped him by putting her arms around his neck. "Thank you for a wonderful day," she said.

He kissed her. He had not intended to behave in such a precipitous fashion, but it was too late to slow things down, not that he wanted to do that. He thought she said, "Don't go," but he could not be sure. One thing he knew for certain, he would stay. They stumbled up the draughty stairs and into the warm sitting room. They were completely alone in the house. There were no children asleep in beds to awake suddenly and disturb them. Hours and hours stretched ahead of them to fill with their needs and desires. They did not tear their clothes off in frenzied haste, as people do in movies. They removed them slowly in the glow of the fire having first turned off the lights.

Later, much later, as they lay in Olivia's big bed, Stephen thought, wonderingly, she is passionate. He lay awake with her sleeping form pressed close to him, and pondered on all the lonely years when no woman had loved and cared for him in this way, and he felt fortunate indeed.

Chapter 27

Shortly after her one hundred and first birthday Hilda died. Pat telephoned Olivia to tell her the news, and neither of them could truthfully say it was a sad event; only the association with the past gave it poignancy.

"I'd like to come to the funeral," said Olivia at once.

"I was hoping you would say that," replied Pat, "then we can have lunch together at Fortnums." They often met for lunch, Olivia travelling to London by train, returning in the late afternoon.

"Thank God, that's over," said Pat, heaving herself into a chair at the restaurant when they finally got a table. She was fatter than ever and the slightest exertion made her breathless, but she still managed to look stylish, more stylish than most of the women having lunch in that elegant place. She looked at Olivia and thought how much she had improved since knowing Stephen. She looked rounder and more relaxed, and had the special glow of a woman who is loved.

"Thank God in more ways than one," continued Pat. "She died peacefully and without pain, despite the arthritis in her joints. It was old age that got her in the end."

As she spoke, an elderly waitress handed her the menu. "Shall we plump for the usual?"

"Yes, let's."

"People can go on for too long," said Pat, "and my precious Hilda did just that. I was her slave during the last years of her life. Did you notice the words the vicar used this morning? '*Well done, thou good and faithful servant*' – very apt, for Hilda was good and faithful to me, and I loved her very much. But . . ." she sighed, "the strange thing is, darling, the roles were reversed and at the end I was her servant. 'Do this, dear,' and 'Do that, dear' from morning 'til night."

Olivia laughed. It was so funny when you thought about it, the old retainer taking the reins from the mistress.

Pat warmed to her theme. "There was no rest from 'Take me for a drive in the car, dear,' or 'Can I have a nice bit of fish for my supper, dear?'" Pat dissolved into laughter. "It was a hard haul."

The church had been almost empty that morning, any friends of Hilda being long since dead. Only the vicar, Pat and Olivia, and an old man who turned up unexpectedly and introduced himself to the two women as Hilda's nephew.

"Do you think he hoped we would ask him to have lunch with us?" Pat asked. "Hilda never mentioned his existence. He was so weird! I think he must have been an impostor."

They were able to accept Hilda's death with resigned flippancy, but Olivia knew that Pat was aware of a real loss, a loving and stable influence that had been taken from her. For Pat, it was comforting to have Olivia's presence on such a day. It was pleasant, sitting in Fortnums, sipping cold white wine and eating delicious scrambled eggs laced with slivers of smoked salmon.

"How is Stephen?" Pat asked. She liked Stephen, had met him several times during the five years Olivia had known him. She knew that he wanted Olivia to be his wife, and she was one of the few people who approved of her niece's decision not to marry him. They spent as much time as possible together, weekends and holidays at Easter and in the summer when the children were with Bill and Pippa. It was Pat's belief that the reason they were so happy and compatible was that marriage had not stultified their romantic feelings for each other, and enforced absences had strengthened their love.

"He's fine," said Olivia in answer to the question, "at least he is not quite so fine at present. He has hurt his back. He doesn't know how he did it, and it is very painful. They are short staffed at school, and he has been very busy. I think he's tired."

Marigold Armitage did not share Pat's views on marriage. Shortly after their visit to Lyme Regis, Stephen talked openly to Marigold. He told her that since his first meeting with Olivia he had felt a bond with her, and he was sure she felt the same way about him. Sadly, however, she had refused to marry him.

"I can understand that marriage is unimportant these days," he said, "but my case is different. A headmaster needs a wife, not a mistress."

"I don't think Olivia has any controversial views on marriage," Marigold told him. "There must be another reason. When her husband came to see me, shortly after I met her, he was very anxious she should return to him. He is a likable fellow, and, at that time, it was obvious that she still cared for him. Their children were three good reasons for her to try again at the marriage. He had hurt her, there is no doubt about that, but I think she has a forgiving nature. When I questioned her about her refusal to make a new start she said the lack of trust between them was too big a burden to bear."

Stephen suddenly had a picture in his mind of Olivia at the hotel in Lyme, her lowered head and flushed face. "Her friend was killed in a car accident," he said thoughtfully. "Alice. Do you think Alice might have something to do with it?"

"Oh, no," replied Marigold decidedly, "she loved Alice. When I went to see her in hospital, after little Marigold was born, she wept for her."

Stephen was too happy to allow any shadow to fall

across his path. He was aware that there was an area in Olivia's life that was out of his reach, as if enclosed by a high wall, and he hoped one day to break down the barrier. In the meantime, he had discovered in Olivia a woman no one else knew existed, not even, he suspected, the man who had been her husband. The years of loneliness had taught him not to take risks with good fortune. He urged Marigold to let the matter rest.

But it was not in Marigold's nature to say nothing. She spoke frankly to Olivia. "Stephen is a fine man and he loves you. He will give you a security you do not have at present. The children like him and that is an advantage. From his point of view he needs you – parents like to see a charming wife hovering in the background. You would have a lovely home, and the role of a headmaster's wife would suit you perfectly."

Olivia's answer was enigmatic. "I can't be completely honest with him," she said, "and he deserves complete honesty."

"That is nonsense, my dear," replied Marigold irritably. She did not understand her at all. Could it be that she still loved Bill and could not contemplate marrying anyone else? She seemed so happy with Stephen, and it was hard to believe that Bill, apparently comfortably settled with his Pippa, could still have a hold on her.

When Stephen saw Olivia shortly after this conversation with Marigold he sensed at once, so in tune were they, that something had upset her. He put his arms around her. "Don't worry, darling. She means well, but she does not understand." He forbore saying that he, like Marigold, did not understand.

Pat and Marigold had never met, but they had something in common: they both loved Olivia. Pat felt that Marigold must be a kindred spirit because she was a woman, like herself, who had achieved something on her own. Also, she was a great admirer of Dominic Platt. "Any woman who can invent a man like that must be all right."

Now, sitting in the stately surroundings of the Fountain Room Olivia told Pat of the anxieties she and Stephen shared about Marigold Armitage. He, who had always appreciated her sharp intellect, began to think that something was slipping away from her. He mentioned it to Olivia who was typing the latest Dominic Platt mystery, and she agreed strange things were happening.

For instance, one day Marigold had forgotten the name of Dominic's disabled son who was so helpful in the investigations. He had been at his father's side through all the books, mentioned on almost every page among thousands of pages. "Come on, Olivia, what is his name?"

"Francis."

"Of course, Francis."

Marigold asked Olivia to fill in bits of the puzzle that were eluding her.

"The professor was on holiday when the murder took place," Olivia told her. "Remember? He was not really away, but everyone thought he was."

"Why did the professor say he had gone on holiday?" Marigold wanted to know.

"He pretended it was because his daughter had fallen out with her lover, that's the whole point. He managed to deceive the police, when all the time . . ." It was hopeless, and all Olivia could do was to put matters right when she typed the story.

Stephen spoke to Bernard of their fears, and characteristically Bernard did not mince matters. "The old girl is losing her marbles," he said.

Tragically, Marigold was aware of what was happening to her. The terrible threat of senility haunted her day and night, and she did not know how to face the enemy, except by trying to fight it and the strain of doing this made her unreasonable and irritable.

"You see," said Olivia patiently, "Dominic suspects Lady Merriman, but does not reveal his suspicions."

"I know that," cried Marigold, provoked, "you don't have to tell me the plot of my own book."

"But the trouble is that she does not know the plot any more," Olivia told Pat.

"So *The Italian Legacy* is mostly being written by you?"

"Of course not. It does not require much brain to correct the inaccuracies. Marigold writes a very comprehensive synopsis before she starts a book. It's all there for her to work on, she is about three quarters of the way through now."

"Oh dear," said Pat, "it is so much sadder than dear Hilda dying of old age. That poor woman."

"And it is particularly hard on Bernard," said Olivia. "He has always played second fiddle to Marigold, and now it is the other way round."

"Is she still writing?"

"She is having a break at present. She often has a rest before she finishes a book, so it is nothing unusual. The publishers have learnt to be patient."

"That means you can go away without feeling guilty," said Pat, "which brings me to something I want to discuss with you. I need a holiday. You know what I have been through during the last two years, now it is time for a change of scene. Not for long though, I don't like to leave London for too long. We have a relation, Olivia, a cousin who Joan and I knew as children. She married and went to live in Vancouver – now she is a widow and a grandmother. For years she has been asking me to go and stay with her, and this time I'm going to accept the invitation. But I don't want to go alone. I want you to go with me."

Olivia stumbled over her words. "I don't think . . ."

Pat interrupted her. "I shall pay for everything. You will not need to put your hand in your pocket unless it is to buy presents for the children. No, don't worry," when Olivia started to protest, "I can afford it, and my reason for asking you is a selfish one. I want your company."

"It would have to be when the children are with Bill and Pippa," said Olivia thoughtfully, "that is the beginning of the Easter holidays, and, of course, Stephen likes to see me then."

"I shall be taking you away from Stephen for two weeks only, and I am sure he will understand. A fortnight is long enough for me, I assure you. We'll stay in my cousin's home in Vancouver for a week, and then we'll travel by train across the Rockies and visit places like Banff and Lake Louise."

Olivia smiled. "It sounds wonderful."

"What about the dog? What happens if you all go away?" Pat had given them the dog, but now, unreasonably, regarded it as an encumbrance.

"Oh, Mary Chalmers is always happy to look after Spot. I don't know what I'd do without Mary."

Pat was paying the bill, and Olivia was murmuring words of thanks when a five-pound note was shoved into her hand. "For George."

"Oh, come now, you can't give to George and not to the girls." Olivia made as if to give the money back.

"I know, I know," Pat was already rummaging in her wallet for two more fivers. "You can't change me," she said apologetically. "The male child will always be the important one to me."

"Just as well you did not have any children," retorted Olivia with spirit. "They would probably all have been girls, and a great disappointment to you."

Chapter 28

Stephen came to the airport to see them off. By this time, Olivia was beginning to wish she had never agreed to go on the holiday. Although Stephen had encouraged her to accept Pat's offer, she knew that he must be hiding his disappointment that she was not spending the time with him. In the five years they had known each other they had always been together when the children were with Bill and Pippa.

Pat, on the other hand, was in good spirits. She was clad in a voluminous cape that made her look even more majestic and imposing than usual, and around her neck dangled an enormous silver cross on a chain. "My spiritual insurance during the flight," she told them.

Considering she was only going away for two weeks she had a great deal of luggage. Olivia had managed to get everything in one case.

"I wish I could help with these," said Stephen wearily surveying all the suitcases. "I feel such a fool." He was walking in the way people walk when they have back problems; neck thrust forward, small agonising steps.

"I'm so sorry," said Pat, noticing, and suddenly anxious.

On the plane, as soon as the air hostess appeared with the trolley, she ordered two large brandies for herself and Olivia. "I'm terrified of flying," she admitted, "and the only thing to do is to get half-drunk."

Olivia accepted the drink gratefully. She felt she should not be abandoning her familiar world, now unimportant, infinitesimal, somewhere beneath her feet. She knew what it meant to have a heavy heart, her heart felt like a stone in her chest. She was trapped in a steel compartment, there was no escape, but, unlike Pat, it was not being in the air that made her afraid. A nameless terror possessed her, and, looking out of the window by her side at the unreal clouds floating past, her eyes filled with tears.

"You are worried about Stephen, aren't you?" said Pat, understanding at once. "He does not look too good, I admit, but backs are hell. By the time you return he will be as right as rain."

"He is going to see a physiotherapist while I'm away," Olivia told her, slightly comforted.

"Well, there you are . . ." Pat knew about Olivia and her doubts and apprehensions. "Relax, and get as much as you can out of this trip. It's a great opportunity for both of us."

Olivia came to a determined decision to follow Pat's advice. She was being so generous, paying for everything; it would be unfair if her enjoyment was marred by Olivia's anxieties. As she sipped the brandy, which gradually gave her a warm sense of well-being and optimism, she reflected that she had always exaggerated difficulties that came her way. Instead of being realistic and facing up to them, she had made compromises. Her real battles had been with herself and her feelings. Stephen had taught her not to fear happiness, had made her understand it was not a delusion, not a confidence trick that must eventually bring disillusionment. He was thankful for his own happiness, gloried in it, and told Olivia to do the same. She owed it to him not to feel uneasy.

She wrote to him from Vancouver.

Just returned from a walk on the beach which is a short distance from here. It is not like an English beach – the sand is dry and grey and scattered with odd-shaped pieces of driftwood that have been stripped of bark by the sea.

Pat and I are staying in the smart part of Vancouver, and my walk along the beach took me past some very opulent looking houses. I wish you could see the gardens of these places, so neat, I think every owner must employ a full-time gardener. There are banks of rhododendrons and azaleas, the most brilliant colours you can imagine. Although the climate in this part of Canada is like our own, unpredictable, everything growing here seems more lush and luxuriant than at home. There is a wisteria covering the house where we are staying that puts Marigold's wisteria to shame, and you know how we always think that is so splendid.

Yesterday, we were invited to one of these grand houses, and when I commented on its beauty the lady owner said, "I hope it is like an English home". This appears to be the criterion, and I could not help being amused when I thought of my shabby little house in Tapworth.

Our hostess is charming and kind, and I hope she is enjoying having us to stay. She is inclined to be a bit bossy, and Pat is clearly irritated. They are too alike, that is the trouble, and I have my usual 'pig in the middle' role. We move on soon to Banff, and I will write to you from there.

You would like this country; it has a nice English feel about it. I have never been to the States but I imagine it is completely different. We at home are inclined to put them in the same bracket, as they are neighbours. All the time, I wish you were here sharing this experience with me. I miss you, and I love your letters, but do not write again to this address. I shall be home soon.

Don't laugh – I am reading Gone with the Wind. *Pat bought me a copy and I cart it around in a string bag. I see looks of amazement when I produce it, because it is so heavy and because I am a rare being who has not read it years ago.*

Please look after your precious self, and I hope the treatment for your back is doing you good. I love you always. Olivia.'

They went to Banff where they stayed at the Banff Springs Hotel, dark, imposing and luxurious. Pat and Olivia shared a room looking out to Mount Rundle. The air outside the oppressively hot hotel was sharp and cold, and there were flurries of snow even at that time of the year. On they went to the Chateau Lake Louise where they sat on a sunny balcony overlooking the enchanting lake. Then to Calgary by bus, a wind buffeted city where they had a meal in a slowly revolving restaurant before, feeling slightly sick, they boarded the plane for London.

The first person Olivia saw when she and Pat emerged from the customs bay at Heathrow was Stephen. He was leaning on the rail, looking for her. Oh God, she thought, he is dying. It was a spontaneous terrible thought that she dismissed instantly.

Silently, she removed her suitcase from the trolley that she and Pat had shared. Pat was going to get a taxi to Queen's Gate, and when it came time to say goodbye they kissed, and Olivia whispered, "Thank you." Pat started checking her luggage, fussing with her cloak in an attempt to hide the compassion in her face.

When Olivia and Stephen reached his car in the car park, she carrying her suitcase, he did not protest when she got into the driver's seat. Sitting beside her, it was evident he was in pain although he did his best to disguise it. She wondered how he had managed to make the journey to the airport.

He said, "Did you get my letter telling you that I have been staying with Bernard and Marigold?"

"No."

"Bernard knew an excellent physiotherapist in Melbury, so it was convenient for me to stay at Platt Cottage. Also, I think it was a cri de coeur from Bernard as Marigold is getting more and more disorientated, and the poor old chap doesn't know how to cope with it on his own."

"All this has happened in two weeks?"

"We can't manage without you, darling."

"And your back? It doesn't seem to be much better."

"I've had an X-ray, I'll tell you about it later. I should get the results tomorrow."

"You are not going to Marigold's house tonight," said Olivia firmly. "You are staying with me."

He agreed. "Until the children return." He never stayed at the house when they were there. He always treated her children with great consideration, and it was to his credit that, despite the headmaster's image and the appropriation of their mother's affection which until he appeared they regarded as entirely their own, they were fond of him. He was consistent, even-tempered and interested in what they had to say.

Olivia and Stephen had a bad night. Stephen's back made it impossible for him to find a comfortable position, and he had difficulty in breathing. Olivia propped him up with pillows. The passion they had known in the past seemed very far away.

In the early hours of the next morning Olivia fell asleep at last, exhausted by the travelling and the stress of the homecoming. When she awoke she saw that Stephen was sitting in the chair by the window of her bedroom. She got out of bed, and knelt beside him. "All right, darling?"

"Fine. I did not want to disturb you."

"When do you know the results of the X-ray?"

"This morning. I have an appointment at the hospital." He took her hand. "Olivia, I must tell you that this is the result of a chest X-ray. It is nothing to do with my back — that seems to have taken second place. The doctors are no longer interested in curing that, although I wish to God they would do something about it."

"A chest X-ray?" A little shiver of fear went through her body.

"I'm afraid they think I have lung cancer."

"Stephen!"

"I have myself to blame. I have smoked for years, cigarettes and finally cigars. I started smoking when I was a midshipman, aged fourteen. We were not told of the risks then."

She realised he had not smoked since her return. "You have given it up?"

"It's ironic, isn't it? It has given me up. All these years I have tried to break the habit, and now the craving has gone."

Fear has driven it away, thought Olivia, her own fear in every fibre of her being.

She drove him to the hospital, and she parked her car opposite an ugly red brick building that was the chest clinic. She sat in the car for a long time, waiting for him. He had been adamant in not wanting her to go in with him. She tried to read, but it was hard to concentrate. The book was *Howards End* by EM Forster, and it would always remind her of the unreality of that day. She got stuck on a page and read it over and over again, and finally gave up. She watched an old man emerge from the clinic, and he leaned against the wall while he had a coughing spasm. Then he lit a cigarette and shuffled on his way. She tried hard not to feel despondent; she knew it was important that Stephen should not be aware of her awful apprehension. It was the beginning of another deception between them.

When Stephen appeared he was smiling and he gave her a wave. When he got into the car beside her, he said quite casually, "It is as they thought, but don't worry, darling, it is encouraging. I have to have treatment, but they say I have every hope of getting better."

She started the car.

He continued in the same business-like tone, "I think we should go and see Bernard and Marigold. It would be convenient if I could stay with them for the time being."

"Of course," she replied in a controlled voice. "You know they will be delighted to have you." She wondered: where do headmasters hide when they are ill?

Marigold, who had been sitting listlessly since she got up that morning, came to life instantly when she saw them. Stephen explained the reason for their visit, and his misfortune made her forget her own problem. Bernard was fetched from the garden.

Excitedly, she said to Stephen, "Tell him what you have just told me."

Obligingly, Stephen repeated what he had said before.

"It is so dreadful," was Marigold's comment. "My poor Stephen."

"Very sorry, old chap," from Bernard.

"It's not so bad," Olivia interrupted, sensing that Stephen would not like too much sympathy. "We feel so much better now we know what we have to face, and that something is going to be done about it. It is a great relief."

"You will let your girls know at once?" Marigold asked Stephen in her old dictatorial manner. It was the question Olivia had wanted to ask him, but had held back.

"No," he said impatiently, "there is no need to worry them." Olivia took his arm, saddened by the lapse in his usual good humour – his irritability showed her, more than anything else, how hopeless and inadequate he felt.

"We'll go home now, Marigold," she said.

The following day she took him for his first treatment, and they sat waiting for him to be called, her hand in his hand.

"You have done so much for me," he spoke in a whisper so the other patients would not hear.

"It's the other way round," she whispered back.

"I only taught you to read!" He was laughing when the nurse came to fetch him.

Bernard took him a few days later for the second treatment. Poor Bernard, longing to help, said proudly, "I had a G and T in the car, ready for him to drink when it was over."

"What a marvellous idea," said Olivia. "Why didn't I think of that?" Gin and tonic, the favourite drink of naval officers that Stephen preferred above all others.

The children returned, and Stephen went to live with Bernard and Marigold. As he could not return to school at the end of the Easter holidays, the deputy headmaster took over from him. "He will do a good job until I am well," Stephen said. He was constantly on the telephone to him, advising him, making suggestions and taking notes. Olivia thought it was a good sign that he still took an interest.

She marvelled that so much had happened in such a short time. Only three weeks had elapsed since she and Pat went to Canada, and now everyone's life had changed. She wished the consultant at the hospital would tell her about Stephen's progress.

During his third treatment a lady approached her. "Are you Mrs France?"

"No," said Olivia, half rising to her feet.

"A relative?"

"A very close friend."

"I see. Do you know who is the next of kin?"

It sounded so ominous that Olivia felt weak with fear. "He has two daughters," she said when she could speak. "Constance is married and lives in Bath. His elder unmarried daughter, Monica, lives in New York. Do you think they should be told?"

"Isn't it possible he has already told them himself?"

Oh, you silly woman, thought Olivia, don't you realise we do everything together? "No," she said firmly, "he has not told them because he does not want them to be worried."

The woman smiled sweetly. "In that case I think we should let him decide when to tell them."

Olivia confided to Mary Chalmers. "The consultant would discuss Stephen's illness with a wife, but not with me. Nobody tells me anything because I am not married to him."

"Why don't you go and see your own doctor?" Mary suggested.

It sounded a good idea, so Olivia went to see the doctor who had looked after her and her father and the children since they moved to Tapworth nearly ten years earlier. He was also a friend, and knew Stephen. "I'm sorry to hear this," he said. "It's rotten luck."

"If I knew what to expect," Olivia told him, "I think I could face it better. It worries me that his two daughters know nothing about his illness. He is being very stubborn about it. Not like himself at all."

"That is because he is under a tremendous strain."

The doctor dialled a number, then after a few moments dialled another number. Olivia sat twisting her hands for what seemed an eternity. Then he started speaking and she listened carefully to his side of the conversation. "I see . . ." A long pause, and then, "I think his friend, Mrs Olivia Randall, should know about this. Have you any objection to my telling her? Also, he has two daughters who should be informed." There was another long pause. "I suggest Mrs Randall gets in touch with them."

When he put the receiver down he looked at Olivia

very seriously. "I'm afraid the news is bad, my dear. The trouble with his back is linked to the main problem, and his chances are not good."

He looked at some notes on his desk, and she looked at her hands in her lap, trying to take in what he had told her.

At last she spoke, slowly and carefully, "What can we expect then? That he will finish this treatment, get better for a while and then get ill again? Please tell me the truth."

"It may be more rapid than that." Then, seeing her stricken face, he went on to say, "Perhaps, from Stephen's point of view, it is for the best. He strikes me as the sort of man who would hate a long illness."

She got to her feet. "Of course you are right," she said wearily. "Thank you for telling me."

That evening she telephoned Stephen's daughter in Bath. "I'm afraid your father is ill, Connie. I can't explain it now, but I think you should come and see him."

She sensed rather than heard the sharp little intake of breath at the other end of the line. "At once? Like tomorrow, you mean?"

"Yes."

Before ringing off Olivia asked her for her sister's telephone number in the States. She waited until eleven o'clock that evening, calculating when she was most likely to find her in. "Monica?"

"Yes?"

"This is Olivia Randall speaking. I'm afraid your

father is ill, and I think you should come and see him."

The next morning Olivia walked over to Platt Cottage. She found Stephen sitting on the sofa, where they had sat together at Marigold's party so many years before. She sat on the floor beside his feet, and took his hand and held it against her cheek.

"Darling, I have something to tell you. I could not help thinking how upset my children would be if I kept something important from them. I thought the girls should know you are having this treatment, so I have telephoned them and they are coming to see you."

She looked up into his face and was suddenly struck by the change in his appearance. "Please do not be cross with me," she pleaded.

"I'm not cross," he said gently. "Of course you did the right thing, and it will be lovely to see them."

Chapter 29

That evening, Olivia went to meet Constance at Melbury Station. She was a plumpish woman dressed in a tweed suit and wearing flat-heeled shoes. She had her father's crisp curly hair, very short and not started to go grey yet. She was the sort of woman who, when the children were older, would be a Justice of the Peace or run the local Citizens Advice Bureau.

Olivia had booked a double room for her in the best hotel in Melbury where her sister would join her when she arrived from New York. Olivia drove her there, and Connie left her luggage in the room.

Then Olivia drove her to Marigold's house, on the way telling her about Stephen but being less frank than the doctor had been with her. The worried look on Connie's face made her think she should not be given the full facts, in case she communicated her anxiety to her father who still had hope.

Olivia did not go into the house with her. "Please explain I have to fetch George from school," she said.

George was a dayboy at a public school nine miles away and his day finished, after prep, at nine o'clock in the evening. Olivia often joked with Stephen that she could never have had a social life, even if she had wanted one, because of the school runs. She took George to school in the morning, picking him up twelve hours later. His sisters were dropped off at a stop to catch the school bus, then met at the same point at half past four. It was difficult to fit in all these commitments with Stephen's visits to the hospital, her time spent with him and now the arrival of his daughters. She hoped the strain did not show in her face, for he would be quick to notice.

She allowed George to accompany her when she drove to Heathrow to meet Monica. The girls stayed at home to do their homework. A blessing was that the days of having to employ a babysitter were over.

Nearly sixteen, George was eager to discuss the event that was dominating their lives. "He is going to die, isn't he?"

"It looks that way."

"Poor Stephen. It is difficult to imagine what he must be thinking." With youth and expectation and the sheer joy of being alive, it was hard for George to contemplate the mysterious nothingness of death. He said, "Of course he is hiding his feelings – that's his way of dealing with it."

"And I have to hide mine, for his sake," said Olivia. "It is a tragic pretence."

Ahead of them was a myriad of little lights, circles of brilliance, dazzling and hurting her eyes. "I expect you think I am driving too slowly," she said. "The truth is I do not like driving at night. All the lights confuse me."

"It will be good when I take my test," said George. "Then I'll do the driving." After a few minutes of silence he said, "Next time you go and see Stephen, Mother, may I go with you?"

"Of course, darling. I would have suggested it, but I did not want you to be upset."

"Is he so changed?"

"I see him every day, so I don't notice the change as much as some people, although yesterday …Yes, I think you should be prepared to see a change."

"Shakespeare wrote '*Love is not love, which alters when it alteration finds*,'" pronounced George. "Have you heard that before, Mother?"

"No, I have not," replied Olivia, "but I think it's beautiful." For the first time, she felt tears sting her eyes. Up to that moment she had been too busy to feel emotion. "Dear George," she said, "what a comfort you are. Stephen would love to see you."

"He's been good to us," he replied.

Monica's plane was delayed, and during the long wait Olivia was glad of George's company. She watched him fondly as he ploughed through a meal of sausages, egg and chips.

Although she had not met Monica before, Olivia had no difficulty in picking her out amongst the people coming through the gate. She looked like her sister, but slimmer and smarter. George pushed the trolley laden with expensive luggage, while his mother explained how she had booked her and her sister into a hotel in Melbury.

"I'll enjoy staying in an English hotel again," said Monica with a smile that made her look like her father. "It is so long since I've been over here. Dad always comes to visit me, instead of the other way round. How is he today?"

"Much the same," Olivia told her, "looking forward to see you." She thought this cool efficient career woman would deal with the situation better than her sister.

She was completely wrong. She collected the sisters the next morning and took them to Platt Cottage. Stephen greeted Monica with warmth and real love. She was shocked and fled into Marigold's dining room where she burst into tears. Olivia, who had followed her into the room, implored her to be brave. "You must not let him see you like this. It would upset him dreadfully."

Constance joined them. "For God's sake, pull yourself together," she urged her sister. "We have to face up to this. If you cannot, you must leave."

Olivia was grateful to her.

Soon after this came a morning when Bernard

telephoned Olivia and said, "I don't think Stephen can come for his treatment today. He's not too good."

Olivia arranged for someone to take the children to school, threw on a jacket, grabbed her handbag and drove quickly to Platt Cottage. She found that Stephen had got up, dressed and was sitting on the edge of the bed.

"I think I'll give it a miss today, darling," he said.

She telephoned the hospital and the person on the other end was sympathetic.

"We think Mr France should be admitted," Olivia was told, "and if you think you can't manage to bring him we will send an ambulance. However, I'm sure he'd rather be driven here by you, Mrs Randall."

"They want you to go to the hospital, Stephen," said Olivia, "and I'm going to take you there."

He gave a deep sigh but he did not protest.

Bernard helped him to the car. "I'll come with you."

"It's very sweet of you, Bernard," said Olivia, "but we will manage, thank you." He was apt to fuss and it made Stephen anxious. He preferred to have Olivia alone, but on this particular morning nothing mattered to him. He did not notice what was happening around him; he was hovering in a shadowy world, desperately trying to maintain a hold on reality. The sheer effort of existing took up so much of his concentration that he was unable to utter a word, and remained silent throughout the journey.

When Olivia stopped in the hospital car park,

Stephen opened the door, somehow managed to lurch out of the car, and then he fell against it, his hands spread out on the roof. She panicked, and called out to the person nearest to them, a man in the process of locking his car.

"Please help . . ."

He was a vicar, wearing a dog collar, and he took one of Stephen's arms and Olivia took the other. Together, they managed to guide him to the swing doors of the hospital entrance.

"There's a wheelchair at the end of the corridor," puffed the vicar. He was a big man with a florid complexion, and beads of sweat glistened on his forehead, It required strength to support the tall Stephen, whose legs were buckling beneath him. Olivia flew to fetch the wheelchair and trundled it back as fast as she could. Stephen was leaning against the wall, and the vicar was holding him so that he did not slip to the floor. Stephen sank into the wheel chair, and she wheeled him to the reception desk, the vicar walking beside her.

"I can't thank you enough," said Olivia, as always remembering her good manners. They shook hands solemnly. She had the strongest feeling that the person slumped in the chair was someone unknown to her, like the kindly vicar who now touched Stephen's bent head, as though blessing him. She seemed to be watching herself from a long way off, like following the actions of a leading lady in a play wondering what was going to happen next. She was very calm, and the nurse who wheeled Stephen into the ward was calm too, but it was part of a daily routine for her.

"When shall I come back?" Olivia asked her.

"Give it a couple of hours," said the nurse. "That will give him time to settle in."

As she walked down the corridor, Olivia thought, I did not kiss him, did not touch him. She went back, and he was still sitting in the wheelchair, waiting for someone to deal with him. She bent down and kissed his cheek that felt moist to her lips. He managed to lift his hand and take one of hers, and then give her a glad little smile.

The nurse was still there, bustling around with clean sheets and pillowcases. "I'll bring his things when I come back," Olivia told her.

On the way home, she stopped at the hotel in Melbury, and was told at the desk that Constance and Monica had gone out. She left a message telling them that she would collect them in two hours' time. Then she went to Platt Cottage and told Bernard and a distrait Marigold what had happened, and packed a few of Stephen's belongings into his travel bag. Pyjamas, dressing-gown, slippers, flannel, toothbrush, razor and shaving soap, ivory-backed hairbrushes marked with his initials in silver. She hoped she had not forgotten anything. When she got home she left the bag in the car, climbed the stairs to her bedroom, and, fully clothed, lay flat on her back on the bed.

She was awoken from a deep sleep by the shrill bell of the telephone by her side.

It was Constance, faintly reproachful, saying, "Are you coming to fetch us?" She was an hour late.

When they reached the hospital, Monica carrying a large bunch of flowers, they found that Stephen was unconscious. So it has come to this, thought Olivia.

The nurse, a different one, gave Monica a vase for the flowers, and she arranged them in it, and placed it on the locker beside her father's bed. He was restless, agitated, waving his arms about and clutching at the air. Olivia tried to imprison one of his hands in her own, but he pulled it free. She felt awkward and wondered if his daughters wanted her to be there at such a time.

It was the old Olivia, wanting to do the right thing and not hurt anyone's feelings.

"Please, please stay with us!" The cry came from the hitherto stoical Constance, who was now visibly showing signs of distress. Olivia decided they did need her there. There was a feeling of apartness between the sisters. They sat on the hard chairs with a big space between them, not sharing their grief.

So the three women embarked on a long vigil. Screens were put around their little area, but they could hear things going on outside them: the departure of visitors, the arrival of supper, and then the trolley bearing pills and sleeping tablets. Suddenly, the lights were dimmed, and there was the daunting prospect of the long night ahead of them.

Another nurse appeared, one of the night staff, an older woman with a comfortable bosom and a little tuft of grey hair showing beneath her cap. She announced that Stephen was to be moved to a side room, and, not comprehending the significance of this, they trotted after the gliding bed, and once more sat on the chairs provided for them.

The nurse took hold of Stephen's hands and put them under the sheets, and he was instantly quieter. "All right, Mr France?" she shouted in his ear.

"He may be able to hear you," she explained, "you should talk to him." She hurried out of the room, apron crackling, stout shoes clumping on the shiny floor.

They were concerned by her suggestion that somewhere at the bottom of the black pit he was in, he could hear them. Evidently just sitting beside a dying man was not enough, something more was expected of them. The difficulty was that they did not know what to say to him. Olivia contemplated whispering the words, 'I love you' but thought his daughters might not like it. It might be hard for them to accept he loved her. He loves me more than anyone in the world, thought Olivia, even his children, but I am an outsider – that's the trouble with me, I am always an outsider.

Monica leaned over the bed, and said, "Can you see the flowers I've brought you, Dad?" but it was obvious that he could not see anything, and she settled back in her chair A tacit decision was reached by the three of them that they would not attempt to speak to him any more.

Olivia sat very still, and spoke to him with her

thoughts. In the place where he was, he would probably receive them more clearly than the spoken word. She said, 'I'm so sorry; I know I should have married you and looked after you, and been the sort of wife you wanted. I have kept things locked up in my mind when I should have brought them out in the open. You would have understood. I realise that now when it is too late.' When she had said these words to him, she went back to the beginning and said them again, and again, and again.

Four hours later, a tray was brought to them with a pot of tea, white cups and saucers, milk and sugar, plain biscuits on a plate. They were pleased to see the nurse again, and they smiled at her, and hoped she would stay a while with them. This time she did not try to reach Stephen – he was quiescent.

"How shall we know when . . .?" asked Constance, but could not continue.

The nurse told them that they might hear a noise at the back of his throat. "Ring the bell when you want me to come," she said. She was gone before they could question her further; all that was left to them was to sit in silence and listen to the sound of Stephen breathing.

Olivia was still talking to him in the special thought language she had devised, but now the message was different. Now she was urging him to die. 'Please, darling, you must die. There is nothing left any more.' She longed for sleep – if only she could go home and sleep. 'Please, darling, let me go home. Just die, darling, and then I can get some sleep.' Surely he would listen? Later, when she remembered this imaginary conversation with him, she was horrified to think she had willed him to die, just so that she could get some rest.

His noisy breathing stopped. Frantically, Monica pressed the bell. They looked away as the nurse dealt with him. The two sisters clung to Olivia, sobbing uncontrollably. She shed no tears, only experienced a great sense of relief. When Constance and Monica had recovered sufficiently she drew them near to the bed, and they stood around it gazing at him. He looked serene and handsome, and the lines of pain and worry had been wiped from his face as if by an unseen hand. Olivia touched his hair, and it was soft and curly, like a child's hair. It is true, she thought, there is something beautiful about death. It is a sort of miracle.

"You can come back later, if you want to," said the nurse, but they agreed they would not do that. They had to pass through the dimly lit ward on their way out, and they could hear the breathing and occasional snores of the sleeping patients, but some were awake, fearful, with the awareness of the living of unknown terrors close at hand. Olivia felt watching eyes as she stepped quietly past the beds.

The cold air struck their faces when they emerged through the swing doors into the blackness.

"Do you feel all right to drive?" asked Constance.

"I'm fine," said Olivia. She was icy. She took them back to their hotel. They looked bedraggled and worn out. A few days before they had been they had been following their usual day-to-day routine, Constance the housewife and mother in Bath and Monica the career woman in New York. An ironical little twist of fate had brought them to this sad conclusion. They still did not wholly understand how it had happened. Monica had lost all her brittle self-assurance, and Constance's face was swollen with crying. Olivia waited with them until a porter came to the door and let them in

When she arrived home she was amazed to find the twins waiting up for her. It was two o'clock in the morning, and she could hardly believe it when she saw them, in their dressing-gowns, wide-awake.

"We guessed what was happening," George explained.

"Oh, Mummy, I'm sorry," said Claire, putting her arms around her mother.

"I'm so lucky to have you," was all Olivia could say.

She went to Platt Cottage early the next morning. She did not want them to hear the news from anyone else. "Died?" said Bernard. "It's hard to take it in."

"What has happened?" asked Marigold pettishly. "Why doesn't someone tell me?" She had been told already, and was told again. She was profoundly shocked, and sat, twisting her hands, looking first at Olivia and then at her husband. "He was a wonderful man," she said.

"Yes."

"Have you had any breakfast, dear?" Bernard asked Olivia. She had not. "Then I'll get you a cup of coffee."

He shuffled off to the kitchen, glad to have something to do.

While he was out of the room, Marigold said, "I feel very sad."

"I know," said Olivia. She put her arms around the older woman, and they remained like that for a few moments.

Then Marigold stirred, and got to her feet. "I think I'll go and put clean sheets on his bed, so it is ready for when he comes back."

When Bernard returned with the coffee, Olivia told him what Marigold had said. "Let her do it," he said. "She doesn't like to be crossed."

Chapter 30

There was nothing more for Olivia to do except attend the funeral. Constance and Monica tackled the arrangements with the calm efficiency and strength that comes to people in the midst of grief. They were so busy that Olivia hardly saw anything of them.

Pat, who had always liked Stephen, came from London to say goodbye to him. "Another funeral," Olivia said to her. "How can I bear it?"

"At least it is a proper wholesome sort of grief," commented Pat, "not like the other thing."

Olivia knew she was talking about Alice, and not about the death of Kenneth or, more recently, dear old Hilda. Pat had not been around at the time of the accident, yet she was perceptive enough to sense that the events of that night were not as straightforward as they appeared. She had always mistrusted the renewed friendship between the two families. Pat thought Alice capable of anything.

"I don't think Marigold should go to the funeral," said George. "She will only get upset."

"George is right," said Pat decisively.

So it was arranged that Marigold should spend the afternoon with Mrs Bracegirdle whom she adored. Olivia had been told that the other Marigold was not going either, although Bernard would be there. "She's not up to it," was his explanation for her staying away.

In the meantime, Pat was enjoying being part of the family, a role she was happy to assume for the few days she was going to spend with them. The slightly chaotic atmosphere and the almost constant ripple of little squabbles gave her an indefinable feeling of well-being, although she knew she would be relieved to return at the end of her visit to the peace of her London house.

Claire was washing her hair, which was very long and very purple. Four times she rinsed it under the bathroom tap, but each time it emerged the same vibrant colour, leaving a faint mark on the side of the bath and on the towel when she dried it. "I can't go with my hair this colour," she wailed, ignoring the fact that it was the shade she had set out to achieve.

"Don't worry," her mother said soothingly. Olivia was feeling particularly loving towards her children at this time.

"It's an appropriate colour for a funeral," Pat pointed out. "I'm sure Stephen would be amused."

"And the black clothes are right too," said Olivia.

But Claire was not so easily comforted. "Black clothes are not right for funerals," she maintained unreasonably. Since entering the teens she had taken to wearing black, except when in school uniform which she endured with very bad grace. She favoured a long skirt to the ankles, like a nun's habit and big black boots that made walking on her slender ankles difficult. Even black lipstick was applied to disguise her soft pout, and her eyes were outlined with kohl pencil. Olivia despaired of ever seeing her pretty daughter in colours again, but the day of Stephen's funeral was to mark the end of Claire's black phase, and the day following it she went shopping and bought herself a multi-coloured skirt and a red top.

The church was packed with Stephen's friends, mostly masters and their wives whom Olivia had never met. His two daughters sat in the front pew, Constance with her husband, a middle-aged business man with a paunch and a bald head, and Monica sitting beside her American partner, rich, flamboyant and caring enough to travel from New York to be with her.

The deputy headmaster read the lesson. He was a weedy, intense-looking man, so different from Stephen. Olivia wondered would he now take his place? He read a passage from *Ecclesiastes*,

> . . . *A time to be born, and a time to die;*
> . . . *A time to kill, and a time to heal;*
> . . . *A time to weep, and a time to laugh;*
> . . . *A time to mourn, and a time to dance* . . .

Inevitably, Olivia's thoughts turned to Alice, as they always did on that sort of occasion. It had been the right time for Stephen to die, for his illness had taken away his contentment, but it had not been the right time for Alice. Alice, who had so much to live for, had been mown down because of a senseless action, a moment of instability which had destroyed her. A fool had killed her. And the child, thought Olivia, the unborn child as well. Kneeling, she shut her eyes, and in the darkness, behind her closed lids, she saw Alice – Alice, as she had been when she first met her, young, with a wide ingenuous smile, the sweep of fair hair lying over one shoulder.

'You were going to take my husband away from me,' Olivia reminded her.

'I was in love with him,' replied Alice. 'I loved him so much, and he loved me. There was nothing either of us could do about such an overpowering love.'

"It's so awful," murmured Olivia, back at Stephen's funeral. Kind Pat leaned over and gave her hand an encouraging squeeze. Perhaps I am having some sort of breakdown, Olivia thought, always talking to people who are not there.

She glanced at the anguished faces of George and Claire. It was the first funeral they had attended, and the sight of the coffin on a pedestal in front of the altar filled them with apprehension.

It was a relief to get out into the sunshine again. Outside the church Olivia felt better, and spoke calmly to Stephen's daughters who invited them all to the hotel, where there was to be a gathering of their father's friends. Bernard was hovering by Olivia's side, and they both made the same excuse – they had to get back to Marigold.

"It seemed unreal to me," she said to Pat, on the way home, "not like the person at all. Do you think that is what he would have wanted?"

"Does it really matter what he wants, now?" Pat was coolly practical. "Something has to be done, and this is the way civilised people have chosen to do it."

"It does not seem very civilised to me," commented George.

"Well . . . it's over now," said Pat briskly, "and this evening I am taking you all out for a meal. I think that is what Stephen would have wanted."

"Oh, no," said Olivia.

"Oh, yes," said Pat firmly. "The twins have been through a hard time, and they deserve better."

When they stepped into the narrow hall, there were four letters lying on the floor beneath the letterbox. Olivia picked them up slowly, three bills and an Airmail blue envelope, forwarded from Vancouver.

"Don't open it, Mummy!" cried Claire, recognising the handwriting.

"I'll read it later," said her mother, and she placed the letter on the hall table, and it was still there, unopened, when they went out that evening.

Pat took them to an expensive restaurant on the river. Little Marigold was there as well, she was collected from

Mrs Bracegirdle's house on the way. It was a cheerful party, and Olivia found herself relaxing and enjoying herself. Each twin was allowed a glass of red wine. "If you are old enough to go to a funeral, you are old enough to drink a glass of wine," Pat told them.

Olivia shared their pleasure, the food and the wine and the happy faces around her. "You are wonderful," she told Pat. "You always do the right thing at the right moment."

"Like giving us Spot," said Marigold.

"You were not born when Pat gave us Spot," George pointed out.

"That was just one of the many kind things you have done for us," said Olivia.

Pat was touched. "It works both ways. You lot are all the family I have left now."

Sitting up in bed that night, pillows at her back and newly acquired spectacles on her nose, Olivia read her letter.

'Olivia, I am staying with Bernard and Marigold as it is convenient for me to visit the man in Melbury, recommended by Bernard, who I hope will do wonders for my back. As you can imagine, these two dear friends are being wonderfully kind to me.

Yesterday, I used my key and went into the house to see that everything is all right. It is, but it seems so empty without the family. I missed Spot's noisy welcome. I even missed him trying to chew my shoelaces!

I went into your bedroom, and sat on your bed and thought

many delicious thoughts. I confess I opened your cupboard and stuck my nose into your clothes, so that I could be as close to you as possible. I ached for you, my darling, and I love you very much. I know you will be back soon, and I long for your return. Without you I am lost! You are everything in the world to me, my own Olivia.

Stephen.'

The house was very quiet, everyone else was asleep, Pat in George's bed, George on a camp bed downstairs, the two girls side by side in their little bedroom, Spot curled up on Olivia's bed. She felt blessed, surrounded by so much love.

She folded Stephen's letter very carefully, and put it back in the blue envelope. This is real, she thought.

She took off her spectacles and laid them on the bedside table. Then she turned off the light and settled down to sleep. Whether it was the good food, the wine or the knowledge that she was loved, sleep came to her almost immediately – deep contented sleep with no ghostly faces to disturb it.

Chapter 31

After Stephen's death Pat and Olivia became, if possible, even closer. They met once a week in London, and Olivia told her everything, or nearly everything. Pat was like a mother to her, but more than a mother, a friend and, despite the difference in their ages, a contemporary. Olivia could talk to her about things she could never have discussed with Joan — Claire, for instance. Joan would not have understood Claire. At a distance of a year Olivia found herself wondering what Stephen would have thought about the perverse character of her daughter. He must have dealt with many wilful boys, but perhaps the sexual obstinacy of this girl would have defeated him. Olivia felt sure that neither Constance nor Monica had presented any problems.

Although Pat adored George, and he would always be her favourite, she recognised in Claire the very young

Patience, the rebellious one who had not obeyed the rules, unlike her sister Joan.

Claire imagined herself in love, and she told her startled mother that she was engaged, and she showed her a silver ring to prove it. Olivia met a silent unassuming boy who wore permanently a leather coat from which emanated a strange odour; she thought it must be a mixture of patchouli and cigarette smoke, but her thoughts turned uneasily to pot. It was so offensive that she had to open the windows wide after he had left the room.

"He puts soap on his hair," Olivia told Pat, "so that he can mould it in spikes, and now Claire is doing the same. Of course he has earrings, and the tattered jeans which are pretty universal – even George wears them."

"What is his name?" asked Pat.

"Tod Banks. I know his parents, and they are nice people. Quite ordinary in fact."

"Ordinary people have extraordinary children, these days," said Pat.

"I don't know whether Tod is very shy or very dim. I can't get through to him at all. Supposing she got pregnant?" Olivia could not hide the anxiety in her voice. "What a tragedy that would be. I think I shall have to talk seriously to her, but that will not be easy as she will be on the defensive at once."

"What about Bill?" Pat wanted to know. "Has she introduced Tod to him?"

"No."

"Do you think you should ask him to talk to her? He is her father, and should share the responsibility."

Olivia sighed. "Now, that is something else I have to tell you."

Pippa had telephoned her with news to impart. "I'm sure the children will have told you that all is not well between Bill and me."

"No, not a word," replied Olivia truthfully.

"How odd," was Pippa's reply She had a knack of making Olivia feel an inadequate mother, now she was implying her children did not confide in her. "Anyway, I think Marigold should stay away for a while – the atmosphere at Mulgrave Terrace is upsetting her, and I don't want her to be upset. You know how I adore that child."

"Oh, dear, I am sorry," said Olivia.

"We have to get the financial aspect sorted out before I go on my way," went on Pippa, "and then no doubt Lady Sylvia Townsend will be moving in here."

Sylvia Townsend – the name was familiar to Olivia. She was a young woman who worked at the House of Commons and was secretary to Edward Preston. Of course, that was how Bill would have met her, through the Prestons, who had made it quite clear, after she and Bill were divorced, that their allegiance was with him.

"Those poor children!" said Pippa reproachfully before she rung off. "What chance have they had?"

Olivia spoke to George about the situation – solid dependable George was the most likely of her children to give a straight answer to her question, "Am I right in thinking all is not well at Mulgrave Terrace?"

"Always at each other's throats," he replied gloomily.

"What about Sylvia Townsend?" It was such a relief that he was sufficiently grown-up for her to speak openly to him.

"Oh, entered the Stepmother's Stakes, that's for sure," said George.

"Is Marigold worried?"

"Well, you know her, she likes people to be at peace with one another. Claire and I are different – we are always baiting each other and are used to bickering, so we take no notice. Marigold gets anxious."

"Do you like Sylvia Townsend?" Olivia could not resist asking him, but he was beginning to get bored with the topic, and "I haven't given her much thought," was all he would say on that score.

Olivia talked to her younger daughter, and between them they decided that, for the time being, Marigold would not accompany her siblings when they visited their father. Bill did not raise any objections to this new arrangement.

As Olivia explained all this, Pat listened attentively. "Poor Bill!" she said then. "What a muddle he has got himself into! But I can see he will not be in the right frame of mind to tackle the problem of Claire and her boyfriend. So, it's up to us, darling, to sort it out." Secretly, she was pleased. There was nothing she liked better than assuming a parental role in the family, her family as she thought of them. She plunged straight in with her remedy. "Talking to her won't do the slightest bit of good," she said. "You must remember she is very young, and does not know nearly as much as you think. What you must do is to make an appointment with your nice doctor, and then take her to see him. That is the only firm line you will have to take with Claire, absolute insistence that she keeps that appointment. Drag her along with you if necessary. Warn him beforehand why she is coming to see him. He will fix her up with the pill, and your troubles will not be over, but much reduced."

Olivia laughed. "Not the old Dutch cap? Thank goodness, Claire does not have to go through that indignity, but it is history repeating itself, isn't it, Pat?"

Claire was surprisingly amenable about going to see the family doctor, the same one who had been so kind when Stephen was ill. Perhaps she was relieved when her mother took over a worry she did not know how to deal with herself.

Olivia sat in the waiting room while the doctor saw her daughter, and then he called her into his surgery, and said, "I have talked to Claire, and I think it will put her mind at rest if she goes on the pill. Sixteen is young, and I have to balance my reluctance against the fact that she will not have to rely on the good sense of another person."

He patted Olivia's shoulder. "Well done," he said. Then he turned to Claire. "You are lucky to have a mother who is so understanding. If you are going to behave in an adult way it is important you think like one as well." This sage advice was not the sort Claire appreciated, and she assumed the what-do-you-know-about-it expression, only too familiar to Olivia. However, she was gratified when her daughter tucked her hand in her arm as they left the surgery, and even gave it a little squeeze as if conveying reluctant thanks.

Claire spent many nights at the home of Tod's parents who had the space and the attitude of mind, neither of which Olivia possessed, that allowed them to agree to their son and his girlfriend sharing a room in their house. Claire was torn between love for her family and love for Tod, and the conflicting emotions did not bring her joy. Eventually, the fault-finding of her twin brother and the quiet disapproval of her mother drove her from home altogether.

Olivia was devastated when Claire moved out, and no encouraging word from Pat that 'it will be all right in the end' could dispel her despair and sense of failure. Claire still came to see them, but it was not the same. They felt she belonged to Tod and his family now.

Claire had been away from home for nearly a year when George drove his mother to the station for her weekly visit to London. After attaining his seventeenth birthday he had passed his driving test on the first attempt, and now Olivia did not feel the car belonged to her any more.

"If I pick you up at the station this evening, Mother, may I have the car today?"

"I suppose so," said Olivia. Her nerves were frayed, and she felt irritated, even with George. "Just don't use all the petrol in the tank."

"All right. All right."

She and Pat did not go out that day. Pat had made a quiche and a salad, and they ate in the kitchen, like old times. Pat was not very active now, and she had given up painting altogether. Suddenly she lost interest, and was quite happy to get rid of all the paraphernalia attached to her work. "I never had a real talent," she explained, "so I don't mind stopping." Fortunately she had enough money to live comfortably without the income she derived from the business.

She had restored the studio to its original purpose, and it was now a gracious drawing room again, furnished with beautiful antiques and pictures. Pat had a 'good eye' for picking up works of art by unknown artists, which later increased in value.

They moved into this room after they had finished lunch. Olivia loved to sit in one of the comfortable armchairs, just savouring the charm of Pat's possessions and the peace and quiet. There was very little peace and quiet at home. Gradually, she felt her anxieties recede.

"If I were you," said Pat, "I would stop worrying about that naughty little girl of yours. She has a place in college, and George is going to university. They will both be fine."

"I know. It's just that I can't help wondering if we forced her into this situation. How could we be sure it was a sexual relationship she really wanted?"

"I'm sure," said Pat, remembering Patience. "Oh, dear, the miseries of being young, second only to the miseries of being old."

She got to her feet heavily. Olivia noticed how much she had aged, and she had lost her old energy. Lately, she had been taking a rest in the afternoon, and after she had lumbered off to her bedroom, Olivia decided to go out and look at the shops.

She walked briskly to South Kensington and took the tube to Green Park. She walked past the Ritz Hotel on her right, and carried on until she came to the imaginative windows of Fortnum and Mason. She studied them all closely, and then moved on to Hatchards bookshop where she browsed for a while, something she would not have dreamed of doing before meeting Stephen.

Out in the street again, she heard a voice, saying her name, "Olivia!"

She stopped. "Captain Nigel?" The old name came automatically to her lips.

"How wonderful to see you," he said, the same words he had used when he met her that evening at Pennel Bridge after a gap of ten years.

"How long is it?" he asked. "Nine years? Ten years?"

Just before Marigold was born, she thought. "Eleven years."

"Really? You haven't changed a bit."

She thought she had, and felt different, but he looked younger than she remembered and less tense.

"Tell me about yourself," said Olivia. An impossible request to make, standing in the street, but he answered, "I married again, and I have three children," thereby giving her all the information she wanted in one short sentence.

"How lovely!"

"Look here," he said, clutching hold of her arm. "I suppose there is no chance of your coming to have a meal with us one evening? I know Alison would love to meet you, and I'd like you to meet her, and see our children."

"I come to London quite often but usually just for the day, to see Pat. I have to get back to Marigold, that is my younger daughter, so it is difficult to go out in the evening."

"I understand," he said. "How is Pat?"

"She's well." How lean he looks, she thought, and could not help thinking of Pat's bulk.

"Look," he said again, "I'll give you our address and telephone number, and if you can see a way of coming, please let us know. We'd love to see you." He was already scribbling on the back of an envelope, which he gave to her and she tucked into her bag.

"Are you sure your wife won't mind a complete stranger descending on her?"

"She will be delighted. She is a very relaxed person, has to be with three young children." There was a note of pride in his voice. He kissed her cheek and squeezed her hand before turning away, and she watched his tall figure striding down the street. He had shown no sign of embarrassment. The past must be forgotten by him, she decided with a pang of envy. Clearly the unexpected encounter had not aroused memories that could cloud his present contentment.

"Of course you must go," said Pat when she heard about the meeting. "I'm longing to know more. What does he look like?"

"Good, very good – bald of course, but younger somehow. And he has three children!"

"That is remarkable," said Pat dryly. She went on, "Thank goodness I don't have to see him. He would be horrified by the size of me. But you must go, darling, and then come back and tell me all about it. George is quite old enough to look after his little sister for one night, and you can stay here which will be very nice for me."

That evening when Olivia arrived at Tapworth Station she was surprised and annoyed that there was no George there to meet her. She peered into the darkness, but there was no sign of the car speeding up the road. She telephoned from the kiosk, but there was no reply from the house.

"Oh, really, it is too bad." She spoke aloud, but there was no one to hear her. The little village station was deserted, and she felt chilled and abandoned standing by the side of the road. There was nothing for it but to walk home.

Her irritation increased when she saw there were no lights on in the house. They had not even bothered to turn on the light in the porch. She expected the usual welcome from Spot, but when she opened the front door with her key she was greeted with emptiness. Where was Marigold? After hanging up her coat she went upstairs to peek into Marigold's bedroom to see if there was evidence that she had been there.

Now that Claire no longer shared her room, Marigold had got into the habit of chucking her clothes on her sister's bed. The first thing that Olivia noticed was that the bed had been cleared of clutter, and the next thing she noticed was Claire's old teddy bear propped against her pillow, regarding her with a triumphant beady eye. In the centre of the room stood two large suitcases.

Olivia flew down the stairs, just in time to see her family tumble through the front door.

"Oh, Mother," cried George, "I'm so sorry I didn't meet you at the station. Claire wanted to go back and explain things to Mrs Banks, and it took longer than we thought."

How could she have doubted him for a second?

Olivia put her arms around Claire, and heard her say, "Mummy, I've missed you so much. It wasn't George's fault. It was right for me to go and see Mrs Banks."

Of course it was right.

"She's home for good," said George, smiling.

They gathered around her, loving her. They were

nearly grown-up; only Marigold, her baby, could still be called a child. The two girls clung to her, and Olivia drew George into the circle and put her head against his chest. He was so tall, a man.

"I'm very happy, and proud," said Olivia. "You'll all be leaving me one day, and it is right that you should, but today we are all together, and it is wonderful."

"Spot will stay," said Marigold, and Spot, hearing his name and sensing the excitement, started to jump up at them, barking furiously.

"Crazy dog," said George, trying to subdue him, "act your age". It was true that Spot was getting old, although he showed few signs of it and still liked to pretend he was a puppy.

Later, the twins went out to meet their friends, and Olivia, still feeling indulgent towards them, allowed them to take the car. When Marigold had finished her prep and gone to bed, Olivia telephoned Pat.

"Claire is back."

"Oh, I'm so glad to hear that, darling," said Pat, "but I told you it would be all right, didn't I? You worry too much."

Chapter 32

Sitting in a taxi on the way to the Benton's house, Olivia wondered what sort of evening lay ahead of her. She remembered that first dinner party when she, her father and Bill had been invited to the house in Pennel Bridge. While taking off her coat in the hall she had raised her eyes to see Alice gliding down the stairs in a shimmering pink dress. And, afterwards, the brittle conversation at the dinner table, so bewildering to her artless ears and so offensive to her father's – surely it would not be like that?

The Bentons lived in a substantial Edwardian house in Belsize Park and, as so many years before, the door was opened by Nigel Benton, and behind him hovered his wife. Alison. Olivia got an impression of red hair and freckles, and then she noticed a comfortably unfashionable shape. In that first meeting, Olivia discerned that Nigel, in his second marriage, had found a very different woman from his first choice.

He made the introductions, taking her coat at the same time. They picked their way through numerous toys scattered in the hall. Dolls, footballs, plastic guns, it was incredibly untidy, and Olivia thought of the suburban orderliness of Alice's home and the uncluttered simplicity of the house in Queen's Gate.

She was taken into the drawing room, the corner of which was filled with more toys. The room had charm though, and suddenly Olivia saw the line of crested plates on a shelf the height of a picture rail. So Nigel had kept some link with the past.

"I'm so glad you managed to come this evening," he told her. "Alison has been looking forward to it, haven't you, darling?"

Alison's broad friendly smile conveyed her pleasure. "Would you like to see the children?" she asked eagerly. "Two of them will still be awake."

"Very much," said Olivia. "I was afraid I would be too late to meet them."

"We'll go up while Nigel is getting us a drink."

She led the way up the staircase, and the first room they entered contained a big old-fashioned wooden cot. The occupant, a girl, was asleep, lying on her stomach, bottom up, so that all that could be seen was a mass of very blonde hair. The floor was covered with piles of clothing, nappies and more toys, and Olivia had to step over them so that she could peep through the bars and get a glimpse of a plump cheek and a snub nose.

"Lovely," she murmured. There was a not unpleasant but faintly sour baby smell in the room, different from the immediately recognisable smell in the next room, the small boy smell. The boy was about four years old, and he was sitting up in bed looking at a picture of a red fire engine in a book. When asked, he told her that his name was Christopher. She sat on the edge of his bed, and they looked at the book together.

"*The biggest fire engine in a fire station is called a Turntable Ladder,*" she read aloud. "*It is often used to rescue people from high places.*" She turned the pages and looked at the brightly coloured pictures. "It's very exciting," she said.

"Stay and read some more."

"I can't because Daddy is waiting for us downstairs, but I will come again."

Christopher's room was large, probably allocated to him because of the railway system snaking across the floor. This room would have been the master bedroom of such a house, and the small room next door, now occupied by the oldest child, the dressing room.

Alison introduced Olivia to her elder daughter, "This is Emma." Emma was also in bed, reading, Olivia observed, a book called *Winter Holiday* by Arthur Ransome. She had not read it because although she had managed to catch up with a great deal of adult reading, she had never felt able to tackle the childhood literature as well.

"Are you enjoying it?" she asked Emma, a brown-eyed child with freckles like her mother.

"It is story of adventure from start to finish," said Emma with the prissiness of a clever eight-year-old.

"What beautiful children!" said Olivia as they went downstairs. "How funny that none of them has inherited your lovely hair."

"We managed to avoid that," said Alison.

Supper in the dining room was a simple affair. Even that room had a high chair in it, and a playpen stuck in one corner. Olivia remembered Nigel as a tidy man and there was evidence of that trait in his character in the house. The pictures on the wall with exact spaces between them, the arrangement of the furniture – she imagined he had done all that when they moved in, then when things became chaotic he had given in with a good grace.

Nigel asked her about the twins and Marigold, and he enquired after Bill. Olivia told him about Pippa, not mentioning the complication of Sylvia. He spoke of Pat with natural affection, recalling how talented she was.

"She's given it all up," Olivia told him.

"That is hard to believe." He turned to his wife. "I've told you, darling, about the cards she used to paint. Birthday and Christmas cards, although they were not as good as the screens. Do you remember those beautiful screens, Olivia?"

"Indeed I do, and I have one of them in my house."

"And where is that?"

She was surprised by the question, but then remembered that many years had passed since they last saw each other and it was extremely likely that she would have moved during that time. "I live in the same house," she said, and when he looked puzzled, added, "the one where you came to see me when I was painting the ceiling."

For the first time he looked uncomfortable, as if a memory from the past had obtruded on his present contentment. "Of course," he said quietly.

There was a pause in the conversation which, up until that moment, had been pleasant and unrestrained. Irrationally, Olivia found herself feeling embarrassed, as if she had made a gaffe.

The awkward little silence was filled by a cry from Alison. "Oh, oh . . ." They all looked towards the doorway where stood a small figure clad in a sleeping suit.

Relieved, Nigel sprang to his feet and gathered the child into his arms and Christopher nuzzled into his father's neck, hiding his eyes from the light. "I'll take him back to bed," said Nigel, leaving the room.

"He'll soon settle him down again," said Alison.

"He's a good father."

"Yes, he adores the children."

"What does he do now? I mean – has he got a job?"

"He's a palaeontologist."

"What?"

"A fossil hunter."

"How silly of me," said Olivia. "That is what he did when I first knew him. Then he became an enthusiastic gardener. Is that still an interest?"

"Very much so," Alison replied. "This house suits us because it has a large garden, unusual for London. I hope you will come again, in the daylight next time, so you can see what wonders Nigel has done to this garden. I inherited the place from my parents, and we like it here very much. Nigel has always been, at heart, a Londoner."

Olivia helped her carry the dishes to the kitchen that was as disorganised as the rest of the house. She thought of her own tiny kitchen that she struggled to keep tidy against tremendous odds. This one was spacious and well equipped, and richly messy. Alison loaded the dishwasher, a luxury Olivia did not have, and left the saucepans in the sink. Then she made two mugs of instant coffee, and they sat down to drink them at a pine table in the centre of the room. Alison cleared a space for them with one easy sweep of her arm, pushing a collection of bills, newspapers and milk bottles to one side of the table.

"Nigel will sit with Christopher until he falls asleep," she said, "and, while he is not with us, do you mind if I ask you something?"

"Go ahead," said Olivia, wondering what was coming next.

"Alice," she said, and the name and the unexpectedness of hearing it from someone she had so recently met, produced a thudding in Olivia's ears.

"Yes?"

"She was your friend, wasn't she?"

"Yes."

"Please tell me about her," pleaded Alison. "You see,

Nigel never mentions her. He talks about Pat, as you have heard this evening, but Alice is another thing altogether – not a word can I get out of him about her. It is as if she never existed. I have tried to ask him about her, but it is as if a curtain comes down when I mention her name. He was married to her, for God's sake, for how long – ten, eleven years? A whole chunk of his life I know nothing about. He knows everything about me, and I have told him all about my past, and I'm not proud of that I can tell you but, at least I have made no secret of it. I believe that people who love each other should have no secrets. I feel like that girl in *Rebecca* who became wracked with jealousy about her husband's first wife who was tragically killed in an accident. Do you remember?"

"I do remember, and I know what you mean," said Olivia slowly.

"I love Nigel," Alison continued, "and we are very happy. I don't want anything to rock the boat. I can't tell you how wonderful he has been. I met him at a time when I was badly in need of help. He was my saviour. He told me that he had been married and his wife had died in a car accident, I thought I would hear the rest in time, but I never did. Of course I know it must have been terrible for him, but I feel he is locking me out because he never talks to me about it. It frightens me – I don't want to be obsessive about it, but I begin to think I am getting that way."

Olivia recalled Nigel's description of his wife.

'Relaxed' he had said, and she thought how often people, men in particular, made wrong judgements about those close to them.

Alison went on, "I can understand him being very affected by the death of his wife, and I try to persuade myself that his reticence to talk about it is a natural reaction – even after all this time. I'm sure you were devastated yourself, as she was your friend."

"It was very sad," Olivia said, "especially as she was pregnant."

"Pregnant? You say she was pregnant?" Alison sounded astonished.

For the second time that evening Olivia felt she had blundered. She did not want to make matters worse, so she said nothing, and Alison was thoughtful.

"I see," she said at last, "I didn't know that she was pregnant. Poor Nigel – that would have upset him very much."

"Perhaps I should not have mentioned it," said Olivia.

"No, I'm glad you did. And I'm sorry to inflict my silly problem on you, reawakening old memories you would probably prefer to remain forgotten. It is just that when Nigel told me you were coming to see us, I thought you might be the person who could help me because you knew him when he was married to Alice."

"One thing I can do," said Olivia, "is to tell you why I think Nigel does not talk about her. It is not because he loved her so much, not because he still misses her and cannot bear her name mentioned – that is what you imagine, isn't it?"

"I suppose I do, yes."

"It is because he wants to block out that part of his life. His memories are not happy ones. He will not be able to forget Alice, none of us can do that; she must remain part of us for the rest of our lives. It helps not to talk about her – it is as simple as that."

"But why?" Alison wanted to know. "What made her so special? Was she so beautiful, so outstanding?"

"She was neither of those things. You are far more attractive than she was, and a nicer person. But she was effective, there's no doubt about that . . ."

"Effective?"

"It's a strange word, I know, to describe an individual, but I can't think of a better one. She had an effect."

"I see," said Alison doubtfully.

"You can't begin to understand because you did not know her. Forget her," Olivia urged. "She is no threat to you, I assure you. I have not seen Nigel so happy for years. He loves you, and he loves his children, and it shows. Life with Alice was complicated; with you he feels it is straightforward. Take my advice, and keep it that way."

"I will." They could hear Nigel tiptoeing down the stairs. "Thank you," she whispered.

"He fell asleep halfway through the story," he said.

"I must go now," said Olivia briskly, standing up. "I've had a lovely evening, but I must get back to Pat."

Nigel laughed. "She'll want to know all about your time with us," he said, putting his arm around his wife's waist. "I know her!"

Olivia remembered Pat's last words to her that evening, "I want to hear every sordid detail," she had said, using a phrase very popular in her generation.

"I want to get back before she goes to bed," said Olivia. "She will be waiting up for me, like the old days,"

"I'll walk with you to Haverstock Hill," said Nigel. "You'll pick up a taxi there."

"Please come again," said his wife, "when the children are all awake, and you can see the garden."

"I hope you will," said Nigel as they walked up the street together. "Too many years have slipped by – we must not allow that to happen again. Alison would like to have you as a friend – it is hard bringing up three children, as you know only too well."

As he had predicted, Pat was eager to hear all about the evening. "I'm glad he is happy," she said about Nigel, "he must be fifty-seven now, but that is not too old to enjoy fatherhood. Although . . ."

"You feel no bitterness now?" Olivia interrupted.

"All gone, years ago," replied Pat cheerfully, "the old hormones sort things out, you know, darling. I was too old for him."

"What a good thing you did not succeed in that

suicide attempt," said Olivia. "What a waste that would have been!"

"Yes," Pat agreed, "emotions can make one behave very foolishly – Nigel's wife, for instance, worrying about Alice. She sticks around, that woman, even beyond the grave. It's about time her soul went to rest."

Then Olivia told her about Nigel's last words to her that evening. They had been standing, arm-in-arm, on the pavement, peering up the street for a lit-up taxi. As they saw one coming towards them, Olivia said, "I can't tell you how lovely it has been to see you again. And you have a marvellous family. I can hardly believe you are the father of three children."

He had replied quietly, "I'm not. I think I should explain. When I met Alison she was a single mother, struggling to bring up a child on her own. I gave Emma my name when I married her mother. Later, we adopted the two other children."

Chapter 33

The happy relaxed atmosphere at Platt Cottage had changed, in a very short time it seemed to Olivia. She did everything she could to help Bernard in his tragic predicament. He insisted on paying her as if she was still working for Marigold, and in return she cooked meals for him, and visited the house every day. She always found time to sit with Marigold and try to talk to her; she felt it was important to keep everything as natural as possible. Bernard made no effort to reach his wife; he felt she was lost to him. Olivia did not know which was worse, the rapidly diminishing intellect of Marigold or the impotent grief of her already bereaved husband.

Help came from Canada in the shape of Peter Armitage, their younger son. He was a sculptor so as a self-employed person it was possible for him to come to England at short notice.

"I'm sure Sandra will make a fuss about him leaving," said Bernard. Olivia knew that Marigold did not care for her daughter-in-law, and, over the years, she had been forced to listen to her whingeing about her. When Marigold did not like someone she was quick to criticise them, and Bernard, who had no mind of his own and agreed with his wife in every particular, cheerfully joined in the shredding of Sandra's character. Olivia often wondered if their complaints were justified, that she had no sense of humour, that she was snappy with her husband and children, and, worst of all, that she was unreasonably jealous. Peter was undeniably the favourite son of his parents; the beautiful fair-haired boy, rather delicate, had been described to Olivia many times. Apparently he had grown into a man of considerable talent and charm, and she wondered if, in the eyes of Marigold and Bernard, any woman would have been good enough for him.

She was about to find out for herself, for, in her capacity as friend of the family, she had volunteered to meet him at the airport. Standing at the barrier, peering at the people herding through the gate, she felt slightly nervous. Olivia had never managed to lose her anxiety about meeting strange people.

She recognised him at once because he looked like Bernard. Not hurrying, dreamy, his rather untidy appearance probably due to the long flight.

"Peter?" she called, and, as he approached, "I'm Olivia."

He smiled, and said, "It is very kind of you to meet me."

"I'm delighted," she said, "I've heard so much about you."

When his luggage had been heaved into the boot of the car, and he was sitting beside her, she said, "They are very excited at Platt Cottage about your arrival."

Bernard and Marigold had been in the habit of visiting each of their sons once a year, Tom, who lived in Australia, married with two children, and Peter who lived in Vancouver with Sandra and the two boys. They understood that Tom's career kept him in Australia, but they blamed Sandra for forcing Peter to stay in Canada. After all, they contended, a sculptor can live anywhere he chooses.

After negotiating the turning on to the motorway, demanding her full attention, Olivia took a surreptitious look at the profile beside her and decided his proud parents had been right in their description of him – it was a handsome sensitive face. She had seen photographs of his work, abstract and sometimes on a large scale. He had made his name by sculpting a bird-like creature in stone that graced the entrance hall of the museum of British Columbia. He was well known in Canada but, as yet, his work had not been exhibited in any other country.

He spoke. "Tell me about my mother."

She paused. "I'm afraid the change in her will be a shock," she said. Perhaps it was as well to prepare him for it.

"Is she aware of what has happened to her?" he asked.

"At first, she was, and she fought against it, fiercely. Now she has become rather apathetic, and maybe that is the best thing for her. Certainly, she seems happier than she was a few months ago."

"You say you think she is happy?"

"Well, perhaps happy is not the right word, and resigned would be better."

He repeated the word. "Resigned. It is hard for me to associate that word with my mother. This must be the worst affliction of old age there is, and to strike someone as vital as Marigold Armitage, it is beyond comprehension."

"Yes, but she has good days when she is almost normal, and you would not think there is anything wrong with her." She did not tell him that the good days were getting less and less frequent, which was why his father, unable to cope with the situation on his own, had asked Peter to visit them.

They drew up outside Platt Cottage, and the moment Olivia had dreaded had arrived. She and Bernard were terrified that Marigold would not recognise her son. She was getting increasingly muddled about names and faces. They need not have worried. As soon as Marigold saw that beloved face, her own face lit up as if a magic hand had removed the lost look which lately had become her habitual expression. Olivia left the happy little group, and returned to her own family.

She continued to go to Platt Cottage every day to

prepare a cold lunch for the three of them; they asked her to stay but she refused. There was too much to do at home to waste time chatting over lunch. The housework had to be done somehow, Spot needed a walk in the afternoon and by then it was time to meet Marigold at the school bus stop. George was away at university, but, rather surprisingly, Claire had opted to attend a local college so that she could continue to live at home. In the evening Olivia returned to Platt Cottage, usually with something in a casserole that she had prepared earlier in the day. After she had set it before the Armitages, she went back to her own house to eat with her daughters. Then after supper she started cooking for the following day. It was a gruelling routine she had set herself, and the only time for reading was when she went to bed, and she usually fell asleep over the book She thought regretfully of the days when she just did secretarial work for Marigold; the present regime was much more exhausting and she was glad she no longer had to fetch George from school at nine o'clock.

It was obvious that Peter welcomed her visits, and she could understand why. Living with parents was unbelievably boring for an active man. Privately, Olivia thought he could have found jobs to do around the house, but apparently he was not that way inclined; too artistic, she decided. She wondered how long he intended to stay, but did not like to ask him. She knew he telephoned his wife at least twice a week, and she heard him talking to his little boys.

One day she mentioned to him that she took Spot for an afternoon walk, and he asked her if he could come with her. Bernard was dozing in his chair and Marigold resting on her bed, so there was nothing to keep him there. So he started collecting her at her house at half past two, in his father's car so that they could set out on their walk from a different place every day. She was used to taking Spot along the lane and back, but these were real hikes and sometimes lasted about two hours. She was reminded of the walks with her father in the New Forest, all those years ago. It was good to have company; children are never interested in walking with their mother. Spot was in seventh heaven, trembling with anticipation when he heard Peter ringing the bell.

On one of the walks she told him about *The Italian Legacy*, completed up to the last three chapters. The publisher was constantly writing to ask when it would be finished. He had not been told about Marigold's mental deterioration.

Olivia had appealed to Bernard, "Should I write and tell him the truth? That there is little likelihood of him ever getting the whole book?"

Bernard had been distressed. "No, no, tell him nothing. Marigold would not like it." He was always very anxious to do as Marigold would have wished before her 'illness', as he referred to her present state.

"Shall we finish it together?" asked Peter. He liked the idea of the 'together' part of such an arrangement.

Olivia told him that they would have the synopsis

to work on. "It should not be too difficult," she said thoughtfully, "but isn't it cheating?"

"I don't think so," he said. "It is the last thing we can do for my mother, and, if she knew about it, she would be pleased."

Somehow Olivia found time in her busy day to spend time with Peter poring over the synopsis, which Marigold, in her once meticulous way, had written for the book. Together, they converted the notes into descriptions, sentences and dialogue, and eventually separate chapters. Every evening they read aloud to Bernard the results of their efforts during the day. They both thought it was important that he should understand what they were doing, that he should feel he was taking part in the plan.

Marigold sat in her chair, saying nothing, her face devoid of expression.

Then one evening, when Peter was reading, she spoke. Her voice was strong, decisive, like the voice of the old Marigold. "What are you doing with my book?" she asked.

They stared at her in astonishment. It was a fleeting moment of lucidity, because immediately she relapsed into her mindless silence. They tried to talk to her, but it was if a light had come on momentarily in a dark room, and they could not switch it on again.

Putting on her coat in the hall, Olivia was close to tears. "We must not go on," she said to Peter. "It is wrong of us."

He took her hand. It was their first physical contact

since their meeting, and both were conscious of the significance of it. "Don't feel that way," he pleaded. "I don't know why she said that — perhaps it is the last sensible remark she will ever make. She asked us what we are doing with her book, well, the answer to that is that we are finishing it for her because she cannot finish it herself. You can be perfectly sure the publishers would not let a new Dominic Platt lie forgotten somewhere in a drawer — they would get someone, a stranger, to write the last three chapters. How much better that we, who love her, take on that task."

She withdrew her hand. "Yes, I'm sure you are right." Suddenly she felt very weary and rather depressed.

Pat was annoyed because Olivia had no time for her weekly visits to London. "You've become too involved with those people," she said peevishly. "They're working you to death, it's ridiculous. I thought that her son came over to sort things out? What has he done for his mother since he arrived? Nothing by the sound of it! I don't like the sound of him."

"He's very nice."

"You think everyone is nice," said Pat. "What does George think of him? I'd get a straight answer from him."

"George has not met him."

All three children met Peter a few days later. They were home for the summer. As usual with any male friend of their mother's, they stared at him with unfeigned interest. "We're taking Spot for a walk," Olivia explained.

She sensed that Peter felt as uncomfortable as she did, and it irked her because there was no need for awkwardness.

"I'm sorry about that," she said as they set off.

Later, she made the mistake of asking the children what they thought of him.

"Seems all right," said George.

But Claire was immediately on her guard. The fact that her mother was interested enough in someone to ask for their opinion made her instantly suspicious. "He fancies you," she announced. And then came the direct heart-stopping question. "Do you fancy him?"

"Of course not," replied Olivia crossly. "He is married with two children. And," she finished triumphantly, "he is five years younger than me."

"That doesn't signify," said George, who knew about such things.

"I don't think Stephen would like it," said Marigold.

"Stephen has been dead for two years," Olivia reminded her, feeling that the utterance of these words was like a betrayal.

"But you must not forget him," said her younger daughter.

Olivia thought how complex were the minds of the modern young, so much more lax in their standards than her own generation, and yet in some respects as moralistic in their views as the Victorians.

She decided that the time had come for her to speak frankly to Bernard and his son. She explained that, with the best will in the world, she could not take on so much now the children were at home. Peter was contrite; he had not realised the strain imposed on Olivia. Being a man he had not thought deeply about how much she had to do, he was just happy to see her at Platt Cottage. He liked to follow her into the kitchen and watch her prepare a meal for them; it seemed right somehow that she busied herself on their behalf. He did not concern himself with her other life, as he thought of it.

Olivia was glad that she had spoken out. She felt that she had been neglecting the girls; many times she had left them to scrounge meals from the refrigerator. Now something would be done that would enable her to spend more time with all three of her children. They led busy social lives, but they liked her to be there when they decided to come home.

Peter arranged through an agency for a lady called Mrs Savage to come and live at Platt Cottage. She was a trained nurse, but his mother was not informed of this fact. She just did not understand why a stranger had come into their midst. "I like Olivia," she said.

Mrs Savage had the spare bedroom, and a television was purchased for her and a comfortable armchair. She had the use of the car, did the shopping and the cooking, and, after a few days of uncertainty, was accepted by Marigold.

On his wedding anniversary Bernard suggested that the four of them should go out to dinner at a restaurant. He suggested the same place by the river where Pat had taken Olivia and the children after Stephen's funeral.

"You and Mother go alone, Dad," said Peter. It's an occasion for just the two of you together. I'll take Olivia somewhere else, and we'll meet afterwards."

"There's no need," Olivia protested.

"I don't want to stay here on my own," he said obstinately, "I want to take Olivia out to dinner."

A little warning signal sounded at the back of her mind that accepting this invitation would not be the right thing to do. However, she ignored it, and said nothing.

"That's settled then," he said with satisfaction.

She had noticed that he liked to get his own way.

He collected her that evening. Marigold and Bernard were sitting in the back seat. When she opened her front door, he said, "You look good." He dropped his parents off at the restaurant by the river, and took Olivia to another one a few miles away.

When they were seated she said, "This is fun. My children are out every single night. It's my turn for a change."

He was delightfully attentive, and his expression when he looked at her made her realise that he was not just taking her out as a repayment for all she had done for his family. She thought nervously that she ought to try and cool down his ardour, put their relationship on a more casual level.

"I have terrible news for you," he said. "I am going home in three days' time."

That's all right then, she thought, relieved, and

instantly feeling relaxed in his company. "You must be looking forward to seeing the family again."

"I did not intend to stay for so long," he admitted. "I found it hard to tear myself away." When she did not reply he went on, "You know why, don't you?"

"Of course I know why," she said briskly. "Because of you mother. It is understandable you don't want to leave her."

"My mother is in the good hands of Mrs Savage, and you are nearby to keep an eye on things. I am not in the least worried about her. At the moment I can think of only one person, and that is you. You must have guessed how I feel about you."

"She said, "I'm afraid you must stop talking like this, otherwise I shall have to go home at once, without finishing this delicious meal."

He laughed. "I don't want you to do that, so I will say no more. We'll talk about Dominic Platt. He's safe enough."

"And safely wrapped up, having solved his last crime. I hope no one will notice where we took over."

"Not a chance," he said, "we did a seamless job on him."

When they left the restaurant, it was raining heavily, and he took her hand and they made a dash for the car. Instead of turning the ignition key and starting the engine, he turned to her and took her face between his hands. Before she could stop him, he kissed her, a long hard kiss, and she did not resist him. She put her hands behind his head, and exulted in his kisses, on her lips, on her face and neck. She caught his hand, as she had done in the far distant past when she had wanted to stay the wandering hands of Adam Bowlby and others like him, usually in the back seat of the car, not the front. "Not here," she said.

"You know I love you," he said.

They drove in silence to pick up Bernard and Marigold. Peter sprang out of the car to help them totter through the rain. They looked a very old pair, and Olivia wondered if they had enjoyed the evening.

"Did you enjoy yourselves?" she asked. Her face was burning, and she felt sure they must guess what had been happening to her.

"Very nice," said Bernard laconically.

"Where are we going now?" asked Marigold.

"Home," said Olivia. "Peter is dropping me off at my house, and then he is taking you both back to Platt Cottage."

"I thought . . ." said Peter, looking sideways into her face.

"No," she said firmly. "Please take me home first."

The next day when she went to Platt Cottage he was there, waiting at the door for her to arrive. "I haven't had any sleep," he told her, "I've been thinking of you all night."

"Please be quiet," she said.

She rummaged around in Marigold's desk until she

found brown paper and string. Then she started to wrap up the finished manuscript. Peter stood beside her, watching her intently.

"Please don't look at me all the time," she said. "You make me feel nervous."

"I want you to feel nervous," he said. "I want you to feel so nervous that you can't speak, can't breathe, that all you can think about is me and how much I love you."

"Someone will hear you," she said.

"You know, as well as I do, that no one in this house is on the same wavelength as you and me. My father is too preoccupied with his own problems to know what is going on around him, and my mother, who would have understood once, is no longer with us. We are alone, the two of us."

"You know that is not true," she said. "There are other people in your life to think about."

"Now you are annoyed with me," he said. "Are you going to punish me by not going for our walk this afternoon?"

It was not in Olivia's nature to inflict punishment. "No, of course not," she said.

She printed the name and address on the parcel. It lay on the top of Marigold's desk, waiting to be taken to the post office.

"Well, that's that," said Peter.

She touched the parcel, as a person at a funeral quickly touches the coffin of an old friend, in a gesture of farewell. "Goodbye, Dominic Platt," she said.

Chapter 34

Olivia did not go for a walk with Peter that afternoon, or any afternoon after that. George broke his leg in two places playing rugger, and he and his mother waited for hours in the Casualty department of Melbury Hospital before he was called to have an X-ray, and the leg put in plaster. Olivia was far too concerned about her son's pain to give a moment's thought to Peter Armitage.

However, it had been an understood thing that she would take him to the airport, and so she was there to collect him and his luggage at the arranged time. She felt happy to leave a rapidly recovering George to the solicitude of his sister. Claire maintained that she shared the pain of her injured twin and, in consequence, an unusual harmony reigned between them. George was lying on the sofa, his leg propped up by cushions, watching the television. Marigold happily acted as their slave, making cups of coffee and providing her brother with endless snacks; his hunger was never satisfied for long.

Bernard was bereft seeing his favourite son depart, and Marigold felt it too. Her eyes filled with tears, and she clung to him, saying, "Don't go," over and over again. There was no doubt that she had a very good idea of what was happening.

"My God," said Peter, when they eventually got on their way, "that was terrible."

After a pause, he asked, "Will you write to me?"

"Why?"

"To tell me how my mother is, so that if there is any dramatic change I will come again."

She promised to write in six months' time. "I hope I will be able to tell you that she is the same as she is now. The doctor seems hopeful that may be the case."

He sat in gloomy silence for what seemed a long time to Olivia. She wondered if he was anticipating his return home with pleasure or mixed feelings. He never said a word against his wife, and she liked him for that. She had no means of knowing, except from rather pointed remarks made by Marigold in the past, whether the marriage was a happy one.

He broke the silence at last. "I have been talking to my father about your relationship with Stephen France. I had no idea you were so close to him."

"Did you know him?" she asked.

"Of course. He was always visiting our house when

Tom and I were young. Neither of us went to his school because we chose to go somewhere other than where Dad worked. We saw Stephen in the holidays, and we both liked him enormously. He had a way with boys, always the same even temper, never patronising."

"I know," she said.

"I certainly never expected to feel jealous of him."

She laughed. "You are ridiculous!"

"I suppose it is a bit ridiculous, as you say, to feel jealous of someone who is dead, but I envy him those four years with you."

"What about my husband, Bill?" she said sarcastically. "Are you jealous of him also?"

"Curiously, I am not," he said. "I think he blotted his copybook, whereas good old Stephen would be the faithful sort." Bill had sometimes referred to Stephen as 'old' and she had not liked it.

"He was not so old," she protested.

"Evidently not."

She had no intention of revealing anything to him of her time spent with Stephen, and she asked him to talk about something else.

"Like how much I am going to miss you?" he asked.

"I'll miss the long walks," she said.

At the airport she sat and read her book, while he went off to check in. He seemed a very long time, but she was quite content to sit and wait for him. She always welcomed this sort of enforced break, when no one could call her away to do something.

Eventually, he returned and at once she noticed a change in him – the downcast air had gone and he seemed uplifted. "My flight has been cancelled," he said.

She felt sorry for him. "How awful for you! Why is that?"

"Bad weather, I suppose," he said.

It had rained throughout the drive to London. "I didn't know flights had to be cancelled because of rain," said Olivia. "I thought it was only fog that caused delays."

"I don't know," he said vaguely. "Anyway the next flight is tomorrow morning."

She imagined him spending the night at the airport, trying to get some sleep lying on two hard seats.

"I'm being put up at the airport hotel," he told her.

"Oh, well, that's something anyway."

"I told them that you would be with me. I said that I wanted you to see me off tomorrow morning, and that is the truth, I do want you to be there when I leave."

"I must get back," she said, "George –"

"You know that George is being well looked after." He caught her arm, "Look, we can't stay her arguing. Come with me while I check into the hotel."

She was weak – that was the trouble. I ought to be on my way home now, she thought; instead she meekly followed him to the car.

She sat in a chair in the foyer while he filled in forms at the reception desk. She and Stephen had stayed together in many hotels, managements no longer cared whether people were married or not. It was very different from the fifties when she and Bill had gone for an illicit weekend at the Bedlington Hotel.

They went up in the lift to the room, a clinical practical hotel bedroom with a double bed (she wondered, had he requested that?) and a message of welcome on the television screen.

"I'm not happy about this," she told him.

He put his arms around her, "Oh, darling, please be happy," he said. "I don't know when I have been so happy."

"Have you told you wife that the plane has been delayed?"

"Yes, I telephoned her as soon as I knew." He kissed her, and she found herself trembling.

"You want to be with me, I can feel it," he said.

He was right, she did want to be with him, and trite phrases came to her mind, such as not wasting the few precious hours that had been granted to them and it was meant that they should be together for this night. Part of her mind made excuses for wanting to stay, but another part told her she should have no part of it.

She managed to release herself from his arms, and to persuade him that it was a good idea for them to go downstairs and have dinner. "I'm so hungry," she said pathetically.

When they were seated at a table he told her that the airline would pick up the tab for the dinner; he would only have to pay for the drinks they ordered. "We'll have a bottle of champagne," he said. He was radiating good spirits.

"I don't like champagne," she said.

"Well, then, my darling, we'll have a bottle of wine."

He gestured for a waiter to come over, and he asked for the wine list.

"While you are looking at that," she said, "I'll go to the ladies'."

"Do you know where it is?"

"I'll find it."

It had the old-fashioned designation 'powder room' over the door, incongruous in such a contemporary hotel. She sat on the loo seat for a long time staring at the door. When she finally emerged she gazed at herself in the mirror. She did not powder her nose or apply lipstick; she left the room quickly and made her way to the reception desk.

"Please could you give me a piece of paper and an envelope?"

"Certainly, madam."

She rummaged in her handbag until she found a pen. She wrote, *'Dear Peter, I'm sorry I have to leave. I hope you have a good flight tomorrow, with no problems. Olivia'*. She wrote on the envelope *'Peter Armitage'*.

"He's having dinner in the dining room," she told the woman behind the desk. "Will you see that he gets this, please?"

Then she went through the swing door, walked briskly to the car park, peered into the darkness and rain for her car, got into it and began the journey back home. When she was about halfway there she stopped shaking.

"Good heavens," said Pat wonderingly when she was told this story. They were having their usual lunch at Fortnums.

"I know," said Olivia, "I surprised myself. I never imagined I would do such a thing."

"Tell me about Peter," said Pat. "What is he like?"

"Young," said Olivia, "younger than me. Very attractive – light build, fair hair and blue eyes. Rather intense – looks a bit like a mature student – doesn't care what he wears, but then I suppose he can be forgiven in that respect because he is a sculptor."

"You should have slept with him," said Pat.

Olivia was shocked. "You always told me that you did not get involved with husbands," she said reprovingly.

"That's true," said Pat, "when I knew the wife. In your case, you did not know his wife. She was a shadowy person in his life whom you had never met. It makes a difference."

"I don't think it does," said Olivia stubbornly. "Surely I have learnt something from my experience with Bill? I couldn't bear to make anyone as unhappy as I was. And she would have known, Pat, as soon as she saw him at the airport she would have had an insight into what had happened while he was in England."

"She will have that anyway," said Pat wisely.

Of course, she is right, thought Olivia. A person as transparent as Peter would not be able to hide his feelings. But he would assure her that nothing had happened, and perhaps they would be able to go on from there.

"Didn't you think it was meant to be," asked Pat, always the incurable romantic, "a twist of fate, bringing you together?"

"I could not make the weather an excuse for spending a night with another woman's husband."

"I'm sure you did the right thing, darling," said Pat. "It was very noble . . ."

"Don't say that!" Olivia raised her voice, and the people at the next table looked up and stared at her.

"Please don't get upset," said Pat hastily. "I just meant that if it had me I should have grasped the moment. God knows," she finished sadly, "there are years and years without such pleasures." This concept made the two women pause with their own thoughts for a moment. "Of course it was a complete con," said Pat thoughtfully.

"What do you mean?"

"You were conned, darling, that is quite obvious. When he went to check in he was told that the flight was overbooked. If he was prepared to give up his seat he would receive a sum of money in compensation, and also he would be put up for the night at the airport hotel. His flight in the morning would be guaranteed. He had a choice, either leave on the flight he had booked for or agree to their proposal. The rest was easy, asking for a double bed, the rooms are all doubles anyway, and telephoning his wife, no doubt with the same story he told you. He must have felt his luck had changed suddenly."

"I feel such a fool," said Olivia miserably.

"That childlike trust is part of your charm," Pat told her. "I love you for it, and so do a lot of other people. Gullibility is not a sin. And don't let this change your feelings about him. I can't help admiring the man for his determination. He got so near, but he could not be expected to know you have inherited the high moral values of Kenneth and my sister. He never had a chance."

In less than a year Olivia saw Peter again. He came to England, this time accompanied by his wife and their two children, and his brother, Tom, travelled from Australia with his family. There were too many of them for Bernard and the long-suffering Mrs Savage to look after in Platt Cottage, so they stayed in a hotel in Melbury. The brothers had come with a purpose, to say goodbye to their mother who was on the edge of stepping into darkness, not the unknown void of death, but the less merciful oblivion of the mind. It was a tragedy too poignant for anyone to contemplate too deeply, and they tried to make it an ordinary holiday for the sake of the four children.

Olivia was introduced to Sandra, and as soon as their hands met she was aware of an interested but half-fearful expression on the woman's face. Olivia knew what the look meant, and she was glad that she was able to meet it unflinchingly. They sat on the sofa together, and Olivia told her of her visit to Vancouver, and how she had liked the city.

Sandra was a big-boned young woman, very different from her slender husband. Olivia recognised at once a lack of sureness in her character, which made her appear brusque. She thought that Marigold and Bernard had been harsh in their assessment of her.

"We all feel very sad about Marigold," said Sandra, "such a wonderful talented woman." She was more charitable towards her mother-in-law than Marigold had ever been towards her.

"You know that her last book is to be published next year? Bernard decided to tell the publishers the position, so they know it is to be her last."

"Yes," said Sandra, "Peter did tell me something about it."

"We managed to write the last three chapters, with Bernard's help of course. Your clever husband did most of the hard work – he said it was the last favour he could do for his mother."

While they were talking, Olivia glanced up and saw Peter, at the other side of the room, looking at her. She felt no regrets, only relief that she could have an amicable conversation with his wife without feelings of guilt. His expression was petulant, like a little boy, thought Olivia, who had been deprived of something he wanted very much.

Part Four

Chapter 35

It was strange talking to Bill on the telephone; Olivia had not spoken to him for so long. He only rang her when he had something important to convey, like six years before when he had called to tell her of his impending marriage to Sylvia Townsend. On that occasion she noticed, to her annoyance, a quickening of her heartbeat and a feeling of breathlessness. This time, when she heard his voice, her heart remained perfectly steady.

He did not come to the house now, as the children, children no longer, visited him when they felt inclined and not according to rules set down by solicitors. All three of them had a deep love for their father and they liked their young stepmother. They enjoyed going to Mulgrave Terrace where there was always a lot going on and interesting people to meet. George was in his final year at Medical School and Claire was working as a costume designer at the BBC. Marigold was a student at the same college her sister had attended, reading Environmental Studies.

So Olivia and Marigold were the only members of the family living in the house at Tapworth, and they had a very good relationship. Independent, but not too independent, not treading on each other's toes, and seldom quarrelling. In disposition they were alike. Marigold was self-effacing and rather shy, and slow to express an opinion unless it concerned saving the rain forests or protecting wild animals about which she felt very strongly.

"Is anything wrong?" Bill asked when he heard Olivia's voice on the telephone.

"No, it is just that I have something to tell you, and I'd rather do it face to face."

He agreed to come and see her that evening, after he finished work. She detected a little sigh before he rang off – he could not believe he was going to hear anything to his advantage.

Nervously, as she waited for his arrival, she started to tidy Marigold's books which were sprawled untidily on the table. Then she decided to leave everything as it was. She listened for the sound of his car, and hurried downstairs to open the door when she heard the bell.

He favoured her with a smile. She noticed that he had put on weight since she last saw him, and he had less hair. Perhaps being married to someone much younger than himself had aged him.

When they were in the sitting room upstairs she did

not ask him if he would like a drink; she knew what he wanted after a busy day in the office. She poured him a whisky with a dash of water, not too strong because he was driving, and a glass of sherry for herself. Doing this task gave her a warm feeling of déjà vu, as if they were back at Carpenters again, waiting for her father to come over for an evening drink.

They sat in opposite armchairs, looking at each other. He is getting older, she thought sadly, and she did not like it. It was hard to see in him now the personable young man she had met on Penzance station all those years ago. That was the worst part of the ageing process, the knowledge that nothing in the past could be brought back and re-examined; it was gone for good.

He was thinking, she has a few grey hairs but she looks good, she is better looking now than when she was young.

"Children all right?" he asked, anxious to find out why he had been summoned.

She nodded. "Yes, fine."

He reflected that she had always had the annoying habit of not getting down to the business in hand; he supposed, as usual, he would have to wait for her to tell him why he was there.

"I talked to George on the telephone," he told her. The twins were very good at keeping in touch with both parents. George, in particular, was protective of his mother.

Bill went on, "And Marigold came to see us. I must

say, she looked a sight. Why does she have to wear those ridiculous clothes?"

"They all do at college, and she looks better than most," Olivia replied loyally.

"I can't imagine what our friends think of her." He was referring to the friends of his wife and himself.

Olivia said, "I expect some of them have daughters of their own, and understand. Do you remember Claire and the widow's weeds? And the purple hair? Look at her now! She is beautiful and very well dressed." Claire had become a cool efficient young woman, sharing a flat with a charming account executive who worked for a well-known advertising agency and wore Harvie and Hudson shirts and drove a company car. He was a far cry from Claire's first love, Tod. Olivia was thankful that Bill had never really known about Tod.

"She looks better than she did, I admit," Bill agreed grudgingly, "but I thought we would escape with Marigold. She seemed a sensible girl."

"She is sensible, and has many qualities."

If Bill knew what these qualities were he was not prepared to admit to their existence. "It is a pity she has not kept her looks," he persevered, "She was a pretty child. And now she is a vegetarian too, which I find hard to understand!"

"She is at an awkward age for girls," said Olivia, beginning to lose patience with him. "In two years' time all her good looks will have returned, and she will probably be eating meat again."

"I hope you are right."

"It sounds as if all your children are a disappointment to you," she said with spirit.

"Not at all," he protested. "I think George has ability. I don't like Claire's clothes, even now, whatever you say. I don't think a girl's skirt should be in line with her crotch!" He sighed. "I expect I'm old-fashioned. As for Marigold, I'm just sorry her delicate features have coarsened so much."

Coarsened! The word had an abrasive sound to it, quite unsuited to Marigold's young sweetness, Olivia felt that it was time for the obligatory chat about the children to come to an end.

"How is Sylvie?" she asked icily.

"She's well," he said shortly, and then, "Now, what is it you have to tell me?"

"It is good news for you," she said. "I shall not need your maintenance any more. You will have to go on giving an allowance to Marigold while she is at college and paying all her expenses, but the payments to me can stop."

It gave her immense pleasure to say this to him. She had never imagined she would be in a position to do so. She saw the old spontaneous smile light up his face.

"I can't pretend I'm not pleased," he said. "Making payments to you and to Pippa as well has been a terrible drain, dragging me down."

And an extravagant young wife, she thought, with no babies to distract her from endless shopping and entertaining.

She wondered if he would ask her if she was intending to marry again, that would be the obvious reason for her not requiring maintenance from him. But he remained silent, and she realised the possibility had not occurred to him.

Presently, she decided to tell him how she could manage in the future without his help. "Pat died, and she made me her sole beneficiary."

"I thought the old boy's allowance would go with her," said Bill.

"That went years ago, but Pat has accumulated a fair bit of money herself and made good investments. Also, the house in Queen's Gate is a valuable property." She did not tell him that she had already accepted an offer for the house.

He was sorry about Pat. He had liked her. "I had no idea . . ." he began.

"I can hardly believe it," said Olivia. "Pat was such an important person to me." Her eyes filled with tears, as they did whenever she contemplated life without Pat. She looked down at her hands, folded in her lap, hoping that Bill would not see her tears.

"I must say you have had your share of misfortunes," he said quite gently, "but I am glad you are not still grieving over your old schoolmaster."

Olivia had never liked the word 'old' applied to Stephen, but she knew that Bill was right in one respect – she no longer grieved for Stephen, and that realisation brought with it a certain sadness and loss.

She said, "If you are not the sort of person who puts flowers on graves and messages in newspapers, and I am not, then death must be the finish. Only thoughts are left. I have stopped grieving, but I will never stop remembering."

"How did she die?" asked Bill, referring to Pat.

"A heart attack. She was very fat and refused to do anything about it. She was seventy-six."

"Good God! It makes me feel so old. Do you remember when she tried to commit suicide?"

"I shall never forget," said Olivia.

Bill was thinking about Pat's sitting room, and the gas fire that made a funny hissing noise, and how he was kissing Olivia when the peal of the bell, echoing through the house, heralded the arrival of Alice.

"What will you do with all that money?" he demanded, as if suddenly aware that she might be stepping back into his world, Mulgrave Terrace, dinner parties and expensive cars, the world he shared with Sylvie.

"I'm going to buy Marigold Armitage's house," she told him. "Bernard is moving into a retirement home by the river, near here so that I can visit him. He is selling Platt Cottage." She did not explain to him that Marigold's strange existence was taking her into very old age, and she was spending her remaining days in a nursing home. During the first year she was there, Olivia and Bernard visited her, sometimes together and sometimes alone, until a time came when they realised their visits caused her distress. Perhaps the sight of their faces stirred a memory in her clouded mind, and the effort of trying to capture it, and failing, made her unhappy. Eventually, they came to a mutual, and very reluctant, decision not to go and see her any more. It was hard for them to accept that, in her confused state, the nurses who looked after her meant more to her than family or friends.

Bill looked around him at the comfortable lived-in room, the worn carpet and the faded curtains. "It seems a strange notion to buy a house like that at this stage in your life," he said.

"I want a nice home again," Olivia explained to him, "like I had at Carpenters. The children will visit me, even if they do not live there, and, hopefully, one day we will have grandchildren who will come to stay." He noticed her use of the word 'we'. "And there is the garden," she added. "I am so looking forward to having a garden."

"This seems a pretty good house to me," he said.

"It is, and we have been happy here, but it is time to move." She sounded determined.

She got up and went to the sideboard where she poured herself another drink.

"Not for me," said Bill, "I'm driving, and I have to go soon."

Walking back to her chair, she said casually, "I met Cap – Nigel Benton. Some time ago, quite by chance, in London."

A shadow passed over his face. "I was never keen on the fellow."

"He often asks about you. He married again, and has

a delightful wife, Alison, and three children, so he is a family man at last, and obviously enjoys it. As a matter of fact, I have seen quite a lot of them since that meeting seven years ago. They have become tremendous friends of mine."

"Really?" He was not interested, or pretended not to be. His mouth drooped, and Olivia knew he was becoming irritated and anxious to leave. But something Nigel had said to her on her last visit to them had made her brave.

"He never mentions Alice," she said. But she had, and Bill looked uncomfortable.

"Alice . . . that all seems so long ago, doesn't it?" she went on. "How long did you grieve for Alice, I wonder?"

"Well, it wasn't grief exactly."

"But you did mourn her, surely?" Olivia persisted. "You must have done, because you loved her."

He didn't respond.

But, suddenly, she was determined to force a response. "You loved her so much that it was your intention to live with her at Mulgrave Terrace."

He looked pained. "I do not have to listen to this."

"I don't understand why neither you nor Nigel will talk about Alice. After all these years surely it is possible to mention her in a natural way."

It was too bad. They had been getting on quite well, and now this had to happen. He was about to get up and depart in a dignified way, always a good ploy, but she stopped him.

"Don't go," she said, and there was an edge to her voice he had never heard before. How she had changed!

He sank into his chair again. "What do you want me to tell you?" he asked.

"Let us, for once, talk openly to each other," Olivia cried. "It may be our last chance."

"Very well," he said seriously, aware that she had hit upon the one thing he had wanted to do for a very long time. "You asked me if I grieved for Alice. I did not. It was a tragic accident, I know, but afterwards I felt as if I had emerged from a long black tunnel. I was free of the terrible hold she had on my life."

"There was so much deception, so many lies," said Olivia sadly. "You allowed me to think Emily Frobisher was the reason for our unhappiness. How could you let me think that when all the time you were in love with Alice?"

He did not answer her question. "I said I wanted you back with me – that was truthful. It was your stubborn pride that got in the way of our being a proper family again."

"There was more to it than pride," she retorted. "Don't forget, you wanted us to separate because of Alice. I didn't know it then, but that was the reason."

"When did you know?" he asked, curious at last.

"Nigel told me. He came here, to this house, to tell me about you and Alice. It was the worst day of my life, and twelve hours later Alice was dead."

"I thought he told you long before that," he said vaguely.

"No."

He had found it easy to forget that uneasy chapter in his life. Over the passage of years, he had managed to convince himself that it did not amount to anything much.

"I know you were fond of Alice," he went on, "but I think you should know that she was not the dear loyal friend you thought she was. She was a very complicated lady indeed."

"I know that, or rather I discovered it when Nigel came to see me."

They were silent, both thinking of that particular day.

"Why did you ring Alice that night?" Bill asked suddenly.

Her heart contracted. "What do you mean?" she whispered.

"The night of the accident. I was there when the telephone rang. Alice answered it, and it was you with a cock and bull story about me having a heart attack."

"You were there?" Suddenly, she could see it all so clearly. Just as she had seen him lying on the floor, now she pictured him sitting on the edge of Alice's four-poster bed with its ridiculous chintz hangings, probably putting on his socks when the telephone rang. They had been making love, for Nigel had left the scene and it was safe for them to be together in that house. Olivia had not driven into the Benton's drive that night, so she had not seen Bill's car, parked close to the hedge so that it could not be observed from the road.

It had happened a long time ago, but thinking about it gave her the familiar anguished torn apart feeling. Perhaps this is the real meaning of grief, thought Olivia, the remembrance of unhappy moments, not the remembrance of happy ones as most people think. She could not be sad about Stephen any more, although she loved him, but she could still feel sad about Bill. The realisation startled her, and she looked at him to see if there was a reflection in his face of her own feelings, but his expression betrayed nothing.

She said slowly, "I telephoned Alice that night, and you heard it all?"

"Well, I could not hear your exact words, but Alice told me what you had said. You can imagine her reaction. It was just up her street. She would have prolonged the fun, dragging you off to hospital, pretending she believed I had been taken there in an ambulance in the last throes of goodness-knows-what. She would have enjoyed making a complete fool of you, but she did not do it because she had other things on her mind."

"You were in the bedroom – in bed – when I rang?" She needed to know that. "Alice answered the telephone by the bed?"

"No," he answered irritably, "you don't understand."

"I want to understand," she said. "Please tell me exactly what happened."

He half rose from his chair. "I haven't time for all this," he said. "I'm late as it is. Sylvie –"

"This is nothing to do with Sylvie!" she cried. She

stopped him from leaving by catching hold of his hand.

They had not touched for years, and both felt the strangeness.

"Please, Bill," she pleaded. "If you have one little bit of feeling left for me, you must tell me what happened."

He looked into her eyes, beseeching him, and he knew he would have to stay.

Chapter 36

Bill told Olivia that he had left the office early that day. That was natural enough as it was the first day of his holiday. His secretary and one of his partners remembered to wish him well – as far as they knew he was going away with his wife and children. His secretary had suspicions that she had not shared with any of her colleagues; she thought his behaviour had been very odd during the last few months.

He was anxious to get to Pennel Bridge as soon as possible, as there were last-minute arrangements to be made before he and Alice moved to Mulgrave Terrace on the following morning. She had telephoned him and told him that Nigel had been informed of their plans, and was leaving the house that afternoon. It meant, she said excitedly, that when the removal people she had instructed arrived in two days' time, there would be no one there to prevent her from taking what she wanted.

"Is that so important?" he asked. It was an aspect of the whole business that made him feel uncomfortable.

"Of course," she said, "you can't expect me to leave what is rightly mine."

He supposed she was right; she was always right, and very practical. He thought of the house he had once regarded as home, and the boxes marked with red and blue stickers, ready for despatch to their separate destinations. The enormity of what he and Alice were doing struck him, as it had done many times before, but now he had a sense of relief that it would soon be over. He often wondered why his life had become so complicated. It had never been his intention to reach this stage and he thought he had made that clear to Alice from the beginning, but she had not listened to him, running ahead of him in her heedless way, choosing the house where they would live and compromising him still further by telling him she was carrying his child. Finally, during their holiday in Madeira she had told Nigel the truth.

"He was devastated," she told Bill during one of her many telephone calls from abroad. He locked himself in his study while he talked to her, having complete faith that his wife would not listen on another line.

Soon after her return Alice told Bill that Nigel had been to see Olivia who now knew everything. "Thank God, at last she's in the picture. She's such a fool, imagining all this time it was that silly Emily Frobisher."

When she made that scathing remark about someone who was supposed to be her friend Bill was shocked, and almost told her he could not go through with it. Instead he went off alone and got very drunk. The next day when Olivia suggested a separation he was not surprised – he could not expect any other reaction.

"Don't worry so much," said Alice. "Everything is going to be all right."

Alice's unfailing optimism steered Bill through a very hard time. His life at home with Olivia was made intolerable by heavy silences and reproachful looks. He was thankful to escape to the office, but even there he sometimes felt his integrity as a solicitor and a professional man was slipping away from him. When he felt everything was too complicated to endure, Alice's soft embrace had persuaded him that it was all worthwhile, that there was sunshine outside for them both.

He listened to her when she told him that they were destined to be together, that life must not be wasted because of foolish sacrifices. He had made a terrible mistake in marrying Olivia, and now he had been given another chance. When he was consumed with doubts about what they were doing, Alice reminded him, in her sharp provocative way, that because of his mistrust in her they had been deprived of years of happiness together.

Now, driving at speed through the rain to Pennel Bridge he felt almost relaxed for the first time after weeks of uncertainty. At last, he and Alice would be together, and there would no more secrecy. He did not intend to stay long with Alice that evening –after all, he reasoned, the marriage was over, and tomorrow was the beginning of a new life for them all.

He parked the car in the usual place, near the hedge, more out of habit than necessity. He entered the house with his key, and saw Alice sitting at the little telephone table in the hall. There was a drink by her side. She replaced the receiver when she saw him, and turned her face away from his kiss.

"What's wrong?" he asked.

"Everything is changed," she said. "I'm not coming with you tomorrow."

He thought she had got cold feet, a complaint he had been suffering from for some time. Now he felt strong, and he comforted her. "Darling, it's going to be all right, I promise you. We'll be together, and that is all that matters."

"No, you don't understand," she said. "I love Nigel. I have always loved him, and I was a fool to get involved with you. I regret it terribly."

Her words were so completely unexpected he found himself unable to speak. Dazedly, he listened while she told him how Nigel had come to the house a few hours earlier to collect some of his clothes. He had been in their bedroom, two suitcases open on the bed, when she walked in and announced that she wanted to stay with him. She was so certain he would take her back. He had done so before after similar escapades, and she thought he would do so again.

She begged him, but he quietly went on packing his shirts and trousers neatly into one of the cases, without saying a word. She wept, and fell to her knees beside the bed, trying to catch hold of his hand. He pushed her away, and calmly walked to the cupboard and removed two of his suits, which he folded into the other case. She told him repeatedly that she loved him, that she had never loved anyone else. She implored him to forgive her.

He closed the suitcases, and picked them up, one in each hand. Then he did say a word, and the word was "No". He walked out of the room, she heard him hurrying down the stairs and then the slamming of the front door. Running to the window, she watched him get into his car and drive away. She had no idea where he had gone, and she was determined to find out.

Bill felt angry but chastened as well. He had given up everything for Alice, and now his dreams for the future were in ruins.

"I watched her going through her address book," he told Olivia eighteen years later, "ringing all their friends to see if he was there. She kept saying, 'I'll get him back, I know I will'. She refused to believe that he would walk out on her."

"There was the child," said Olivia. "That must be what made the difference. He could not accept the child."

"You may be right," said Bill. "He knew it could not be his."

"You were the father."

"Why do you say that?" he demanded, as if stung by an unfair accusation. "Edward Preston could have that honour, or your father for that matter."

"No!"

"It is not beyond the bounds of possibility. Of course Alice convinced me that it was my child she was carrying, but later I was not so sure. One thing I realise now, when you told her you were pregnant she was determined to become pregnant also."

"How horrible!" Olivia shuddered.

He took up the story again. "After trying all their friends, and getting a negative answer every time, she started on hotels. In between the calls I reminded her of the house I had purchased for us in Melbury, and the plans we had made together. She ignored me.

The hours went by, and the only time she got up from her seat was to wander into the dining room to get another drink. I was tired and hungry, but there was no suggestion of finding anything for me to eat, and I decided not to drink on an empty stomach. One of us had to stay sober. Looking back, I don't know why I stayed. I supposed I hoped she would change her mind.

When it was nearly midnight, I could tell the people at the other end were showing signs of irritability at being disturbed at such an hour. I wondered if she would be forced to give up and call it a day. After all, Nigel could be anywhere in the country – the chances of her locating him must have been very slight. Then, in that strange uncanny way she had, she hit the jackpot. Nigel had booked in that afternoon at a small hotel on the other side of Melbury.

So, there it was, she knew where he was spending the night, and she was hell bent on going to see him to make him change his mind. Then the telephone rang. After all the calls she had made it was quite a shock getting an incoming one. I remember I thought it could only be Nigel at that time of night.

She answered it, and mouthed to me that it was you. I remembered that I had intended to go and see you and your father, but now there seemed no point. I wondered what I would say to you. I watched Alice as she was talking to you, and she became serious and agitated in turn. I heard the words 'hospital' and 'ambulance' and I became alarmed. I thought something had happened to one of the children.

When she put the receiver down, she started to laugh. She became almost hysterical. You remember how excited she used to get? She told me what you had said, but I was in such a bewildered state I could hardly take it in. It was beyond my understanding.

'I must go there at once,' she said getting to her feet. 'I can't leave you lying on the floor, can I? Of course the ambulance may have collected you by the time I get there, but I can go with Olivia to the hospital. Or perhaps I should ring and ask for an ambulance to go to your house, just in case they have not got her message? What do you think?'

'For God's sake –'

'But, of course, I am not going to do either of those things. I am going to see Nigel. Olivia is your responsibility, my darling, and I wish you luck with her.'

I asked her to calm down, and stay where she was. She had been drinking and should not drive. She would not listen, and left the house without even bothering to put on a coat. It was still pouring with rain.

I followed her outside, and watched her back the car out of the garage. Before she drove off, she wound down the window and said, 'Go back to your mad wife!'. I suppose those were her last words."

Yes, thought Olivia, she could imagine Alice uttering those words.

"I followed in my car," went on Bill, "but she was going too fast for me. I heard the terrible noise of the crash and, as I approached the corner, I saw the pile-up in the road ahead of me. I knew it was hopeless. I got out of the car, but there was nothing I could do. I was able to make sure the occupants of the other car were in fairly good shape, just suffering from shock, and I told them I would go and get help. I drove to the nearest garage, and telephoned the police and the ambulance service. I told the police where Nigel was staying, so that they could get hold of him. Then I went to get you."

How strange, thought Olivia, that after such a night his first impulse had been to find her.

"I wish you had told me," she said.

"I often wondered what made you do it. A sort of practical joke?"

"No, not a joke."

"What, then?"

"Alice was right in a way," explained Olivia. "It was a kind of madness. Everything had got too much for me and I lost my way. Perhaps it was a desire to be noticed, something had to be done to show I existed. Everyone should be allowed to lose their cool once in a lifetime, and that night was the time I lost mine. I had this fixed determination to confront Alice and I devised a ridiculous ruse to get her to come and see me. I might have known it would never work."

"She was too clever to be fooled by anyone."

"I always thought . . ." She did not finish the sentence. It was useless expecting him to understand all those troubled years when she had been obsessed by that single loss of judgement, years of regret and guilt which led to this moment of truth.

"Why did Alice set out to destroy us?" she asked. "Pat, my father, you and me — what sort of person would do that? She did not have an unhappy childhood as I remember from what she told me, so there is nothing to account for it."

"Her mother was a nutcase," said Bill gloomily.

"But not evil, surely?" Olivia recalled the limp hand of Maureen lying in hers at their first meeting in Cornwall. Maureen and George, gone forever, like her own parents.

"No, I don't think old Maureen was evil," replied Bill impatiently. "There is no point in trying to find some half-baked psychological excuse for Alice's character. She was herself, and that's all there is to it. Life was a game for her, and she revelled in it. I do not think she was motivated by anything other than a terrible mischievousness. She adored making other people participate in her games, especially people who did not begin to understand the rules. You and your father, for instance." He stared into her face, as if seeing her for the first time after a long absence. He said slowly, "We were all right when she was not around. She could not work her magic when she was not on the spot."

"That's true," Olivia agreed, remembering the happiness of their holiday in Scotland.

"She once said she was a witch."

"That was to amuse the children," he replied.

"Could it have been an insight into her character?"

"Oh, she knew what she was doing, all right," Bill said, "and the only hope for ordinary mortals was to distance themselves from her. I think I always knew that. We managed to get rid of her after the business with Pat, but then she reappeared on the scene and you insisted on welcoming her back."

"I was not entirely to blame," said Olivia defensively.

"No, of course not."

"What about her father?" she asked, changing the subject. "She thought the world of him."

"Ah, her father," said Bill. "Now your shrink might make something of that connection. He died while serving a stretch in prison."

"I thought the business partner embezzled all the money?"

"No, Alice's dad was the fraudster. Charlie Mount. He changed his name, added the 'joy' because he thought it had more panache. When my father met his widow, Maureen, she had lost everything, money, status, pride, everything. He rescued her, but it was too late. She was a broken reed."

Olivia wondered why she had never heard any of this before. What must they have been like, she and Bill, during the first years of their marriage? Skimming the surface of their life with work, children and day-to-day activities, and never getting down to communicating with each other. She thought of Charlie Mount changing his name to Mountjoy. It was absurdly pretentious, and Alice had gone along with it. For the first time, Olivia perceived a rather sad pathetic side to Alice's character.

"Perhaps we should blame Charlie Mount for everything."

"Perhaps."

"And you told Nigel that she was on her way to see him, because she wanted him to take her back, when the accident happened?"

"How do you know that?" Bill asked.

"It was something Nigel said to me the last time I saw him. I mentioned you, and he told me that he had seen you in Melbury, and I wondered why . . ."

"Yes, said Bill, "I went to see him at his hotel, the day

412

after Alice's death. I thought it right I should tell him the circumstances."

Olivia did not reply, silenced by the strange logic of a man who felt it right to tell the truth to someone who, by his own admission, he did not like particularly, and yet had kept his wife completely in the dark.

"He was very calm about it," went on Bill. "If there is any guilt to be borne, he is the one who should bear it, but I don't suppose he has given it a second thought."

"I think he has," said Olivia.

He got to his feet. "I must go. Sylvie will be fussing, wondering where I am."

"Thank you for coming."

"What about the new arrangement?" He did not want her to forget it.

"I'll telephone my solicitor in the morning."

"I'm sorry about Pat," said Bill. "She was a game old girl. I'm glad we had this talk, and I agree we did not talk enough. If we had, things might have been different."

He went down the stairs ahead of her. She thought how she had once found the nape of his neck so endearing, and she noticed his hair still grew into a little peak at the back, but now there was a small bald patch above it.

She stood on the steps and watched the rear lights of his car disappear down the road. It was a mild soft night, and a little breeze cooled her hot cheeks. She took a deep breath. At last she understood. Bill had never really wanted to leave her – he had just had a foolish affair that escalated into something he had not had the strength of mind to resist. If they had talked together their marriage might have been saved but, at that time in their lives, neither of them had understood the devious workings of Alice's mind, or that she would never accept the concept that Bill was not prepared to leave his wife and children. He had been lost in a tangle of misunderstandings, and the pathetic shadowy figure of Emily Frobisher had just added to his difficulties.

Olivia remembered Pat saying to her, that Christmas so many years ago: "Are you sure you are not mistaken? Why don't you confront these people so you know exactly what is going on?" Olivia wished she had taken her advice. Her distress had made her blind but Bill and Alice, between them, had covered her eyes so that her vision was clouded. They had all shared the blame for something that was now so much in the past it no longer mattered. Olivia felt a moment of triumph – it no longer mattered.

Peering into the darkness she thought of happier things, plans which, although not adventurous, excited her.

She would get another dog, to replace Spot who had eventually succumbed to old age. The children had been urging her to get a puppy, and now was the time to do it. She thought affectionately of Spot when he was a youngster, darting this way and that on the little patch of grass in front of the house, his end-of-the-day run, while she waited impatiently for him to do what he had to do and then come bounding back to her.

Then her thoughts turned to Platt Cottage and, in particular, the garden that would soon belong to her. She remembered walking around it with Marigold, after they had finished working on the latest book, and how she had envied the pleasure Marigold derived from it. It was a pleasure that had been denied to Olivia for eighteen years. How her father would have loved the garden at Platt Cottage! It grieved her to think of it.

It was time to begin preparing Marigold's supper, and she anticipated with delight her return from college, the sound of her key in the lock, the bang of books dumped on the floor, Marigold's greeting, warm and loving, "Mother! I'm home!"

Still she stayed for a while, staring at the clear night sky with the black trees outlined against it and the silver streak of the river beyond. It was quiet, with the stillness of the evening, after people had returned from work, before they went out again to enjoy themselves. So it had always been, and would be in years to come when nothing in the present would matter any more. That thought, and the night air which had become suddenly chilly, made Olivia give a little shiver, and she quickly returned to the house, shutting the door firmly behind her.

THE END

Direct to your home!

If you enjoyed this book why not
visit our website:

www.poolbeg.com

and get another book delivered straight to
your home or to a friend's home!

www.poolbeg.com

All orders are despatched within 24 hours.

Published by Poolbeg.com

STILL WATERS RUN DEEP

NANCY ROSS

A scandal has broken – the secret mistress of Roderick Macauley, MP, has just sold her diary to the newspapers. He may have to resign.

Bridget, Macauley's daughter, sets off for Pondings, the family home. Her only thought is to be with her mother Duibhne in this crisis. But the political scandal is just the tip of the iceberg. Other secrets are lurking that will rock the family to the core.

Delphine Blake, reporter on *The Daily Graphic*, stumbles upon an even more startling story – the truth about the cool, beautiful Duibhne Macauley – or Lady Duibhne Shannon, as she was formerly known.

As Duibhne's extraordinary story unfolds, we learn that her serenity is like the polished, unruffled surface of a lake, hiding powerful currents and sinister secrets in its depths.

ISBN 1-84223-106-5

Published by Poolbeg.com

THE ENCHANTED ISLAND

NANCY ROSS

'It seemed to her that this short episode in her life had the substance of a dream – a dream from which she feared she must now awaken.'

Christabel first meets Ambrose Silveridge at a dinner party. The Silveridge name is synonymous with immense wealth and generosity. But Christabel is attracted to his striking good looks and how he overshadows everyone else at the table.

After a whirlwind romance, Ambrose proposes, but the forceful Lady Silveridge shows her displeasure at her son's choice of wife. By marrying Christabel he will lose his birthright. Christabel is enraged and her angered response drives the couple apart.

Hurt and confused, she goes to stay with her Aunt Bell on the tiny island, La Isla de la Fuga, the Island of Escape. Among its inhabitants she finds friendship and understanding and learns an intriguing tale of love which endures against all odds.

Can the love between Christabel and Ambrose overcome the obstacles in its path?

ISBN 1-84223-132-4

Published by Poolbeg.com

Love & Friendship

NANCY ROSS

"With guilt and revulsion I explore the pockets of his suit jacket. Dan was with me for the births of both of our sons. I understood the things that hurt him and that pleased him. We shared everything, or so I thought. So, how did it change? Why did we lie apart now?"

So ponders a young wife and mother who through the 'Pat-a-Dog' scheme and her beguiling cocker spaniel befriends Maeve Bailey, an old woman who has made the difficult decision to join her failing husband in an expensive retirement home. Despite the difference in their ages, the two women become firm friends. The young woman learns of Maeve's early life on the London stage, her two marriages and the heartbreak that ensued.

And as her marriage crisis deepens, Maeve offers her support by asking for help to write down her memoirs. At least, for the time being, she might find some distraction and comfort in the elderly woman's revelations of a very different marriage, a long time ago.

ISBN 1-84223-145-6